Healing the Orphaned Heart

Rebecca Lange

Published by Rebecca Lange, 2022.

Table of Contents

I tried to be an actress, Mama, but it just didn't work out... maybe it was the sarcasm.

1

Bound for the Unkown West

" **W** hy do I have to leave? Why didn't my father name you as my guardians?" Rose Williams's voice quivered as she looked up at her governess and the family's longtime butler, Charlotte and Thomas Graham. Tears shimmered in her eyes, catching the pale morning light spilling through the train station's high windows.

A departing whistle echoed through the cavernous space, a cruel reminder that *her* train would leave within the half-hour. Yet Rose couldn't move, not until she asked the questions clawing at her heart one more time.

Why hadn't her father, planned for this? Why had he left nothing in place beyond the cold, distant formalities of a will? Why hadn't he realized how utterly alone she would be once he was gone?

Now, orphaned at seventeen, Rose had no choice but to leave Boston and journey halfway across the country to live with her father's brother, a man she barely remembered. Her stomach twisted. Uncle John was a reverend who had moved his family to Idaho Springs, Colorado, shortly before Rose's mother passed away. She had been only five then. Twelve long years had slipped by without a single visit. And now he, his wife, and their sons were the only blood kin she had left.

Charlotte cupped Rose's trembling hands in both of hers, offering a tender, aching smile.

"Your uncle is your closest living relative, my dear. As much as Thomas and I would love to keep you with us, family must come first." Her voice softened. "You know we love you more than words can express. And I'm certain your aunt and uncle will care for you."

"And what if they don't?" Rose whispered, lowering her gaze. "I barely remember them. I'm to live with people who are nearly strangers, and Uncle John will decide everything. My dowry. My future. Even my husband." Her breath caught. "I may not have any say at all."

Her composure shattered. Tears spilled fast and hot as she pressed her face against Thomas's chest. He hesitated only a heartbeat, before wrapping his arms around her, propriety forgotten. Thomas had served the Williams family for twenty years, since before Rose was born. He had watched her toddle through the halls, listened to her laughter, soothed her fears after her mother's death. Though she was the daughter of one of Boston's wealthiest men and he merely a servant, Thomas had loved her as though she were his own.

Charlotte turned away, dabbing her eyes with a handkerchief. When Rose finally stepped back, Thomas brushed a tear from her cheek with a gentleness that broke her all over again.

"We love you dearly, Rose," he murmured. "You've grown into a fine young woman with a tender heart. Life has dealt you more sorrow than most, but I've seen your courage. You'll weather this storm, too."

Charlotte nodded firmly. "You've endured heartache and disappointment, yet each time you've risen stronger. We believe in you, sweet girl. If anyone can find her footing in a new life, it's you."

Thomas's smile turned wistful. "And don't fear your aunt and uncle. I remember them well. Your father was always the quieter, more serious one. Your Uncle John was spirited—warm, good-humored. He may surprise you."

Rose searched his face, her brows tightening with worry.

"But can I trust them? What if they're like Father... so buried in duty they forget I exist? Can I trust what Uncle John wrote in his letter?"

Thomas's expression gentled even further.

"Listen to your heart, sweet Rose. It will tell you more than you think."

"But hearts can be deceived."

"They can," he admitted softly. "But more often, they warn us when something is wrong, or when someone's intentions are not what they seem. Trust in the Lord, child. He will not forsake you."

Rose nodded, though her throat ached with unshed tears. She embraced them both again, clinging to the only true family she had ever known. Charlotte kissed her cheek, lingering.

"Do you have everything packed?"

"I believe so."

Thomas summoned two porters and instructed them to handle her trunks with care. He and Charlotte couldn't stay to watch the train depart, not without breaking entirely, and they were due that afternoon at their new position.

After Thomas tipped the men, Rose gathered her courage. She squared her shoulders and took one last lingering look at the two people, who had been her home. Then, swallowing her tears, she followed the porters toward the platform.

The train whistle cut through the cold morning air, a sharp, merciless farewell. *She could do this. She had to.* What other choice did she have? Rose took a trembling breath and turned toward a station window, just in time to see Charlotte crumple into Thomas's arms, weeping. The sight pierced her like a blade.

They had been her family—her protectors, her confidants. And now she was losing them too, just as she had lost her father. She pressed a gloved hand to her lips, willing the tears to stay down. No. She mustn't break here. Not in front of strangers.

Drawing her shoulders back, she stepped onto the crowded platform. The station pulsed with movement, the hiss of steam, the shouts of porters, the hum of weary travelers embracing or letting go. A child laughed nearby. A woman sobbed into her husband's coat. Everyone seemed to be clinging to someone. Everyone except the one person Rose most longed to see.

Her gaze swept the platform with rising panic. Where was Andrew? He had promised he would come, promised he wouldn't let her leave without saying goodbye. Her chest tightened as she glanced at the ticking station clock. Time was slipping away. Her eyes stung, but she held herself together. Too many curious faces surrounded her. She needed dignity, composure, anything to keep from unraveling.

Instead, she focused on gratitude. In the two short, chaotic weeks since her father's death, Thomas and Charlotte had done everything they could to soften her upheaval, arranging her travel, packing her trunks, even coaxing her father's solicitor to release enough funds to ensure her comfort. Without them, she would have been utterly lost.

"Miss Williams," one of the porters said politely, drawing her attention. "Which compartment will you be riding in?"

"First class," she replied quietly, glancing toward the elegant car at the front of the train. Thomas had insisted on it, wanting her to have privacy and the smallest measure of comfort amidst her heartbreak. He had even secured a private section so she would not be forced to share the space with strangers.

The porters nodded and began loading her trunks. Rose clasped her hands tightly and scanned the bustling platform again, her pulse quickening. Still no sign of Andrew. The clock struck another merciless minute, five left until departure. The thought of leaving without saying goodbye made her breath hitch painfully.

A flicker of movement drew her eye. A young man, standing some ten feet away, was watching her. He was tall and broad shouldered, his chestnut hair tousled by the breeze, his posture relaxed but confident. When their gazes met, he didn't look away. Something in his expression, curiosity sharpened with bold admiration, made her skin prickle.

Rose turned quickly, pretending not to notice, but she could feel his gaze lingering like a touch. Handsome or not, his audacity unsettled her.

Where are you, Andrew? she thought, her eyes darted once more toward the station entrance. Nothing. Only strangers. Only the steady rush of travelers boarding and disembarking. Her heart sank. She swallowed hard against the tightness in her throat and blinked away fresh tears.

Gathering her courage, she stepped toward the train, her gloved fingers tightening around the handle of her small traveling case. She placed her foot on the first step—

"Rose!"

She froze. Her name, shouted above the crowd, made her whirl around. Relief flooded her so swiftly it nearly stole her breath.

Andrew was running toward her, weaving between porters and passengers. His dark hair was wind-tossed, his coat unbuttoned, his expression frantic, and she had never been so happy to see anyone in her life.

Without thinking, she rushed to meet him. Propriety vanished. When he reached her, she threw her arms around his neck, and he caught her up, lifting her clear off the ground in a fierce, unrestrained embrace.

For a heartbeat, the noise of the station faded into nothing. There was only Andrew, his warmth, his strength, the familiar comfort of him. He set her down gently but kept his hands on her shoulders.

"I'm so sorry I'm late," he said breathlessly. "My employer refused to let me go. I told him I'd work late this evening to make up for it. In the end, I just... left. I may not have a position when I return, but I couldn't break my promise to you."

Rose's eyes widened. "Andrew, you didn't. What will you do if you lose your job?"

He gave a faint, rueful smile. "I'll manage somehow. I'll find something else. I only wish I could go with you."

Before she could respond, the shriek of the whistle split the air, signaling the train's imminent departure. They both turned toward it. Andrew took her hand, guiding her back to the steps.

"Come on," he said softly. "You'll miss it." He helped her onto the first step, then climbed halfway after her. Before she could speak, he pulled her close and kissed her. The world dropped away.

It was a brief, desperate kiss, his lips warm and trembling against hers, but when he pulled back, the raw tenderness in his eyes made her breath falter.

"I love you, Rose," he whispered, voice breaking. "I want to marry you someday. I know I can't give you the life you deserve, and your father would never have approved of me... but I needed you to know."

Rose stared at him, stunned. For years they had been closest friends, nothing more. Never had he spoken of love.

"Andrew..." she began, but he was already back on the platform as the train shuddered beneath her feet.

"I'll follow you as soon as I can!" he called. "Maybe your uncle will be more understanding than your father was. I love you!"

She tried to answer, to tell him she couldn't return those feelings, that she treasured him too dearly to let their friendship become something else, but the whistle drowned her voice. The train lurched, wheels grinding to life.

"Andrew!" she cried, reaching for him as he waved, his figure blurred through tears and smoke. Within seconds, he was swallowed by the crowd, disappearing into the distance.

Rose remained on the carriage platform, gripping the brass handrail as the world around her lurched into motion. The wheels groaned, the engine rumbled, and slowly Boston began to slip away.

The station blurred first, then the familiar rooftops, then the city itself, dissolving into a haze of brick, smoke, and distance. Her home. Her memories. Her heart.

She stood there until the platform was nothing more than a dark smudge behind her, until the last chimney vanished around a bend in the tracks. Only then did she force her fingers to release the railing and make herself turn away.

With a trembling breath, she stepped into her private compartment and gently closed the door, shutting out the world beyond the foggy glass. The quiet felt deafening. She sank into the velvet seat, the plush fabric swallowing her slight weight as though inviting her to rest, but rest was impossible.

The moment she lowered her face into her hands, the tears spilled over, hot and uncontrollable. They slipped between her fingers and soaked her gloves, each one carrying a piece of Boston with it.

How was she to bear this? Leaving everyone she loved—everything she had ever known? Venturing alone into a world that felt far too wide, too uncertain, too unforgiving? Her shoulders shook, and for the first time since her father's death, she let herself cry without restraint.

The train clattered on, indifferent to her grief, carrying her farther and farther from the life she'd been forced to leave behind. And Rose, adrift and trembling, could only weep for the home she feared she might never see again.

Eventually, Rose had no tears left to shed. Her heart still ached, an ache that pulsed with every breath, but the sobs had softened, leaving behind a dull, lingering heaviness. She reached for her handkerchief and gently blotted her swollen eyes before drawing a long, steadying breath.

The rhythmic clatter of the wheels beneath her became almost soothing, a steady heartbeat reminding her that life, however altered, must continue.

She smoothed her skirts, gathered her composure, and rose. Perhaps a visit to the washroom would help her feel a bit more presentable.

The first-class carriage was divided into several private compartments, each spacious enough to accommodate a family and designed so the cushioned seats could be converted into sleeping berths for longer journeys. For a young woman traveling alone, the arrangement was a blessing, a small sanctuary of privacy amid bustling passage.

Her father's faithful butler, Thomas, had thought of every detail before her departure. Even now, she could almost hear his gentle voice urging her to be cautious, but not afraid. The memory coaxed a bittersweet smile to her lips.

Taking up her reticule, Rose slid open the compartment door and stepped into the narrow aisle. The gentle sway of the train made her grip the wall rail for balance as she walked forward.

A few passengers passed her in quiet conversation. Others sat by the windows, absorbed in newspapers or gazing at the rolling countryside streaking by. The air carried a faint blend of coal smoke and polished wood, an oddly comforting mixture.

Just ahead, an elderly woman stood near one of the doors, slowly turning in place, her expression clouded with confusion.

"Excuse me, madam," Rose said softly, stepping closer. "You seem a little distressed. May I be of assistance?"

The woman turned toward her, relief washing over her lined features.

"Oh, dear girl, yes! I went to the washroom, and now I cannot remember where my compartment is. These corridors all look the same."

Rose smiled kindly. "Do you have your ticket with you?"

The woman blinked, then gave a light, self-deprecating laugh.

"Mercy, what a silly old goose I am. Of course I do." She reached into her reticule and withdrew a folded slip of paper with trembling fingers. "Would you be so kind as to read it? My eyesight isn't what it once was."

"Certainly," Rose replied, unfolding the ticket and scanning the section number. "You're only a few doors away. Allow me to escort you." She offered her arm, which the older woman accepted with grateful warmth. Together they made their way down the aisle, their footsteps muffled by the carpet runner.

When they reached the correct compartment, Rose lifted her hand to slide the door open, only for it to move before she touched it. A young man appeared in the doorway, his fair hair catching the lamplight.

"Grandmother!" he exclaimed. "I was just about to look for you. Did you wander off again?"

The elderly woman chuckled and swatted his arm lightly.

"I did, Daryl, but this lovely young lady came to my rescue. Isn't she a darling?"

Heat rushed to Rose's cheeks, and she lowered her gaze modestly.

"Thank you for helping my grandmother," the young man said, his voice rich and smooth. When she lifted her eyes, they met a pair of striking green ones. His expression was open and kind, though a spark of curiosity glimmered there as well.

"There's no need to thank me," Rose replied, recovering her composure. "I was happy to assist."

His grandmother beamed between them.

"You should escort this dear girl back to her compartment, Daryl. It's the least we can do."

The young man's mouth curved into a charming grin.

"As you wish, Grandmother. I'd be delighted."

Rose shook her head at once, though she couldn't quite keep a shy smile from touching her lips.

"That's very kind of you, sir, but there's no need to trouble yourself. I'll find my way perfectly well."

"Are you quite sure?" he asked, his tone courteous with just a hint of teasing.

"Quite," she replied softly but firmly. She turned to the elderly woman with a respectful nod. "It was a pleasure meeting you, madam."

"The pleasure was mine, my dear," the woman said warmly. "Safe travels."

With another polite smile, Rose inclined her head to both of them and continued down the corridor toward the washroom. Yet as she walked, her thoughts drifted—no longer toward Boston or her tears, but toward a pair of vivid green eyes and a grin that lingered in her mind as though it might reappear before the journey was through.

When Rose stepped back into the aisle several minutes later, the train swaying gently beneath her feet, she halted in surprise. A group of five men stood clustered near the end of the corridor. The moment they spotted her, they moved as one, closing in with deliberate, coordinated steps, as though they had been waiting for precisely this moment.

"Miss Williams," one of them called out, his tone far too eager to be polite. "Who was the young man who kissed you before the train departed?"

Before she could answer, another pushed forward.

"Are the two of you engaged? Tell us, do you think your late father would have approved of a man of such modest standing?"

Rose froze. Her pulse quickened. *Journalists.* Her stomach dropped. Oh, how she despised them—their shameless prying, their hunger for scandal, their utter disregard for human decency.

"Forgive me," she said tightly, forcing civility into her trembling voice, "but I'm not answering any questions at present." She attempted to slip past them, but the men shifted together like a flock of carrion birds, blocking her way.

"Miss Williams," another demanded, thrusting a notebook nearly into her chest, "how did your father contract typhus? Did you know he was ill?"

"Where are you going now that he's gone?" someone else pressed sharply. "Have you truly no family left in Boston?"

Rose bit back rising frustration, her fingers tightening around the handle of her reticule.

"Please, gentlemen," she said, though her voice wavered. "Leave me be. I have nothing to say to you."

Her plea only amused them. They stepped closer, hemming her in until her back brushed the polished wood paneling.

"Do you suppose the young man who kissed you," one sneered, "is after your fortune? Is that why you let him force his affections on you before an entire station of witnesses?"

Heat rushed to her cheeks. Anger flared through her fear.

"That man is my dearest friend," she said sharply. "And I would advise you to mind your tone."

Another leaned in, smirking. "Who is he, then? Do you consider it proper for a young lady of breeding to show such familiarity with a man who is neither fiancé nor husband?"

"Has he accosted you before today?" came a third voice, oily, mocking, vile.

Her composure snapped. "He has never accosted me," she retorted hotly. "But I cannot say the same of *you*. Now step aside!" She shoved one of them hard enough that he stumbled, but he caught her wrist instantly, his grip cruel and possessive. "Unhand me!" she cried, struggling. "Leave me alone!"

She twisted free, fury and panic crashing together inside her chest. She tried again to force her way through, but the men only grinned, delighted by her distress.

One reached out and ran the back of his fingers along her cheek. Revulsion flooded her.

"Get your filthy hands off me!" she shouted, slapping his hand away. He laughed and reached for her again, but this time she was faster. Snatching her small perfume bottle from her reticule, she aimed at his face and sprayed.

"Ahhh!" he howled, clutching at his stinging eyes. "You little—!"

She seized her chance to flee. But before she could take more than a step, two of the others grabbed her by the arms and dragged her backward into an empty compartment. The door slammed shut. One yanked the curtain across the window, blotting out the corridor.

"Let go of me!" she gasped, fighting wildly, but their hands only tightened.

"You're a feisty little thing, aren't you?" one drawled, his gaze sweeping over her with vile satisfaction. "Do you think it's wise for such a pretty young heiress to travel alone?"

Her mind reeled. This was wrong, so horribly wrong. Journalists had hounded her before, of course, but never like this. Never with this... menace. Her voice trembled, but she forced herself to stand tall.

"Which newspaper do you represent? I'll be writing to your editor the moment we stop."

2

Under Federal Protection

Their laughter was coarse and cruel. "Who said we're reporters?" one asked, dark mockery dripping from every word. His eyes dragged over her slowly, too slowly. "Maybe we just prefer our stories unprinted." He lunged suddenly, shoving her down onto one of the seats. The reek of sweat and tobacco rolled over her, turning her stomach.

"Stay away from me!" she gasped, twisting as he leaned over her. His face hovered inches from hers, breath hot and foul.

Before he could touch her, Rose snatched the nearest object, the small leather-bound book she always carried, and swung with all her strength. The crack of impact was sharp and gloriously satisfying. He reeled back with a snarl, clutching the side of his face.

"You arrogant little beast!" he spat, ripping the book from her grasp and hurling it to the floor. The others advanced, their shadows blotting out the lamplight.

Rose's heart pounded so violently she could scarcely breathe. But she refused to cower. If she had to fight, she would fight with everything she had, because deep down, she knew she might very well be fighting for her life.

"That is enough!" The roar of a commanding voice split the air like a crack of thunder. The men surrounding Rose jerked around, startled. Heart hammering, Rose, still pressed against the wall, edged sideways, desperate to put even a few inches of distance between herself and her attackers. Her breath came in sharp, trembling bursts.

Framed in the doorway stood the young man she had noticed earlier, the one who had watched her from the platform before the train departed. But now, there was no idle curiosity in his expression. His jaw was set, his shoulders squared in rigid readiness, and his brown eyes blazed with righteous fury.

"This young lady," he said, his voice low but ringing with authority, "has asked you repeatedly to leave her alone. I don't care who you claim to be or whom you work for, you have no right to treat her in such a vile and indecent manner. You've accosted her long enough. It's time you left."

One of the men sneered, swaggering forward.

"And who might you be to tell us what to do?"

"That," the young man replied evenly, without the faintest hesitation, "is none of your concern. Now, leave."

The leader, the brute who had tried to force himself on her, let out a derisive snort.

"So that's it. A gallant type. One of those self-styled heroes who thinks a bit of chivalry will win a girl's trust, and her purse strings. Trying to make her think she needs you, is that it?"

The young man didn't flinch. He didn't even spare the speaker a glance. Instead, he stepped forward again, fully placing himself between Rose and the men who had tormented her. Rose's breath hitched, part shock, part overwhelming gratitude.

Before any of the attackers could answer, another voice rumbled from the corridor—deep, commanding, and instantly chilling.

"Gentlemen, your train ride is over. You'll be meeting the sheriff at our next stop." Two broad-shouldered men stepped into view, long dusters sweeping behind them and silver badges gleaming beneath the carriage lamps. U.S. Marshals.

Rose's knees nearly gave way with relief. Her fingers tightened around the wall rail as her attackers paled visibly.

The marshals stepped inside with calm, lethal assurance, transforming the cramped compartment from a cage of terror into a place of ironclad order. Four deputies followed, along with the conductor, whose face was drawn with anger and shame.

Everything happened in a blur. The nearest marshal seized the leader by the collar and slammed him against the wall with practiced ease. The sharp click of handcuffs rang through the compartment.

"Make one more sound," the marshal growled, "and you'll ride the rest of the way in the stock car."

The man's protest died instantly. Another deputy twisted the next attacker's arm behind his back with merciless precision. The remaining three were stripped of notebooks, pens, and anything even remotely suspicious before being bound as well.

Their jeers, curses, and sputtered excuses grew faint as they were marched down the aisle, and out of sight. Within seconds, the menace that had suffocated the air was gone, leaving behind only the sway of the train and Rose's ragged breathing.

Rose leaned heavily against the wall, trembling from head to toe. Her breath came in uneven bursts. Her fingers numb from gripping her reticule so tightly. The conductor turned to her, stricken.

"Miss Williams, I am deeply sorry. I had no idea those men meant you harm. Had I known of your prominence in Boston, I would have ensured guards in first class."

"No need for guards," one marshal said firmly. "We'll see this young lady safely to her destination."

Rose managed a faint, grateful smile. "Thank you," she whispered.

The young man who had intervened stepped closer, concern softening his strong features. "Are you all right, miss?"

"I think so," she answered, though her voice wavered. A sudden wash of heat swept over her, and her knees buckled. "Perhaps... perhaps not."

A marshal caught her gently by the arm. "Easy. Sit before you fall."

Between the marshals and her rescuer, they guided her back to her compartment. She sank onto the cushioned seat, feeling fragile, weightless, and breakable.

"We'll stay with you awhile," one marshal said reassuringly.

Rose shook her head weakly. "I don't wish to be a burden. Surely you have duties to attend to."

"You're no burden, Miss Williams," he replied with a small, comforting smile. "We're bound for San Francisco, with a stop in Denver. We'll see your aunt and uncle receive you safe and sound."

Her brow furrowed. "You... know where I'm going?"

The marshal beside her—tall, with warm brown eyes—nodded.

"Your father contacted our headquarters in Boston several weeks ago. He requested protection for your journey west. Personal assignments aren't typical, but your father supported the U.S. Marshals Service generously. He was close friends with two of our chief deputies. We were ordered to accompany this train and ensure you came to no harm."

Rose stared, stunned. "You were assigned to travel all the way to the West Coast... for me?"

"Not precisely," said the second marshal with a faint smile. "We'd already been reassigned to the western division. Chief Deputy Walton, whom I believe you know, asked us to leave early so we could look after you. We'll report to our new post in October. Until then, we're making ourselves useful, checking in on federal prisons and reservations along the route."

Recognition softened her expression. She remembered Chief Deputy Walton, the steady-eyed, silver-haired lawman who had visited her father so often.

"Deputy Walton was always so kind. Please give him my gratitude when you next correspond. And thank you, truly."

"It's our pleasure, Miss Williams," the marshal said warmly. "I'm Christopher Moore, and this is my partner, Anthony Jones."

Their steady presence eased the trembling in her hands. For the first time since the attack began, Rose felt something close to safety. Her gaze drifted to the young man seated across from her. Though his expression had been fierce when he stepped in, his composure never wavered. There was strength in the set of his shoulders, yet a quiet warmth in his eyes.

"Thank you," she said softly. "For stepping in when you did. I confess, that was... rather frightening."

"That's perfectly understandable," Marshal Moore said. "Those men were despicable. Journalists can be intrusive, but they had no right to invade your privacy."

Rose shook her head slightly. "I don't believe they were journalists. One of them said something that made me doubt—"

Her words made the marshals exchange swift, sharp glances. Marshal Jones immediately stepped into the corridor, signaling deputies with a grim expression.

Her rescuer turned back to her, offering a gentle smile.

"Forgive me, I haven't introduced myself. My name is Grant Adams."

"Mr. Adams," she murmured, tasting the name softly.

He nodded. "I live in Idaho Springs, not far from your uncle's parsonage. We're neighbors, or as close as neighbors can be when the land between our properties stretches for miles. Your family and mine cross paths often." A warm glint lit his eyes. "Your uncle and aunt speak of you fondly."

Rose blushed and looked down, smoothing a crease in her skirt.

"I haven't seen them in twelve years. What are they like?"

Grant leaned forward slightly, voice sincere and reassuring.

"They're wonderful—warm, witty, compassionate. You'll find your aunt an absolute treasure and your uncle one of the sincerest men alive. Their eldest son, Paul, is studying for the ministry in Denver. He's earned a small congregation, and my little sister's heart, too."

A faint smile touched Rose's lips. "Truly?"

He chuckled. "Truly. I expect a wedding announcement any day now. Their youngest, Jordan, works on my father's ranch. A restless soul, but a good one. He's traveling with Paul at present, but he'll be back before long."

Rose's expression gentled. "And... do you know how they feel about my coming to live with them?"

Grant's eyes softened with warmth. "They're overjoyed. After raising four sons, your aunt is thrilled at the thought of having a young lady in the household again. They've kept fond memories of you. They're eager to welcome you home, though they wish, as we all do, that the circumstances were kinder."

Her throat tightened. She swallowed, nodding faintly. Marshal Moore offered her a small smile.

"Miss Williams—"

"Please," she whispered. "Call me Rose."

Grant's voice dropped, unexpectedly gentle. "That's a beautiful name."

Heat rose to her cheeks again, and she looked down, pretending to adjust her lace cuff. But her heart gave a small, unsteady flutter she could not quite hide. Something warm unfurled within her, something fragile, tentative... yet unmistakably full of hope.

Grant had to admit—Rose Williams was a remarkably beautiful young woman. Her hair, the color of sunlight woven through silk, framed her face in soft waves, and her blue eyes shimmered like morning light dancing upon water.

Even now, with fatigue shadowing her features and worry tightening her delicate expression, he sensed that her true smile, unrestrained and sincere, could brighten an entire room. He found himself wanting, fiercely, to see that smile for himself.

"Your uncle once mentioned," he began gently, hoping to draw her thoughts toward softer memories, "that your grandfather was a duke in England before he renounced his title and immigrated to America. Is that true?"

She nodded faintly. "Yes, that's correct."

Grant leaned forward, his voice warm with curiosity.

"I would love to hear that story."

Her lips curved, but only slightly, and her voice held a quiet sadness.

"I'm afraid I don't know much about it. Father rarely spoke of England, or the life they left behind. My grandfather passed away before I was born."

Before Grant could respond, the compartment door slid open. Marshal Jones stepped inside, his expression grave.

"Did you find out who those men were?" Marshal Moore asked, immediately rising to his feet.

Jones nodded once. "Only one of them is an actual reporter. The other four were hired to accompany him and... harass Miss Williams."

Marshal Moore's eyes darkened. "Harass her? For what purpose?"

Jones exhaled sharply, frustration tightening his jaw.

"Apparently, the owner of the *Boston Codex* holds a personal vendetta against the late Dr. Williams. Her father sued the paper multiple times for printing false reports about his hospital and its high-profile patients, and he won every case."

Grant's jaw clenched. "So, this man decided to take revenge on the daughter."

"Yes." Jones reached into his coat and withdrew a folded newspaper. "We found this in the reporter's bag, along with a note confirming their instructions."

Marshal Moore unfolded the paper, his brow furrowing. "Where's the article?"

"Second-to-last page."

Grant stepped beside him, reading over his shoulder. Cold anger surged through his veins as the bold headline came into view:

Wealthy Heiress Leaving Boston – Will She Take Her Dowry With Her?

After the sudden death of Dr. Edward Williams, his only daughter, Rose, finds herself orphaned and alone. Introduced to society just last year, Miss Williams's father had not yet secured a suitor for her at the time of his passing.

According to information received by this correspondent, the young heiress is expected to relocate to Colorado to live under the guardianship of her aunt and uncle.

Reverend John Williams, of Idaho Springs near Denver, will not only manage her dowry but also determine the choice of her future husband.

Grant's hand curled into a fist. "Why would they publish this?" he demanded. "What purpose does that last line serve except to make her a target? They've turned her into prey."

A sharp gasp sounded behind them. Rose sprang to her feet, her face draining of all color.

"How will I ever be safe again?" she whispered.

"You will be safe," Marshal Moore said firmly. "We'll make certain of it."

"How?" Rose's voice shook, fragile as paper. Tears pooled in her eyes. "This article is practically an invitation for fortune-seekers. Every opportunist west of Boston will know exactly where to find me. I can't go to my aunt and uncle now, I'll endanger them, too!" Her breaths grew quicker, short, shallow gasps. Moore stepped toward her at once, steadying her by the arm.

"Miss Williams—Rose—breathe slowly," he urged. "You're all right. Nothing will happen to you."

But her trembling only worsened. Her vision blurred. Her knees buckled.

"Easy," Moore murmured, catching her before she collapsed. "Stay with me, Rose. Look at me."

With Marshal Jones's help, they eased her onto the seat and gently laid her back, raising her legs to help her breathe. For several tense moments, her breath came in rapid, uneven bursts before, slowly, mercifully, it began to steady. Her complexion, however, remained ghostly pale.

Grant's heart thundered. Panic surged hot and sharp through him.

"I'll fetch a doctor," he said abruptly, rushing into the corridor. He nearly collided with the conductor hurrying from the adjoining car.

"Is there a doctor aboard?" Grant demanded.

The conductor nodded. "Yes, sir, Car B, near the dining compartment." He disappeared and returned moments later with a tall man carrying a black medical bag.

"Shane!" Grant exclaimed. "I didn't know you were in Boston."

The doctor clasped his hand briefly. "My grandfather passed away. My great-uncle asked me to attend the funeral. What's happened?"

As they hurried back toward the compartment, Grant explained in low, urgent tones everything that had transpired.

When they entered, Rose lay reclined against the seat, her eyes open but glassy with shock. Her breathing came shallow and trembling, each breath sounding as though it cost her dearly.

"Rose," Grant said softly as he crouched beside her, his voice laden with worry, "this is Dr. Shane Hunter. He's a family friend, and one of the best physicians in Colorado."

Shane stepped forward, calm and steady, the sort of presence that soothed by simply existing.

"Miss Williams," he said in a low, reassuring tone, "can you tell me what happened?"

Rose parted her lips, but her voice broke before it could form a word. Tears spilled down her cheeks. She turned her face away, overwhelmed and unable to speak.

Marshal Moore filled the silence, his voice firm, edged with sympathy and anger.

"She's suffered a severe shock. The men who attacked her weren't all reporters, only one was. The others were hired agitators. They were acting under orders from the owner of a Boston newspaper who harbored a personal grudge against her late father."

Shane's jaw tightened, fury flickering across his otherwise composed features.

"I see," he murmured darkly. "That explains quite a bit." He set his medical bag on the seat and turned to the others with a voice that brooked no argument. "Gentlemen, please step outside. She needs air and privacy."

The marshals obeyed immediately. Grant hesitated, unwilling to leave her, but the gravity in Shane's voice pushed him to rise. He stepped into the corridor with the marshals.

As Shane drew the curtain across the glass door, Rose's soft, uneven sobs drifted through. Fragile, heartbreaking sounds that made Grant clench his fists helplessly at his sides.

The steady rhythm of the train continued beneath them, indifferent and constant, but inside that small compartment, the world felt unbearably fragile.

HEALING THE ORPHANED HEART

Grant lingered near the window, his back rigid, his fists clenched so tightly his knuckles whitened. Outside, the sun dipped low over the endless sweep of plains, casting the horizon in hues of gold and bruised rose. The view should have been calming, should have reminded him of the vast, steady peace of the West. But all he felt was fury.

What kind of man—what kind of creature—would stoop so low as to torment a grieving young woman simply because her father had defended his honor? To hound her across states, to twist her vulnerability into spectacle, to set hired thugs upon her like wolves? He exhaled sharply, jaw tightening.

Rose Williams did not deserve this. She did not deserve fear or sorrow or the weight of yet another threat pressing upon her from the world beyond Boston. She had already lost her father, her home, the life she had known. And now strangers sought to exploit her grief as though she were nothing more than a headline, an opportunity.

His chest ached at the memory of how fragile she had looked moments ago, tears carving silent paths down her pale cheeks. He didn't yet know what role he might play in her life—he wasn't foolish enough to mistake a few exchanged words for fate. And yet... something within him had shifted the instant he saw her on that platform: alone, afraid, desperately scanning the crowd for someone who might not come.

Whatever the future held, one truth had carved itself into his heart with the certainty of iron: he would do *everything* in his power to protect Rose Williams from the shadows gathering around her. Whether she knew it or not, she wasn't alone. Not anymore.

Dr. Shane Hunter emerged from the compartment a short while later, and the three men waiting in the corridor straightened immediately. His expression remained controlled, but faint lines of concern creased his brow.

"I've given her a mild sedative to calm her nerves," he said quietly. "She's resting now—sound asleep. She should wake in a few hours feeling weak, but steadier."

Grant released a breath he hadn't realized he'd been holding.

"Thank goodness," he murmured. Then, glancing at his friend, he added, "I must say, Shane, I don't believe it's mere coincidence that you and I ended up on this train. What are the odds of traveling to the same town as the young lady who needed our help?"

A faint smile touched Shane's lips. He glanced upward, acknowledging an unseen hand.

"I'd say the Man upstairs arranged that. Providence orders things far better than we ever could."

Marshal Jones folded his arms. "Well, Providence or not, we've got work to do. We'll reach the next station in two hours. Once there, we'll turn those five men over to the local sheriff. Harassment, unlawful restraint, attempted assault, the charges will be significant." He cast a meaningful look at Moore.

"We were originally bound for San Francisco after a brief stopover, but that may need to change. Miss Williams clearly requires continued protection. We'll wire headquarters in Boston, explain the situation, and delay our reassignment until further notice."

Grant's jaw tightened. "You believe someone leaked her travel plans to the *Boston Codex*, then?"

Marshal Moore nodded grimly. "It's the only explanation. Someone with access to her father's household or correspondence. Whoever it was sold that information straight to the paper."

Shane's expression darkened. "Despicable," he muttered. "To turn a grieving young woman into a target simply because of her inheritance... there's no conscience in that."

A heavy silence settled over the men. The rhythmic clatter of the train filled the space between them, a steady reminder that their journey, and Rose's danger, was far from over.

Rose slept soundly until the train slowed its approach to the next station. The gentle jolt of the wheels shifting against the rails stirred her, and she blinked awake, momentarily disoriented. For a breath, she did not know where she was. Then the soft rumble of the train and the fading ache in her chest reminded her.

She turned toward the window. A small frontier town slid into view, its dusty main street lit by lampposts just beginning to glow, its wooden storefronts lined with a scattering of curious onlookers watching the train roll in.

While Marshals Moore and Jones departed with their deputies to deliver the handcuffed men to the sheriff, Grant and Dr. Hunter remained aboard to watch over her. The bustle on the platform eased as passengers dispersed into the evening.

Shane turned to her with a gentle smile.

"Rose, a bit of fresh air might help. You've been through quite an ordeal. A few steps outside could do you good."

Her gaze drifted uneasily toward the platform.

"I'm not sure that's wise," she whispered. "I'd rather stay here."

"Just a short walk," Shane assured her kindly. "You'll feel stronger for it. And we won't leave your side."

Grant stepped forward, offering his hand with quiet confidence.

"He's right. A breath of open air will steady you. I'll help you down."

She hesitated, her heart still bruised, her mind still fragile, but she found no reason to distrust them. After a small pause, she nodded.

"All right."

Grant guided her down the narrow steps, his hand firm beneath hers. The air that greeted her was cool and clean, stirred by a soft breeze scented faintly of pine and distant fields. The sun was sinking toward the horizon, casting warm shades of gold and rose across the clouds. The evening light washed over her face, lending a touch of color to her pale cheeks.

Instinctively, when Grant offered his arm, she rested her hand upon it. The gesture felt grounding—steadying—in a way she desperately needed.

The two men kept their tone light as they strolled a short distance along the platform. They spoke of Colorado's crisp mountain air, of wide-open landscapes, of the contrast between Boston society's rigid expectations and the West's generous hospitality. Their words wove a warm cocoon around her, easing some of the tightness in her chest.

But it wasn't until she looked up and saw Marshals Moore and Jones returning from the sheriff's office—tall, composed, unshakably calm—that a true wave of safety washed over her. Their presence alone, steady as bedrock, was enough to settle her completely. She felt a fragile but certain truth unfurl gently within her: She was protected. And, at least for this moment, she was safe.

Marshal Moore met her gaze and offered a small, reassuring nod, his eyes warm with unspoken concern. To her great dismay, Rose's heart skipped a beat. She looked away at once, feigning interest in the steady stream of passengers walking along the platform.

Don't be foolish, Rose, she scolded herself. *He is at least fifteen years your senior—seasoned, self-assured, and a federal marshal whose work sends him from one end of the country to the other. This is nothing more than a fleeting infatuation. That is all.*

He had saved her. He had spoken gently when she was frightened. And he had treated her with a respect she seldom received from men who claimed refinement. Any young woman, *any sensible young woman*, might feel a flutter of admiration after such gallantry.

Yes. That was all it was. A simple, temporary admiration.

And yet... as he approached, boots striking the platform with steady, unhurried confidence, she found herself smoothing her skirt, tucking an errant curl behind her ear, and willing the warmth in her cheeks to fade.

Compose yourself, she urged sternly. *You are not a child. You must not let your heart run away with you.*

Despite her rational resolve, she could not entirely suppress the truth blooming quietly in her chest. Some feelings, unexpected, impossible, inconvenient, rose of their own accord, no matter how she tried to smother them. And no amount of sensible reasoning could fully silence them.

3
Rescued, Rattled and Held

When Grant, Dr. Hunter, and the two marshals escorted Rose back toward her compartment, they found the narrow aisle swarming with journalists. Men clutched notebooks and pencils, their eager voices rising in a discordant hum that filled the corridor like the irritating buzz of locusts.

The moment Rose appeared, necks craned and murmurs rippled through the crowd. In an instant, the four men closed ranks around her, Grant and Marshal Moore at the front, Marshals Jones and Shane behind, forming a protective barrier that shielded her from both the crush of bodies and the hungry gleam in far too many eyes.

"Gentlemen," Marshal Moore said, his voice clipped and stern, "Miss Williams is not to be questioned. You've already caused enough disruption aboard this train."

One of the reporters bristled, opening his mouth to protest, but Moore's cold, unyielding stare silenced him before a single word escaped. Jones stepped forward, his tone harder still.

"If you value your professional integrity, you'll vacate this car immediately."

A ripple of murmuring swept through the men. The marshals explained, calmly, crisply, the earlier assault and the deceitful pretenses under which the five impostors had cornered her. Faces shifted around them: confusion, then shock, and finally something close to shame.

"We had no idea," one reporter said quietly, removing his hat. "Miss Williams... you have our sincerest apologies."

Another, young, earnest, ink smudged across his fingers, shook his head in disgust.

"The *Boston Codex* has gone too far. We'll make certain the public hears the truth."

Rose's eyes widened, surprise and gratitude flickering across her pale features. She managed a trembling smile, touched by their unexpected integrity.

Two men tipped their hats respectfully before stepping off the train. The rest followed, their expressions subdued. Within moments, the corridor was blessedly clear again, the noise dissipating like a storm drifting over open plains.

Rose exhaled, the tension in her shoulders easing, though only slightly. Exhaustion tugged at every limb, her emotions still stretched thin.

"I... I would like to freshen up," she murmured.

"Of course," Grant said at once.

The men escorted her to the washroom, stopping by the door and positioning themselves discreetly along the corridor, vigilant, immovable, unspoken guardians. No one would disturb her again. Not while they breathed.

Inside, Rose drew a long, shaky breath. The washroom was mercifully large. Along one wall stood a broad table lined with porcelain basins and neatly folded towels. A long mirror stretched above them, reflecting the flickering gaslights. Opposite were three private stalls with polished doors and brass locks.

She hurried into one, bolted the door, and rested her forehead against the cool panel. She needed stillness, just a few minutes where no one could corner her, question her, or look at her with greedy ambition.

A faint creak sounded from the next stall, light footsteps, the rustle of skirts. Likely another woman. Even so, Rose's body tensed, her senses still raw from the ordeal.

She finished quickly and stepped out. At the table, she filled a basin with cool water. The ordinary act steadied her slightly. She lifted her hands to splash her face just as the stall beside hers opened.

A plain but pleasant-looking young woman emerged, offering a shy smile before washing her hands and slipping out. Relief swept through Rose's trembling chest. She turned back to her basin.

Then another sound broke the quiet—the slow, deliberate creak of the third stall door.

Rose glanced toward the mirror. And froze. A man stepped out.

For one terrible heartbeat, disbelief rooted her in place. The sight was so wrong—so impossible—that her mind refused to accept it. Then cold, slicing terror flooded her veins.

She screamed and spun toward the door.

The man lunged, reaching it first. The bolt slid into place with a horrifying click that echoed through the tiled room.

"Let me out!" she cried, rushing toward him and the door.

He caught her around the waist and yanked her backward. Outside, she heard pounding, someone shaking the knob, then a heavy fist striking the door.

"Rose!" Marshal Moore's voice thundered.

She struggled wildly, but the man's grip only tightened.

"You ain't goin' no place, darlin'." he hissed, his sour breath brushing her cheek. Panic surged so fiercely she thought she might faint. Her eyes darted around the room, searching, desperate, for anything she could use as a weapon.

Another slam rattled the door. Before she could scream again, his hand clamped over her mouth.

"Quiet," he whispered, venom dripping from each syllable. His other hand fumbled at the buttons of her bodice. Her heart pounded so violently she feared it might give out.

Think, Rose, think! She forced her body to go still, if only for a moment, just long enough to make him believe she'd given in. Her fingers crept toward her hair... searching... finding the long pin holding it in place.

The instant he leaned closer, his mouth descending toward hers, she struck. With a cry of fury and terror, she drove the sharp end of the pin deep into the back of his hand and bit him savagely along the cheek.

He roared, jerking backward.

Rose gasped for air, trembling so violently she could hardly stand. She bolted toward the exit, but he lunged again, snagging her arm.

"Please," she pleaded, voice breaking. "Just let me go!"

He leered. "If I make you mine now," he growled, "you'll be weddin' me, sure as sunrise."

Revulsion and raw rage ignited inside her. Acting on pure instinct, Rose snatched one of the porcelain basins from the table and smashed it across his head. Water exploded everywhere as the bowl shattered. He cursed and staggered, clutching his temple.

At that moment, the door burst open, splintering from its frame. Marshal Moore, Marshal Jones, and the conductor stormed inside, Grant close behind.

"Get him!" Moore commanded.

Jones and Grant lunged, tackling the assailant before he could regain his footing. The struggle was brief and brutal, the man pinned, cuffed, and hauled upright within seconds.

Moore turned to Rose just as she swayed on her feet. She trembled uncontrollably. Her hands pressed against her chest as though trying to hold herself together. He caught her before her legs gave out, pulling her safely against him.

"It's over," he murmured, voice low and steady. "You're safe now."

Deputies dragged the intruder away. Silence settled over the washroom, broken only by Rose's ragged, uneven breaths.

Then the tears came, great, shuddering sobs that tore through her like a storm. Moore tightened his hold, heedless of propriety, gently smoothing her hair as he whispered steady reassurance.

"It's all right. You're all right."

When her sobs finally subsided, she drew back, cheeks burning with embarrassment.

"I'm so sorry," she said hoarsely.

He shook his head. "Rose, never apologize for surviving. You've every right to your tears." His hand lingered on her shoulder, a quiet, steady reassurance. "Take a moment to compose yourself. Shall I wait here?"

She nodded, unable to speak. While he turned to inspect the broken door, Rose filled a fresh basin, splashed her tear-stained face, and patted it dry. When she caught her reflection, disheveled hair, pale cheeks, eyes red and swollen, she hardly recognized herself. Her gaze dropped to the floor. Her hairpin glinted faintly in a puddle of water. She bent to retrieve it, hands shaking, and fastened it back into place. Then, with trembling fingers, she rebuttoned her dress.

When she turned, Moore stood waiting by the door, posture steady, expression gentle.

"Ready?" he asked softly.

She nodded.

He escorted her back to her compartment. Grant and Marshal Jones joined them moments later. Dr. Hunter entered soon after, his face a mixture of concern and profound relief.

Rose sank into her seat, exhaustion settling over her like a heavy cloak. Around her, the men exchanged grim, protective looks, a silent vow forming between them.

For the first time since her father's death, she understood just how dangerous her journey westward might truly be, and how precious these unexpected guardians had already become in her fight to survive it.

Marshal Moore leaned forward, resting his elbows on his knees, his eyes searching Rose's pale face.

"Can you tell us what happened?"

Her hands trembled, her voice quivered, but she gathered what strength she had and recounted the ordeal: the man hiding in the washroom, the sudden attack, her desperate fight to escape. When she finished, the compartment fell silent except for the rhythmic clatter of the train wheels.

Then a thought struck her. Her throat tightened.

"Is this what my life will be now?" she whispered. Her wide, frightened eyes darted from one man to the next. "Will every man see me as prey because I inherited my father's fortune? Has everyone read that dreadful article in the *Boston Codex*?"

Marshal Jones exchanged a grave look with his partner. Then he reached into his pocket and handed a folded note to Moore.

"We found this in the coat of the man who attacked you. The owner of the *Codex* personally contacted him."

Christopher unfolded the note, his jaw tightening with every line.

Jones continued, "According to this letter, he wasn't supposed to hurt you, just frighten you. Supposedly it was meant to 'send a message.'"

Grant let out a sharp breath, anger flashing in his eyes.

"What a disgusting piece of prairie coal," he spat.

Christopher refolded the paper with a grim shake of his head.

"What is this world coming to?" he muttered.

Dr. Hunter leaned forward, voice gentle. "Rose, I've heard much about your father. He was well known in Boston, among the medical community and the universities back east. You must have been very proud of him."

She lowered her gaze, her expression torn between affection and sorrow.

"He was well liked by his colleagues and patients," she said softly.

"He was a surgeon, wasn't he?" Shane asked.

"Yes."

"I heard he operated on many prominent people, perhaps even President Garfield."

Rose shook her head faintly. "No, not on the president. His staff requested my father after the shooting, but President Garfield wasn't stable enough to be moved. And Father... he was overwhelmed with patients in Boston. He couldn't spare the time for travel."

Grant frowned thoughtfully.

"President Garfield died from his wound, didn't he?"

Rose suspected their questions were meant more to soothe her nerves, than satisfy curiosity, and she was quietly grateful. She nodded.

"He seemed to improve for a time, but the doctors couldn't locate the bullet, even after several attempts. The official report said he died of infection. Father believed it was because the physicians didn't wash their hands properly."

Christopher raised his brows. "He believed that was the cause?"

"Yes," she said, a flicker of passion entering her voice. "Father was adamant about cleanliness, his operating rooms, his tools, everything. He studied the work of Dr. Ignaz Semmelweiss, an Austrian physician. Semmelweiss discovered that when doctors washed their hands before treating patients, mortality rates dropped drastically. Father admired him deeply, though few in the medical field took those findings seriously."

Shane nodded with approval.

"My great-uncle has come to the same conclusion. He insists on washing before every procedure, though many of his colleagues scoff. They'll learn soon enough."

A quiet smile touched Rose's lips. "That sounds like something my father would have said."

Marshal Jones tilted his head. "Were you and your father close?"

Rose hesitated, then released a slow sigh.

"Not exactly. After my mother died, Father retreated into his work. He spent hours locked away in his study or away at conventions. He avoided social gatherings entirely unless he had to go. Our butler once told me Mother had kept the house warm and lively. After she passed, that warmth vanished."

Christopher nodded. "He sounds like a man devoted to his calling."

"He was," Rose agreed. "But I think it was easier for him to bury himself in work than face his grief. Perhaps I reminded him too much of her... and it became painful to be near me."

"I'm sorry, Rose," Jones said gently.

She gave a weary shrug. "It is what it is."

Christopher's voice softened. "He did make sure you were cared for, though?"

"Yes," she said. "Our butler and my governess loved me as their own. The staff were kind. When I turned sixteen, Father tried to reconnect. He insisted on introducing me to society and was determined to secure a suitable match."

Grant's brow furrowed. "You were being courted at sixteen?"

"He wanted me well matched," Rose said with a faint, rueful smile. "He had strong opinions about which young men were suitable. Whenever I took interest in someone, he disapproved. When I turned seventeen, he allowed three suitors to call, but I found them insufferable. And then, quite suddenly, he fell ill."

"Typhus," Christopher said quietly.

Rose nodded. "He often visited the poor districts, treating the sick for free. He must have caught it there. I received a letter from the hospital saying he was dying... that I wasn't allowed to see him. I never even got to say goodbye." Her voice fractured.

Christopher reached across and gently took her hand.

"I'm truly sorry, Rose."

She managed a tremulous smile. "Thank you. I try not to dwell on it. We weren't close... but I wish we had parted in peace."

Marshal Jones cleared his throat. "Did he leave you anything personal? Something to remember him by?"

"Not much," she admitted. "He dictated a final letter through his nurse. He wrote that he cared for me, that Uncle John would become my guardian, and that all his assets were to go into my dowry. He instructed the butler and solicitor to sell everything except what I wished to keep and to settle his debts with the staff. The remainder was to be placed in a joint account in my name and Uncle John's."

Grant shook his head slowly. "And all this turmoil... simply because your father dared to hold a corrupt newspaper accountable."

Rose nodded. "My father dismissed his financial advisor for leaking information to the *Boston Codex*. The story was published without consent. Father sued—and won. The settlement cost the owner dearly. He never forgave it."

"Your father sounds like a man of integrity," Grant said softly, admiration clear in his voice.

A genuine smile warmed Rose's face. "He was. Despite his flaws, he treated everyone with dignity, regardless of station. He invested in ventures not for profit but to help others. He supported hospitals, paid debts, funded new businesses... all quietly."

Grant nodded. "And yet he was distant with you."

"Yes," she said gently, "but he set an example I'll never forget. He told me money and status should never determine a person's worth. My closest childhood friend was the son of one of our housekeepers. His father was a drunk, but Father never forbade our friendship." She drew a steadier breath. "I only hope Uncle John will let me use part of my dowry to continue Father's work."

Grant smiled warmly. "He will, Rose. John Williams isn't the sort to control your life. He's fair, level-headed, and kind."

She looked uncertain. "He only has sons. It's easy to be lenient with them."

"John and Lizzie won't treat you as a burden," Grant said firmly. "They'll protect you, yes, but they won't dictate your choices. That's simply not who they are."

"How can you be so sure?"

He smiled. "Because the West isn't like Boston. People care less about titles and reputations. They care about honesty, hard work, and survival. Idaho Springs is simpler, and kinder, than the world you've left behind."

Christopher nodded. "He's right. Life out west has its hardships, but it also has freedom. Sometimes that makes all the difference."

Rose listened, her heart swelling with a fragile but growing hope. Maybe, just maybe, her life in Colorado would not be the lonely exile she had feared. Perhaps it might even become a new beginning.

To ensure Rose's safety through the night, the two marshals agreed to stand watch outside her compartment, each taking half the shift. Marshal Moore volunteered for the first, while his partner, Anthony Jones, returned to his seat a few cars down to rest before dawn.

The train swayed gently as it carved its path through the darkness. The rhythmic clatter of the wheels echoed faintly through the nearly silent corridor, the lamps casting soft pools of golden light that flickered with each subtle motion of the carriage.

Christopher stood with his back against the doorframe of Rose's compartment, alert yet composed, one hand resting loosely near the revolver at his hip. His eyes scanned the shadows with the steady, practiced vigilance of a man long accustomed to danger.

He had been standing barely an hour when a muffled cry shattered the stillness.

"No... leave me alone," Rose whimpered from within the compartment. Her voice trembled, pitched with rising fear. "Please, get away from me. Help! Somebody, help me!"

Christopher's calm broke at once. He pushed the door open and slipped inside, moving swiftly and quietly through the dark.

Rose tossed and turned on the narrow bed, her face ghostly pale in the sliver of moonlight filtering through the curtain. Her hands clawed desperately at the sheets, her breathing ragged, as though fighting off an unseen assailant.

Christopher knelt beside her, careful not to startle her further.

"Rose," he said softly, laying a gentle but steady hand on her shoulder. "It's me, Marshal Moore."

At his touch, she jolted upright with a gasp, her chest rising and falling in sharp, uneven bursts. Her eyes were wide, wild, unfocused. For several frantic heartbeats she seemed not to know where she was. Her gaze darted around the small compartment in panicked confusion.

Then, slowly, recognition dawned. She pressed a trembling hand to her chest.

"It... it was just a dream," she whispered, her voice cracking with lingering terror. Christopher immediately withdrew his hand, giving her space so she wouldn't feel cornered or embarrassed.

"You're safe now," he said gently. "Nothing can reach you here. Will you be all right?"

Rose swallowed hard and nodded, though her voice trembled.

"Y-yes. I think so. Thank you. And... thank you for waking me."

He inclined his head in a quiet, reassuring gesture.

"Try to rest. I'll be right outside." With that, Christopher slipped from the compartment and eased the door shut behind him, resuming his post with renewed vigilance, more determined than ever to keep nightmares, both real and imagined, from touching her again.

Inside, Rose sank back against her pillow, her breath unsteady as she covered her face with her hands. Relief and humiliation tangled painfully in her chest, relief that Marshal Moore had come the instant she cried out, and humiliation that he had found her so vulnerable, so unguarded.

She prayed it had been too dark for him to see the tears streaking her cheeks... to notice the way she shook like a frightened child.

He must think me fragile... foolish... weak. The thought made her throat tighten.

The carriage swayed softly, the steady clack of the rails beneath her weaving a lullaby she was far too tense to accept. Sleep did not return easily. Each time she closed her eyes, the day's horrors leapt back, shadows looming behind washroom doors, the cold grip of a stranger's hands, the echo of her own terrified cries.

Even the moments of kindness that followed, the marshals' protection, Grant's steady presence, Shane's calm reassurance, were overshadowed by the raw fear embedded deep in her bones. She shifted beneath the blanket, pressing her palms to her eyes as if she could block the memories themselves.

You are safe, she told herself. *He said you are safe. He is just outside your door.*

But safety felt like a fragile promise, shaken easily by darkness and exhaustion. Only after a long, aching stretch of time did the relentless replay of the day begin to soften. The motion of the train, its gentle rocking, its steady heartbeat, gradually threaded through her frayed nerves. Her breathing slowed. Her muscles loosened. At last, with a final, shuddering sigh, Rose's eyes fluttered closed. And this time, sleep took her.

Morning came with the train slowing to a crawl, the pale light of dawn spilling softly through the curtains. Rose stirred, her lashes fluttering as she blinked awake. A faint calm settled over her, fragile, but real.

From the other side of the compartment door drifted the gentle murmur of voices: a woman's, high-pitched and familiar, followed by the deep, steady timbre of Marshal Moore.

Rose smiled sleepily. She knew that voice, the elderly woman she had helped the previous afternoon. She could picture the scene easily: the poor dear turned around once again in the long corridor, and Marshal Moore, ever patient, guiding her back with quiet reassurance. Through the door, his voice carried warm and steady, like the hum of the rails beneath them.

Another voice joined the conversation—lighter, amused, unmistakably youthful.

"There you are, Grandmother," the young man said, laughter in his tone. "That is the last time I let you go to the lavatory alone."

"Oh, Daryl, don't fuss," the older woman scolded affectionately. "If I hadn't wandered off, I wouldn't have met this charming, handsome marshal."

Two masculine laughs followed, one rich and youthful, the other low and warm.

"Thank you for assisting my grandmother," Daryl said.

"It was my pleasure," Christopher replied, and Rose could hear the smile in his voice. She lay back against her pillow for a moment longer, letting the sound wash over her, kind voices, gentle banter, morning light. After the terror of the day before, it felt like waking into a different world. A safer one.

4

When the Marshal
Caught Her

Rose couldn't help smiling. *How kind he is,* she thought. *So calm... so considerate.* His gentle patience with the elderly woman warmed her heart more than she cared to admit. She decided to take advantage of the moment, while he was still engaged in conversation just outside, to slip quietly to the washroom without drawing attention. She dressed quickly, smoothing her hair and straightening the bodice of her traveling gown, wanting to appear composed after the restless night.

Just as she reached for her reticule, she froze. Her soap and towel, she had forgotten them. With a small sigh at her own scatterbrained state, she stepped back inside the compartment and set the reticule on the seat.

"Which trunk did I pack them in?" she murmured, scanning the overhead shelf. After a moment's thought, she remembered. Not one of her largest trunks, but still heavy enough to give her pause.

She slipped off her shoes for better balance, stepped up onto the cushioned seat, and reached for the trunk. Her fingertips brushed the handle. She eased it forward, hoping to lower it just enough to retrieve her things. She never got the chance.

The train gave a sudden, violent jolt and screeched to an abrupt halt. Rose gasped, pitching off balance. She slipped, falling backward in a helpless tumble as the trunk slid free, hurtling toward her in a heavy blur.

She threw up her arms in reflex, bracing for impact, but instead of pain, she collided with solid warmth and strength. Two strong arms closed around her, catching her in mid-fall and drawing her against a broad, steady chest. The trunk struck the floor with a thunderous crash that rattled the windows.

For a breathless instant, she found herself staring up into Marshal Moore's face, mere inches from her own. His eyes were wide with alarm... and unmistakably touched with amusement.

Her cheeks ignited. He must have seen the entire ridiculous spectacle. Before either of them could speak, the conductor appeared in the doorway, flustered and red-faced.

"Is everything all right in here?"

Rose shut her eyes, mortified beyond measure. She became acutely aware she was still held in the marshal's arms, his grip secure and protective, as though he had no intention of letting her fall even now. She tried to shift away, but his arms reflexively tightened, drawing her a fraction closer. A tiny, involuntary gasp escaped her.

"We're fine," Christopher replied calmly, his voice steady despite the adrenaline still thrumming beneath it. "Miss Williams was reaching for her trunk when the train stopped suddenly. I caught her before she fell. Fortunately, no harm done."

"Thank goodness," the conductor breathed, visibly relieved. "The brake line stuck for a moment. Everything's in order now." He tipped his hat and hurried down the aisle.

Rose remained suspended in the marshal's arms for another heartbeat, long enough for her breath to tangle, long enough for her heart to forget its duties, before her wits finally scrambled back into place.

Her dignity, bruised but stubborn, rallied at last, reminding her sternly that a respectable young lady ought not remain cradled against a man's chest, no matter how steady or safe he felt.

Once the conductor was gone, Marshal Moore turned back to her with a faint, amused smile tugging at his lips.

"You know," he said lightly, "if you'd like me to put you down, you can simply ask."

Her face went scarlet.

"I... I didn't want to interrupt your conversation," she managed, mortified by how breathless she sounded.

"That was very considerate of you." His grin widened, warm, teasing, as he slowly and carefully set her back onto her feet, as though she were something fragile and precious he dared not mishandle.

Rose steadied herself, smoothing her skirts with trembling fingers, and slipping back into her shoes. When she finally dared to look up, she found his brown eyes bright with humor, and something softer beneath it. For a disarming heartbeat, she forgot how to breathe. Her stomach fluttered, her pulse leapt traitorously in her throat.

"I'm so sorry," she murmured, stepping back as quickly as dignity allowed.

"It could have happened to anyone," he said gently. "Please don't trouble yourself over it."

His kindness only flustered her more. She gave a small, nervous smile, then turned to the fallen trunk and retrieved her towel and soap with as much composure as she could muster.

"If you'll excuse me..." she said softly, attempting a graceful exit.

"I'll come with you," he replied at once, so naturally she wondered if he even realized how protective it sounded.

She hesitated, startled by how reassuring those four simple words felt. Then she nodded. Together, they walked down the corridor toward the washroom. Ever vigilant, Christopher strode a half-step ahead, glancing over his shoulder now and then to ensure she was safe. When they reached the door he knocked, paused, and stepped inside first. He checked each stall, each corner, then turned back to her.

"It's all clear," he said with a nod, holding the door open. "You may go in."

And once again, Rose found her heart fluttering, not from fear, but from the quiet, steadfast way he watched over her.

⁓

Once alone, Rose poured cool water into the basin and splashed it onto her face, hoping the chill would calm the warmth still burning in her cheeks. The washbowl gleamed beneath the soft morning light, and the room, freshly cleaned after yesterday's chaos, was once again orderly and serene. Her thoughts, however, were anything but.

Her heart still raced. No matter how she tried to steady herself, the memory lingered—the startling strength of Marshal Moore's arms around her, the steadiness of his grip, the faint scent of soap and leather that clung to him... the way he had held her as though her safety mattered more than anything else in the world.

Get ahold of yourself, Rose, she scolded silently, gripping the edge of the basin. *You're only flustered because he rescued you. Again.* She lifted her gaze to the mirror. Her reflection stared back: pale cheeks, weary eyes, and a small tremor at the corner of her mouth she couldn't quite quell.

"He doesn't see you that way," she whispered. "To him, you're just a girl he's been assigned to protect. You are not yourself right now," she murmured. Grief, fear, exhaustion, they all churned within her, tugging her heart in reckless directions.

Taking one last steadying breath, she straightened her shoulders, dabbed her face dry, smoothed her hair, adjusted her dress, and collected the scattered pieces of her composure.

At least, she reminded herself firmly, *the marshal's duty will end soon enough, once I reach the safety of my aunt and uncle's home in Colorado.*

She *should* have felt comfort in the thought. She *should* have welcomed the promise of a quiet life far from danger. And yet... even as she insisted on it, a small, treacherous part of her heart whispered otherwise, a part that wished his duty would never end.

When Rose and Marshal Moore returned to her compartment, Marshal Jones, Grant, and Dr. Hunter were already waiting.

"Good morning," Jones greeted, rising as the door slid back. "Shall we break our fast? We've reserved a table in the restaurant carriage."

Rose nodded, and the five of them made their way down the aisle together.

The restaurant compartment, one bright, elegant link between first class and the rest of the train, was already humming with soft conversation and the clink of porcelain. Their table sat at the far end, near a window where the morning light fell clean across linen, silver, and steaming pots of tea.

As Rose took her seat, she noticed several small faces peering shyly through the door pane: children in thin coats, their eyes solemn, their cheeks pinked from the morning chill. The sight tugged at her heart.

The conductor passed just then. Rose lifted a hand.

"Excuse me, why aren't those children coming in?"

He followed her gaze and sighed.

"They're from the emigrant cars, miss. Their parents spent all they had on passage. The dining car is for first-class patrons only."

"Please let them in," Rose said at once. "I'll pay for their meals."

The conductor looked stricken.

"I'm sorry, Miss Williams. The rules are strict. Non–first-class passengers simply aren't permitted to dine here."

"Oh." Rose hesitated, only a heartbeat. "Then... may I pay for their food, and have it sent to them?"

The man shifted uneasily. "We can arrange trays to the emigrant compartments, yes. But it isn't only those children who are hungry. There are many families aboard with very little. If you wished to feed them all, it would—well, it would be considerable."

"I'm not concerned with the cost," she said quietly. "Please see that two meals a day are delivered to every family in need for the remainder of their journey." She lowered her voice. "And I'd prefer to remain anonymous."

For a long moment, the conductor only stared.

"Two meals a day?" he echoed under his breath. He caught himself, straightened, and tipped his cap. "Very good, miss. I'll work with the kitchen and porters at once."

"Thank you."

Around the table, four men tried, and failed, to hide their smiles.

"That's very kind of you, Rose," Marshal Jones said softly. Moore, Grant, and Dr. Hunter nodded in agreement. "I'm certain those families will remember it."

"It saddens me there are so many to remember," she murmured, glancing again toward the doors as the children were ushered away. "A society that thrives ought not look past its hungry."

A waiter arrived with a tray and an easy, almost oblivious confidence.

"The government looks after such folks, does it not?" he ventured as he set out cups and saucers.

Rose met his eye, her tone gentle but unwavering.

"We hide them," she said. "Poorhouses—crowded, harsh, unfit for anyone. Many insist poverty is sloth, when often it is misfortune: a failed harvest, a landlord's rent, a tax beyond bearing. Shame follows hunger. Shame drives men to drink. Drink begets violence, and soon there is even less bread for the table." Her voice softened. "We blame the wound for bleeding."

The waiter blinked, chastened, and slipped away. Only then did she realize how quiet the table had become. The men were very still, watching her with something like respect. Heat rose to her cheeks.

"My best friend and his parents lived in a poorhouse for years," she added, lowering her voice. "When my father discovered it, he purchased a small cottage and let it to them for almost nothing." Her throat tightened, and she reached for her cup to steady her hands.

They began to eat. Conversation around them ebbed and flowed, the clink of china, murmured greetings, the soft drone of travelers beginning a new day. But within their own circle, a thoughtful hush had settled.

Rose's thoughts drifted, back to the men who had harassed her, the *Boston Codex*, and the way bitterness and greed could so easily be sharpened into weapons. Unfair. The word rang inside her like a struck bell.

Would she ever feel safe again? Would every platform, every corridor, hide another hand reaching for her?

She lifted her gaze through her lashes. Marshal Moore sat across from her, listening to Jones describe the night watch. His profile was steady, unshowy, grounded by the quiet assurance she felt even from a distance.

A faint blush crept from Rose's collar to her cheekbones. Each time he had pulled her from danger, her heart had taken longer to settle. It frightened her, not the feeling itself, but the audacity of it: to find comfort in a man whose life belonged to law, duty, and the rails.

She turned toward the window, letting the rush of late-morning light and blurred fields calm her breathing. A light touch on her sleeve made her start.

"Rose?" Moore's voice was low, pitched only for her. "Are you quite well? You seemed... far away."

She tried to smile. "I am well enough," she said, and then realized, with some surprise, that it was true. So long as he stood within reach, she felt steadier than she had in days. But she could not explain the tangle inside her: terror braided to gratitude, gratitude warming into something more dangerous. And beneath it all, guilt—for Andrew's earnest promise on the platform, for a friendship she cherished and a love she could not return. Her fingers tightened around her napkin.

"Only a little... overtired," she added, choosing the safer truth.

Moore nodded, accepting her answer without pressing.

"If the noise is too much, we can return to your compartment and take our coffee there," he offered gently. "Jones will see to the account."

"Thank you," she murmured, comforted by both the suggestion and the warmth beneath it. And for the first time that morning, she felt herself breathe a little easier.

A few minutes later, the conductor returned, slightly breathless, a ledger tucked beneath his arm and his cap askew from hurry.

"Arrangements are in motion, Miss, ah—ma'am," he corrected himself quickly, recalling her request for anonymity. "We've compiled a list of families by compartment. The kitchen will send bread and broth at midday, porridge for the little ones, and a proper stew for supper. Discreetly." He tapped the ledger. "No names mentioned."

"Perfect," Rose said, her shoulders loosening with relief. "And if any prefer tea to coffee, see that they have it."

"We will." He hesitated, shifting his weight. "There are also two elderly ladies in the third emigrant car who... well, they look like they might need a shawl more than a second roll."

"Then they shall have *both*," Rose replied without missing a beat. "Ask the porter to fetch whatever is needed from the dry-goods trunk. I'll reimburse the cost."

The conductor nodded briskly, made a quick note, and bowed himself away with renewed purpose. Grant leaned back, amusement softening his features.

"You realize you've put half the train crew to work."

"Good," Rose replied, allowing herself a small, genuine smile. "Let them be busy with kindness for a change."

"Spoken like your father, I imagine," Dr. Hunter said warmly.

This time, the words did not tug painfully at old wounds. Instead, they settled around her like a gentle cloak. For once, they steadied her.

5

Rescued

When the meal ended, Marshal Moore rose and offered his arm, his manner courteous but unmistakably protective. "Shall we return to your compartment now?"

"Yes," she answered, rising. "I think I would like that."

They moved down the aisle together, her gloved hand resting lightly in the crook of his arm. Rose glanced out the window as they walked, the sweep of late-morning light stretching across the racing horizon.

Fear still paced the edges of her thoughts, a restless shadow that refused to fully leave her. But it no longer held the center of her heart. In its place stood something steadier, choice, perhaps. Or the first fragile shape of courage.

And when Marshal Moore's hand closed gently, almost unconsciously, over her gloved fingers, the clatter of the train softened into a calmer rhythm. A rhythm she could breathe by.

Rose had barely taken her seat, her mind still whirling from everything she had endured, when she realized the four men were watching her with quiet, attentive concern. Flustered, she drew a slow breath. Had they asked her something?

As if sensing her distraction, Marshal Moore leaned forward slightly, his voice gentle but steady.

"Are you all right? Your mind keeps wandering off."

Rose hesitated, unsure how to answer. *Was* she all right? How could she explain the tangle within her heart, the fear, the confusion, and that other feeling she scarcely dared to name? Each time Marshal Moore came to her aid, each time his calm voice and steady hands anchored her, the terror inside her softened into something warmer. Something perilous. Something she had no business feeling. But how could she confess any of that with all four men watching her?

Perhaps if she focused only on the fear, they might stop looking at her with such piercing kindness. Their collective gaze stirred the butterflies in her stomach into a frenzy.

"Am I all right?" she repeated softly. "I'm... not sure I know how to answer that. I'm frightened—angry too. I don't want to live a life where I must always depend on someone else's protection. I simply wish to live in peace." Her voice wavered, but she pressed on.

"It's difficult enough to leave the life I've known, the people who loved me, and begin again somewhere I've never been. Aside from you, Grant, and Dr. Hunter, I don't know a soul in Colorado. I don't even remember my relatives." She lifted her gaze to Christopher Moore, her heart full of fear, longing, and something unspoken.

Gently, he reached across the table and gave her hand a reassuring squeeze before letting it go.

"You'll find your life again, Rose," he said with quiet conviction. "In time, I believe you'll come to love your new home. You're a strong young lady. The losses and hardships you've faced will serve you well in everything ahead."

"What if they don't?" she whispered. "I'm going to a place where people will look at me and see only a girl who has everything, someone to envy, not to know."

No one spoke at first. Encouraged by the silence, Rose felt something loosen in her chest. The words poured out of her as if a dam had broken.

"I didn't have many friends in Boston. No one cared to truly know me. Whenever I thought I had found a friend, and dared to open up, they told me to stop feeling sorry for myself. They thought I had no right to complain. They couldn't imagine that a girl with a wealthy father and a fine house could have troubles of her own." Her voice softened.

"No one cared that I had no mother. No one cared that my father cared more for his work than for me. He left me in the hands of others, kind hands, yes, but... they were not his."

A long sigh escaped her, and then, almost as if speaking to herself, she continued.

"I'll never forget the trouble I had at school. I was six years old. A group of boys attacked me."

Christopher's expression hardened. "Attacked you?"

She nodded faintly.

"They were several years older. They said I was a 'dumb rich girl.' They beat me for it. People think money brings happiness, but a grand house means nothing if there's no love inside it. I was fortunate to have Thomas, our butler, and Charlotte, my governess. They were my family." Her eyes shimmered with the memory's sting.

"Why would a group of boys ambush a little girl?" Moore asked, anger tightening his voice. "Where were the adults?"

"Thomas was late that day. He always took me to and from school, but a delay kept him. I stayed on the grounds—it should have been safe. The boys must have been watching. They waited until the teachers were gone, then cornered me behind the building." She swallowed, forcing the words out.

"They demanded money. I told them I had none. They didn't believe me. They searched my satchel, threw my books on the ground. When they found nothing, they demanded I bring them money the next day. I refused. That's when they started hitting me with sturdy sticks. One even had a cane."

All four men inhaled sharply.

"Two of them held me down while the others struck me," Rose whispered. "They thought they could beat me into obedience. Even then, I knew that if I gave in once, they'd do it again. I had to stand my ground." Her jaw tightened at the memory.

"They slapped my face, and no matter how I begged them to stop, they only laughed. Finally, a teacher saw what was happening. He grabbed two of the boys by their collars, and the rest fled. Another teacher came running, and just then... Thomas arrived." Her gaze drifted, far away.

"I'll never forget the look on his face, rage and heartbreak together. He looked as though he could have killed them."

Marshal Jones's voice was taut with anger.

"I hope they were punished. Severely. With a belt, a strap, or even the cane they brought."

Grant nodded grimly. Rose looked between them, her expression calm but resolute.

"And what good would that have done? Beating children to teach them not to be violent? Adults tell children not to strike others, yet use the same hand to discipline them. Shouldn't we lead by example?"

The four men exchanged thoughtful glances, chastened by her quiet wisdom. Feeling lighter, Rose straightened.

"Thomas took me home and sent a servant to fetch my father. He came at once and treated my wounds himself. Everyone in the household was horrified. When Father saw me, tears filled his eyes. He tried to be gentle, but the pain was terrible." Her voice softened to a fragile whisper.

"That was the only time after my mother's death that he held me. He sat beside me and simply... held me."

Marshal Jones regarded her with quiet compassion.

"No one has shown you that kind of affection since?"

A faint smile touched her lips. "Our servants did," she said softly. "They were the ones who truly loved me. I don't know what would have become of me without them."

When the train finally rolled into Denver, Rose's stomach tightened. This was the last stop of her long, harrowing journey by rail. From here, the final miles would be by stagecoach into the mountains, into Idaho Springs, where her uncle lived.

Dr. Hunter and Grant had tried to reassure her that all would be well, that her uncle was a kind and godly man, but comfort could only reach so far. No matter how she tried, a small knot of dread refused to loosen. What if he was stern? Cold? Distant, as her father had been? What if she had traded one lonely house for another?

The four men helped her down from the train. Warm summer air brushed her face, fragrant and bright, yet the sunlight did little to dispel the chill gripping her chest. The station bustled around her, porters shouting numbers, steam hissing from the engine, horses stamping at the hitching rails. The noise pressed in from every side.

Her gloved hands twisted together as she scanned the platform, searching for a man she barely remembered. Then a familiar voice—deep, warm, unmistakably kind—called behind her.

"Rose?"

She turned sharply—and froze. The man approaching looked so much like her father that, for a fleeting instant, her heart lurched into her throat. The same broad shoulders, the same hazel eyes, the same dark hair streaked with silver.

But the resemblance ended there. Where her father's gaze had grown cold and weary, her uncle's eyes were gentle—alight with affection, relief, and a spark of humor beneath the brim of his hat.

Her throat tightened. "Uncle John…"

Before she could say another word, he stepped forward and gathered her into his arms. His embrace was warm and strong, protective in a way she had not felt since childhood, and the tenderness of it undid her completely. She bit her lip hard, but the tears spilled anyway, fast and hot, as she buried her face against his chest. He simply held her, saying nothing, letting her weep until the storm inside her eased.

When at last she drew back, he kept one steady hand on her shoulder and gently tipped her chin upward.

"You look so much like your mother," he said softly, his own eyes shining. "For a moment, I thought I was looking right at her. Lily had those same beautiful blue eyes. Everything about you reminds me of her."

A trembling smile touched Rose's lips.

"And you... you look so much like Father."

John's expression softened, though sorrow flickered at the edges.

"I'm sorry about him, Rose," he murmured. "It isn't fair that you've had to lose both your parents so young."

She shrugged faintly, honesty outweighing sentiment.

"It is what it is. I hardly knew him, really."

Surprise flickered across her uncle's features, but after a moment he nodded, respecting her truth.

"Come," he said at last, giving her hand a gentle squeeze. "We've still a few hours to go by stagecoach. Let's get your luggage sorted." He called two porters over, directing them as they collected her trunks, then turned back to her with a reassuring smile, trying, she sensed, to dispel her worry.

"The stagecoach leaves in an hour," he said. "Plenty of time for a cup of tea."

Rose nodded, relief and apprehension tangling in her chest, and followed him toward the station doors.

They had not gone far when several men slipped out of the milling crowd, forming a loose ring around her. Their movements were too smooth, too coordinated, nothing about them felt casual. Their smiles were thin. Practiced.

Rose stepped back. Then again. Her shoulders struck the wall behind her.

"Miss Williams," one called, raising his voice. "How was your trip West?"

"Are you eager to begin your new life in Colorado?" another added brightly, notebook in hand.

Journalists. Or so they claimed.

"Leave me alone," Rose said firmly, trying to slip past them. But they shifted with her, blocking her path.

"Why did you attack the journalists on the train?" one demanded with a sneer. "Is that how you treat the press when someone tries to interview you?"

Rose blinked, stunned. "What are you talking about?"

"Are you *denying* that you assaulted two reporters?" another shot back. "We have the Codex's story right here." He waved a folded newspaper in her face.

Shock flared into white-hot fury.

"Assaulted? They were the ones who attacked me, and only one of them was even a real journalist. Perhaps it's time you stop believing everything printed in that dreadful paper."

Unease flickered across a few faces. But two men, standing slightly apart, wore smirks that told her they weren't here for truth. They were here for sport.

Rose drew herself up, her voice firm.

"If you're truly journalists, show me your badges. Which newspapers do you represent?"

The men hesitated. None replied.

"That's what I thought," she said sharply. "Now step aside."

But when she tried to slip through the gap, one man lunged, seizing her wrists and shoving her back against the wall.

"You've got a sharp tongue for someone so delicate," he hissed.

Before she could cry out, a thunderous voice cracked across the platform.

"That's enough!" Uncle John was there in an instant, his face dark with fury. He grabbed the man by the coat and tore him away from her, stepping bodily between Rose and the group.

"You will not lay a hand on my niece," he growled. "Now back away before I lose my temper."

The men fell back, startled by the force of his anger, but the one who had grabbed her stubbornly held his ground.

"We only want an interview, Mr. Williams. Surely—"

"You've had your answer," John snapped. "Now go."

"Mr. Williams—"

"Enough, Murphy." The new voice came from behind the group. Two men approached, calm, composed, professional in bearing. One carried a notebook. The other wore a press badge pinned on his lapel.

"It's pathetic," the first said, glaring at Murphy. "You call yourself a journalist, but you're nothing more than a hired bully."

The second nodded sharply. "We know exactly what's going on. We saw the Codex's call to action, how the owner urged his correspondents to intimidate Miss Williams. It's despicable."

Murphy scoffed. "You don't know what you're talking about."

"Don't we?" the man countered. "You're giving honest reporters a bad name. Now get out of here before someone calls the sheriff."

"Already done," John said flatly. His stance did not shift an inch. He was every inch the protective uncle, unmovable as stone.

Murphy hesitated, jaw working, then jerked his head at his companions. One by one, they slunk away, swallowed by the restless crowd of the station.

As soon as the harassers retreated into the crowd, the two legitimate journalists turned toward Rose. Gone were the sharp, probing expressions she had come to expect from the press. Their faces held only concern—quiet, genuine, unguarded.

"We're truly sorry for what you just endured, Miss Williams," the taller man said. "The owner of the *Boston Codex* is playing a dangerous game. Ever since he lost those lawsuits to your father, he's been trying to turn the entire industry against you both."

The second nodded, his voice low.

"The *Circadian Patriot* out of Harrisburg has already issued warnings. They're urging every respectable paper not to fall for the Codex's smear campaign. What happened on that train wasn't journalism, it was hired intimidation."

John straightened, still protective, still wary.

"And which paper do you write for?"

"The *Digest*, out of Colorado Springs," the taller reporter replied, presenting his badge as proof. John inspected it carefully before offering a curt nod. Only then did the iron tension in his shoulders ease.

Rose's strength slipped away all at once. She sank to the ground, her back pressing against the sun-warmed wall of the station. Her breath came in shallow, uneven pulls. Her hands trembled uncontrollably in her lap. The stares, the accusations, the grip on her wrists, it all came crashing back over her in a sickening wave.

John knelt beside her without hesitation. His hand found her arm—steady, warm.

"It's over now," he murmured. "You're safe."

She swallowed hard, fighting to pull air into her lungs.

"They... they came out of nowhere."

John's expression hardened, resolve cutting sharp lines across his face. He turned slightly toward the journalists.

"Please tell me everything you know about the incident on the train," he said quietly, and they filled him in. He shook his head before turning back to Rose, his hazel eyes darkening with controlled fury.

"So, it's true. A group of men harassed you?"

Rose nodded, her voice barely above a whisper. "Yes."

John's jaw tightened as if he were clamping down on words too sharp for her ears. His hand slid from her arm to her shoulder, firm, protective.

"Then hear me now," he said, voice low and unshakable. "Whoever is behind this vile, cowardly business will answer, to me, and to the law. No one will threaten you again without finding consequences waiting for them."

Her lips parted, trembling. Tears filled her eyes, not from fear this time, but from the overwhelming relief of not being alone. Of being defended without reservation. For the first time since she had stepped onto the train in Boston, Rose truly felt what it meant to be protected, not by an escort, not by duty, not by circumstance... but by family.

"After they were released from jail," one of the reporters explained, "the so-called journalist returned to Boston and wrote an article claiming Miss Williams attacked and assaulted him." He turned to Rose with a sympathetic smile. "Would you care to share your side of the story?"

Rose hesitated for only a moment, then nodded. Her voice was steady as she recounted what had happened on the train: the harassment, the invasive questions, the way they had cornered her in the corridor and forced her into the compartment. Her composure only faltered once, when she described the moment, she had been forced to defend herself with the only weapon she had.

"I only protected myself," she finished quietly. "They accosted me. I didn't attack anyone."

Grant and the two marshals immediately stepped forward, confirming every detail with firm, unquestionable authority. John Williams's expression darkened, the muscles in his jaw tightening.

"That is outrageous," he said sharply. He turned to Dr. Hunter. "Shane, your uncle is a judge here in Denver, isn't he? Could you contact him, see if there's any legal action, we can take against this... filth?"

"Of course," Shane replied at once, already reaching for his notebook. "I'll send word to him this afternoon."

Rose shook her head, exhaustion slipping into her tone.

"Uncle John, it won't make a difference. These men can't be reasoned with. If they were true journalists, perhaps, but they're not. They're hired hands working for the owner of the *Boston Codex*. He's only trying to avenge himself for losing to my father in court."

Both reporters nodded solemnly. The older of the two, Kendrick Smith, cleared his throat softly.

"That may be true, Miss Williams. The tragedy is that these men used private information about you to turn you into a target, a prize, even. We doubt the Codex's owner realized how dangerous that could be when he sent them after you." His voice lowered. "But waiting until after your father's death... well, that suggests something darker at play."

Marshal Jones stepped forward, arms folding across his chest.

"Gentlemen, your names?"

"Kendrick Smith," the older man said with a respectful nod.

"Albert Miller," the younger added.

John turned to the marshals, hope and frustration tangled in his voice.

"There must be a way to make the *Boston Codex* retract what they printed, to force them to issue a correction, at the very least."

Jones sighed, shaking his head.

"It isn't that simple, sir. The article was written carefully, just vague enough to twist the truth without making a direct accusation. Editors like that will claim their words were misunderstood. And if they print a follow-up, it will be to protect themselves, not her."

Rose lowered her gaze, her hands tightening in her lap.

"I'm so sorry if this brings danger to you or Aunt Elizabeth. I never wanted to be a burden to anyone."

Her uncle's expression softened instantly. He crouched before her, lifting her chin so she had no choice but to meet his eyes.

"You are not a burden, Rose. Do you understand me?" His voice was tender but unyielding. "Your aunt and I have been waiting for the day we could welcome you into our home. Nothing those men say or do will ever change that. Anyone who thinks they can harass you to gain your dowry will find themselves sorely mistaken. We love you, and we always have."

He brushed a tear from her cheek with his thumb. Rose's breath hitched. She glanced at Grant, who met her gaze and gave a small, knowing nod, as though to say, *See? I told you so.* Warmth bloomed in her chest, unexpected, steadying.

John's features softened, a smile easing across his face.

"Do you know what your grandfather used to say?"

She shook her head.

He straightened, pride warming his tone. "'A Williams always stands up for their family.' We protect our own. We don't yield to threats or fear—we face them head-on."

Tears pricked Rose's eyes again. She pressed her lips together, frustrated by how easily emotion rose these days. Her uncle pulled her into his arms.

"Don't worry, my dear girl. You're not alone in this. We'll protect you, and we'll love you, in every way we can."

Kendrick Smith nodded earnestly.

"We'll look into the matter further, Miss Williams. If we uncover anything about who sent those men, or why, you'll be the first to know."

An hour later, John Williams helped his niece into the waiting stagecoach. Shane, Grant, and the two marshals, climbed in behind them. The interior was cramped but serviceable: worn benches, narrow windows, and close quarters made warmer by the unspoken camaraderie among them. John made sure Rose had the seat nearest the window so she could watch the landscape unfold around her.

As the stage lurched forward and Denver faded behind them, conversation drifted lightly through the compartment—travel anecdotes, stories of mountain roads, the unpredictable moods of the Rockies. The miles slipped steadily beneath the wheels.

But the gentle rocking and the warmth of the crowded interior soon overcame Rose. Her head grew heavy, her breathing slowed, and she drifted into sleep. John watched her for a moment, his expression softened by tenderness and sorrow. When her head tipped forward, he slipped an arm around her shoulders and guided her gently to rest against his chest.

"She's been through a great deal," he murmured, brushing a loose strand of hair from her forehead. "You can see the weight of it in her eyes."

Marshal Moore nodded. "Yes, sir. This journey has tested her in every way, but God's been watching over her."

"I believe that," John replied quietly. "And I thank Him for sending you all to protect her. I can't bear to think what might have happened otherwise."

Shane Hunter offered a faint, thoughtful smile.

"She's stronger than she realizes. Most young women would have broken long before now, but she keeps standing back up."

John's gaze drifted to Rose's peaceful face, her lashes still faintly damp from earlier tears.

"She's endured too much heartache for one so young. Lizzie and I have been longing to have her with us again. When she was a little girl, she was bright and spirited, always eager, always curious. It broke our hearts to leave Boston. Lily, her mother, was a treasure, truly one of a kind." He exhaled, pain and regret shadowing his features.

"After Lily passed, I begged Edward to come West or at least let Rose live with us. I told him she needed warmth, a family to anchor her. But he refused. Said she was well cared for." His voice lowered. "From what I've gathered, I'm afraid he wasn't the father he ought to have been."

The men exchanged quiet, solemn looks. Marshal Moore's voice was low.

"No... he wasn't."

John nodded, his eyes returning to his niece, sleeping without knowing the grief and fierce devotion in his expression.

"What she needs now is love. And laughter. She's had far too little of either." His voice thickened with emotion. "I intend to see she finds both again."

No one spoke. The stagecoach rattled on, wheels clattering over hard-packed road. Outside, the Colorado plains stretched toward rising foothills, sunlight catching on golden grasses. Far ahead, the blue shadows of the Rockies rose tall and eternal, welcoming her home.

John tightened his arm around Rose just slightly, an unspoken vow settling deep in his heart. This time, she would be safe. This time, she would be cherished. This time... she would be loved.

Rose stirred awake as the stagecoach jolted to a halt. For a moment she blinked in confusion, unsure where she was or how long she had slept. Then she realized her head had been resting on her uncle's chest. She sat upright at once, mortified, brushing a loose curl behind her ear.

"Oh, Uncle John, I'm so sorry, I didn't mean to fall asleep on you."

He chuckled softly and gave her arm a gentle squeeze.

"Nonsense, my dear girl. After the journey you've had, I'm only glad you found a little rest."

Her cheeks warmed, but she managed a shy smile. The coach door swung open, letting in a rush of crisp mountain air tinged with pine and woodsmoke. Rose turned toward the window, and her breath caught.

The world outside glowed beneath the golden sweep of sunset. The sky blushed in shades of rose and violet, painting the Rockies in breathtaking silhouette. Their distant, snow-touched peaks shimmered like silver crowns. The foothills rolled gently below them, wild, rugged, and astonishingly beautiful. Pines dotted the slopes like brushstrokes.

Gone were the brick buildings and narrow alleys of Boston. Gone the noise, the soot, the crowded harbor. In their place stretched a landscape open and unspoiled. Quiet. Vast. Alive. A whisper escaped her lips.

"It's... beautiful."

Uncle John smiled at her wonder. "Welcome to Idaho Springs, Rose," he said softly. "Welcome home."

When the coach door opened fully, her uncle stepped down first, followed by Dr. Hunter and Grant. They turned to help her descend the steps, the marshals close behind, their watchful eyes scanning the street.

As Rose's boots touched the packed dirt, she drew a slow, steadying breath. The main road was nothing like Boston's bustling streets. It was a broad, dusty stretch lined with wooden buildings, their porches shaded and their windows glowing warmly in the fading light.

Instead of elegant carriages and polished cobblestones, creaking wagons rolled by. Horses stood tethered at hitching posts. A dog dozed, on the boardwalk near the general store, while two boys chased each other with sticks outside the barbershop.

Across the way she spotted a modest saloon and hotel, a cheerful café with lace curtains fluttering in the breeze, a small post office beside a brick-fronted bank, and much to her delight, a tiny library with a hand-painted sign and books displayed proudly in the window.

Farther down the street rose the graceful spire of a whitewashed church, half hidden among aspens and pine. The sight drew another quiet breath from her. *So, this is Idaho Springs.*

Her uncle turned at the sound. "It's small," he admitted with a smile. "But you'll find it has everything a person truly needs... and more kindness than most expect."

Before she could respond, a cheerful voice rang out.

"Reverend Williams! Fine to see you back in town. And is that your niece I've been hearing about?" An older woman bustled toward them, gray hair neatly pinned beneath a bonnet, apron tied around her waist as if she'd left her kitchen mid-task.

"Mable," John greeted warmly. "Good to see you. And yes, this is my niece, Rose."

Mable's eyes twinkled.

"Well bless my heart, aren't you the prettiest thing this town's seen in years! Look at those eyes. John, you'd best be ready to chase off half the young men once word gets around."

Rose flushed scarlet, lowering her gaze, while her uncle barked a warm laugh.

"I was just thinking that," he teased. "Seems I'd better start checking the rifles at the general store."

Mable swatted his arm. "Oh, hush, Reverend, or the poor girl will think every fellow in town is a scoundrel."

Just then, several miners and cowboys stepped out of the saloon across the street. Their laughter faded as they caught sight of the newcomer. A few removed their hats respectfully. Others simply stared in open curiosity.

Feeling their gazes, Rose instinctively edged closer to her uncle. Mable leaned in with a mischievous glint.

"See? Barely five minutes in town and you're already turning heads."

Rose's blush deepened, but the woman's good-natured teasing drew a shy smile from her all the same.

"John," Mrs. Colton said warmly, "she's just lovely. I'm eager to get to know her better."

Her uncle nodded proudly. "I've no doubt she'll be a wonderful addition to our little town."

Soon more townsfolk approached, shopkeepers closing for the evening, families out for a stroll, children tugging at their mothers' hands for a closer look. John greeted them all by name, his introductions gentle and full of pride. Rose offered polite smiles and shy handshakes as each person welcomed her with sincere affection.

With every warm word and kind face, something inside her eased. Fear loosened by slow degrees. These people were curious, yes, but with no malice, only neighborly interest and simple goodwill.

When the last of the introductions were complete, John thanked everyone for stopping and promised to see them at Sunday service. He gestured to the marshals and Grant.

"Gentlemen, if you'll come along, we've plenty of room at the parsonage for supper and a good night's rest."

Grant offered to help carry Rose's trunks, and John accepted with an appreciative nod.

"Thank you, son. That's a kindness to us both."

Shane tipped his hat. "I'll stop by the clinic first—my great-uncle will want to know I've returned. But I'll come by later to check on Miss Williams."

Rose smiled. "Thank you, Dr. Hunter. Truly, I'm all right."

He returned the smile before disappearing down the street.

6

Lines Not to Cross

As Rose walked beside her uncle toward the parsonage, the evening air wrapped around her like a gentle embrace. It carried the crisp scent of pine, the faint sweetness of woodsmoke, and the peaceful hush of a town settling into night. Golden light softened the rooftops and set the distant mountains aglow.

With each step, something fragile and miraculous unfurled within her, a steady, almost timid hope. Perhaps this place, this small and beautiful mountain town, could be the home she had been searching for.

As soon as Uncle John opened the door to his home, Rose was greeted by an explosion of movement, two dogs bounding toward her with unrestrained enthusiasm. They barked joyfully, tails wagging so vigorously, their entire bodies wiggled. Startled at first, Rose let out a breathless laugh and instinctively crouched to greet them.

The pair, one a golden retriever with warm, honey-colored fur, the other a sleek border collie with bright, intelligent eyes, pressed eagerly against her hands, nudging her palms with their wet noses, begging for affection.

"Well, hello there," she murmured, scratching behind their ears. "Aren't you two lovely?" At her touch, both dogs melted with devotion, licking her hands and circling her as though personally welcoming her home.

But when Marshal Moore and Marshal Jones stepped through the doorway, everything changed in an instant. The dogs stiffened, hackles lifting, their bodies tense as they moved to stand protectively in front of Rose, rumbling low growls vibrating the air.

Rose froze, unsure, but her uncle only chuckled.

"That's odd," John said, snapping his fingers for the dogs to heel. "They've never done that before. Looks like Rose just gained herself two new protectors."

Marshal Moore eyed the dogs warily. "They're friendly, I assume?"

"Perfectly," John assured him, though the amusement in his eyes was unmistakable. "So long as no one means harm to the person they're guarding."

"Guarding?" Moore echoed.

"Yes," John said, folding his arms. "If someone tries to frighten, snatch, or touch the person they're protecting in a way they don't approve of, they'll growl first. If that warning isn't heeded..." He grinned. "They'll drag the offender straight into the lake."

Marshal Jones let out a laugh. "That's... surprisingly effective training. You teach them yourself?"

"Our two youngest boys did," John replied proudly. "They trained the dogs to react to tones of voice, distress calls, even body movements. They'll only bite or hold someone down if the person they protect cries out in pain."

Moore looked impressed—and intrigued.

"Remarkable. And you think they'd protect Rose already? They've only just met her."

"They can sense when someone needs them," John said simply. "They're good judges of character. And they know a bruised heart when they see one. I'd say they've chosen her already."

Moore's lips curved into a playful grin. "Shall we test the theory?"

Rose turned sharply toward him, startled. "What—?"

Before she could finish, Moore stepped forward, wrapped an arm lightly around her waist, and drew her gently back against him.

Rose gasped, eyes wide, but before she could speak, the dogs exploded into furious barking. Their warning snarls sharpened as they lunged forward, teeth bared, only to be halted by John's commanding voice.

Moore released her at once, taking a quick step back with both palms raised. Rose stumbled away, her cheeks flaming, while John shook his head, fighting laughter.

"Just as I said," he remarked dryly. "Let that be your warning, Marshal Moore. They take their duties very seriously."

Moore chuckled and shot Rose a teasing wink.

"Duly noted, Reverend. I'll tread carefully around your niece, and her bodyguards."

Rose opened her mouth to reply, but quick footsteps pattered down the hall.

"Rose!" a warm, bright voice called. A woman appeared, a graceful figure with soft brown hair pinned neatly back, her eyes kind and shining. She hurried forward, wiping her hands on her apron. "Oh, thank heavens, you're finally here!"

Before Rose could so much as stand upright, she was swept into an affectionate embrace.

"We've been so worried," Aunt Elizabeth murmured, holding her tightly, as if trying to make up for every lost year. "It's so good to have you home, sweetheart."

Rose pressed her cheek against her aunt's shoulder, touched beyond words.

"Thank you," she whispered.

Aunt Elizabeth drew back with a radiant smile.

"And please, call me Aunt Lizzie. Everyone else does." She looked her over, eyes softening. "My, my... 'stunning' doesn't begin to describe you."

John rested a proud hand on Rose's shoulder.

"I told her she looks just like Lily."

"Oh, she does," Aunt Lizzie agreed, emotion flickering in her eyes. "So very much." Then her smile brightened with a playful glint. "And mark my words, half the young men in this town will be lining up to court you."

Rose's smile faltered, her stomach tightening. *If only that were true*, she thought. *Men chased fortunes, not affection.* She lowered her gaze, falling suddenly quiet.

Sensing that something was wrong, Aunt Lizzie gave her hand a gentle squeeze before turning to the guests.

"And you must be the marshals John mentioned in his telegram. We're grateful you're here."

Marshal Jones inclined his head.

"We'll contact headquarters tomorrow. With everything that's happened, I imagine we'll be told to stay on for a while yet."

"You're welcome for as long as needed," John said warmly. Then he glanced at his wife. "Lizzie, could you show them to the guest rooms?"

"Of course." She turned toward Grant with a smile. "And would you mind helping John carry Rose's luggage upstairs?"

Grant tipped his hat. "With pleasure."

Rose followed her uncle up the staircase. At the end of a short hall, he opened a small corner room with a white-painted door and a brass knob worn smooth by years of use. The moment she stepped inside, she drew a quiet breath.

It was smaller than anything she'd known in Boston, no gilded moldings, no lofty ceilings, but warmth radiated from every corner. A delicate quilt of pinks, blues, and ivory lay across the bed. A vase of wildflowers, daisies and asters, filled the air with a sweet scent. Sunlight spilled through lace curtains. Lavender lingered softly in the room like a memory.

But it was the view that stole her breath. She crossed to the back window and pushed aside the curtain. Her uncle's white steepled church was to the left, a shimmering lake to the right, evergreens whispering along its edges, and beyond that the mountains rising tall and ancient, their snow-capped peaks glowing in the last streaks of sunset.

"It's beautiful," she whispered.

John stood beside her, smiling. "Your aunt made the quilt," he said gently. "She wanted something that would feel like home to you."

Rose touched the careful stitching, her throat thickening. "It's exquisite."

"She spent weeks on it," John said softly. "Lizzie wanted you to feel welcome the moment you stepped through the door."

Rose swallowed hard, overwhelmed. Home. She had not expected to feel it again, not so soon, not so strongly.

The scent of supper drew her into the dining room, warm bread, roasted herbs, and something sweet baking. Candlelight danced over the table set with roast chicken, buttery potatoes, steaming bread, and jars of preserves.

Conversation flowed easily. Laughter warmed the room. Rose found herself smiling, really smiling, not from politeness but from genuine comfort.

When the plates were cleared, Grant rose and bowed.

"I'll take my leave now, Reverend. My horse is waiting."

John stood too, shaking his hand. "Thank you again, son. We're in your debt."

Grant's expression softened.

"It was my pleasure, sir." He turned to Rose. "It was an honor, Miss Williams. I'm glad I could help you reach home."

A small flutter stirred in her chest, soft, unexpected.

"And thank you, Mr. Adams," she said quietly. "I won't forget your kindness."

He tipped his hat and stepped into the evening. Rose watched him go, feeling that the world before her held not only fear and uncertainty... but possibility.

Once Grant had left, Rose turned to her uncle with a hopeful smile.

"Would it be alright if I took a short walk? Just to the lake and back?"

Before anyone could reply, Sally and Lucy, who had been dozing near the hearth, shot to their feet. They bounded toward her, tails wagging so vigorously their whole bodies swayed. Sally barked cheerfully while Lucy nudged Rose's hand as if giving eager permission. Rose laughed softly.

"It seems I already have volunteers to accompany me."

John grinned and exchanged a knowing look with his wife.

"Sally and Lucy have made their choice. I'd say you're officially their favorite person now."

"I'm honored," Rose said with a playful bow, reaching for her shawl. She had barely settled it across her shoulders when movement at the edge of her vision made her glance back.

Marshal Moore stepped forward, hands clasped lightly behind his back. His voice was warm, casual on the surface, but a sincere undertone threaded through it.

"I'll join you. It's nearly dusk, and though those two look quite capable," he nodded to the dogs, "I'd feel better knowing you weren't alone."

John lifted an eyebrow, folding his arms across his chest with exaggerated sternness.

"All right, Marshal, but remember what I said about those dogs. They don't take kindly to any fellow who gets too close to the young lady they're guarding."

Lucy punctuated the warning with a low, approving rumble. Moore flashed a harmless grin.

"Understood, Reverend. I'll behave myself."

The exchange drew a bright, effortless laugh from Rose, a sound that made Aunt Lizzie clasp a hand over her heart and share a delighted look with her husband. Marshal Moore pressed a hand dramatically to his chest.

"I see someone would enjoy watching me get dragged into the lake."

His teasing tone drew a blush to Rose's cheeks, but she managed a shy, mischievous smile.

"Perhaps," she said lightly, as he opened the door for her. "But only a little."

John chuckled behind them.

"Careful, Marshal, she's got a wicked streak, that one."

Rose shot her uncle a look of mock indignation, though her eyes sparkled.

With Sally and Lucy trotting proudly at her sides, heads high, ears alert, and Marshal Moore walking at a respectful, dog-approved distance next to her, Rose stepped into the cool evening air. The sky was brushed in lavender and gold, the mountains cut into the horizon in rugged silhouette. Pine scented the breeze, and the soft crunch of gravel kept time with the dogs' rhythmic steps.

HEALING THE ORPHANED HEART

As shadows lengthened and the first stars began to glimmer, Rose felt something she had not felt since childhood: a weight lifting, her heart opening, peace settling over her like a familiar, long-lost cloak.

John and Elizabeth stood in the doorway, watching Rose and Marshal Moore disappear down the winding path toward the lake. Sally and Lucy darted joyfully through the twilight, zigzagging, circling Rose, racing one another in playful bursts, yet always returning to her side, as if tethered by instinct.

Fireflies flickered at the edges of the yard. A hush settled over the land. But it did little to settle John's heart. He exhaled heavily, folding his arms.

"I'm worried about her, Lizzie. She's not the same cheerful girl we remember."

His wife's warm smile faded. "She's been through so much, John. Losing her father alone would wound any young woman."

"That's not what worries me." His voice was low, troubled. Elizabeth turned to him, concern deepening the gentle lines around her eyes.

"Then what is it? What happened to her?"

So, he told her. Everything he had learned on the journey home: the harassment on the train, the Codex's malicious article, the men at the station who had cornered her, the fear that flickered behind her brave composure. As the words spilled out, Elizabeth's expression shifted—from shock... to aching sorrow... to fierce, unyielding resolve.

"They'd better not mess with our girl," she said, her voice low but steely. "I don't care who they are or how powerful that newspaper owner thinks he is. If anyone dares to harm her or threaten her again, they'll answer to me first."

John let out a soft, touched chuckle.

"I agree. We may have to fight off the wolves to keep her safe."

Lizzie folded her arms tightly, her jaw set as she watched Rose vanish behind the trees.

"Then let them come. They'll find this family doesn't frighten easily."

John nodded. "Grant told me something else too." He hesitated, then sighed deeply. "Rose was afraid to come here, worried that, as her guardian, I might try to control her life or marry her off without her consent."

Elizabeth inhaled sharply. "Oh, the poor lamb."

"Edward... he tried," John said quietly. "But he made mistakes. He was broken after Lily died, and he raised Rose with distance when what she needed was closeness. Love." He rubbed a hand over his face, sorrow clouding his expression. "Thank the Lord he had the sense to contact marshal headquarters before he passed. I shudder to think what might've happened to her without those men."

Elizabeth shook her head, grief and anger mingling in her gaze.

"What kind of cruel heart does something like this to a young woman? Who writes lies about her and sends men after her, knowing she's vulnerable?"

"Selfishness," John replied grimly. "And greed. Those two sins can turn any man into a monster." He straightened, his voice firm. "But I promise you this, Lizzie, no one will marry that girl unless I'm certain it's her choice. She'll have freedom here. Love, if she wants it. Peace, if she can find it."

Elizabeth reached for his hand and squeezed it fiercely.

"Then we'll make this home a refuge for her. A place where she can heal. And if any outsider tries to harm her again..." Her eyes burned with fire. "They'll find the whole of Idaho Springs standing in their way."

John's lips softened into a tender smile.

"You've always had the heart of a lioness, Lizzie."

She lifted her chin with quiet pride. "Only when it comes to my family."

Outside, the last rays of sunset shimmered across the lake, turning the water into a sheet of rippling gold. Rose walked beside Marshal Moore, her shawl gathered close around her shoulders, while the dogs trotted ahead, their tails waving like banners in the fading light.

"Your aunt and uncle seem like fine people," Moore remarked, warmth touching his tone.

"They are," Rose said softly. She glanced back toward the parsonage, where lamplight now glowed through the windows, casting a soft amber halo around the home. "Grant was right. I can trust them. It doesn't feel like I'm intruding on their lives... more like I'm being added to them."

Moore smiled at that. "I'm glad to hear it."

Just then, Lucy bounded back with a stick clamped proudly in her mouth. Rose took it, gave it a playful toss across the grass, and laughed as both dogs bolted after it, their paws kicking up little clouds of dust.

"It feels good to be wanted," she murmured. Moore turned slightly, studying her with a gentleness that warmed her heart.

"Of course you're wanted, Rose. Anyone with eyes can see how deeply your aunt and uncle care for you already."

She smiled faintly, though her gaze drifted toward the mountains now bathed in violet twilight.

"I suppose I'm still getting used to it. Seeing Uncle John defend me in Denver... it surprised me. No one has ever stood up for me like that, not with such conviction." Her voice grew quieter. "My father would never have done that. He always let our butler handle matters. Confrontation wasn't something he faced himself." Her tone softened, tinged with old disappointment.

"He only fought when the Boston Codex printed lies about him. Even then, everything was done through lawyers and letters. He fought with intellect, not passion... and never with his own voice."

Moore's eyes darkened with empathy. "He must have been a proud man."

She nodded slowly. "Proud, and brilliant. But sometimes too distant to see the cost of his pride."

For a while, they walked without speaking. The only sounds were the whisper of grass beneath their feet and the playful splashes as the dogs chased the stick into the shallows. The scent of pine and wild sage drifted around them, warm and clean.

"I must admit," Rose said at last, her voice thoughtful, "it always annoyed me that, simply because I was Dr. Edward Williams's daughter, I became the favorite target of every journalist in Boston. After my debut, I couldn't step outside without notebooks thrust in my face or some dreadful gossip column waiting to dissect my day."

Moore chuckled softly. "Well, to be fair, you are a beautiful, captivating young woman. That alone would have drawn attention. And your father's prominence only magnified it." His humor faded, replaced by quiet gravity. "But what they did to you on that train... was inexcusable."

Rose shook her head, frustration tightening her voice.

"The nerve, to twist everything into a spectacle, to make me seem like some prize to be hunted. I'll never understand how people can be so cruel."

Moore stopped walking and turned toward her. His expression was gentle but unwavering, the look of a man who wanted his words to matter.

"You can't control the cruelty of others, Rose. But you can rise above it. And you already have."

She looked up at him, her blue eyes reflecting the pale shimmer of the lake.

"Do you really think so?"

"I know so," he said simply.

A quiet hush settled over them, a silence that felt safe rather than empty. The wind stirred the tall grass, the mountains loomed like ancient guardians in the distance, and Rose felt the weight of her fear loosen, just a little.

Sally and Lucy bounded in excited circles around Rose, tails wagging furiously, urging her to throw the stick again. Laughing, she obliged, winding her arm back and sending it sailing through the dusky air.

But before the stick even hit the ground, Marshal Moore swept in behind her and, with an unmistakably mischievous grin, wrapped his arms around her waist. A startled cry burst from her lips as he lifted her clean off her feet and slung her, quite unceremoniously, over his broad shoulder.

"Marshal Moore!" she yelped, half laughing, half indignant. "How dare you? Put me down this instant!"

Her outburst froze the dogs in their tracks. They halted mid-run, ears pricking sharply. Then, as one, they bolted back toward her. The moment they saw their mistress draped over the marshal's shoulder, chaos erupted.

"Oh no," Christopher muttered, just before both dogs launched themselves at him. Their teeth sank firmly into his jacket, tugging with surprising and very determined strength. He stumbled backward, trying to keep his balance, and finally released Rose so she tumbled harmlessly onto the soft grass.

"Easy, girls, easy!" he attempted, but it was far too late. With a mighty splash, the marshal went sprawling into the lake, dragged by two fiercely loyal canine guardians.

Rose rolled to her side, skirts in a tangle, watching in stunned disbelief. Then Christopher surfaced, soaked from crown to boots, hair plastered to his forehead—and her composure shattered. She burst into helpless laughter.

"Good girls," she managed between gasps, pressing a hand over her mouth as Sally and Lucy shook themselves vigorously on shore, spraying droplets everywhere before trotting proudly back to her side.

Marshal Moore waded toward the bank, dripping and thoroughly defeated. He tried, truly tried, to look stern, but her laughter was too infectious. A grin tugged at his lips, then broke into a warm, rueful chuckle.

"That's what you get for not behaving around me," she teased, eyes sparkling wickedly. "My uncle did warn you. Are you happy now that you're all wet?"

He raked a hand through his soaked hair, feigning indignation.

"You'd best be careful, young lady," he said as he stepped toward her, water streaming from his sleeves. His tone was teasing, but the way his gaze held hers made her cheeks grow warm. She instinctively stepped back, though her smile didn't fade.

"I think you're the one who should be careful, Marshal," she countered with playful defiance. "You'd better not cross my protectors again."

"Protectors, hmm?" His grin deepened. "We'll see about that."

Before she could react, he lunged. But this time she was ready. Laughing, she gathered her skirts and darted out of reach, running toward the path. The dogs barked excitedly, unsure whose side they were meant to be on.

When she glanced back, she saw him holding something in his hand, two small, wet biscuits.

"Oh, you're bribing them now?" she called, scandalized and amused in equal measure.

"Every lawman knows how to make peace with his enemies," he replied, tossing the treats to Sally and Lucy, who accepted the offering without the slightest hesitation.

"Traitors!" Rose laughed, turning to flee again.

He splashed after her across the damp grass. "Not fair! You had a head start!"

She spun just long enough to flash him a triumphant grin, then whistled sharply. The dogs abandoned their snacks mid-chew and barreled straight for the marshal. This time they didn't drag him into the lake, but they tackled him with enough enthusiasm to send him sprawling in the grass once again. Pinned beneath two panting, triumphant dogs, Christopher groaned.

"All right, all right, you win!"

Rose was laughing so hard she could barely breathe.

"You see, Marshal Moore," she managed between fits of laughter, "you should never underestimate a woman with loyal friends."

The dogs barked in approval, tails thumping the ground like victory drums. Still laughing, cheeks flushed and eyes bright, Rose turned and ran toward the parsonage, her laughter echoing through the cool evening air. Sally and Lucy bounded after her, galloping proudly at her heels.

Behind them, soaked, defeated, and smiling despite himself, Marshal Christopher Moore sat in the grass, very aware that he had just lost a battle he hadn't entirely minded losing.

7

Abusive Punishment

A few moments later, the front door swung open, and Reverend Williams stepped out onto the porch with Marshal Jones beside him. Both men halted.

There, trudging up the path, was Christopher Moore, dripping from hat to boots, his coat plastered to him like a second skin, water trailing from his sleeves in mournful rivulets. Even his hat drooped pitifully in his hand, as though sharing in his defeat.

John arched a single eyebrow. A look perfectly balanced between reproach, and amusement.

"You're playing with fire, Marshal," he said, folding his arms. "May I ask why you felt the need to get that close to my niece?"

Christopher drew himself up, attempting dignity, an effort somewhat undermined by the water dripping steadily from his chin onto the porch steps.

"Reverend, I swear, I meant no disrespect." He cleared his throat, trying for seriousness. "I was only attempting to make her laugh. You said yourself she needed humor tonight."

A beat of silence passed. Jones pressed a knuckle to his mouth to stifle a chuckle. John's sternness wavered, softening into a sigh.

"I did say that," he admitted. "And heaven knows the girl could use every smile she can find." But then his gaze sharpened again. "Just remember, humor can be a dangerous thing when hearts are tender. Be careful not to confuse kindness with flirtation... or let her confuse it."

Christopher's shoulders eased, though he nodded solemnly. "I understand, sir. Truly."

John studied him a moment longer, eyes searching, measuring the sincerity behind the young marshal's soaked and sheepish expression. Whatever he saw there seemed to satisfy him. With a final, quiet nod, he turned back toward the house.

"Come inside before you freeze. Lizzie will have something warm for you." He stepped in, leaving the door open.

Marshal Jones remained on the porch, watching Christopher with the calm, unreadable stare of a man who'd seen far too much, and understood even more. When Reverend Williams was out of earshot, he stepped closer.

"Listen, Moore," he said quietly. "She's a sweet girl, and she's been through more than her share of hardship. Don't let your fondness for her, whatever form it takes, blur the line of propriety."

Christopher blinked, genuinely startled.

"Fondness?" He scoffed lightly, though color rose at the back of his neck. "Anthony, she's barely more than a child. I'd never—"

Jones arched a brow, unconvinced. "She's a young woman, Chris. A lovely one. And she's looking at you like you hung the moon." His voice softened. "I know you mean your teasing to be harmless. But she's fragile right now, clinging to anyone who treats her gently. Reverend Williams knows it, too. That's why he spoke up."

Christopher let out a slow breath and rubbed the back of his neck, water still dripping from his sleeve.

"I truly didn't mean to cause trouble. I only wanted to make her laugh. She needed it."

Jones's mouth quirked. "I'm not scolding you. Just reminding you to be careful. You've always had a soft spot for the vulnerable. It's one of your best qualities. Just make sure your chivalry isn't mistaken for courtship, by her or her uncle."

A wry, almost embarrassed chuckle escaped Christopher. "Understood. Loud and clear."

Jones clapped him once on the shoulder and headed inside. Christopher turned toward the doorway, and nearly collided with Sally and Lucy, who had reappeared in the entryway, tails wagging like banners. They stopped, staring up at him as though assessing the state of the drowned creature before them, then gave a pair of sharp, almost triumphant barks.

Christopher narrowed his eyes at them. "Don't start," he muttered. "I've suffered enough humiliation for one evening."

The dogs tilted their heads... and then, unmistakably, gave matching doggish grins before trotting off after Rose, their nails clicking cheerfully across the wooden floor. Christopher watched them go, dripping, defeated, and, despite himself, smiling.

Rose woke early the next morning, long before the household began to stir. A soft, silvery mist drifted across the lake and fields, dissolving the line between water and sky. The dawn light, faint and drowsy, filtered through the trees in pale ribbons, giving the world a dreamlike glow.

She stretched, rubbed the sleep from her eyes, then smiled. Curled up together on the braided rug beside her bed, Sally and Lucy slept soundly, noses tucked beneath their paws. Sally let out a tiny snore, her tail twitching as though chasing rabbits in some pleasant dream. Lucy's ear flicked once before settling again. The sight warmed Rose's heart.

Not even twenty-four hours, and they've claimed me as theirs.

It was a beautiful early August morning, cool, quiet, untouched, and something in her chest urged her outside. She wanted to breathe the crisp mountain air, to walk freely without fear for the first time in weeks.

I should enjoy this freedom while I can, she thought with a wry smile. It wouldn't be long before half the eligible bachelors of Idaho Springs began knocking at her uncle's door. Mable's teasing from the night before echoed in her mind, stirring a flutter of nerves. Out here, at least, she could slip away unnoticed.

Since Sally and Lucy were still asleep, she chose not to wake them. They had guarded her well the night before, they deserved their rest. She hurried to the small vanity in the corner, poured water from the pitcher into a bowl, and quickly washed her face and brushed her teeth. Then she dressed in a simple morning gown and shawl, brushed and pinned her hair with practiced ease, and tiptoed downstairs.

The house held the soft hush of early morning, wood settling, distant birds calling, the faint clatter of dishes from the kitchen.

Passing her uncle's study, she saw him already at his desk, glasses perched on his nose. From the kitchen drifted the warm, quiet humming of her aunt.

Rose hesitated. Should she tell someone? After everything that had happened, leaving without a word felt strange. But the morning was so peaceful, and the walk would be brief. She didn't want to disturb anyone.

She found a scrap of paper, and pencil, and wrote neatly: *Gone for a short walk to the lake. I'll be back soon. —Rose*

She placed the note where it could not be missed and weighed it down with the salt cellar. Then she slipped out the front door. The crisp air kissed her cheeks. The world felt wide and open, full of promises rather than peril. With her first step down the soft path, she felt something inside her begin, slowly, to heal.

The air was so clean it almost startled her, pine resin, damp earth, cold mountain stone. She breathed deeply, savoring it. *This is what fresh air is supposed to be.* Rather than heading straight for the lake, curiosity tugged her elsewhere. She wanted to explore, to glimpse more of the place she would now call home.

She walked along the forest's edge, confident in her excellent sense of direction. As long as she did not stray far, she could not lose her way. Pulling her shawl tighter against the cool bite of morning, she ventured toward the trees.

Birdsong echoed through the branches, a layered chorus welcoming her. Sunlight filtered through the canopy in trembling beams, stirring motes of dust that glittered like tiny stars. She followed a narrow path worn by many feet, or perhaps by deer, until she reached a leaning post with a weathered sign:

NO TRESPASSING!
You Are About to Enter Private Land.
Trespassers Will Be Punished.
Jonas Adams

Rose blinked, then let out a soft laugh. "Sounds like, Grant's father doesn't like visitors." She was about to turn back when a sharp, frightened squeal froze her mid-step. An animal, small, terrified, somewhere close. Heart tightening, she scanned the underbrush. Nothing. Until the cry came again, faint but urgent.

She hesitated for only a moment before following the sound through the trees. When she stepped into a small clearing, the rising sun struck her full in the face, blinding her. She took one step forward, and the ground vanished beneath her foot.

Rose gasped, arms flailing as her heel slipped over the grassy lip of a deep, narrow pit. Instinct seized her. She lunged sideways, catching hold of a sturdy but whippy branch from the nearest tree. Her boots scrabbled against the loose soil.

For one breathless moment, she hung there, half over the pit, half over solid earth, her heart pounding in her ears. She hauled herself back, collapsing to her knees. After several deep breaths, she forced herself to look. A tiny rabbit darted frantically along the dirt walls, unable to climb out. Its squeaks tugged at her heart.

"Oh, poor thing," she whispered. Determined, she tested the branch's strength, then wrapped her shawl around it for a better grip and carefully lowered herself into the pit. The rabbit panicked further at her approach. Rose tried to corner it gently, but it darted wildly around her skirts.

"Please, hold still," she murmured. On a lucky leap, the rabbit bounded toward her, and she reacted instantly, dropping low, sweeping her skirt out, catching it in a fold. The creature wriggled, but she covered it with her free hand. Now came the hard part.

Bracing her feet against the dirt wall, she climbed, inch by inch, up the side of the pit, clinging to the branch with one hand and securing the trembling bundle with the other. Her arms shook, her boots slipped, but she refused to give up.

At last, she reached the rim and rolled onto the dewy grass. She freed the rabbit, and it shot into the forest like a streak of light. Rose collapsed onto her back, breathless.

"That," she whispered to the empty clearing, "was not how I expected my morning to go."

She pushed herself upright, still brushing dirt and needles from her skirt, when a deep, irritable voice cut through the quiet: "What are you doing here?"

She startled, spinning toward the sound. The sun blazed behind the speaker, turning him into a dark silhouette atop a horse. But she recognized the voice instantly.

"Grant?" she squinted.

He nudged his horse closer. "Didn't you see the sign," he snapped, "or can't you read? No trespassing means you don't enter."

Rose stepped back, stunned. Before she could answer, a soft gasp sounded from behind him, Grant's younger sister, staring with wide, uneasy eyes. Rose lifted her chin, her voice tight with effort.

"I wasn't aware it was a crime to go for a walk."

"That doesn't explain why you're trespassing."

"I didn't intend to trespass," she shot back. "I followed the sound of a distressed animal. I found a rabbit trapped in that pit and rescued it."

A hard scoff came from the man across from her.

"Did it never occur to you that the rabbit was trapped there on purpose? Out here, we hunt. You just cost us our supper."

Rose's eyes widened, then narrowed with sharp incredulity.

"Yes," she said dryly, "because clearly you're so impoverished that you must rely on baby rabbits to survive."

Behind him, the girl stifled a snort before covering her mouth. He released another scoff.

"You'd better watch that tone, young lady."

Rose's temper flared. "How about *you* watch yours? You've been nothing but rude since the moment you appeared. What exactly have I done to deserve this treatment?"

"You have no business here."

The words hit like a slap—cold, harsh, unprovoked.

"Yes," she said through gritted teeth, "you've made that quite clear." Without another word, she turned sharply and stormed away, fury blazing in her chest. Pine needles crunched beneath her boots as she marched through the trees without looking back. If Grant Adams's intention had been to make her feel unwelcome, he had succeeded brilliantly.

As soon as the girl vanished into the trees, Jennifer Adams turned sharply toward her brother, her dark brows rising in disbelief.

"Why were you so rude to her?"

The young man shot her a furious look, reins pulled tight in his fists.

"She trespassed. And I believe the sign on our border is perfectly clear."

Jennifer scoffed. "Oh, please. That old sign has been there since Pa put it up twenty years ago. We've never enforced it, and you know it. It's a warning, not a noose. As usual, you are being unreasonable."

Her brother gritted his teeth and nudged his horse forward, but Jennifer kept pace beside him, refusing to let him escape the conversation.

"And your behavior just now?" she pressed, her voice rising with indignation. "It was downright embarrassing. I know you hate helping out on the ranch, and I know you think getting up early to check fences and livestock is somehow beneath you, but that does not give you the right to snap at strangers."

"I don't need a lecture," he growled.

"Well, you're getting one," Jennifer fired back. "Do you even know who that young woman was?"

"I don't care."

Jennifer let out a groan of frustration and circled her horse around to block his path, forcing him to look at her.

"You should care," she insisted. "Because from what I've heard, that was Paul's cousin, Reverend Williams' niece. The same girl, the marshals escorted from Denver. The girl who just came to live at the parsonage."

He blinked, momentarily thrown, but quickly masked it with another scowl. Jennifer shook her head in disbelief.

"Honestly, brother... way to welcome new folks to our little town."

He opened his mouth to respond, but she was already nudging her horse ahead, posture stiff with disapproval. The young man followed reluctantly, his jaw still tight. He did not bother to look back toward the forest.

Rose was ready to explode. Grant Adams was a rude, arrogant excuse for a human being. How could she have been so breathtakingly wrong about him? He had seemed so kind during her journey to Colorado, gentle, even, and his protectiveness on the train had touched her deeply. But clearly, she had been mistaken. He was not the gentleman she had imagined.

Fuming, she stormed deeper into the forest, the cool morning air doing nothing to soothe the burn in her chest. When she reached a fallen tree, its broad trunk stretching across a shallow dip in the ground, she seized the chance to distract herself.

Balancing along the rough bark, she moved carefully, arms outstretched, willing the concentration to quiet her racing thoughts. She was almost to the other side when four figures burst from the thick brush. Indians.

A startled gasp tore from her throat. Her boot skidded on the bark, but before she could hit the ground, a pair of strong hands caught her around the waist and steadied her. Her breath froze.

She had never seen Native people in person before, but she knew well, too well, what the newspapers in Boston had claimed about them. She also knew how gravely they had suffered, how deeply they had been wronged and displaced by white settlers.

Still trembling, she straightened and tried to calm her pounding heart. Lifting her chin, she summoned a timid but genuine smile.

"Thank you... for catching me," she said softly. "I appreciate your help."

The four young men simply stared at her, their dark eyes watchful, unreadable. Rose swallowed.

"Forgive me, but... do you speak English?"

For a moment, no one answered. Then the one who had caught her tilted his head, glanced sideways at his companions, and finally smiled.

"Yes," he said warmly. "Sorry for scaring you. That wasn't our intention." He winked at the other three, and they nodded in agreement.

Rose blinked, surprised both by his perfect English and by the mischievous glint in his eyes. Slowly, she smiled back.

"You're... not scared of us?" he asked curiously. "Most white people are terrified."

"I don't frighten easily," she answered truthfully. "And I enjoy meeting new people." She hesitated, then asked gently, "What tribe do you belong to?"

"We are Cheyenne," he replied with quiet pride. "The white man may have forced us onto a reservation, one we must share with other tribes, but we keep to ourselves as much as we can. We still hold to our traditions."

Rose's chest tightened with sympathy.

"I'm truly sorry," she said softly. "For everything you've endured. For how you were treated... and likely still are. None of it was right."

The young man studied her face for several long seconds, his sharp gaze slowly softening.

"Who are you?" he asked at last.

"My name is Rose Williams. I'm the niece of Reverend John Williams."

Recognition sparked in his eyes. "Ah. The Reverend," he said, grinning. "A fine man. And with an excellent sense of humor, for a white man, at least."

Rose laughed, relieved by the shift in tone.

"My name is Ahanu," he said, tapping his chest. "And these are Calian, Denali, and Kosumi."

She smiled warmly. "Is it too forward of me to ask what your names mean?"

"Not at all." Ahanu pointed to each one in turn. "My name means *he laughs*. Calian means *warrior of life*. Denali means *great one*, and Kosumi," he gestured toward the youngest, "means *fishes for salmon with a spear*."

Rose's eyes sparkled. She turned back to Ahanu.

"Well... your name suits you. You seem like someone with a great sense of humor, mischievous, and probably the sort who finds trouble more often than he avoids it."

Ahanu burst into hearty laughter.

"She saw right through you, Ahanu," Calian teased with a grin. "You always get yourself into trouble."

Ahanu shot him a playful glare but kept laughing, his eyes warm and bright as they remained fixed on Rose.

Shouts rang through the trees, sharp, angry, and the thunder of hooves followed. Within seconds, the quiet clearing was swarmed by mounted soldiers. Rose stiffened as the horses circled the four young Cheyenne men, dust rising in choking clouds.

A high-ranking officer, broad-shouldered, red-faced, already scowling, swung down from his horse.

"What are you doing outside the reservation?" he barked. "You know you're not permitted out in groups larger than two. Who authorized this?"

Ahanu said nothing. His jaw set, his eyes burned with restrained fury. The officer strode forward and, without warning, slapped Ahanu hard across the face.

"Did you swallow your tongue, Savage?"

Outrage exploded through Rose. Before she even thought, she stepped between them, arms spread protectively.

"There is absolutely no need to mistreat these young men, Colonel," she snapped.

The colonel turned his head. His expression shifted from irritation to pure venom the moment he saw her, as if the very sight of her daring to speak enraged him further. He seized her arm and yanked her aside.

"You accosted a white girl?" he thundered at the Cheyenne boys. "You filthy savages will pay for that."

Calian opened his mouth to protest, but a soldier behind him struck him brutally with the butt of his rifle. Calian crumpled to the ground, coughing in agony. Rose dropped to her knees beside him, her voice shaking with fury.

"How dare you attack him like that? What kind of barbarian strikes an unarmed man?"

Ahanu shook his head desperately. "Don't defend us," he warned. "It will only make things—"

Before he could finish, the same soldier slammed his rifle into Ahanu's back. The young man fell forward with a cry, the breath knocked from his lungs.

Rose shot to her feet, spinning on the soldier. Without hesitation, she grabbed the rifle from his hands and hurled it away.

"You are a coward," she hissed through gritted teeth. "Striking a man from behind? How pathetic."

The colonel strode forward and seized her arm again.

"Stand aside, Miss. This is army business, far beyond your understanding."

"I will not!" she shouted, wrenching free. "You have no right to treat human beings like animals! They did not accost me, they saved me!"

For a moment, the colonel simply stared at her, stunned. Then slowly, his lips curled into a vile grin.

"You've got spirit," he drawled, sliding an arm around her waist. "I've always liked a feisty woman." He leaned in to kiss her, but Rose slapped him so hard the crack echoed through the clearing.

"How dare you?" she spat. "You disgrace your uniform. A man who abuses his rank, assaults women, and brutalizes innocent people has no honor, and no place in the military."

His eyes went flat and murderous.

"You listen here," he growled, grabbing both her wrists in a bruising grip. "Interfering in army matters is a federal offense. Get out of my sight before I—" He shoved her violently to the ground.

"Rose!" Ahanu tried to crawl toward her, but another soldier slammed his weapon into his back again, knocking him flat. The colonel kicked him hard in the stomach. Ahanu gasped, curling instinctively around the pain.

Rose staggered to her feet, shaking but defiant. She had never been one to look away from suffering, and she would not start now.

"You are going to regret this, Colonel," she said, her voice low but fierce. "I will report your actions to your superiors. Every one of them. You have disgraced your command."

The colonel sneered, then struck her across the face. The blow sent her sprawling, her vision flashing white.

"Captain!" he roared, jabbing a finger in her direction. "Take this woman and administer the punishment for interference and insubordination. The same as any man."

The young captain paled. "Sir, she's a woman."

"I don't care. That is an order."

The captain's jaw clenched. He lifted his chin.

"No, sir. I will not obey that order. She is right, you are abusing your authority. I will not assist in this."

Silence rippled through the soldiers. The colonel lunged forward and punched the captain across the face, sending him staggering.

"You will pay for your disobedience," he spat. "Take the Indians back to the reservation! I'll see every last one of you court-martialed for this treachery. And I'll send a wire to Lieutenant General Hilton myself."

Two soldiers moved toward Ahanu and Calian. Rose tried to rise again, but she was dizzy from the blow.

"Second Lieutenant Wright!" the colonel barked. "Take that woman and carry out the punishment!"

The young lieutenant stepped forward, then shook his head. "No, sir. I won't."

The colonel's fury broke loose. He grabbed the lieutenant by the throat and slammed him against a tree so hard the young man's head cracked against the bark. Rose cried out helplessly, horror twisting her stomach.

"Cowards! All of you!" the colonel roared, releasing the lieutenant only to shove him aside. "Corporal! Sergeant!" He jabbed a finger at the two soldiers who had struck the Cheyenne boys. "Take this woman. Now. And follow me."

The two men seized Rose by the arms, their grips bruising, and dragged her after the colonel as he stormed deeper into the trees.

Rose's breath came in shallow, frightened gasps, but her eyes stayed fierce. She would not go quietly. Not now. Not ever.

HEALING THE ORPHANED HEART

The moment the colonel and the two soldiers disappeared into the trees with Rose, the clearing fell into a tense, horrified hush. Captain Ray exhaled a shaky breath and turned sharply to the young Cheyenne men, his eyes blazing.

"Ahanu," he said urgently. "Do you know who that young woman is?"

Ahanu nodded, rubbing the sore spots on his back where the soldier's rifle had struck.

"Yes. She is the niece of Reverend Williams."

The captain's face drained of color. "My word..." He scrubbed a hand over his face. "Then we have to act quickly." He spun toward the young lieutenant the colonel had assaulted.

"Second Lieutenant Wright, ride to Reverend Williams's home. Immediately. Tell him everything. He'll know what to do."

Still shaken but resolute, Wright nodded. "Yes, sir." He stumbled to his horse, mounted, and galloped hard toward town.

Captain Ray turned next to his men. "I'm heading straight to the telegraph office. We need to report the colonel before he sends his lies to Lieutenant General Hilton. If we're quick, the general will hear from us first."

Calian winced as he stood but stepped forward.

"Captain Ray," he said, breath tight, "let Ahanu and me run to the Adams ranch. It's closer than the parsonage. Someone there may reach her faster."

Ahanu nodded firmly. "The marshals stayed near town. And the Adams ranch hands know these woods. If anyone can catch the colonel before he harms her further, it's them."

The captain hesitated only a second, long enough for fear to flicker across his features, then barked: "Go. Both of you. Hurry."

Ahanu and Calian sprinted into the forest, swift and sure-footed. Ray turned to the remaining soldiers, men pale with shame and fear.

"The rest of you, back to the reservation," he said quietly. "Until a higher-ranking officer intervenes, we cannot follow him. If we do, he'll take it out on you, and heaven knows what that monster is capable of."

One soldier swallowed hard. "Sir... what if he hurts her?"

Captain Ray's jaw tightened, grief and fury warring in his eyes.

"He already has," he said grimly. "But once the general sees my report, the colonel's career, and his freedom, will be finished."

He mounted his horse, kicked it forward, and thundered toward town, praying they weren't already too late.

"Grant!" Ahanu's voice cracked through the quiet yard like a whip. Grant, tightening his saddle near the barn, jerked upright. Jennifer had just dismounted, and both siblings spun toward the two Cheyenne men racing from the trees.

Ahanu reached them breathlessly, chest heaving, eyes blazing.

"Colonel Bricks has taken Rose Williams," he gasped. "He intends to punish her."

Jennifer clapped her hands over her mouth, horror widening her eyes. Grant froze, just long enough for the shock to sharpen into something dark and dangerous.

"What?" he barked. "Where is she? Where did he take her?"

Calian stepped forward, speaking in a rush.

"We saw everything. She defended us, stood between us and the colonel. He ordered his men to seize her. One of our boys followed them. The colonel never noticed. Calian can find him."

Grant swung into his saddle in one furious motion.

"Jen, give him your horse."

Jennifer didn't hesitate. She thrust the reins toward Calian, hands shaking.

"Go. Bring her back!"

Calian vaulted onto the horse, and the moment he had the reins, Grant kicked his own mount into a hard gallop. The two men tore across the yard and vanished into the forest, straight toward danger. Ahanu paused only long enough to meet Jennifer's terrified gaze.

"I'll catch up," he promised, then slipped into the trees like a shadow.

Left alone, Jennifer pressed a trembling hand to her heart.

"Please, Lord," she whispered. "Let them find her in time."

Jonas Adams stepped out of the barn moments later, wiping his hands on a rag. He stopped short when he saw Jennifer alone, pale and shaken.

"Where's Grant?" he asked, confusion giving way to concern. Jennifer swallowed.

"Trying to rescue Rose Williams," she whispered.

Then, in a rush, she relayed everything, Colonel Bricks, the assault, Rose dragged away. For a heartbeat, Jonas stood utterly still. Then the change came. The gentle, steady man she knew hardened into someone fierce, his jaw clenching, eyes flashing like steel.

"Has anyone informed the sheriff?" he demanded.

Jennifer shook her head helplessly. "I don't know. Everything happened so fast."

Jonas didn't waste his breath. He spun toward the barn.

"Saddle my horse, now!"

A ranch hand sprinted into action. Moments later, Jonas swung into the saddle with practiced ease.

"That devil will not get away with this," he growled. "If he lays so much as a finger on that girl... I swear, Jennifer, we'll tear him apart."

Jennifer nodded, eyes brimming. "Please, Pa... get help before it is too late."

His expression softened for a heartbeat.

"I will. And when the truth reaches Bricks's superiors, may they lock that swine in irons." He kicked his horse forward, hooves pounding like thunder as he charged toward Idaho Springs. Rose Williams had a town behind her now, and Jonas Adams led the charge.

Calian lifted his chin, scanning the trees. He closed his eyes, listening intently. A mockingbird's cry pierced the forest. He angled his head, then cupped his hands and released another sharp hawk call into the air. Silence—then the mockingbird answered. Calian's eyes snapped open.

"This way."

Grant urged his horse after him, branches whipping past as they plunged deeper into the woods. The canopy thickened, shadows stretching long across the ground. Minutes later, they found a trembling boy crouching between two bushes.

"Nodin," Calian breathed, rushing to him. The boy, barely thirteen, looked up with wide, haunted eyes. Relief washed over his face when he saw them. Grant slid off his horse.

"Where is she?"

Nodin's hands shook as he pointed toward an old, sprawling oak.

"Over there," he whispered.

Grant's stomach dropped.

"I—I wanted to run to her," Nodin stammered, "but I didn't know if soldiers were waiting. If they caught me... I didn't want to bring trouble on my family."

Calian knelt beside him, placing a steadying hand on his shoulder.

"You did the right thing," he said softly. "You kept watch. You helped us find her."

Nodin's lip trembled. "I listened the whole time. Waiting. Then I heard your hawk call... and I knew you were close."

"It took us too long," Calian murmured, guilt flickering in his voice. "But we're here now."

Grant was off his horse before it had fully stopped. He sprinted across the clearing toward the still figure lying in the grass.

"Rose!"

She lay curled on her side, breaths shallow, a faint moan escaping her. He knelt beside her, terrified of what he might see, and the sight nearly stole his breath. Her face was bruised and bloodied, one cheek swollen, her lip split. Dark welts marred her skin. She looked fragile, broken.

Calian and Nodin stood behind him, stricken. Grant reached to lift her, but the moment his hands brushed her legs, Rose whimpered, a soft, wounded sound that tore through him. He jerked his hands back immediately, heart twisting.

"What did they do to her?" he demanded, voice shaking with fury. Nodin swallowed hard.

"The colonel... slapped her over and over," he whispered. "Then he ordered the soldiers to tie her hands and bind her to the tree. They beat her back... her legs... her feet. With heavy sticks."

Grant's jaw clenched so hard it hurt.

"They hit her legs for so long," Nodin whispered, tears gathering. "I thought they meant to kill her. And when they stopped, I hoped he'd be satisfied, but then he used his riding crop."

Grant closed his eyes, agony and rage twisting inside him.

"He whipped her harder than the others had struck her," Nodin continued. "He tried to force her to beg him to stop, to beg for forgiveness, but she refused. So, he hit her again."

Grant's fists tightened until his knuckles whitened.

"It wasn't over," Nodin said, voice breaking. "When he finished whipping her, they untied her and let her fall. Then he sent the soldiers back to the fort."

Grant's head snapped up sharply. "Tell me," he said in a low, lethal voice, "that he didn't... violate her."

"No," Nodin said quickly. "He didn't do that. But he took off her shoes... and beat the soles of her feet. She whimpered, but she never begged. Then he dropped his crop and knelt over her. I—I couldn't see what he did. But she screamed."

Grant's heart nearly stopped. A sick, burning rage flared through him.

"When he turned her on her back again," Nodin finished, "I knew he meant to hurt her more. So, I moved closer and made the sound of a mountain lion. It scared his horse. The horse bolted, he chased it... and then he rode away."

Silence followed, broken only by Rose's small, pained breaths. Grant drew in a shuddering breath and turned to Calian.

"Go back to the ranch. Tell Jennifer to send a cowboy with a wagon, we can't move her on horseback."

Calian took a deep breath. "The captain sent a man to Reverend Williams. He'll know by now. They'll bring a buckboard."

"Good," Grant said hoarsely. "Calian, meet them and show her uncle the way."

Calian nodded once and sprinted into the forest. Grant knelt beside Rose again, gently taking her limp hand.

"You're safe now," he whispered, voice cracking. "I've got you. We'll get you home."

Nodin lingered, fearful and small.

"You should go back," Grant said softly. "To the reservation. You've done more than enough."

The boy nodded, then slipped into the shadows. Grant brushed his thumb across Rose's knuckles.

"Hold on, Rose," he whispered. "Your family is coming. And I swear—that man will never touch you again."

8

Carried From the Woods

Calian stepped out of the shadows just as John Williams and Second Lieutenant Wright pushed through the thinning line of trees. Sweat beaded along John's brow despite the cool air, every second felt like an eternity.

"Calian," he called, breath unsteady. "Do you know where Rose is?"

The young man's jaw tightened. He nodded once and turned without a word. They followed him with the buckboard. Before long, the forest grew too dense for the wagon, and they abandoned it, continuing on foot through brambles and roots that clawed at their boots.

Terrible thoughts swarmed John's mind with every hurried step. He tried to steel himself, tried to imagine Rose frightened or shaken, but never, not once, did his mind conjure anything close to the truth of what they found. The sight hit him like a physical blow.

Rose lay curled slightly on her side at the base of a tree, her dress torn, her face mottled with bruises. Grant knelt beside her, pale and shaken.

"Rose..." John's voice cracked. "Oh, my goodness, what have they done to you?" He was on his knees beside her before he realized he had dropped to the ground. Rose blinked weakly, her lashes trembling, and finally focused on him.

"Uncle John..." she whispered. Even that small sound was ragged. "I was only defending Ahanu and Calian and their friends. I wasn't interfering in army business..."

John's fists curled so tightly his knuckles turned white.

"Even if you had interfered, it would not justify this. Nobody deserves such brutal punishment." His voice trembled with fury. "The colonel had no right. And he will answer for every mark he put on you."

Grant lifted his head, his expression bleak.

"She's been drifting in and out since I got here. I didn't want to move her and make anything worse."

John leaned closer, gently cupping the side of Rose's face.

"Where does it hurt, sweetheart?"

"Everywhere," she whispered. "My back... my legs... my feet." She swallowed hard, eyes glistening as she fought the tears. "I—I can't move them."

John hesitated only a moment before lifting the hem of her dress slightly. What he saw made him reel. Her stockings were soaked through, dark and wet, and blood had seeped down to her torn, raw feet. His stomach twisted violently.

"Dear mercy..." Wright muttered behind him.

"We need to get her to Dr. Hunter. Fast," John said, his voice low and urgent. Grant nodded. He and John slid their arms beneath her as carefully as humanly possible, but the moment their hands brushed her battered legs, Rose's body jolted. A broken cry tore from her throat, followed by a shuddering whimper that made all three men freeze. They exchanged helpless glances.

"How are we going to get her to the buckboard?" John asked tightly. "We can't carry her like this, not without causing her agony."

Grant swallowed, thinking quickly. "We can lay her across the back of my horse. It's the only way to avoid touching her legs at all. She won't have to bear her own weight."

John exhaled shakily. "Yes. Yes, do it."

Grant clicked to his horse, who obediently lowered himself. Together, the men lifted Rose again, supporting her under her torso and shoulders, keeping her legs suspended. Even that small movement wrung a gasp of agony from her. They eased her across the horse's back, her cheek pressing against the animal's warm hide. Rose's hands shook as she clutched weakly at the saddle.

John stood beside her, heart shattering.

"Rose... sweetheart... don't hold it in," he murmured, brushing a strand of hair from her face. "We know it hurts. You can scream if you need to. Let it out."

But she shook her head, jaw clenched with desperate, stubborn resolve, not wanting to be a burden, not wanting to frighten anyone, not wanting to seem weak. John's throat tightened. He wished, more than anything, that she didn't feel the need to be strong. Not like this.

Grant led the horse with painstaking care, guiding it slowly through thick bushes and tangled undergrowth. Every branch that brushed against Rose, every jostle of the horse's steady gait made him wince, imagining how each movement must send new bolts of pain through her battered legs. He murmured softly to the animal, keeping it calm, keeping it steady.

It took far longer to retrace their path back to the buckboard. The sun had shifted by the time they finally broke through the trees and reached the waiting conveyance. Lizzie had sent what she could—pillows, folded quilts, and extra linens were stacked inside, ready to soften the hard wooden wagon.

"Easy... easy," John murmured as he and Grant lifted Rose from the horse's back. Her sharp gasp and trembling breath tore at their hearts. They laid her onto the layered bedding as gently as if she were made of glass.

Grant climbed into the back with her at once, bracing himself behind her so she wouldn't slide or shift. Even the smallest jolt would be agony. John's expression was grim.

"The drive back is going to hurt her," Grant warned quietly. "The path isn't even."

John closed his eyes briefly to steady himself. When he opened them again, fury burned there, raw and barely restrained.

"Why did these barbaric swine beat her legs?" he growled. "Of all things—her legs?"

Calian stood near the horses, his posture rigid, his dark eyes frozen with a cold fury that could have cut steel.

"They didn't want her to walk home," he said in a low, flat voice. "They wanted the pain to stay. They wanted her to suffer long after they were finished." His throat bobbed as he swallowed hard. "She was tortured because of us. Because she stood up for us." His voice cracked. "If we hadn't left the reservation with more than two people... if we hadn't startled her... none of this would have happened."

John shook his head sharply. "No. Do not take the blame on yourselves. Men like that colonel look for excuses to strike. If it hadn't been you, he would've found another target. He enjoys hurting those who are weaker. It's in his nature. None of this is on you."

Grant exhaled through gritted teeth.

"I'm surprised he hasn't been brought up on charges before. How that monster managed to become a colonel is beyond me." He shook his head bitterly. "Either his superiors are blind, or they chose to look the other way." He glanced toward the trees, then back at Calian.

"We can't take the horses with us," Grant said quietly. "Can you bring them back to the ranch before returning to the reservation?"

Calian nodded firmly. "I will. And I'll tell Ahanu and Nodin what happened. Tell them where you're taking her."

John's jaw tightened. "Let them know she's going straight to Dr. Hunter's clinic in town. And tell them we fully intend to see that lowlife removed from command, for good this time."

Calian's expression hardened with resolve. "We will pray for her. And we will pray for justice." He clicked to the horses and led them away as John climbed to the driver's seat, determination burning in every line of his face. The wheels creaked. The carriage lurched forward. And Rose, already trembling with pain, braced herself, consciously or not, for the agonizing journey ahead.

⚬⟋

No matter how carefully Grant tried to steady her, the carriage still jolted and lurched along the uneven mountain road. Every bump sent a fresh wave of fear through him. Rose lay across his lap, barely conscious, her skin far too pale, her breath faint and shallow.

John sat on the driver's seat, gripping the reins so hard his knuckles whitened. Tears streaked his weathered face as he prayed aloud, his voice breaking with each word.

"Lord, please... spare this child. Don't let her suffer more. Don't let her slip away. Keep her safe. Keep her with us."

Grant swallowed against the tightness in his throat. Rose's head shifted weakly with each jolt, and he tried to cradle her closer, shielding her from the worst of it. But the road was merciless. When the carriage hit a deep rut, Rose's lashes fluttered, and then her eyes rolled fully shut. She went limp.

For one terrifying heartbeat, Grant thought she had stopped breathing. Then he felt the faint rise and fall of her chest and exhaled shakily.

"She's unconscious," he called to John, relief and dread tangled in his voice. "Thank goodness... at least she won't feel the worst of this."

John bowed his head, whispering another fervent prayer. Hoofbeats pounded from behind, growing louder. Within moments, two riders came into view, Marshal Moore and Marshal Jones, galloping hard to catch up. They pulled alongside the buckboard, anxiety etched into every line of their faces. Marshal Moore leaned down from his saddle, eyes scanning Rose with barely contained panic.

"How is she?" he demanded. "Is she still alive?"

"She fainted," Grant said. "Which is a mercy. She doesn't need to stay awake for this pain." His voice sharpened. "Has that brute been arrested?"

"Not yet," Jones replied grimly. "We're waiting on word from marshal headquarters in Denver and from Lieutenant General Hilton. Braxton Goodwing has sent a dozen telegrams already."

Moore added, "Your father arrived in town as we were leaving. He was headed to the sheriff, but Duncan Bailey already knew. Mr. Adams wired a relative in Washington, someone high enough to make noise."

"Good." Grant's jaw clenched. "Everyone needs to hear about this. The army ought to hang that colonel."

Moore nodded grimly. "They just might. Word is spreading fast." His gaze moved back to Rose, lingering with a mixture of fury and anguish. "Shane and his great-uncle are waiting at the clinic," he said. "They're ready the moment you arrive. They'll take care of her, Grant. They'll do everything they can."

Grant tightened his hold on Rose, his voice raw.

"They'd better hurry. She's losing strength and more blood."

The marshals spurred their horses ahead to clear the way. The buckboard rattled on toward town, carrying a broken girl, a desperate guardian, and a young man whose heart burned with fear, rage, and a vow that this would never happen to her again.

When the carriage jolted to a halt outside the small, white-washed clinic, Shane Hunter burst through the doorway, sleeves rolled up and worry etched plainly across his face.

"Bring her in, quickly. Is she still conscious?"

Grant and John both shook their heads.

Shane exhaled sharply. "Good. She's better off not feeling any of this. Bring her straight to the surgery room."

Grant didn't waste a second. He scooped Rose into his arms, wrapping her gently in one of the quilts to shield her from the cool mountain air. Even through the fabric, he could feel how limp she was, how frighteningly light. Her head lolled against his chest as he hurried inside.

The clinic smelled of antiseptic herbs, carbolic, and wood smoke. Lamplight flickered over glass jars and metal instruments, casting long shadows across the narrow hallway. Shane strode ahead, pushing open the door to the surgery room.

"Set her here," he said, motioning to the examination table. Grant laid Rose down as gently as human hands could manage. The moment her trembling body touched the cold surface, he flinched, wanting to shield her again, to gather her close and keep her safe. But Shane was already moving.

"Grant," the doctor said firmly, "I need space to work. Please wait outside."

Grant didn't move. His hands hovered above Rose's shoulders, unable to leave her. Her hair, tangled and streaked with dirt, clung to her cheek. Her lips were pale. She looked heartbreakingly fragile.

"Son," John said gently, placing a hand on his arm, "let him do his job."

Grant's throat tightened. He lowered his head, then forced himself to step back. Shane guided him toward the door, his tone softening.

"We'll do everything we can for her. I promise." The door closed with a heavy click, shutting Grant and John out into the dimly lit waiting room. The sudden silence was suffocating. Grant braced his palms on his knees, breath coming hard.

Please, Lord. Don't take her. Not like this.

John sank into a wooden chair and covered his face with both hands. The old wall clock ticked above them, each second scraping across the raw edges of their fear. Behind the closed door came muffled voices, the clink of instruments, the splash of water, every sound a reminder that Rose was fighting for her life.

"Get some chloroform so she doesn't wake," Henry Hunter instructed the nearest nurse. His tone was steady, but a muscle in his jaw twitched, a small crack in the seasoned doctor's composure.

"Yes, Doctor." She uncorked the small brown bottle. The sharp, sweet scent of chloroform filled the air as she moistened a folded cloth. She positioned herself beside Rose's head, watching the fragile rise and fall of her breathing.

Shane and Henry moved with swift efficiency, their experienced hands grim and sure. They removed the outer layers of Rose's clothing with the utmost care, preserving her modesty while exposing what needed treatment. Her chemise remained, but Henry cut away the ruined fabric clinging to her back, sticky with dried blood. The sight beneath it made both men pause.

Angry welts striped her skin from shoulder to waist, some split open, others swollen beneath deep, darkening bruises. The cruel imprint of a riding crop was unmistakable. Shane drew a slow breath.

"Heaven forbid..."

Henry nodded grimly. "We'll deal with the crop wounds first. Then her legs."

Her stockings were soaked with blood, fabric fused to skin. Rather than tear them away, Shane carefully cut the stockings open from ankle to thigh. They peeled the remnants free, revealing long, vicious welts. Purple bruises blooming beneath torn flesh. Cuts where the sticks and crop had broken skin. Dried blood flaked away at the slightest touch.

The nurse pressed the chloroform cloth gently over Rose's nose and mouth, brushing a stray curl from her damp forehead.

"Sleep, sweetheart," she whispered. "Don't feel this."

As chloroform carried Rose deeper into unconsciousness, the two doctors exchanged a solemn glance, silent acknowledgment of the cruelty before them.

"This was punishment meant to break her," Shane murmured, fury trembling beneath the surface. "But she endured it."

Henry's expression hardened. "Then we'll make certain she survives it."

Together, they bent to their work, treating, cleansing, stitching, with the precision of men who refused to let brutality have the final word.

When they reached her feet, even Henry, who had practiced medicine during wars and frontier raids, let out a low, involuntary gasp. Her feet were mangled. The soles were bloody and raw, the skin flayed. Deep bruising marred her heels and arches. Several small puncture wounds oozed sluggishly, deliberate injuries.

"Have mercy..." Henry whispered, his voice hoarse with rage. "What kind of monster does this to a young woman?"

The two nurses exchanged stricken glances but worked quickly, preparing basins of warm water and antiseptic. Shane swallowed hard and reached for the cloths. Together with the nurses, he began cleaning Rose's feet. Even in unconsciousness, Rose flinched at each touch, her fingers twitching weakly.

Henry examined her face for fractures. "She took several blows, but it doesn't appear he broke anything."

It was the only mercy they found. The work was slow and grueling. Blood mixed with water until the basins ran dark. Cut by cut, they disinfected, trimmed torn edges of skin, and stitched the deepest wounds.

Two hours passed before they were done. By the time Shane tied the final stitch, sweat beaded his brow. Henry wiped his hands on a cloth, shoulders sagging in exhaustion. Her back was no longer covered in blood, but in careful rows of stitches and covered with a thin sheet. Her legs were wrapped in soft linen. Her feet cocooned in thick layers of sterile cloth. She looked so small now. So fragile. Too pale.

Shane stood over her, jaw clenched, grief and fury burning behind his eyes.

"We'll do everything we can," he whispered. "I swear we will."

⸻

John had just finished speaking with the marshals when the clinic door swung open. A tall, broad-shouldered older man stepped inside, his presence commanding enough to silence the room. His uniform bore the insignia of one of the highest ranks, and even before John fully registered it, he knew. Lieutenant General Hilton.

Behind him came Captain Ray and Second Lieutenant Wright, both grim. A heartbeat later, Sheriff Bailey hurried inside, hat in hand, fury tight in his expression.

"Where is the young lady?" Hilton asked without preamble, his voice edged with urgency. Before anyone could answer, a side door opened and a nurse stepped into the waiting room. She paused, startled by the sudden assembly of high-ranking men. John stepped forward.

"Nurse Joni," he said gently, "this is Lieutenant General Hilton. He's here about my niece."

Her eyes widened. She dipped her head respectfully, then crossed to a cabinet to gather more bandages.

"She's in the surgery room, sir," she reported. "We're finishing her treatment now."

"She is not fully bandaged yet?" Hilton pressed.

The nurse swallowed. "No, sir. Not yet."

"Then I must see her injuries before they're covered," he said grimly. "I need to assess the extent of the damage if I'm to determine how we proceed."

The room went still. No one questioned him. Just then, the door burst open again and Braxton Goodwing, the telegraphist, stumbled in, chest heaving, face flushed.

"Lieutenant General Hilton," he gasped, clutching a telegram. "This just came from Washington, with instructions to deliver immediately. It's from President Arthur himself."

A murmur rippled through the room. Hilton took the telegram, scanned it, and his jaw tightened. Whatever the

President had written only strengthened the resolve already burning in the general's face. He handed the paper to Captain Ray.

"Read that," he ordered. Then he nodded to the nurse. "Please take me to the patient. Now."

The nurse hurried back through the surgery door. Hilton followed, pausing at the threshold with military precision, waiting for permission to enter.

In the waiting room, every man, John, the marshals, the sheriff, and the two young officers, stood suspended in breathless silence, praying that justice was unmistakably on its way.

"Cover the bandages with the healing ointment and place them carefully on her back and legs," Henry instructed the moment the nurse stepped back into the surgery room. His voice remained steady, but the tension in his jaw betrayed how deeply shaken he truly was.

"Dr. Hunter," the nurse said quietly, "Lieutenant General Hilton is here. He wishes to see her injuries. Should I allow him in?"

Shane exchanged a quick, heavy glance with his great-uncle. The request carried enormous weight, military protocol, legal responsibility, and Rose's dignity were all at stake. After a moment, Henry gave a firm nod.

"Yes," he said. "But only Lieutenant General Hilton. No one else."

The nurse dipped her head and slipped back out. A moment later, she returned and lifted a hand to usher the general inside.

Lieutenant General Hilton entered with measured, controlled steps, his presence filling the small room. Authority radiated from him, an unyielding gravity that made even the seasoned medical staff stand a little straighter. He nodded respectfully to the nurses, then looked at Henry and Shane.

"Doctors," he greeted quietly.

Henry acknowledged him with a solemn incline of his head. Shane stepped back to stand at his great-uncle's side. Gently, almost reverently, Henry reached for the sheet covering Rose's back. Shane steadied his breath, bracing himself despite having already witnessed the damage.

As the sheet peeled away, Hilton's face, trained into military discipline, hardened. The welts, the rows of stitches, the dark bruises, the raw, flayed skin along her legs and feet... even a man who had witnessed battlefield horrors could not hide the sharp flash of shock in his eyes. Shane swallowed hard.

"This," Henry said gravely, "is what Colonel Bricks ordered done to her."

The lieutenant general clasped his hands behind his back, but the muscle in his jaw ticked violently. He stepped closer, his voice low and taut with barely restrained fury.

"No civilized army," he said, "would ever tolerate this." He drew a long, steady breath, then looked at the doctors with grim resolve. "Continue your work. I have seen enough." His gaze returned to Rose once more, softening for the briefest heartbeat, before he stepped toward the door, carrying with him the full weight of what he had witnessed and the unmistakable promise of consequences to come.

The door had scarcely clicked shut when his voice rang through the clinic, firm and commanding.

"Captain."

Captain Ray appeared almost instantly, spine straightening.

"Yes, sir."

Hilton's tone held the cold precision of a man accustomed to swift, unflinching justice.

"Take the second lieutenant, the sheriff, and the two marshals. Arrest the coward responsible and the two soldiers who carried out his orders."

The captain's jaw tightened. "Colonel Bricks will resist, sir."

"Then," Hilton said, withdrawing the folded telegram from his coat and pressing it into Ray's hand, "you show him the telegram from the President." His voice dropped lower, steely and unmistakably lethal in its calm. "Inform him that President Arthur demands an immediate accounting. If Bricks so much as raises his voice, remind him that I am waiting in town, and I expect to see him behind bars before the hour is out."

"Yes, sir," Captain Ray answered, his voice hardening with purpose.

"We will conduct a pre-trial here in Idaho Springs," the lieutenant general continued. "After that, he will be transported to Denver, and then to Washington to face formal charges." The order left no room for argument.

Captain Ray saluted sharply, then strode away, quickly joined by Second Lieutenant Wright, Sheriff Bailey, Marshal Moore, and Marshal Jones. Their footsteps echoed down the corridor, five men armed with authority, determination, and righteous fury.

Hilton remained where he stood for a moment longer, his gaze drifting back toward the closed surgery room door.

"Justice," he murmured, "will be served."

9

When the General Listened

Once Rose's wounds were cleaned and wrapped in layer upon layer of bandages, the physicians carried her carefully into the adjoining recovery room. It was a quieter space, entered through a narrow side door from the surgery. Only once she had been settled onto a clean bed did the nurses step aside and allow her aunt and uncle to come in.

Elizabeth's breath hitched the instant she saw her niece's still form. She pressed a trembling hand to her mouth, tears spilling freely. With a broken sob, she hurried to Rose's side, pulled up a chair, and took her hand into her own.

"Oh, my darling girl..." she whispered, stroking Rose's fingers with heartbreaking tenderness.

John moved slowly, almost reverently, sinking into the chair on the other side of the bed. The sight of Rose, so pale, so unmoving, carved deep lines into his face. He laid a steady hand on her forearm, his thumb brushing softly against the linen bandages.

A nurse approached, draping a light blanket over Rose's damaged legs and tucking it carefully around her. The room filled with the hush of soft footsteps, the rustle of cloth, and the warm glow of lamplight.

A moment later, Shane entered the recovery room, his expression drawn with fatigue and the weight of everything he had witnessed. Behind him stepped Lieutenant General Hilton, posture rigid yet respectful.

"I'll remain here awhile," the general said, voice low but resolute. "There are questions I'll need to ask the young lady once she wakes. Matters that must be documented at once."

Henry Hunter inclined his head. "Of course, sir. You may stay as long as needed."

John looked up and gave a quiet nod. Justice required testimony, and testimony required clarity. When Rose woke, however painful, it had to be done.

Hilton pulled a straight-backed chair to the corner of the room, positioning himself with a clear view of the bed. Even seated, his presence anchored the room with authority and purpose.

Lizzie leaned closer, brushing a loose strand of hair from Rose's forehead.

"Rest now, sweetheart," she whispered, voice thick with love and fury. "We're right here. You're safe. You're safe."

John bowed his head, murmuring a quiet prayer over the girl between them, while Shane stood close, watching with a physician's vigilance. Beyond the walls, hushed voices and hurried footsteps signaled the beginning of something larger, arrests, justice, consequences. But inside the small recovery room, time held still, suspended around the battered young woman fighting for each breath. Her family waited, steadfast, grieving, and ready to guard her with their lives.

Not long after, Rose shifted with a faint whimper, her breath catching in her throat. The movement pulled her sharply from unconsciousness, and her eyes fluttered open, unfocused at first, then slowly sharpening.

The first face she saw was not her uncle's or her aunt's, but that of a tall, commanding man seated near the foot of her bed. His expression was carved from discipline, yet his eyes, commanding, steady, unexpectedly gentle, held compassion.

"Miss Williams," he said quietly, leaning forward, "I am Lieutenant General Hilton. If you feel able, I'd like to ask you a few questions. Only as much as you can manage."

Rose swallowed, her throat dry.

"I... I think I can manage," she whispered. She shifted slightly, searching for a position that didn't send fire lancing up her back and legs. When she turned her head, she saw her aunt and uncle sitting close, John on one side, Lizzie on the other. Their eyes, full of love and fear and relief, undid her completely. Tears welled and spilled, and she pressed her face into the pillow, trembling with exhaustion and emotion.

"Oh, darling," Lizzie murmured, smoothing her hair. "We're here, sweetheart."

"You're safe now," John added softly, brushing her forearm. "It's over."

Hilton waited in respectful silence.

"Take your time, Miss Williams," he said gently. "No answer is worth more pain."

When Rose finally managed to speak again, her voice was fragile but steady. She told him everything, every step of the horror she had endured. Her hands shook as she recounted it. At her weakest moments, Lizzie clasped her fingers tightly.

Hilton never interrupted or looked away. His jaw tightened when she described the beatings, the threats, the soldiers forced to obey. When she told of the final blows, her voice faltered. John bowed his head, visibly fighting his anger. When she finished, silence settled like a held breath.

"Thank you, Miss Williams," Hilton said at last, his voice low with restrained fury and genuine respect. "You have shown remarkable courage. Rest now. I will see to the rest." He rose, placed a steady hand briefly on hers, then turned to Reverend Williams.

"Reverend," he said, "I'll be remaining in Idaho Springs until this matter is resolved. Would you show me to the hotel?"

"Of course, Lieutenant General," John replied quietly. "This way."

As the two men left, Lizzie stayed at Rose's bedside, holding her hand and humming a soft lullaby, one Rose dimly remembered from childhood visits. Outside, murmured voices and the creak of boots filled the hall. Marshal Moore stood sentry at the door, expression carved in stone. Several soldiers stood with him, forming a silent wall of protection.

Inside, Rose's eyes drifted shut again, exhaustion pulling her under. This time, she slept with her family at her side, and an entire town standing guard.

Christopher had drifted into an uneasy doze in the chair outside the recovery room when a soft, strangled whimper snapped him awake. His eyes flew open at once. Through the cracked door, Rose's voice rose, breathless, frightened.

"Stop... please don't, help! Help me!"

Before the echo faded, Christopher was through the door. Rose writhed beneath the blankets. Her face twisted with terror. Her bandaged legs kicked weakly as she tried to push herself up, too fast. Pain shot through her, and she cried out.

"No... no... don't touch me—"

He reached her side and gently pressed his hands on her shoulders, careful not to hurt her.

"Rose," he whispered urgently, "it's me. It's Marshal Moore. You're safe. No one's hurting you. I swear it."

But she didn't hear him, not yet. The nightmare held her fast. She thrashed again, gasping.

"Rose," he said louder, voice firm but warm, "open your eyes. Look at me. You're safe."

Her eyelids flickered. Slowly, achingly, her gaze lifted to his. Confusion. Terror. Then recognition.

"It... it was just a nightmare," he murmured, his hand drifting softly over her hair. "You're safe. No one will ever hurt you like that again. Not while I draw breath."

Her breathing steadied. A faint, trembling smile appeared, small but real, before exhaustion pulled her eyes shut again. Christopher stayed beside her for a moment more, watching her features soften. The sight of her, so bruised, so undeserving of any of it, twisted something deep inside him.

He had seen horrors before. But nothing had struck him like this gentle girl lying broken in a place where she should have been safe. He brushed a tear from her cheek with a feather-light touch, then stepped back, settling into the chair outside her door. He wouldn't sleep again that night. Not while she needed watching. Not while he still breathed.

Only Rose's aunt and uncle, and the two marshals, were allowed to visit her during the first week. Dr. Hunter insisted on strict limits. Rest was as vital as medicine. She needed quiet, not well-meaning visitors or questions she wasn't ready to answer.

She slept for long stretches, drifting in and out of consciousness as her body fought to heal. Her back and legs required constant attention. Several times a day, the Hunters and their nurses checked her bandages, examined her wounds, and watched for signs of infection.

On the fourth morning, the fear became reality. Rose woke with a fever, her face flushed, her breathing shallow. She trembled beneath the blankets, her skin alternately hot and clammy. When Shane laid a hand lightly to her brow, he called sharply for his great-uncle.

The two physicians conferred in urgent whispers, paging through medical journals stacked on a nearby table. They had known this was a risk, given the brutality of her wounds and the unsanitary conditions under which she'd been beaten, but they had to decide quickly how to treat it.

Nearly an hour passed before the elder doctor made a soft exclamation.

"Here," he said, tapping a pamphlet. "Dr. Joseph Lister, a surgeon from Edinburgh. He reports success preventing infection using a carbolic acid spray. Claims it creates an antiseptic environment, kills germs before they can settle."

Shane leaned over the page. "Carbolic acid... yes. Some doctors on the East Coast have begun trying it."

Henry nodded. "And so had Dr. Williams, from what I understand." He exhaled softly. "If only more surgeons had listened sooner."

Without hesitation, they called for the nurses and ordered preparations for a second procedure, to clean and remove any dead or infected tissue before the fever could climb further out of control.

When John and Lizzie arrived at the clinic that morning, they found Rose back in the recovery room, pale, exhausted, but sleeping peacefully under the influence of medication. Fresh bandages wrapped her wounds. The sharp scent of antiseptic lingered softly in the air. Henry met them at the doorway, wiping his hands with a cloth soaked in diluted carbolic acid.

"She's stable now," he assured them, though worry still shadowed his tone. "The fever hasn't worsened since the procedure. We acted in time."

Lizzie pressed a trembling hand to her heart.

"Oh, thank goodness."

"But," Henry added firmly, "I must ask something of you both. Please do not touch her, not her hands, not her hair, unless you wash thoroughly first. Hot water, soap, and this," he lifted the cloth, "a carbolic rinse."

John nodded immediately. "Of course."

"We're following Dr. Lister's method now," Henry continued. "Every instrument, every cloth, every hand that comes near her will be cleansed. It's her best chance."

Lizzie swallowed, eyes shining with gratitude.

"Whatever you need us to do, we'll do it."

The elder doctor's voice gentled. "With care, rest, and prayer... she will recover. But it will take time."

John stepped to Rose's bedside, close, but careful not to touch, and whispered a quiet prayer of thanks, while Lizzie bowed her head beside him. Outside the door, Marshal Moore listened as well, relief finally softening the tension that had lived in his shoulders since Rose first arrived at the clinic. For the first time since the ordeal began, hope settled over the little building like the faint warmth of morning light.

Early on Sunday morning, Lizzie set out for the clinic. She had barely slept, but she needed to be with Rose. John understood. He watched her go with a soft, worried smile, then returned to his study to pray over his sermon. Two hours before church, he knew he must abandon the message he had prepared. Today called for something different, something from the heart.

The church filled quickly, as it always did, but today curiosity hummed through the pews. People turned their heads when Lieutenant General Hilton entered with the captain and second lieutenant beside him. Soldiers rarely attended John's services, they had their own chaplain, so their presence lent a solemn weight.

HEALING THE ORPHANED HEART

When John stepped behind the pulpit, he swept his gaze slowly across the congregation. His heart was heavy, but resolute.

"My friends," he began, "Lizzie sends her apologies for not being here this morning. You all know her heart. She believes family matters are sacred above all else, and she felt our niece needed her more than we did today."

A warm murmur rippled through the pews.

"I struggled for days with what to speak about," he continued. "But my heart urged me to share something deeply personal, and to address the recent events that have weighed on our community." He paused, gathering strength.

"Before we came to Colorado, Boston was our home. We lived close to my brother and his family. He and his dear wife had a daughter, a precious little girl, full of life, bright as sunshine. Rose." His smile wavered, touched with memory. "Lizzie loved her like her own." He breathed in slowly.

"When I accepted this congregation, leaving Boston was a blessing, but also a deep ache. We prayed long and hard before answering the call to come West."

Faces softened across the sanctuary.

"Soon after we arrived, we learned that my sister-in-law had passed. It broke our hearts, not only because we lost her, but because Rose lost her mother so young." He looked down for a long moment.

"I wrote to my brother, begged him to let Rose come live with us. But he refused. His letters grew fewer, and eventually... they stopped."

Silence settled, heavy and compassionate.

"A few weeks ago, we learned my brother had died of typhus. And that Rose was being sent here, alone except for us. The sweet five-year-old we kissed goodbye so long ago has returned to us a grown young woman, lovely, brave, and strong." He swallowed tightly.

"And since her arrival, I have learned things she never should have had to bear. And as many of you now know... she endured a terrible ordeal the day after she set foot in Idaho Springs."

Gasps fluttered softly across the room.

"I will not burden you with details," he said gently. "But know this: she was not harmed because of anything she did wrong. She was harmed because she stood up for what was right. She refused to stay silent when four young Cheyenne men were mistreated. She chose compassion—and paid dearly for it." John's voice broke. He pressed his fingers briefly to his eyes. There wasn't a dry eye in the sanctuary.

"I don't share this to seek pity. Rose doesn't even know I'm telling you this, and I'm sure she'll wring my neck once she finds out."

A soft ripple of laughter eased the tension.

"She has her mother's fire. And I believe—without doubt—that if she had to make that choice again, she would still defend those young men... even knowing the cost." He rested his hands on the pulpit.

"When she recovers, she will walk among us, into town, through the forests, along the lake. Though she is spirited, she has also newly arrived, newly orphaned, and newly burdened with enemies who wish her harm." His voice gentled.

"Lizzie and I would be deeply grateful if those in this room would keep an eye out for her. Step in if something seems wrong. Intervene if someone seeks to trouble her. Better to step in one time too many than one time too late." Warmth threaded through his closing words.

"Rose is family, ours, and I hope... yours. Lizzie tells me she finally feels like she has a daughter. And she cannot bear the thought of losing her." The final words echoed through the hushed sanctuary. "So let us be her shield. Let us be a community that lifts up the vulnerable, protects the innocent, and stands together in compassion and righteousness."

Lizzie had just finished reading a Psalm when a soft knock sounded at the door. She closed the small Bible and rested it on her lap.

"Come in," she called gently.

The elder Dr. Hunter stepped inside, expression warm but intent. Shane followed with a tray of ointments and fresh bandages.

"How is our patient today?" the elder doctor asked.

"A little better," Lizzie replied hopefully.

"Good," he murmured. "Shane, close the door. Let's have a proper look."

Shane obeyed, then joined him at Rose's bedside. Rose swallowed nervously but nodded for them to proceed.

They worked with practiced gentleness. Lizzie steadied Rose as the doctors untied the linens and eased the blankets aside. Even the slightest movement sent a ripple of pain through her back and legs, and she drew a sharp breath, gripping the sheet.

"I know, dear," Lizzie whispered, brushing her hair. "You're doing wonderfully."

Despite her discomfort, Rose noticed the elder doctor's expression soften as he examined her.

"The swelling is down considerably," he said. "And these bruises, though vivid, are beginning to fade. That is an excellent sign."

Shane leaned in to inspect her cheekbones and jaw. The mottling was still severe, but the heat had left her skin. He dipped his fingers into ointment and gently smoothed it over her tender cheek.

"This will help the swelling and bruising."

Rose exhaled shakily. "Thank you."

Together, the doctors replaced the bandages on her back and legs. The cool salve soothed the worst of the sting. When they finished, the elder Dr. Hunter straightened with a satisfied nod.

"You're healing well, Rose," he said. "Slowly, perhaps, but well. It will be time before you feel like yourself again."

Rose's eyes brightened. "May I sit up?"

"Yes," he replied, lifting a cautioning hand. "But only with support. We'll arrange pillows behind your back and beneath your legs. And whenever it becomes too painful, lie on your stomach again."

Rose nodded gratefully.

"I'll send a nurse to help," he added. "Fresh linens, pillows, whatever you need. Only ask."

She managed a faint, earnest smile. "Thank you, Dr. Hunter. Truly."

He returned the smile and gave her hand a gentle squeeze.

"If you require anything, anything at all, your aunt knows where to find us. We live just upstairs."

HEALING THE ORPHANED HEART

After they left, Lizzie smoothed the blanket over Rose's legs. The room felt warmer somehow, proof that healing, though slow, had begun.

~

The nurse returned shortly after. With Lizzie's help, she gently washed and dressed Rose in fresh linens, then guided her into a seated position. The simple act of feeling clean and upright again felt like a small miracle.

Rose eased back against the arranged pillows. Though she had slept more in the last week than in the entire previous month, lying exclusively on her stomach had grown increasingly uncomfortable. Her face still throbbed when she moved too quickly, and she was grateful there wasn't a mirror in the room. She doubted she could bear her reflection, yet.

Lizzie had barely settled into the chair beside her when a knock sounded. Uncle John stepped inside, his expression warm and relieved.

"How are you feeling, Rose?"

"A little better," she replied. "How was church?"

"Good," he said, taking her hand briefly as he sat on the edge of the bed. "Many people asked after you. And now that Dr. Hunter has given his permission... don't be surprised if you have visitors today, and in the days ahead."

"Why?" she demanded, suspicion sharpening. "Uncle John... did you tell them about me? About what happened?" She shot him a disapproving look.

He winced, though a mischievous smile tugged at his mouth.

"I did. And I also told them you had no idea I planned to speak of it, and that you might want to murder me when you found out."

Despite herself, Rose let out a soft, breathy laugh.

"That thought is crossing my mind right now."

He grinned and winked. "I kept details to myself, I promise. But a little extra watching out won't hurt. The people of Idaho Springs are protective of their own. And you belong here now."

Her expression softened. "Thank you, Uncle John."

10

The Court at Her Bedside

Footsteps echoed in the hallway just before Grant appeared in the doorway with his family. John rose and gestured them inside.

"Rose, this is Jonas Adams and his wife, Cornelia. They own the largest ranch in the state."

"It is a pleasure to meet you, Miss Williams," Mr. Adams said warmly. "I've heard many fine things about you."

"It's nice to meet you as well, sir."

"We've brought a picnic with us," Mrs. Adams added, smiling as she held up a basket. "If it's all right with your doctors, we'd love to share it with you."

"Jonas, John," she went on with a nod toward the men, "let's bring everything inside so we can set it up."

The four adults stepped out, leaving Grant and his sister to gather chairs and pull them closer to the bed.

"I'm Jennifer," the young woman said as she sat. "I'm terribly sorry about how we first met, and I'd also like to apologize for my brother's behavior. He doesn't always think before he speaks, and he lashes out more often than he should."

Rose's eyes darkened at the memory. Grant shot his sister a confused look.

"What are you talking about?"

"You don't remember?" Rose's tone held both hurt and bewilderment. "I couldn't see your faces because of the sun, but I certainly remember your harsh words. You said I had no business on your land. You accused me of trespassing."

Jennifer's eyes widened. "Oh, Rose, no. That wasn't Grant. That was our older brother, Grayson. He's a lawyer in Denver, and he hates coming home because Father expects everyone to pitch in on the ranch. He gets... well, difficult. Embarrassingly so."

"But he sounded like Grant," Rose murmured.

"Their voices are almost identical," Jennifer said. "But Grant is never that rude."

"You thought it was me?" Grant asked quietly.

Heat flooded Rose's cheeks. She lowered her gaze.

"I'm so sorry. I didn't know you had an older brother... and the voice—" She shook her head. "I should have known better. You were so kind during the journey here. It startled me to think you could speak that way."

Grant's expression softened into a charming smile that sent her heartbeat racing.

"Don't fret over it. Grayson and I have plenty in common, but as Jen said, he hates ranch work. That alone sours his mood."

Jennifer sighed. "I should've scolded him before he left. Maybe if I had, this wouldn't have happened." Her eyes welled with tears.

Rose reached for her hand. "None of this was your fault. You couldn't control what he did. And it might have happened on my way home regardless."

Jennifer squeezed her fingers, visibly relieved.

"Thank you, Rose. I'm looking forward to getting to know you better. And I can't wait for us to be related." She nudged her brother playfully. "Right, Grant?"

Grant grinned at Rose, his gaze warm and lingering. Rose blinked, caught completely off guard.

"R–related?" she stammered, turning scarlet.

Jennifer laughed lightly. "When I marry your cousin Paul, of course. Didn't your aunt and uncle mention it?"

"Oh, no, they didn't," Rose managed. "Grant told me on the train. I haven't seen Paul and Jordan yet, so it slipped my mind."

Grant's smile widened. "What did you think Jen meant?"

Rose could feel her face light up like fireworks on the Fourth of July, but before she could answer, the adults returned carrying baskets and a table, filling the room with cheerful chatter and the comforting aroma of warm bread and roasted chicken.

Mrs. Colton arrived just as the last of the picnic baskets were being cleared away. She swept into the room with her usual brisk warmth, and Grant and Jennifer immediately stepped aside so she could take the chair beside Rose's bed.

"Oh, honey," she breathed, reaching for Rose's hand. "I am so terribly sorry for what happened to you. That despicable vermin ought to be tossed straight into hell where he belongs. Any man who strikes a girl is a coward, plain and simple."

A faint laugh escaped Rose. "Thank you, Mrs. Colton." The older woman gave her hand a tender squeeze. She didn't linger long, she sensed Rose was growing tired, but she made every minute count, leaning forward to press a gentle kiss to Rose's forehead.

"My husband and I will be moving to the outskirts of Denver next month," she said with a nostalgic sigh. "My daughter will take over the café. Our son wants us close to him, so we're letting him build us a little house on his land. I'll miss Idaho Springs something fierce, but we're looking forward to this next adventure. And you," she pointed a finger lovingly at Rose, "you better not hesitate if ever you want a place to rest. We'd love to have you stay with us."

Rose brightened. "That's very kind of you, Mrs. Colton."

"Oh, bring Jennifer along," the lady added breezily. "My two oldest granddaughters and I can arrange a little social gathering. Introduce you to some nice young men." She winked. "A girl as sweet and pretty as you ought not be kept hidden away."

Heat crept up Rose's cheeks.

"That's not necessary," she murmured, flustered. "Jennifer is getting married soon, and I'm in no hurry at all to meet anyone."

From the doorway, Mr. Adams inserted himself into the conversation with impeccable timing.

"Rose will meet her Romeo before long," he declared with a grin. "Suitors will be lining up like hungry wolves, and I hope you've got your guns loaded, John!"

Uncle John let out a hearty laugh.

"Perhaps Grant could be one of those suitors," he teased. "Wouldn't that be something, Jonas?"

"It would indeed," Jonas agreed with a mischievous gleam. "Well? What do you think, son?"

Grant spluttered, his neck reddening. "Dad! Why would you two put us on the spot like that? Rose and I aren't even courting!"

Rose groaned and immediately buried her burning face in her pillow. How had the conversation veered into such humiliating territory?

"You two are awful," Jennifer scolded, planting her hands on her hips as though chastising a pair of unruly boys. "Leave poor Rose alone. If she's meant to become my sister, it will happen naturally. There's no reason to embarrass her half to death."

The older men only chuckled in satisfaction, clearly pleased with themselves. Mrs. Colton rose and smoothed her skirts.

"I'd best go, dear. But remember what I said, you're always welcome with us. And if these men give you trouble," she shot Jonas and Uncle John a pointed glare, "just pack a bag and come stay with me. I'll hide you from them."

Rose peeked out from her pillow and cast her uncle a mock glare.

"Thank you, Mrs. Colton. I might have to take you up on that."

The room erupted in laughter, warm, foolish, comfortable laughter, and for the first time since her ordeal, Rose felt the heaviness in her chest lift just a little.

***

Rose had barely finished her breakfast the following morning when a firm knock sounded at her door. Before she could respond, it opened, and her aunt and uncle stepped inside, followed by the two marshals, Lieutenant General Hilton, and a distinguished man she had never seen before. The room felt suddenly crowded, their solemn faces sending a ripple of dread through her.

"Miss Williams," Lieutenant General Hilton began, "this is General Winter. He has come from Washington to join the pre-trial today."

Rose inclined her head politely. "General."

General Winter stepped closer, his expression grave but gentle. He reached out and turned her face slightly so he could examine the fading marks on her cheeks.

"Did the colonel use anything other than his hand when he struck your face?"

Rose shook her head, but unease bloomed in her chest. The atmosphere in the room had shifted. This was no friendly morning visit. Something was coming, something she did not want to face.

"Miss Williams," the general continued, stepping back, "we need you present at the pre-trial today. Your testimony is required."

The words struck like a blow. Rose's breath caught. Her fingers tightened around the blanket.

"No," she whispered, shaking her head more firmly. "Please don't make me do that." Tears burned behind her eyes, but she fought them desperately. The very thought of seeing the colonel again, of being in the same room, even guarded, made her stomach twist with cold terror.

"You must join us," General Winter insisted gently. "Everyone needs to hear what happened directly from you. Your statement will ensure that justice is carried out."

"I can't," Rose said, her voice cracking. "I can't face him. Please... don't ask me to." Panic clawed up her throat, her heart pounding like a trapped bird.

"We will all be with you," the general said softly, taking a half step closer. "You will not be left alone with your tormentors. I give you, my word." He reached out as if to offer reassurance. Rose flinched away, shrinking back against her pillows.

"I'm sorry... I'm sorry, but I can't. Please, leave me alone. You can't force me."

Lieutenant General Hilton exchanged a look with Marshal Moore, one Rose didn't fully understand.

"Marshal Moore," the lieutenant general said quietly.

Christopher immediately stepped forward, his expression full of concern rather than command.

"Rose..." he began softly. But she recoiled from him too. Panic was in full control now. She slid toward the opposite edge of the bed, trying to escape, breathing too fast to steady herself.

"Rose, wait—!" Marshal Moore rounded the bed just as she pushed herself upright. The moment her feet touched the floor, a white-hot stab of pain shot up her legs. She cried out, her knees buckling beneath her.

Christopher lunged forward just in time. He caught her before she struck the floor and gathered her gently into his arms. She trembled violently, half from pain, half from fear.

"Easy," he murmured, his voice low and steady. "It's all right. I've got you." He carried her back onto the bed as if she weighed nothing, laying her carefully against the pillows. Her breaths came in jagged, uneven bursts.

Lieutenant General Hilton exhaled slowly, regret shadowing his stern features.

"We will give you a moment to recover, Miss Williams," he said quietly. "No decisions will be made while you are in distress."

Aunt Lizzie hurried to Rose's side, brushing back her hair with trembling fingers, while Uncle John stood protectively at the foot of the bed, his jaw tight.

Marshal Moore stepped back only one pace, but his eyes never left Rose. His expression was a complicated mixture of anger, directed at the colonel, and aching concern for her.

"Rest for now," General Winter added more gently. "We will discuss this again once you've calmed."

The men withdrew a few steps, giving her space, but the question of the trial hung in the air like a storm cloud waiting to break.

***

While Shane and Henry tended to Rose inside the room, everyone else waited in the hallway. Lizzie faced the gathered men. Her eyes were red, her hands trembled, but her voice held steady.

"Can this not wait?" she pleaded. "Please, postpone it until she is stronger."

Lieutenant General Hilton stepped forward, his expression grave but not unkind.

"Mrs. Williams, I understand your concern, truly. But waiting will not lessen her fear. Trauma grows in the dark. If we delay, she may never be able to face what was done to her. I give you my word, she will not be left alone for a single moment. Marshals Moore and Jones will remain at her side, and the instant she has finished speaking, she will be brought straight back here."

Lizzie shook her head, distraught.

"But why must she be present at all? She already told you everything, you know what happened."

"Yes, she told us," Hilton said gently. "But President Arthur issued direct instructions. General Winter is here on his orders to oversee the pre-trial and hear the young woman's account himself." His jaw tightened. "Several journalists from major papers have arrived as well. The President wants the truth spoken plainly, before witnesses, before officers, before the people."

Lizzie stared at him, bewildered and afraid.

"Journalists? Reporters? She cannot endure that. She's barely strong enough to sit."

"We want people to know," Hilton continued, voice firm but not unfeeling, "that it is never acceptable for a soldier, officer, or anyone sworn to uphold the law to take justice into his own hands. What Colonel Bricks did was not discipline. It was cruelty. Vengeance. Evil." His eyes softened.

"Your niece deserves to see the man who hurt her lose his authority. She deserves to see him stripped of power, publicly, before he is transported to Denver and then Washington for a full military tribunal."

At that moment, the door to Rose's room opened. Both Dr. Hunter and Shane stepped out. The elder physician wiped his hands on a cloth, his expression thunderous.

"We've tended to her," he said sharply. "But I must warn you, Miss Williams is terrified. Her nerves are frayed, and she is in no condition to be hauled before her attackers. If you force her into that courtroom, she may break entirely." He folded his arms.

"My professional recommendation is that you ask the judge and witnesses to come to her instead. Let her speak where she feels safe, away from the men who brutalized her. Anything else would be reckless."

Shane nodded, his jaw tight.

"Her pulse spiked the second she realized she might have to face him. She's strong, but pushing her now could undo all the progress she's made."

Lieutenant General Hilton exchanged a long, weighted look with General Winter. Finally, the higher-ranking officer inclined his head, slow and deliberate.

"Very well," General Winter said. "We will bring the court to her."

Lizzie sagged with relief, pressing a trembling hand to her heart.

"Thank you," she whispered. "You have no idea what this means to us and her."

Hilton's tone remained solemn. "It is the least we can do, for her courage, and for justice."

***

Rose looked up when Uncle John and Aunt Lizzie entered the room, Marshal Moore following closely behind. The moment her eyes landed on him, her pulse lurched. She shrank instinctively against the pillows, her breath turning shallow.

"Please... don't take me to the trial," she whispered. "I don't want to see him again."

Aunt Lizzie hurried to her side, sitting on the edge of the bed with a deep maternal tenderness. She took Rose's hand and gave it a gentle squeeze.

"No one is taking you anywhere, sweetheart," she promised. "Dr. Hunter believes it's safer for you to testify here. The general agreed. Right now, the judge is being brought over. You'll speak from your room, with all of us right beside you. Will that be all right?"

Rose lifted her gaze from her aunt's hands to Uncle John's worried eyes. Compassion and quiet resolve radiated from his face. When he nodded, the tightness in her chest eased, just a fraction.

"You won't face him today," he said softly. "We won't allow it."

She swallowed, her shoulders sagging with relief.

"Thank you," she murmured.

Before she could gather herself further, a knock sounded. Aunt Lizzie called, "Come in."

Two well-dressed gentlemen stepped inside, the journalists she had met in Denver. Kendrick Smith removed his hat immediately, his expression respectful and tinged with sorrow.

"It's good to see you again, Miss Williams," he said with a polite nod. "Though we wish it were under far better circumstances."

His colleague, Mr. Miller, nodded gravely.

"We're here only to listen," he assured her. "Nothing more."

Marshal Moore stepped a little closer to the head of her bed, positioning himself like a silent shield. Rose noticed, and though fear still trembled in her ribs, a fragile sense of protection blossomed. She drew a slow breath.

"All right," she whispered. "I can do this. As long as... as long as I don't have to see him."

"You won't," Moore said firmly, voice low and resolute. "Not today. Not ever without your consent."

The reassurance settled over her like a warm blanket, giving her the strength to face what would come next.

Rose looked around the room, at the two generals, her aunt and uncle, the Hunters, the marshals standing solidly behind her, the judge, and the journalists with notebooks poised. Every face held the same expression: encouragement and steady support. She drew in a breath and met the judge's gaze.

"Miss Williams," he said gently, "can you tell us what happened the day after you arrived in Idaho Springs? Please share everything you recall."

Rose nodded. Though her hands trembled in her lap, her voice remained steady. She recounted everything, her morning walk, the confrontation with Colonel Bricks, the soldiers' violence, the beatings, the humiliation, and the terror of knowing no one was coming to save her. Silence settled thickly over the room.

When she risked a glance at General Winter, she saw controlled fury in his eyes, anger directed entirely at the cruelty she had suffered.

When she finished, the judge leaned forward.

"Miss Williams," he said, voice heavy, "did any of the men who assaulted you give you the chance to defend yourself? Did anyone ask for your side? Offer fairness or explanation?"

She shook her head. "No. The colonel demanded I beg for forgiveness. When I refused, he beat me harder. He never once asked what happened or whether the Indians were guilty of anything. He wanted power, control."

The judge's expression darkened.

"Did you ever offer the forgiveness he tried to force from you?"

Rose inhaled, lifting her chin with quiet resolve.

"No. My uncle taught me my grandfather's motto—that a Williams always stands up and protects their own. We do not bow to threats or cruelty. We face them."

Uncle John reached over and squeezed her hand, his eyes shining with fierce pride. The judge regarded her for a long moment.

"And if you were placed in a similar position again, knowing the consequences, would you still stand your ground and defend what is right?"

"Absolutely," Rose replied without hesitation. "I would rather suffer for the truth than surrender to evil."

Admiration rippled through the room.

"Thank you, Miss Williams," the judge said. "That will be all."

Rose exhaled shakily. Relief washed through her so powerfully it nearly brought tears to her eyes. She sank back against her pillows as everyone rose. One by one, the generals, Marshal Jones, the physicians, judge, and journalists filed silently out to reconvene the pre-trial, each carrying Rose's words with them like a spark of fire.

Only Aunt Lizzie remained, smoothing Rose's hair. Marshal Moore lingered in the doorway, still standing guard.

Lizzie's eyes were soft with pride. "I am so proud of you, Rose," she whispered, brushing a stray curl from her niece's forehead. Rose tried to smile, though exhaustion weighed heavy.

"I'm just grateful I didn't have to be there in person," she murmured. "I don't ever want to see that awful man again."

Lizzie opened her mouth to respond, but a sudden commotion erupted in the hallway. Shouting. Heavy boots pounding. Before either woman could react, the door to her room slammed open. A stranger, wild-eyed, breathless, furious, staggered inside as though fleeing pursuit.

Rose gasped, her heart jolting painfully. Marshal Moore moved faster than she had ever seen. In a single instinctive motion, he drew his gun and placed himself between Rose and the intruder.

"Don't you come any closer!" he barked. The man lunged anyway. Moore holstered his weapon instantly—firing would be too dangerous this close to Rose—and hurled himself forward instead. The two crashed to the floor with a resounding thud. Moore pinned him with practiced ease, twisting the man's arm behind his back.

"What's your business here?" Moore growled. The man spat a curse. Moore snapped steel cuffs around his wrists a heartbeat later. Sheriff Bailey and his deputy burst in moments later, weapons drawn.

"Marshal Moore?" the sheriff demanded. Moore yanked the intruder to his feet.

"Caught him breaking into the recovery room," he said coldly. "He was headed straight for Miss Williams."

The sheriff's expression hardened. He seized the man by the collar and dragged him toward the hall.

"You'll answer for this in my jail," he snarled.

As the intruder's curses faded down the corridor, Moore exhaled, his shoulders lowering from battle-ready tension. He turned back toward the bed and froze. Rose trembled violently, her hands knotted in the blanket pulled tight beneath her chin. She swallowed hard.

"Will these attacks never end?"

Marshal Moore stepped closer, his voice gentle but steady, pure reassurance.

"They will, Rose," he promised. "I give you my word, we'll stop every last one of them."

Lizzie sat beside her again, taking Rose's hand.

"You're safe now, sweetheart. Truly safe."

Rose nodded, though her heart still raced. She sank back against the pillows, breathing through the panic, reminding herself she was surrounded by people who would die before letting harm touch her again. But as the clinic settled into silence, one question lingered in her mind like a cold shadow:

How many more enemies had her ordeal awakened? And how long until peace finally found her?

11

Between Guardians and Suitors

Lieutenant General Hilton and General Winter returned to the clinic shortly after the pre-trial concluded. Both men carried the grave look of those who had just witnessed something appalling. The sheriff had evidently reached them before they stepped inside.

Marshal Moore paced the small waiting area, agitation tightening his jaw.

"How are we going to keep Rose safe?" he demanded as soon as they entered. "We can't force her into a marriage to hide her away. Marriage isn't a shield, not from this."

General Winter folded his arms, his expression thunderous.

"The real question," he said grimly, "is whether marriage would even help. A determined criminal would still attempt kidnapping, knowing he could extort her husband for ransom."

Lieutenant General Hilton nodded sharply, fury simmering beneath his controlled demeanor.

"The man who made her a target, whoever he is, is either wicked beyond measure or entirely lacking in sense. Perhaps both."

Before anyone could respond, the door swung open and Marshal Jones strode in with the sheriff. Behind them were Reverend Williams and two young men who looked very much like him, strong features, brown hair, and the unmistakable Williams fire in their eyes.

"Lieutenant General, General Winter," John said, his voice tight, "these are our sons, Paul and Jordan."

The officers greeted them with solemn nods before General Winter turned toward the sheriff.

"Did the stranger reveal anything? His purpose? His employer?"

The sheriff exhaled and ran a hand through his hair, weary frustration etched across his face.

"Not much. He said only that someone in Boston hired him to kidnap Miss Williams and bring her back East."

Aunt Lizzie gasped from her place near the wall, the color draining from her cheeks. Even John, steady, even-tempered John, looked horrified.

Paul clenched his jaw. "Kidnap her? For what possible reason?"

John turned to the sheriff, his voice low but laced with dread.

"And he gave nothing else? No name? No description? No motive? We can assume it's connected to her dowry, but it could be something worse."

The sheriff shook his head. "He's stubborn. Determined to keep his employer a secret. We'll question him further, but so far, he's given us little beyond the fact that he was paid."

Jordan's fists clenched at his sides.

"So, someone deliberately sent a man after our cousin. Someone who wants her back under their control. Someone willing to use force."

A heavy silence fell over the room, the weight of the threat settling over every person present. Lieutenant General Hilton's voice cut through the tension like a blade.

"Then we will not rest until we identify who is behind this. Miss Williams deserves peace, and justice. Until she has both, none of us are finished."

General Winter nodded, his eyes narrowing. Sheriff Bailey clenched his fists at his sides.

"We'll tighten security and increase patrols," the sheriff said. "No one will lay a hand on her again."

Marshal Moore swallowed hard, determination burning in his expression.

"They won't get close to her. Not while I'm alive."

Aunt Lizzie gripped her husband's arm, her voice trembling but fierce.

"Whoever wants to harm our Rose is about to learn they've picked the wrong family."

And for the first time since Rose had been attacked, John allowed himself a small, grim smile.

"They will indeed."

Rose had slept for nearly two hours. When she finally stirred again, blinking her eyes open, she found her aunt and uncle beside her bed, and two young men standing just behind them.

"Rose," Uncle John said with a gentle smile, "you probably don't remember your cousins, but this is Paul and Jordan."

She focused on the pair as they stepped closer. Paul had their father's warm brown eyes and the steady kindness she vaguely remembered from childhood summers. Jordan shared that same gentleness but carried a spark of mischief in his bright green eyes. Both offered her soft, affectionate smiles.

"It's good to see you again, Rose," Paul said, his voice warm with familiarity. "You've certainly grown up since the last time we saw you."

"Do you remember me?" Jordan asked lightly.

"Of course," she murmured, though her voice was faint. "You were older... four and five years older, I think."

Paul laughed. "That's right. And you were the cutest, and feistiest, little girl I'd ever met." He glanced at his father. "Pa, do you remember the time you scolded Jordan and sent him to stand in the corner?"

Her aunt and uncle exchanged looks before laughter bubbled up from both of them.

"How could I forget?" John replied, shaking his head at the memory. "The moment I turned around, Rose stomped her tiny foot and said, 'Uncle John, why are you mad at Jordan? He's just a boy, and you're a grown-up. I thought reverends were supposed to be nice and hand out cookies to children.'"

Rose groaned and covered her warm face with her hands while everyone else laughed.

"And your uncle, being the soft-hearted man he is," Aunt Lizzie added fondly, "pulled you onto his lap and explained that even reverends must be stern sometimes, because parents correct their children out of love. Then he handed you a piece of candy from his pocket."

"And you," John finished with a chuckle, pointing at her, "said, 'Thank you. It's not a cookie, but it'll do.'"

Another burst of laughter swept the room. Jordan leaned one elbow casually on the foot of the bed, grinning.

"You loved your cookies," he teased. "And you knew exactly how to get them without stealing. One sweet, wide-eyed look, and anyone within five feet was doomed."

Paul nodded. "Those big blue eyes and that perfectly innocent smile, you had every adult in Boston wrapped around your finger. We practically tripped over ourselves trying to please you."

The two generals and the marshals, who had lingered quietly at the back of the room, smiled in amusement, as if they could clearly imagine the scene. Rose blushed hotter than ever, wishing the pillow would swallow her whole.

Later that afternoon, Lieutenant General Hilton and General Winter stepped forward to say their goodbyes. Both offered Rose solemn yet encouraging words, wishing her swift healing. They would travel to Denver the following morning with the officers accompanying them, and a contingent of soldiers would escort the disgraced colonel and the two soldiers involved to Washington, where military justice would take its full course.

As they left, Rose eased back against her pillows, her heart warmed by laughter, love, and the quiet strength of family surrounding her. Despite everything she had endured, hope, fragile but real, glimmered at the edges of her thoughts once more.

When Aunt Lizzie, Uncle John, Paul, and Jordan left for the night, only Marshal Moore remained behind. The moment the door clicked shut, Rose's nerves tightened. Being alone with him, made her pulse flutter in a way she wished she could control.

Ever since the attack, her feelings for him had grown stronger, unbidden and entirely unwelcome. She tried to reason with herself, reminding her stubborn heart that forming an attachment to a man who would eventually move on to San Francisco was foolish. But her heart refused to listen.

Every time she glanced at his handsome face, her heartbeat hitched. Butterflies stirred relentlessly in her stomach whenever he spoke to her in that gentle, protective tone. She wished Marshal Jones were the one stationed at her door. She felt safer admitting that to herself than confessing why she didn't want Moore around.

Rose avoided meeting his eyes as much as possible. Those warm brown eyes, steady, compassionate, impossible to read fully, made her thoughts scatter the moment they settled on her. His faint, quiet smile only made matters worse, melting her heart in the most inconvenient way imaginable.

She felt like some ridiculous schoolgirl, not a young woman recovering from trauma. And she knew, with aching certainty, that he was too old for her, that their lives were too different. Falling for him, even a little, was dangerous. But knowing and feeling were entirely different battles, and her heart had no intention of surrendering quietly.

Her silent turmoil was thankfully interrupted when the door opened again. The younger Dr. Hunter stepped inside, his expression serious but kind.

"My uncle asked me to remain with you and Marshal Moore tonight," Shane said, moving farther into the room. "He wants to make certain there's no repeat of earlier events."

Relief washed through Rose so swiftly she nearly sagged against her pillows. Having a doctor in the room felt like a lifeline, one that steadied her racing thoughts and, perhaps, shielded her from feelings she wasn't ready to face.

Marshal Moore glanced at her with concern, completely unaware of the storm he stirred inside her. Rose, trying to be composed, smoothed her blanket and nodded.

"Thank you, Dr. Hunter. I... appreciate it." For now, she could breathe again.

Three days after the trial, Rose was finally released from the clinic, though several more days passed before she could put any real pressure on her feet. She spent long, quiet hours sitting on a bench beside the lake, the sun warming her face while the cool breeze carried the scent of pine and wild sage.

Sally and Lucy never left her side. One resting her head on Rose's lap, the other lying watchfully at her feet. And whether it was Jordan, one of the marshals, her aunt, or her uncle, someone was always with her, ready to help if she needed it.

One afternoon, weeks later, Rose sat in the gentle sunlight, rubbing the dogs' soft ears, when she heard footsteps on the path. She turned and smiled as the younger Dr. Hunter approached, his medical bag in hand but his expression lighter than usual.

"How are you feeling today, Rose?" he asked, taking in her relaxed posture and the faint pink returning to her cheeks.

"A great deal better, Dr. Hunter. Thank you," she replied.

He chuckled quietly. "Please, call me Shane. I've been patching you up long enough to earn that privilege, don't you think?"

He came around the bench and sat at the opposite end, giving her plenty of room but still close enough to speak softly.

"I actually came with... a question."

Rose tilted her head in mild curiosity, smoothing her skirt.

"A question?"

"I'm sure you've heard the town is holding a dance next week," he began. "And I wondered if you would do me the honor of being my date for the evening."

Her cheeks warmed instantly, and she glanced down at her bandaged feet.

"Do you really think I'll be ready to dance by then?"

"I believe so," he said with quiet confidence. "You're healing remarkably well. But even if your feet tire, we can simply sit and enjoy the music. I imagine you'll have no shortage of people wanting to speak or dance with you, but," his voice softened, "I wanted to make sure I was the one who picked you up and escorted you home that night." He paused, then added with a playful glint in his eye, "Unless, of course, someone else has beaten me to it?"

Rose shook her head, smiling shyly.

"No one else has asked me. And I'd be delighted to go with you. I only... don't know how to country dance."

Shane laughed lightly. "That won't be a problem. It's easier than it looks, and I'd be happy to teach you. Besides, we don't only dance reels and squares. There are always a few waltzes mixed in, perfectly gentle, perfectly slow." He gave her a warm, reassuring smile. "You'll do beautifully."

Rose felt her heart dip and flutter, part shyness, part anticipation, and part gratitude for the simple kindness that surrounded her in this new place. She looked out over the shimmering lake, sunlight dancing on the surface like diamonds, and wondered if perhaps, at long last, life was beginning to mend itself.

Not long after Shane left, Rose heard the rhythmic thud of hooves drifting across the quiet lakeside. She turned her head and saw Grant approaching, his posture straight, his expression warm as sunlight caught in his brown eyes. He pulled his horse to a stop behind the bench, swung down effortlessly, and offered her a charming smile.

"It's good to see you out and about, Rose," he said, stepping closer. "You look like you're recovering well."

"I am, thank you," she replied. "I'm grateful I can look in the mirror again and not see those horrible bruises."

"I'm glad too," he said softly. "But the injuries couldn't hide your beautiful face, regardless."

Heat crept into her cheeks, and she lowered her gaze to her folded hands. Compliments from Grant had a strange way of warming her and unsettling her at the same time.

"Are you here to see my uncle?"

He shook his head and sat on the bench beside her.

"No. I'm here to see you." His smile gentled. "I'd like to invite you to the dance next weekend."

"Oh." Her breath caught, and she hesitated. She didn't know how to let him down gently, and the last thing she wanted was to hurt him. But he looked directly into her eyes, and something in his expression shifted, an understanding, as if he could already read her answer.

"Someone already asked you?" he asked quietly.

She nodded. "Shane was here earlier. I'm sorry, Grant."

He didn't look away. Instead, he squeezed her hand—warm, steady, reassuring.

"That's unfortunate—for me, at least. My dad told me to ask you while you were still in the hospital, but I didn't want to do that when you were recovering." A teasing glimmer lit his eyes. "May I ask for a dance at least?"

Relief loosened her shoulders. "Yes, of course. But as I told Shane, I don't know how to country dance."

"It's not hard," he assured her. "How many dances will you give me?" He flashed one of those winning smiles that made her pulse skip. She grinned back.

"As many as you want, unless Shane plans to claim all of them, which I doubt. I don't have any expectations of overexerting myself."

He chuckled. "You don't know the men of this town. It'll be hard for either of us to claim even one dance. You're a pretty young lady, and they'll be standing in line."

Rose shook her head incredulously.

"I think you give me too much credit. I don't get that kind of attention from men. The men in Boston always made it clear their interest in me was because of my father and his wealth, not because of me."

"Oh, Rose," he said gently, "you have a lot to learn about the folks in this town." He leaned back, resting one arm across the top of the bench. "I've already heard several young men raving about you, hoping to get a chance to dance with you at least once. Many are dreaming of courting you. And several of our cowboys can't wait to meet you officially."

Rose stared at him, stunned. "Why? They don't know me."

Grant's smile turned amused. "Word travels fast in Idaho Springs. What you did for the Cheyenne spread like wildfire. And have you seen the latest edition of the Denver Pillar?"

Rose stiffened. "No... I told the conductor not to tell anyone."

"He didn't," Grant said with a soft laugh. "But the families you helped insisted on knowing who their angel was. Someone spoke, and now the whole region knows about a kind young lady who paid for meals for those who couldn't afford them on the journey to Colorado."

Her cheeks burned. She folded her arms self-consciously.

"It was nothing. I felt guilty knowing I had so much while those children had nothing."

"That's not all." Grant leaned closer, his voice dropping conspiratorially. "There's a rumor around town that you asked the general to allow the Cheyenne to leave the reservation and hunt so they can feed their people properly. My father said permission has been granted."

Rose's face lit up. "Truly? That is wonderful."

He nodded. "I told you. Nothing stays quiet around here." He pointed a playful finger at her. "And there's more. Before I came to see you, Dad told me he and your uncle have been negotiating with the government to buy more land for the reservation, so the Cheyenne have room to hunt on their own grounds. He admitted he joined the effort because you suggested using some of your father's money to purchase the land."

Rose's eyes widened, touched and overwhelmed at once.

"Your father is incredibly kind."

"He felt guilty he hadn't thought of it himself," Grant said with a fond grin. "He's convinced you're an angel, sent here to remind us all, of what matters in this life."

Her face flushed a deeper shade of crimson. She met Grant's gaze briefly before looking away again. He was watching her with warmth, amusement, and something gentler beneath, something that made her heart flutter unexpectedly.

"So," he continued quietly, "people know about you. About your heart. Even if you didn't want the attention. Kindness has a way of being seen. You're truly beautiful inside and out, Rose. And the folks in this town are good, hardworking people. You fit right in here." He paused. "I'd be honored if you'd call me your friend."

For a moment, Rose forgot to breathe. *Friend.* A perfectly ordinary word. A perfectly kind offer. Yet something inside her tightened. Friendship was all he meant. And she shouldn't care. She didn't want a courting relationship, not with him, not with anyone. And yet... the word stung more than she wished it did. She forced a smile, hoping he couldn't see the brief flicker of hurt in her eyes.

"Rose, you look breathtaking." Lizzie's voice trembled as she pressed a hand to her heart. Her niece stood in front of the mirror, radiant in the soft pink ballgown she had brought from Boston. The satin skirt fell gracefully to the floor, the fitted bodice hugged her slender waist, and delicate embroidery shimmered in the lantern light. Her hair was pinned up in an elegant twist, with a few soft curls framing her face, and the long white gloves made her appear as though she had stepped straight out of a painting.

"You look like an angel," Lizzie whispered. "I daresay Shane, and every other young man at that dance, won't be able to tear their eyes away from you."

Rose blushed and shook her head.

"You're far too kind, Aunt Lizzie. I'm sure you're exaggerating. I've seen the girls in this town. Many of them are far prettier than I am."

Lizzie let out a soft, incredulous scoff.

"You truly don't see it, do you? If your mother had lived, you would have known what it feels like to be watched by a woman who can't help but glow with pride over her beautiful daughter. You inherited Lily's grace, you know."

Rose's expression softened. "My governess and the maids always told me I was pretty... but that was because they loved me."

"Perhaps," Lizzie said, eyes twinkling, "but tonight everyone else will prove it. And I'm looking forward to seeing your face when they do."

Since both women were fully dressed, they descended the staircase together. Lizzie walked a half-step behind Rose, eager to witness everyone's reaction, and oh, it was worth it.

Conversation in the parlor halted at once. John, the marshals, Paul, Jordan, and even Jonas Adams, who had stopped by to deliver something, froze as Rose made her way down the stairs. Their expressions ranged from stunned to outright enchanted.

Shane had just arrived and nearly forgot to remove his hat. His mouth parted slightly, admiration unmistakable. Beside him, Marshal Moore looked equally captivated, though he tried, and failed, to mask it behind a composed smile.

John let out a low whistle and took Rose's hand with fatherly pride.

"We'd better not let you out of our sight tonight," he said warmly. Turning to Shane, he added, "I hope you're ready to fight for your right to dance with her, son."

Jordan stepped forward with a grin so charming it might have melted snow.

"You'd better bring your gun, Pa," he teased. Then, looking at Rose, "Too bad we're cousins. If we weren't, I might've asked if I could court you myself."

"Oh, stop it," Rose said, nudging him lightly, though her cheeks flamed. Jordan gently caught her arms and met her gaze with sudden sincerity.

"I'm not joking, Rose. You're going to make a lot of hearts flutter tonight."

Rose blinked, startled, before looking to Lizzie, who merely nodded, her smile saying, *I told you so.*

"Shane," Jordan continued, turning toward the young doctor with mock severity, "you'd best keep this girl safe. We'll all be watching, but you're the one who invited her, so her well-being is on your shoulders tonight."

Shane pressed a hand to his heart and gave Rose a playful wink.

"I'll do my very best, I promise."

Rose's face burned like a campfire at dusk, but the warmth came from excitement, not fear.

It truly was a wonderful evening. Just as Aunt Lizzie predicted, Rose drew every eye the moment she stepped inside. Heads turned, whispers floated through the hall, and Shane had a hard time claiming even a single dance. Her discomfort and modesty only made her more captivating, at least, that was what Aunt Lizzie whispered conspiratorially in her ear.

After several lively dances, Rose finally retreated to a chair to rest her aching feet. She had barely taken a sip of water when, yet another young man approached, hope shining in his eyes.

She hesitated. A part of her wanted, desperately, to say no. But she could not bring herself to be rude, so she rose and allowed him to escort her.

The moment he slipped an arm around her waist, unease tightened in her chest. The sharp scent of alcohol clung to him.

"I'm glad I finally get the chance to meet you, Rose," he said, staring at her with unsettling intensity. "I'm one of Jonas Adams's cowboys. Grant and the family have been talking about you nonstop." His crooked smile deepened. "But you're even prettier than they let on."

She forced a polite smile, scanning the room. Relief flickered through her at the sight of Grant watching her, his brow furrowed. Marshal Moore's eyes were sharper still, tracking her every movement with quiet vigilance.

"My name is Devon," the cowboy continued. "I'd say your bruises are healing nicely." He reached out and tilted her chin, far too intimate for a stranger. "You smell incredible," he murmured, brushing her cheek with the back of his finger.

Rose stiffened, heat rising, not the pleasant kind. She pulled away, but Devon's grip only tightened. He leaned in, attempting to kiss her. She shoved him back.

"Devon," she said sharply, "I'm dancing with you because you asked politely, not because I'm interested. You have no right to step that close to me. I do not want you to kiss me. Please show some respect."

He blinked, stunned. When he released her, she wasted no time and fled toward the hallway leading to the ladies' washroom. She was almost there when a hand clamped around her arm. Devon. He yanked her backward.

"Please let go of me," Rose said, pulling against him. He slid an arm around her waist, dragging her toward the exit.

"I'm meeting some friends at the saloon. I want you to come with me."

"No. I don't drink, and I came for the dance, nothing else."

"But I *want* you to come with me, Rose Williams." His grip tightened. Panic surged.

"Let go of me this instant!" She pushed, but he seized the back of her head, pulling her closer.

"The young lady has asked you repeatedly to let her go."

Devon froze. Marshal Moore stood in the hallway, gun drawn but angled down, his eyes burning with fury. "If you don't want to spend the night in jail for accosting a woman," he said, voice low and lethal, "I suggest you release her. Now." He extended his hand toward her. "Come to me."

She didn't hesitate. She rushed to him, and Moore's arm swept around her shoulders, firm, protective, steadying. The tremor in her breathing eased the moment he touched her.

"You just want her for yourself, Marshal," Devon snarled, reaching for her again. Moore shifted instantly, placing Rose behind him.

Grant stepped out of the ballroom at that exact moment, his expression as cold and sharp as a drawn blade.

"Devon," he said, voice clipped with warning, "I suggest you leave. And if you want to keep your job, you had better never treat a lady like that again."

Devon scoffed. "I don't need *her*. Plenty of ladies in town would be happy to take her place."

"Then why are you still here?" Jordan asked coolly as he appeared beside them.

Rose startled, her cousins were there, along with Shane, forming a solid wall between her and the drunken cowboy. Devon looked around. Finding no support in the sea of hostile stares, he let out an indignant huff and shoved open the door.

Silence lingered only a moment before Rose's breath trembled in relief, but her body kept shaking, adrenaline still sharp in her veins. Marshal Moore turned toward her, concern etched on his face.

"You're safe now," he said quietly. Only then did Rose trust her knees again.

12

From Prey to Beloved

"Rose, there's a letter for you on the table," Aunt Lizzie told her, the day after the dance.

"Thank you." Rose retrieved the envelope and slipped outside to the bench by the lake. With her aunt occupied in the kitchen, Paul visiting Jennifer Adams, and her uncle and Jordan delivering supplies to an older widow, miles outside town. She finally had privacy. Sally and Lucy played in the yard as she opened the letter. It was from Andrew.

Dearest Rose,

...

She read every word, each line twisting deeper, sharper. By the time she reached the end, the letter slipped from her hands. He hadn't asked if she was well. Hadn't wondered whether she was safe. Hadn't mentioned the news in the papers or the attack that nearly cost her life. Instead, he blamed her. Blamed her for leaving. Blamed her for not funding his trip to come after her. He blamed her for the trouble he caused with the Boston Codex—he was the one who had sold her travel plans to the newspaper.

A deep ache formed in her chest. Had he ever cared for her at all? She didn't have long to ponder before a voice she had prayed not to hear again slithered into her ear.

"Good to see you out and about, Rose." Devon's arms clamped around her from behind, trapping her against the back of the bench. His breath brushed her ear. "Maybe we can have some alone time now."

Rose stiffened. "Marshal Moore and Marshal Jones are both nearby," she snapped, twisting to break free.

"I don't think they're outside right now." His grip tightened. "I've been watching you. Your uncle's gone, and so are your cousins. Looks like it's just you and me."

Terror shot through her. His mouth brushed her neck before he yanked her upright.

"Let's go for a ride. I've got a friend in another town, he said he'd marry us."

"Leave me alone!" Rose cried. "Help! Somebody, help me!"

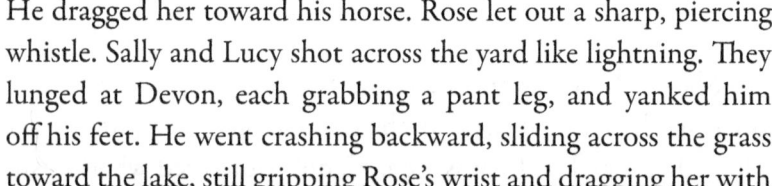

He dragged her toward his horse. Rose let out a sharp, piercing whistle. Sally and Lucy shot across the yard like lightning. They lunged at Devon, each grabbing a pant leg, and yanked him off his feet. He went crashing backward, sliding across the grass toward the lake, still gripping Rose's wrist and dragging her with him. She clawed at the earth, screaming.

Devon suddenly wailed in agony. Marshal Jones had driven his boot onto the man's lower arm, applying enough pressure to make him release her. At the same moment, strong arms wrapped around Rose's waist, lifting her clean off the ground and out of

Devon's reach. She landed hard against Marshal Moore's chest as he pulled her close. By the time she caught her breath, Marshal Jones had Devon by the collar.

"Stay with Rose, Moore," Jones ordered, hauling the cowboy upright. "I'll take this piece of prairie coal to the sheriff."

As the men disappeared, Christopher cupped Rose's cheek.

"Are you all right, Rose?"

She shook her head, tears rising. "Men will never see me for me, will they? I'm nothing but... prey." Her voice cracked. "Something to claim or use. I'm tired of it."

"Rose, no—"

She shoved the letter against his chest. "Read it."

He did. His jaw tightened like iron. "Rose—"

"Why is my worth tied to money? Why can't anyone see me?" Her voice shook harder. "How am I supposed to trust any man's affections now? How do I know they're real? Was everything said to me at the dance yesterday nothing but empty flattery?"

"No," he said firmly. "Some were foolish boys trying to impress you, but not all."

She scoffed bitterly. "The ones who 'care', treat me like a helpless child. The rest want my dowry. And I'm expected to choose one!" Her emotional wounds burst open at once. Tears streamed down her cheeks. "I just want to be loved. Truly loved. Is that so impossible?"

"Rose—"

"All my life I longed for my father to care. For a husband who would love me fiercely." She choked on her next breath. "But I was foolish. The only thing men love about me is my inheritance." Her voice blackened with anguish. "Why did my father leave me such a curse?" She sobbed harder. Sally and Lucy pressed against her legs, whining, but she barely felt them. Christopher reached for her, but she flinched back.

"I don't need your pity. Just leave me, like everyone else has. You'll get reassigned soon enough, and I'll be married off to someone who wants my dowry." She turned away. "I don't need anyone."

He caught her hand, gentle, but immovable.

"Rose, listen—"

"No!" She tried to pull free. "Let go! None of this matters. I'll never be loved for who I am. I may as well give up now—"

"Rose, stop." His voice softened, urgent but tender. "You do deserve love. Fierce, passionate love. The kind that lifts your spirit, not crushes it. Men should earn the right to love you—because you have so much to give."

She stopped struggling. Slowly, he released her hand.

"You're longing for love," he said quietly, "because your heart is full of it."

She stared at him, confused, shaken, until his next words stole the breath from her lungs.

"And you are not a child to me, Rose. I have tried so hard not to see you the way I do... but I can't help it."

Her lips parted. "What... what do you mean?"

He stepped closer, voice barely above a whisper.

"I see you as a woman. A remarkable, brave, breathtaking woman. You've taken a place in my heart you shouldn't have."

Her pulse thundered.

"I love you, Rose."

Before she could speak, he cupped her face and kissed her, fiercely, desperately, as though the confession had cracked open something he could no longer contain. For a heartbeat she froze. Then everything inside her broke free.

She kissed him back with longing, full of all the hope she had buried for years. The world slipped away. There was only warmth and breath and the overwhelming rightness of him. When breath finally forced them apart, he rested his forehead against hers.

"I should stop," he murmured, breathless. "I didn't expect you to be such an experienced kisser."

"I'm not," she whispered. "I was only kissed once. By Andrew. The day I left Boston."

Christopher groaned softly. "Then I need to be careful. Because your spirit is fire, Rose Williams. And if I'm careless, I'll let it burn me alive."

She smiled through her tears. He took her hand and guided her to the bench, wrapping his arm around her shoulders. She leaned into him, letting his warmth soothe the rawest parts of her heart.

"Christopher," she whispered, "what happens now?"

"We keep this quiet," he said gently. "Until I figure out how to navigate this. I'm not supposed to fall for the woman I'm protecting. And I definitely shouldn't be kissing her." He kissed her forehead. "But how," he murmured, "how could I not?"

Rose laughed softly, her cheeks warm.

"If I had known a breakdown would lead to this, I might have had one weeks ago."

He chuckled.

"So all that today was a scheme to make me confess?"

"No," she said, smiling. "But I'm not unhappy with the result."

He kissed her again, slow, tender, promising.

"We should head inside," he said at last. "Your aunt will be wondering where you've gone. And... I don't think my partner should catch us like this."

Her laughter drifted through the trees as he helped her to her feet, their fingers lacing together as naturally as breathing.

"Look who I found in town looking for you," Jordan announced as he stepped into the dining room, where Rose was setting out plates. Rose turned—and froze. Jordan stepped aside.

"Hello, Rose."

She dropped the plate. It shattered across the floor.

"Andrew?" Her voice was barely a whisper. "What are you doing here?"

He smiled—or tried to. The expression was forced, the eyes behind it tight with offense, irritation... and something darker.

"Is that how you greet your best friend?" He stepped toward her. Rose immediately backed away, right into Christopher's steady presence.

One glance at him told her everything: he had already read the danger, already understood her fear. But her aunt and uncle noticed nothing. They greeted Andrew warmly. Aunt Lizzie knelt to gather the shards. Rose dropped down beside her.

"Aunt Lizzie, please, let me do that. I dropped it."

"It's fine, sweetheart. Go welcome your guest."

Guest. The word lodged in Rose's throat like a stone. She straightened slowly. Andrew watched her, expectant, possessive. Uncle John stepped forward with a broad smile.

"Look at you, Andrew. All grown up. My goodness, it's been years." He clapped the young man's back.

Rose swallowed hard. Guilt and anger twisted together inside her. She should have shown them the letter. Now it was too late. She drew a breath, lifted her chin, and faced Andrew squarely.

"We need to talk," she said quietly, but with iron beneath. His brows lifted. He nodded.

"Of course. Let me take my bag to the hotel, and I'll be right back."

"Nonsense," Uncle John said cheerfully. "You'll stay with us. And join us for supper. I'm sure you and Rose have plenty to catch up on."

Rose felt the blood drain from her face. She turned helplessly toward Christopher. He met her gaze, concern flickering deep in his warm brown eyes. He gave her a small nod that steadied her heart: *You're not alone.*

Rose exhaled shakily, then gestured toward the door, her voice clipped.

"Andrew, step outside with me. We'll talk there." She whistled sharply. Sally and Lucy shot to her side instantly, tails high, ears alert, guardians to the bone.

Andrew opened his mouth, perhaps to object, but Rose had already walked past him, stiff-backed and trembling, the dogs flanking her like sentries. Christopher followed them out, silent, but unmistakably protective. Whatever waited outside, she would not face it alone.

13

Between Betrayal and Belonging

As soon as they stepped outside, Rose folded her arms and leveled a cold stare at Andrew. Christopher stayed close behind her, quiet, watchful, a presence that steadied her just by being there. Andrew's eyes flicked irritably to the marshal.

"Can't we talk alone?" he asked, barely veiling his displeasure.

"No," Rose said sharply. "Marshal Moore is here for my protection. Protection I now need because someone decided to inform the press about me and my plans."

Andrew blinked, feigning innocence. "And you think you need protection from me?"

Rose's jaw tightened. "You tell me. What are you doing here, Andrew? I received your letter yesterday. How can you be here already? You claimed you didn't have money for the journey."

"I wrote the letter two weeks ago," he said quickly.

"And why are you here now?" she pressed. "Are you looking for more information you can sell to the press?"

His face flushed. "I told you, I'm sorry I shared anything."

"Yes, after you spent half a page guilt-tripping me for not paying your way to Colorado and accusing me of not caring because I didn't write to you." Her voice sharpened. "In case you don't remember, society frowns on young women writing letters to men they aren't engaged to. And even if it didn't, do you think I had nothing else to worry about? I was assaulted by soldiers for defending the Cheyenne. I didn't need the *Boston Codex* inventing an engagement scandal on top of everything else." She arched a brow. "Or was that exactly what you were hoping for?"

Andrew's mouth opened soundlessly.

"I—Rose—I didn't know. I'm so sorry."

"Of course you didn't know," she said flatly. "You were too busy accusing me of being arrogant."

"Rose—"

"I'm done talking about the letter." She drew a steadying breath. "How is your upcoming wedding?"

He swallowed. "It's over."

"I'm sorry," she said, though her tone held little warmth. "I hope that's not the reason you came."

Irritation flashed across his face. "Why would you assume something like that? I'm your friend, Rose. I care about you."

She laughed once, short and humorless.

"Your letter is proof enough of how much you 'care.' You can't fool me anymore. Your friendship was genuine... until my father's finances became public and people realized he was extraordinarily wealthy. From the moment I entered society, you changed. Every smile, every compliment, it was all about securing your future."

His face twisted. "What happened to you here? Why are you so unforgiving? This isn't like you."

"No. It isn't like me," Rose agreed softly, steel beneath her words. "But I also never expected venom from the person I trusted most. Your letter revealed your true heart. And I'm grateful, Andrew. It's freed me from illusions I clung to out of loneliness."

"Rose, listen—"

"No." She lifted a hand to stop him. "I don't want to hear excuses or apologies rewritten to sound better. I'm done with your lies, your guilt tactics, and your attempts to manipulate me. Please respect my wishes and stay at the hotel tonight. You do not need to be here."

His expression darkened into something cold and resentful.

"Your aunt and uncle invited me. That's where I'll stay."

Rose's heart sank, but she only shook her head. Some people would twist anything to feel wronged.

"Time for supper!" Uncle John called cheerfully from the porch. Instantly, Andrew smoothed his features into a pleasant smile and strode toward the house as if nothing unpleasant had been said.

Rose's throat burned. The anger had drained, leaving only hurt. Christopher touched her shoulder, warm, steady. No words, just quiet assurance. She drew one shaky breath and let him guide her back toward the house.

When Rose saw Andrew seated beside her at the table, smiling as though nothing had happened, her stomach twisted so violently she nearly retched. Her appetite vanished. She could not sit there, shoulder to shoulder with the boy she had once trusted more than anyone outside her family... the boy who had written her that letter.

"I—excuse me," she murmured, rising so quickly her chair scraped across the floor. She kept her head down as she hurried through the hall and up the stairs. The moment she closed her bedroom door, her composure shattered. She flung herself onto the bed, burying her face in the pillow as hot tears spilled freely. How foolish she had been. How painfully, unforgivably wrong.

Her shoulders shook with sobs, sobs for the friend she had lost, for the naïve girl she'd been, for the hurt she could no longer pretend wasn't real. A soft knock came at the door. Rose sat up quickly, swiping at her tears with trembling fingers.

"Come in."

Aunt Lizzie stepped inside, concern etched in every line of her face. She crossed the room quietly and sat on the edge of the bed.

"What's wrong, my dear?"

Rose hesitated. She didn't want to tarnish someone her aunt and uncle had known for years... but she also couldn't bear to lie. With a silent plea for understanding, she reached for the folded letter on her nightstand and handed it to her aunt.

Lizzie read it slowly. Her expression changed with every line, concern, disbelief, then a flash of fury Rose had never seen in her gentle aunt.

"Oh, Rose..." she breathed, shaking her head. "So, all these years, he's been pretending to be your friend? Is that what this means?"

Rose's throat tightened. "It seems that way."

Her aunt set the letter aside and pulled Rose into a warm embrace.

"I am so sorry. And I'm sorry we invited him to stay with us. Had we known—"

"It isn't your fault," Rose whispered, leaning into her aunt's comforting hold. "You had no way of knowing. I didn't either. Until yesterday." She pulled back, wiping her damp cheeks.

"He hurt me, Aunt Lizzie. Not because he found someone else to marry, but because he accused me of not caring, because he tried to guilt me as if I had wronged him, because he judged me without asking what I was going through. And then... to discover he may have only seen me as an opportunity, someone wealthy he could manipulate—" Her voice broke. "It feels like I lost the last piece of my old life."

Aunt Lizzie cupped her cheek tenderly.

"You didn't lose anything worthwhile, sweetheart. You simply learned the truth. And though it hurts, it frees you."

Rose nodded faintly, though pain still clouded her eyes.

"Shall I bring your supper up here?" her aunt asked gently.

Rose blew out a shaky breath. "That would be very kind, yes. I can't sit at the table with him and pretend nothing happened. And I... I don't want to know what information he sold to afford his journey here." Her voice trembled again. "I don't think I can trust a single word he says."

Aunt Lizzie drew her close once more.

"You don't have to see him tonight. Rest, and try to eat something. Your uncle and I will handle the rest."

As her aunt slipped out to fetch supper, Rose lay back against her pillows, staring at the ceiling, her chest aching. Betrayal had a taste she had never known before, and it was bitter, cold, and sharp. But somewhere beneath that hollow ache, a new resolve quietly took root. Andrew might have wounded her, but she would not let him break her.

Soon after, Lizzie returned with two plates of supper and set them on the small table by the window before settling again beside her niece on the bed. Before either woman could speak, a knock sounded at the door.

It opened, and Uncle John stepped inside, followed by Marshals Moore and Jones. One look at Rose's swollen eyes told them enough.

"What's going on?" John asked, his voice tight with worry.

Aunt Lizzie's gaze met Rose's. "He needs to know."

Rose nodded slowly. Her hands trembled as she handed her uncle the letter. He skimmed the page, his jaw tightening, his brows drawing together until he reached the end.

"If this is how he feels about you... why did he come all this way?" John asked, disbelief roughening his voice.

"Because Andrew wants me to feel guilty," Rose replied softly. "He's hoping I'll forget the cruelty in his letter, that I'll pretend nothing has changed between us. That perhaps, after what I've been through, I'd cling to any familiarity, even his." Her voice cracked. "But I see him clearly now. His visit has nothing to do with affection."

Marshal Jones exhaled sharply. "So, he's just another would-be suitor hoping to get his hands on your inheritance."

"And we invited him to stay," John muttered, pressing a hand to his forehead. "Heaven forbid."

Rose shook her head quickly. "It's only for one night. I'll stay out of his way. In the morning, he can be asked to leave politely. Just... please don't tell Jordan until Andrew is gone. He values your family, and I don't want Jordan to feel angry or trapped between loyalties."

John looked torn. "But how are we supposed to sit at table with him and pretend all is well? After reading that vicious letter?"

"I know," Rose whispered. "I know it's asking a great deal. But... as strange as it sounds, I don't want to lose the good memories I have of him. When we were children, his friendship was a lifeline during some very lonely years. Adulthood has not brought out the best in him, and I see now that his affection never grew with mine. He betrayed my trust, and it hurts more than I can say." Her eyes filled again, but she blinked the tears away.

"But I have all of you now. You've given me a home... a family I never dreamed I'd have." She offered a faint but earnest smile. "Because of that, his cruelty is easier to bear than it might have been."

"Oh, sweetheart..." John stepped forward and pulled her into his arms. Rose sank into the embrace, letting its safety and warmth steady her.

"We love you, Rose," he murmured against her hair. She closed her eyes, clinging to him as the ache in her chest eased a little.

"And I love you," she whispered. "Thank you... for giving me a family again."

Marshal Moore's expression softened. Marshal Jones nodded solemnly. Lizzie brushed a tear from her cheek. In that small room, with lamplight warming the walls and supper cooling on the table, Rose felt, for the first time since arriving in Colorado, that she truly belonged.

Rose breathed deeply as she stepped out of the house, grateful for the quiet evening air. The sun had already slipped behind the mountains, leaving a cool hush over the yard. Summer was fading. She could feel autumn waiting just beyond the tree line.

Christopher walked beside her, his hand brushing hers until he finally took it, warm, steady, grounding.

"Will you be okay?" he asked gently.

She considered his question. "It will take some time," she admitted. "But I meant what I told my aunt and uncle. Andrew's letter and his visit... they were necessary. They forced me to acknowledge what I'd suspected for a long while."

"Do you feel any regret?" Christopher's voice was quiet, almost cautious. Rose mulled it over, then lifted her face toward him.

"Regret isn't the right word," she said softly. "I'm... a little sad that he only kissed me once. It was romantic at the train station. He pulled me close when we said goodbye. His kiss gave me butterflies."

She watched him from the corner of her eye. Christopher froze mid-step. His brows drew together, his jaw tightened just enough to be noticeable. Rose bit the inside of her cheek to keep from smiling.

Pretending not to notice, she continued sweetly, "Age-wise, he was certainly more suitable than the present company. But I suppose we can't always have everything we want."

Christopher stopped dead and turned to face her.

"I would recommend," he growled, though amusement tugged at his mouth, "that you be very careful now, young lady."

"Careful?" she echoed, widening her eyes. "Why would you say that? I'm only answering your question. Unless..." She tilted her head. "Did you prefer that I lie?" She glanced up at him with a playful side-eye that should have been illegal. His eyes narrowed in warning, sending a delicious shiver down her spine.

"I don't know what it is," she mused with theatrical innocence, "but Andrew used to give me that same look sometimes. Did I say something wrong?" She barely finished the sentence before laughter bubbled out of her, too delighted to hold in.

She spun to dart away, but she underestimated him. Christopher caught her hand in one swift, fluid motion, drew her back, and pulled her flush against him with a force that stole her breath. Her hands splayed against his chest, warm, solid, and she felt his heartbeat, strong and rapid, matching her own. He didn't give her time to tease again. He kissed her.

Not gently. Not hesitantly. With heat. With hunger. With a fierce, desperate passion that curled her toes and sent sparks trembling through her entire being.

Her pulse roared in her ears as she melted into him, throwing her arms around his neck, letting herself get lost, completely, recklessly, lost. Christopher's arms tightened around her as he lifted her effortlessly off the ground. His lips moved against hers in a slow, consuming rhythm that left her trembling. When she finally pulled back for breath, her chest heaving, his voice emerged in a low rumble.

"You were holding back this time." His eyes were dark, dangerous, tender, and overwhelmed.

"Yes," she whispered. "I didn't want you to accuse me of making you lose control." She winked at him, breathless.

"Too late." He let out a low laugh, still holding her suspended for a heartbeat before lowering her gently to the ground. Even when her feet touched the earth again, she could still feel the imprint of his hands, his kiss, his closeness.

Despite the age difference, despite the complications, despite everything... her heart was unquestionably his.

Grateful that Jordan and Andrew still hadn't returned from town when she and Christopher came back from their walk, Rose slipped quietly inside. After a softly murmured goodnight at the base of the stairs, one last brush of fingers, one last stolen glance, she climbed to her room. Exhaustion weighed on her limbs. The emotional turmoil of the last two days had drained every bit of strength from her. She barely remembered crawling beneath the quilt before sleep, claimed her.

14

Love Beneath the Badge

Rose woke hours later with a start. Someone had sat down on her bed. The mattress dipped beneath a weight that wasn't her own. Still half-dreaming, she pushed her hair from her face, expecting Sally's tail or Lucy's cold nose. Instead, Andrew's face hovered inches above her. Glaring. Wild-eyed. Reeking of whiskey.

Rose's breath seized. A scream built in her throat, but his hand clamped over her mouth before a sound escaped. His body crushed hers into the mattress, pinning her beneath him as his leg trapped both of hers.

"Andrew—" Her voice broke against his palm. He silenced her by smashing his mouth over hers. It wasn't a kiss. It was a violation. Hard. Possessive. Sickening. Her stomach, lurched. His free hand fumbled at the buttons of her nightgown, ripping through the fabric. Panic exploded in her chest. She twisted, desperate, but he shoved her down harder.

"Stop fighting," he slurred, his breath hot against her cheek. "You owe me this. You always have."

No. No. Terror snapped through her, cold and clear. She sank her teeth into his hand, hard. Andrew cursed and jerked back, his fingers clamping down on her shoulders.

"You little—"

The door shoved open, and two low growls rumbled through the room. Sally and Lucy launched. Both dogs hit him at once, teeth ripping through his sleeves as they yanked him off the bed and dragged him across the floorboards. Andrew screamed, flailing, but the dogs held firm. The door exploded open with a bang, slamming hard against the wall.

Marshal Moore reached him first, ripping Andrew out from under the dogs and throwing him face-down onto the planks. Marshal Jones was right behind him, snapping iron cuffs around Andrew's wrists before he could regain his breath. Uncle John and Aunt Lizzie rushed in moments later, pale with horror.

Rose scrambled back until she collided with the headboard, shaking violently and clutching the blanket to her throat.

"Rose." John crossed the room in three strides and gathered her into his arms. She collapsed against him, sobbing. Her entire body trembled. "You're safe now, sweetheart. We're here. He won't touch you again."

Christopher stepped closer, just as Marshal Jones hauled Andrew out of sight. His jaw was clenched so tightly it looked painful.

"Marshal Jones is taking him to the sheriff," he said grimly.

"Good." John's voice shook with rage. "Make sure they lock him up for the rest of his natural life."

"No..." Rose whispered, shaking her head fiercely. "No. I don't want a trial. Just lock him up overnight and send him back to Boston tomorrow. I don't want him here another moment."

John stared, stunned. "Rose, he—he tried to— He deserves punishment."

"Yes," Christopher said gently but firmly. "What he tried to do is unforgivable. Intent alone carries weight. You can't dismiss it just because he was drunk."

"I'm not excusing him," she insisted, her voice raw. "But I can't go through another trial. I won't. I don't want to see him again. And you know how courts treat women. There's no physical injury, just torn buttons and bruised pride. His lawyer would twist everything, smear me, make it look as if I encouraged him."

Aunt Lizzie's eyes welled. "It's monstrous that virtue must be defended harder than the crime itself."

John scrubbed a hand over his face, shoulders sagging. "How is this justice?"

"It isn't," Christopher murmured. "But we can protect her. Control the narrative. Ensure Andrew never comes near her again. And make certain everyone in town knows he is not welcome."

John exhaled slowly. "Then that's what we'll do."

Rose sagged against her uncle, exhausted, trembling. The boy who had once been her closest friend was dragged away into the night. Safe for the moment, but shaken to her core. Yet when she lifted her gaze, Christopher was watching her. The fury in his eyes softened at once into something gentler, protective... something that stirred deep inside her chest. She wasn't alone. Not anymore.

A day after Andrew left Idaho Springs, and just as life was beginning to feel calm again, the newest edition of the *Denver Pillar* arrived. And with it came fresh devastation.

By noon, the whole town was in an uproar.

The mayor wasted no time calling a town meeting, and within the hour the saloon was packed to bursting. Men stood in clusters. Women filled every chair. The mayor slammed the newspaper onto the table.

"These attacks against our newest resident," he began sharply, "are downright disgraceful. This first-page article is nothing but lies and filth, and I say we demand a recall and sue the Pillar for slander!"

"Hear, hear!" the room thundered. Boots stomped. Fists hit tables. Voices rose in outrage. John cast a glance toward Rose, seated near the back. Her shoulders were stiff, her complexion pale as parchment. Even from across the room, he could see the devastation in her eyes. She had endured too much already, far too much, and now this. Another blow. Another betrayal.

Before he could reach her, Rose stood abruptly and slipped out, the back door, disappearing into the crisp air. Marshal Moore and Marshal Jones exchanged looks and followed her immediately. John's heart twisted, torn between pride in his town and anguish for his niece. Idaho Springs loved her. But she couldn't bear another wound.

"What happened?" a farmer asked.

Lizzie nodded toward the mayor, who raised the newspaper again. He cleared his throat and read aloud, voice tight with fury:

> *"'Young man in love travels from Boston to Idaho Springs, Colorado, in hopes of sweeping the woman of his dreams off her feet—only to be cast into prison for giving in to her irresistible playfulness, luring him into her bed...'"*

Gasps rippled through the saloon. "That is outrageous," the farmer spat, slamming his fist onto the table. "Rose Williams is one of the sweetest young women I've ever met. I don't know her well, but I know without a shadow of a doubt this is a lie. Do these journalists even care about facts? Or only their next scandal?" He shook his head. "We should all write to the paper and demand they retract this shameful slander."

"Great idea, Preston!" the mayor declared. "All in favor?"

Every hand shot up.

"Good. Now, we need counter-reporting. Jonas, I'm sure you've got connections that aren't tangled up with the Pillar or the Boston Codex?"

Jonas Adams stood, jaw set. "Yes. I'll contact them immediately. Someone reputable needs to print the truth before people swallow more of these lies."

"Excellent." The mayor swept his gaze across the room. "Anyone with connections to honest papers or legal experts, speak up. The article defending Rose should come from us. And we'll let John, Lizzie, and Rose look it over before publication."

People nodded, murmuring their agreement.

"We'll send it to trustworthy newspapers across the country," the mayor continued. "Let the liars in Denver and Boston face the consequences. And as for that young man trying to smear her name with his guilt-ridden drivel," he lifted the paper, "he should be exposed as well."

John hesitated. "We could include his letter. But Rose won't want to expose him by name. She knows what public humiliation feels like, and she won't want to stoop to his level."

"We'll omit his name," the mayor said. "The shame will still reach him." He closed the newspaper with a snap. "That's all for today. Thank you, everyone, for standing together. Let's move quickly. It's time we defend the name and honor of Rose Williams."

The saloon erupted into cheers, loud, fierce, loyal. Lizzie wiped her eyes. John wrapped an arm around her shoulders, pulling her close. Their niece had found her place. Not just a home, but a community that would stand, shoulder to shoulder, to protect her honor.

Rose had disappeared into her room the instant she returned home. Her heart still pounded with the humiliation and hurt of the latest article, and she wanted, needed, to be alone, if only for a few fleeting minutes. But with both marshals sitting downstairs, ever watchful and always hovering nearby, there was only one way to vanish without alerting them. The window.

Rose pushed it open and hesitated for only a heartbeat before reaching for the thick branch of the old maple that grew close to the house. She had never climbed a tree in her life, certainly not in a dress, but desperate times called for desperate measures. She eased herself over the sill, bracing her slippered feet against the bark.

It did not go gracefully. Her skirt snagged twice, her shoe slipped once, and she scraped both arms on the way down. By the time her boots touched the ground, adrenaline left her shaky and breathless, but free. And that was all she wanted. Freedom. A moment without protection, without questions, without eyes on her.

She hurried away from the house, her breath fogging in the cooling dusk, and followed the familiar path to her favorite place, a quiet clearing beside a fallen tree trunk at the edge of the woods. She sank onto the trunk with a weary exhale, willing her mind to go still. A twig snapped. Rose turned abruptly.

Two figures stepped out from between the trees, tall, graceful, familiar. Ahanu and Calian approached with quiet smiles, their presence as gentle as the breeze stirring the branches overhead.

"Ahanu, Calian," she breathed, relief softening her tone. "How are you?"

"We are well," Ahanu replied, his dark eyes warm. "How is our white sister?"

Rose's shoulders sagged. "Every time I believe things are finally falling into place, something else happens. I'm so tired of it all." She gave a weak laugh. "Forgive me, I shouldn't complain. Everything you've endured... it makes my troubles seem silly."

The young men exchanged a glance before stepping closer.

"Rose," Calian said quietly, "your struggles are not small. What happened to you should never happen to any young woman." His voice deepened. "Your pain is real. Do not diminish it because ours was different."

Ahanu nodded. "You were willing to suffer for us. Willingly. That is something our people will never forget and can never repay."

Rose's eyes stung. "There is nothing to repay. You were treated unjustly, and I'm relieved the colonel will never harm anyone again. I only hope things are easier for you now."

"They are," Ahanu said. Then, with a mischievous tilt of his lips, he nudged her shoulder. "But don't ignore what Calian said. You are modest, yes, but the entire reservation speaks of you with honor. Our elders wish to give you an Indian name. We hope you will visit soon."

"I—I'd be honored," Rose whispered, genuinely touched. "Truly."

"You deserve it," Calian insisted. Then, glancing around the clearing, he frowned. "Where are your protectors? You never travel alone."

Rose winced. "I... left by myself."

Both young men stared at her as if she had grown wings.

"I needed time alone," she said helplessly. "So..." She lifted her arms to show the scrapes. "I climbed out my window and down the tree."

Ahanu blinked. "You did not."

"I did."

Calian inspected the scratches in astonishment. Then both men burst into laughter, deep, rolling, delighted.

"She is a warrior," Calian declared, grinning.

"And a rebel," Ahanu added.

Rose flushed but couldn't help smiling. Their laughter faded, replaced by a brotherly seriousness.

"We will escort you home," Ahanu said firmly.

"No, really, I'll be all right—"

"It is decided," Calian interrupted, shaking his head. "If we let you return alone, your protectors will skin us alive."

Ahanu smirked. "Isn't that what white men do? Walk a young woman home?"

Rose swallowed, nerves fluttering. "I suppose so." But she couldn't help worrying how Christopher, especially Christopher, would react when he discovered she had escaped through a window, wandered off alone, and been found by two Cheyenne warriors before he even realized she was missing. And yet... somehow... the thought made her smile.

A short time later, Lucy and Sally came barreling toward her the instant Rose and the Indians stepped out of the trees. Their joyous barking shattered the forest quiet, tails whipping the air as they pressed against her skirts in frantic welcome. Rose knelt to stroke their heads, grateful for their enthusiastic affection.

She didn't see Marshal Moore or Marshal Jones, but she knew they had to be nearby. The dogs were never outside unsupervised anymore, not since Andrew's attack.

"Thank you for walking me home," Rose said softly, turning to Ahanu and Calian. "I'll be all right now."

Calian crossed his arms, raising an eyebrow.

"Are you sure we should leave you? You're not planning to sneak off again, are you?" His tone was stern, but the dancing mischief in his dark eyes made her smile.

"I promise," she said, lifting one hand as if taking an oath, "I'll stay put."

Ahanu exchanged a knowing glance with his friend, one of those silent conversations only companions who had survived hardship together could share. Then he stepped closer, placing his palm lightly against his heart in a gesture of respect.

"You are strong, Rose," he said. "Stronger than you know. But even warriors need their tribe. Do not walk alone when danger still hunts you."

Her throat tightened at his unexpected tenderness.

"I won't," she whispered.

Satisfied, the two young men gave her small nods, then turned and slipped back toward the trees, their silhouettes melting into the shadowy green as silently as they had appeared.

Rose watched them disappear, her heart full, grateful for their friendship, grateful for their protection... and dreading the reaction she was about to receive from the two marshals who were, without question, already looking for her.

The dogs pressed against her legs, nudging her toward the porch as if urging her to hurry.

"I know, girls," Rose murmured, stroking their heads. "Let's face the storm together." With a steadying breath, she walked toward the house, unsure whether the greeting awaiting her would be scolding, worry... or something deeper.

Rose walked toward the door, then hesitated. Instead of going through the house, she decided to slip in the same way she had left, hoping to avoid the marshals altogether. Maybe they hadn't noticed she was missing yet.

She approached the tree, bracing herself for the climb back to her window. It would be far more difficult going up than coming down, especially in a dress and with her scratched arms stinging, but she was determined. She had just reached for the next branch when strong hands suddenly encircled her waist and lifted her clean off the trunk.

She gasped as she found herself pulled firmly against Christopher's chest. His expression, stern, breathless, and unmistakably relieved, sent a shiver down her spine.

"You are in very big trouble, Miss Williams," he said quietly, though a tremor of emotion undercut the reprimand. "We've been looking everywhere for you."

Rose folded her arms with exaggerated primness, though her heart thudded at the sight of him.

"Well, clearly not everywhere, since you didn't find me," she countered, a mischievous sparkle in her eyes. Before Christopher could respond, Marshal Jones barreled toward them, equally breathless.

"Rose Williams," he panted, bracing his hands on his knees for half a second before straightening. "Why would you sneak away like that? You had us worried sick. You, young lady, need to be disciplined."

Her stubborn pride crackled to life. "I am not a child, Marshal Jones, and I do not answer to you or Marshal Moore. You're here to protect me, not to order me about like a wayward schoolgirl."

"Your aunt and uncle and Chief Deputy Walton asked us to keep you safe," Marshal Jones shot back. "Running off into the woods without saying a word, climbing out your window of all things, was foolish and dangerous. If you're so grown up, why didn't you use the front door?"

She narrowed her eyes. "Because if I walked out the front door and told you I didn't want company, you would have followed me anyway."

The two marshals exchanged a glance—guilty, grudging, and proving her point. Rose lifted her chin triumphantly.

"Exactly. Now let go of me." She pushed past Christopher and strode toward the house, skirts swishing indignantly. Halfway to the door, she turned back, her voice deceptively sweet. "Tell me, are you actually upset with me, or are you upset because I outsmarted you both and reminded you how very old you are compared to me? Perhaps your pride is stinging because you can't keep up with a girl half your size?"

The marshals stared at her in stunned silence. Then both men broke into slow, reluctant grins. Realizing she had gone too far, Rose spun and fled for the house. She made it through the door and was about to rush up the stairs when Christopher caught her around the waist, lifted her clean off her feet, and, before she could even yelp, swung her over his shoulder.

"Marshal Moore!" she squeaked, pounding her fists against his back. "Put me down this instant!"

Marshal Jones—blast him—closed the kitchen door before she could whistle for the dogs. Sally and Lucy barked in outrage, trapped on the other side.

"This isn't fair!" she protested, wriggling.

"I think it's more than fair," Marshal Jones replied calmly, arms crossed as he sauntered behind them. "Someone with such a quick tongue and sharp wit should be able to talk her way out of a little trouble... don't you think?"

She glared daggers at him. "You have no right to—Christopher Moore, put me down!"

"Hmm," Christopher mused. "After such reckless behavior, I think a consequence is in order. Don't you agree, Jones? The lake seems awfully refreshing this evening."

Jones nodded solemnly. "I do believe it's calling her name."

Rose froze. "You wouldn't dare," she breathed.

They dared. Christopher carried her straight out the door and toward the lake, ignoring her sputtering outrage. She wriggled, threatened, bargained, and shrieked his full name in increasingly dramatic tones, but the marshal only tightened his hold.

The moment she felt the cold lick of water around his boots, panic sharpened her voice.

"Marshal Moore, I swear, I will never speak to you again!"

He only chuckled. A heartbeat later, he swung her off his shoulder and tossed her... straight into Marshal Jones's waiting arms. She landed with a shocked cry, clutching his shoulders as he held her securely above the water, grinning like a schoolboy.

Christopher stood ankle-deep, laughing outright. Jones carried her back to dry land and set her gently on her feet with a playful wink. Rose's cheeks burned hotter than a July sun. Before she could unleash another storm of indignation, Christopher stepped in front of her, his voice deliciously low and soft.

"This was just a warning, Rose. A playful one." His eyes glinted with warmth and something that made her stomach flutter. "But if you ever run off like that again... you won't land in Marshal Jones's arms."

Rose's breath hitched.

He leaned closer, murmuring only for her, "You'll go straight into the lake."

Her pulse thundered, her indignation melting into a dangerous mixture of flustered, furious... and undeniably thrilled.

When Uncle John and Aunt Lizzie told Rose what the town had decided—that they would stand up, loudly and publicly, on her behalf, she had been skeptical. But it didn't take long to realize that the people of Idaho Springs defended their own with fierce, uncompromising loyalty.

Letters began leaving town within the hour. Telegrams were drafted, copied, and fired off one after another. Families who barely scraped by sent messages, anyway, determined to add their voices. The post office was overwhelmed, the telegraph operator worked past midnight, and newspapers in Denver and Boston soon received hundreds of outraged complaints demanding accountability.

By the next morning, the *Idaho Springs Gazette* released a special edition devoted entirely to Rose. The article detailed her generosity on the train, her bravery in defending the Cheyenne, the abuse and threats she had endured, and the manipulation by the Boston journalist whose lies had set everything in motion. It condemned the reporters who had twisted the truth and practically encouraged desperate men to hunt her for profit.

A fierce warning followed: any man who arrived in Idaho Springs to pursue Rose without ever having met her would be turned away at once. Any attempt to violate her, to force a marriage, would be punished to the full extent of the law, and anyone with dishonorable intentions would face not only her uncle and the authorities, but every man in Idaho Springs.

Yet it was not written with anger alone, but with affection, her character defended vigorously, her kindness exalted, her reputation shielded like something precious.

Once printed, copies flew across the country, sent to allied newspapers, sympathetic editors, influential leaders, and anyone who might help set the record straight. Within days, the story spread far beyond Colorado. Major newspapers in Chicago, St. Louis, New York, and even San Francisco published the counter-report, calling out the dishonesty of the Denver Pillar and the Boston Codex. The backlash was swift and merciless.

Journalists who had written the vicious rumors were fired. Editors printed public apologies, long, humiliating retractions promising to leave 'the young Miss Williams' alone and to verify all future reports before publishing. Several papers condemned the Boston writer who had sparked the scandal, labeling his work unprofessional, irresponsible, and indecent. The two articles that had tried so hard to ruin her name were pulled from circulation entirely.

Rose could scarcely comprehend it. Her hands trembled as she read the articles piled on the kitchen table, one after another praising her courage or apologizing for believing lies. When she finally looked up, tears shone in her eyes, her breath unsteady.

"They... they did this for me," she whispered. Lizzie wrapped an arm around her shoulders.

"Every single one of them."

Marshal Jones, leaning in the doorway, nodded firmly.

"Idaho Springs doesn't let its own get trampled."

Christopher's gaze softened as he studied Rose's stunned expression.

"You're not a target anymore," he said quietly. "You're defended. Fiercely."

Her chin wobbled, and she pressed a trembling hand to her mouth as a quiet sob escaped.

"I've never had anyone fight for me like this before."

Uncle John stepped forward and kissed her forehead.

"You have a whole town fighting for you now, sweetheart."

The weight she had carried for months, the fear, the shame, the aching betrayal, shifted. Not gone, but gentled. Supported. Shared. Rose felt safe. Truly, deeply safe. And for the first time, she believed that maybe, just maybe, she belonged.

Uncle John and Aunt Lizzie organized a church dance every year to celebrate the end of summer and welcome autumn. Idaho Springs had endured a punishing drought that season, wells low, crops stunted, but the townspeople were determined not to let hardship steal their joy. Everyone brought whatever little they could, and spirits remained high.

At Rose's request, her uncle had used some of her funds to quietly support struggling families. She herself had spent long days helping with harvests beside a group of young adults, even though the fields yielded far less than anyone hoped.

On the day of the dance, the sun baked the town relentlessly. Citizens moved slowly, weary from the heat, but all knew that once the sun set behind the mountains, the air would finally cool.

Rose worked from morning to late afternoon, decorating the church, preparing food with Aunt Lizzie, carrying dishes and decorations back and forth until her head spun. Twice she grew dizzy, but she pushed through it. Duty and excitement kept her going.

She had just set down a tray of pastries inside the church when she stepped out—and froze. Christopher stood near the entrance, deep in conversation with an older marshal she had never seen before.

She took a step toward them, ready to say hello, then halted as soon as she realized they were talking about her. Heart tightening, she slipped behind a cluster of bushes beside the building, lowering herself to stay hidden. The leaves trembled from her uneven breathing.

"I understand that you like her, Son," the older marshal said, voice low and firm, "but a relationship between you two is not possible. We're transferring you to San Francisco immediately."

Rose stopped breathing.

Christopher stiffened. "How do you even know that I have feelings for Rose Williams, Father?"

Father. Rose clutched the branch in front of her, knuckles white.

"Your partner is at your side for a reason," the older man replied. "Not only to watch your back, but to ensure you obey the Code. You know you are not allowed to fall for someone under your protection. And while feelings happen, acting on them must never occur."

"Anthony told you?" Christopher's voice sharpened.

"He sent me a telegram," his father confirmed. "He expressed his concerns... and the frustrations of Rose's uncle. John Williams is worried about the bond forming between you. He's afraid you'll break her heart."

Christopher scowled. "I care for her, Father. And she cares for me. I want to be with her."

Rose's vision blurred with tears.

"Are you certain it isn't infatuation?" his father asked gently. "She is beautiful, young, and vulnerable. You protected her when she was frightened and alone. Of course she would feel drawn to you, you're her hero. But that doesn't make it love. It makes it gratitude. It makes it, longing. She's a child compared to you, Christopher."

Rose pressed a hand over her mouth to stifle a wounded gasp.

"I don't want to lose her," Christopher said, quiet but desperate.

"How do you imagine it working?" his father pressed. "You're a marshal. Your assignments take you across the country. Your job is dangerous. After everything she has endured, could she survive the fear of losing you? Right now, she would promise anything, because it all feels romantic. But if you were killed on duty, it would destroy her."

"I could resign," Christopher murmured. "Become sheriff here."

His father exhaled heavily. "Christopher... you have dreamed of this job your entire life. You are exceptional at it. You bring justice and compassion into a violent world. You would never be content settling down in a small town. Even with a lovely young wife, you'd feel unfulfilled, and that would breed resentment. This life, this calling, fits you. You know it."

Christopher said nothing.

"And you just signed on for another term," his father continued gently. "You're bound to the Marshals for at least four more years. Do you want her to wait that long? And even if she would... do you think her aunt and uncle would let her go so soon?"

Rose closed her eyes. Tears slipped down her cheeks.

"She's more mature than you think," Christopher protested weakly.

"Son, be reasonable. She's lived through trauma and danger. You protected her when she was frightened and alone. She clings to that, she clings to you. But that isn't the kind of love that builds a life. And if you truly care for her... you won't drag her into a future built on fear and uncertainty."

Before Christopher could answer, footsteps approached. Rose peeked through the branches just as a young woman rushed toward Christopher, threw her arms around him, and kissed him squarely on the mouth.

Rose stumbled backward, breath shattering.

"Grace," Christopher managed, stunned. "What are you doing here?"

"I heard you were coming back to San Francisco," she said brightly, looping her arm possessively through his. "I couldn't wait to see you again. So, I asked my parents, and your father, if we could come pick you up together."

"But... why?"

"I missed you, of course."

Christopher stared at her. "Missed me? Grace, I haven't heard from you in a year. Not since I proposed to you."

Rose didn't wait to hear another word. Her heart broke too loudly for her to stay hidden. With a strangled breath, she turned and fled, running blindly toward the dark line of trees, tears streaming down her face as she vanished into the shadows.

"Didn't you miss me too?" Grace asked, bottom lip jutting in a practiced pout. Christopher exhaled slowly, rubbing the back of his neck.

"Of course I missed you, Grace. I cared deeply for you. But that isn't the point." His voice was gentle, but firm. "I proposed to you, and you turned me down. You told me you didn't want to court anymore."

Grace's expression softened, wounded. "I needed time to think," she insisted. "About us... about what I wanted. I wasn't ready to be committed again so soon. Not after everything. You know what happened to my late husband. I needed to be sure I could handle the fear of losing someone else, especially someone in a profession as dangerous as yours."

Her mother slipped her gloved hand around Grace's arm, offering a sympathetic smile.

"Darling, why don't we step inside for a moment? Let Christopher finish talking with his father."

Grace lingered, soft and pleading, as though expecting Christopher to follow. When he didn't, her shoulders dipped. Then she allowed herself to be guided toward the church doors. Her father trailed behind, casting a wary glance back at Christopher.

Christopher turned to his father, disbelief cutting through his voice.

"You told her I was coming home, didn't you? Why would you allow her to come with you and put me on the spot like this?"

Marshal Moore Sr. folded his arms, unruffled.

"You two go way back. You and Grace courted for a year, nearly got engaged, if you recall. Yes, she hesitated, but she never stopped caring for you."

"I love Rose," Christopher said quietly but firmly. "Not Grace. Rose."

His father exhaled heavily, as if dreading the words he had just heard.

"Son... I'm sorry, but there is no future for you and that girl. She doesn't deserve another heartbreak. And neither do you. Grace loves you. She's steady, she's proven, and the two of you can take time to rediscover each other before you consider proposing again."

"That's not what I want," Christopher argued. "Rose—"

"You're thinking with your heart, not your head," his father interrupted gently but firmly. "And you're forgetting your duty. If you refuse your new assignment, your superiors will discipline you. You should never have let Rose know how you felt. And the moment you sensed anything shifting inside you, you should have requested a transfer. You know the rules, they exist for a reason."

Christopher's jaw tightened. "I couldn't just walk away from her."

"I know," his father said softly. "But you must look at this realistically. Leaving will hurt her, yes, but she will move on. She's young, Christopher. Too young. And her aunt and uncle barely know you. You cannot expect them to hand her over to a man who lives a dangerous life and moves from place to place." Marshal Moore Sr. reached out, resting a firm, fatherly hand on his son's shoulder.

"Please try to make peace with what needs to happen. You're a marshal. You bring justice to those who cannot defend themselves. That is your calling, your destiny. And Rose... Rose deserves a life of stability and peace, not a future spent waiting, worrying, and fearing the day she loses the man she loves to a bullet on the frontier." He squeezed Christopher's shoulder gently.

"Remember this: I love you, Son. Everything I'm saying, I'm saying because I want what's best for you. And I want what's best for her."

15

When Her Heart
Finally Broke

Rose didn't even know where she was going. She only knew
she had to get away, away from the church, away from the
voices, away from the truth she had overheard. Her heart felt
flayed open, raw and pounding, every beat sending a fresh wave
of agony through her chest. Tears streamed faster, the farther she
ran, blurring the path and trees until everything became a smear,
of spinning color.

She tried to breathe, but her lungs wouldn't obey. Every gulp
of air came sharp and shallow, as though she were drowning
above water. Marshal Jones had told Christopher's father about
her? Christopher had been engaged? Why hadn't he told her?
Why had he kissed her? Held her? Confessed love if he already
belonged to someone else? Was she a convenience? A diversion?
Another man charmed by the idea of her dowry?

Her thoughts tangled into a suffocating knot. Words she
had tried so hard to ignore began echoing in her mind, her
father's cold warnings, Andrew's bitter accusations, Devon's vile
whispers. And now Christopher's father... calling her a child.

Saying she would ruin Christopher's life. Saying there was no future for her with the man she loved.

Her uncle's last sermon rose in her memory as though someone whispered it directly into her ear.

"True love sometimes means letting someone go, even if it breaks your heart. God sees the whole path when we only see one step." Was this what he'd meant? Had God been trying to warn her all along? Was that why her uncle had preached so passionately about marriage? Was he, like everyone else, deciding her life for her behind closed doors?

She stumbled, dazed, her breath turning ragged. She felt betrayed on all sides, by the man she loved, by the uncle she trusted more than anyone, by a world determined to treat her like a fragile little girl incapable of her own choices.

Her throat tightened painfully. She tried to lick her lips, but they were cracked and dry. The edges of the world blurred gray. A low rushing sound filled her ears, drowning out her thoughts. She reached out blindly, as though she could steady herself against the air, but caught nothing. Her knees buckled. *No... not now.*

Her body refused to listen. Her vision shrank to a narrow tunnel of darkness. Then, hands. Warm, steady, anchoring. One pair gripping her arms, another bracing her back.

"Rose... Rose, try to breathe slowly." Ahanu's voice flowed over her like cool water. She felt him lower to one knee, supporting her weight as gently as if she were a child. Calian's hand brushed her hair back from her damp forehead.

"Easy, Takoda. We're here. You're safe."

Takoda. Her Indian name. Hearing it broke through the panic. She blinked hard, forcing the shadows back until their familiar faces swam into view, full of concern and brotherly protectiveness that expected nothing from her except to breathe.

Just one week earlier, she had stood surrounded by the Cheyenne elders, receiving the name they had chosen for her, Takoda: friend to everyone.

Ahanu tightened his hold as another tremor shook her.

"Slow breaths. In... then out."

Calian's hand moved in steady circles over her back.

"You do not need to stand. Let us hold you until the fear passes."

Rose clung to their voices, letting their calm anchor her until the roaring in her ears dimmed and her heart slowed enough for her to draw a real breath. Only then did she whisper, voice trembling, "How... how did you find me?"

Ahanu exchanged a glance with Calian.

"We saw you run. We knew that look. It is the look of someone whose heart has been wounded." His eyes softened. "You came to the forest to weep alone. But Takoda is not meant to suffer alone."

Calian and Ahanu both lifted their heads when the rumble of wheels broke through the quiet of the trees. A buggy approached quickly, and beside it, a rider urged his horse forward at a gallop.

Grant reined in hard the moment he spotted Rose in the arms of the two Cheyenne men. He dismounted in one swift motion.

"What happened?" His voice was sharp with alarm.

"We're not sure," Calian replied. "We saw Rose running this way. She nearly collapsed before we reached her."

Grant stepped closer, lowering himself so his eyes met hers.

"Rose," he murmured, gentler now, "can you tell me what happened?"

Rose tried to speak but only shook her head.

"Water... please," she whispered, her lips dry and trembling.

Grant didn't hesitate. He grabbed the metal flask from his saddle, uncapped it quickly, and tipped a small amount to her lips so she wouldn't choke. Rose swallowed gratefully, though her hands still shook. By then, the buggy had come to a stop. Mr. Adams and Jennifer climbed down in an instant and hurried toward them.

"What on earth happened?" Mr. Adams demanded.

"We don't know yet," Ahanu said calmly. "She ran until she couldn't."

Mr. Adams looked at Rose with fatherly concern.

"We should take her home to her aunt and uncle."

Rose tried to stand, but her knees buckled again. Grant caught her before she hit the ground, gathering her gently into his arms.

"No, please," she begged, shaking her head weakly. "I don't want to go home. I can't."

Grant's hold tightened protectively.

"Why not, Rose? What happened?"

"They—He," her voice broke. "I don't want to see him. I can't face them. They hurt me... they betrayed me."

Mr. Adams's brow furrowed. "Who betrayed you, child?"

She swallowed hard, new tears spilling down her cheeks.

"Uncle John... and the marshals. Please... please don't take me back. Not now. I can't."

Grant shared a worried glance with his father before turning his attention fully back to the trembling girl in his arms.

"Rose..." his voice softened. "All right. You don't have to go home."

She sagged against him in relief. Grant looked at his father.

"I can take her to the ranch. Nana is there. She'll know how to help." Then, to Rose, he added, "You'll be safe with her. I promise."

Mr. Adams nodded once, decisively.

"Yes. Take her to your grandmother. She's the best person for her right now. We'll go on to the dance and quietly let her aunt and uncle know she's safe, so they don't panic. I'll also send Shane to check on her as soon as I can."

Rose tried to straighten to thank the two Cheyenne men, but Grant kept an arm around her to steady her. Ahanu lifted her carefully so Grant could mount.

"Thank you," she whispered to her Indian brothers, her voice wobbling but sincere.

"We would do anything for our white sister," Calian said, touching her arm gently. "Take care, Takoda. We will visit you tomorrow."

Grant nodded respectfully to both men. Then he nudged his horse forward, securing Rose in his arms as he turned toward the Adams ranch and rode away, dusk settling behind them like a curtain.

"Grant, what happened? Why is Rose Williams here?" Clementine Adams hurried to his side the moment he stepped through the doorway, Rose limp in his arms, her eyes closed, and her head resting against his shoulder as though she had no strength left.

Grant carried her into the guest room and laid her carefully on the bed. Clementine brushed a few damp strands of hair from Rose's brow, her heart twisting at the girl's pallor.

"I'm not entirely sure," Grant admitted, raking a hand through his hair in frustration. "Two Cheyenne found her running through the woods, said she nearly collapsed in their arms. We rode up right after. She could barely speak." His voice lowered, thick with worry. "She said she didn't want to go home. That she couldn't. She said her uncle... and the marshals... betrayed her."

Clementine's breath caught. She remembered the handsome marshals from church, remembered the way one of them had watched Rose as though she were the center of his world. Pieces began falling into place, too quickly and painfully to ignore.

"Oh, that poor child," she murmured, placing her hand softly on Rose's cheek. "She's been through more than most grown women endure in a lifetime. And now this. Is anyone getting the doctor?"

"Yes," Grant replied. "Mom, Dad, and Jen are still heading toward town. Dad said he'd send Shane over the moment he saw him."

"Good," Clementine said firmly, her determination returning. "The girl is shaking with exhaustion and heartbreak. She needs rest, water, and someone who will listen to her." She gave Grant a look, strong, grandmotherly, full of understanding and quiet warning all at once.

"Help me get her comfortable. I'll fetch one of Jennifer's nightgowns. Once Dr. Hunter arrives, he can help me change her into something clean and cool."

Grant nodded, lingering by Rose's bedside. He gently took her hand and gave it a reassuring squeeze.

"You're safe now, Rose," he whispered, more to himself than anyone else. "We've got you."

And Clementine, watching the worry in her grandson's eyes, knew perfectly well: whatever had shattered Rose Williams tonight... it was only the beginning.

"She needs to drink a great deal of water," Shane said after finishing his examination. He spoke quietly, his concern evident as he pulled the blanket a little higher over Rose's shoulder. "Her body is severely dehydrated, and the heat today only made things worse. I spoke with her aunt, and she told me Rose worked from morning until late afternoon and barely stopped long enough to drink anything."

Clementine exchanged a worried glance with Grant.

"Lizzie said she reminded her several times to sit down and drink," Shane went on, "but you know Rose, once she sets her mind on helping, she pushes herself until she has nothing left. Between the heat, the strenuous work, and then the long run... her body simply gave out. She needs rest more than anything."

Grant gestured toward the bed. "Should we move her back home? She might rest better there."

Shane shook his head immediately.

"No. Not tonight." His usually steady voice softened. "Rose was delirious when I arrived. She kept mumbling, and though most of it was jumbled, one thing was clear, something happened today that shook her badly."

Grant's jaw tightened. "She said something similar to Ahanu and Calian... that she couldn't go back. That she'd been betrayed."

Shane exhaled slowly. "Exactly. And in her current state, physically weak, emotionally distressed, it would be cruel to take her somewhere she's terrified to be. She needs quiet, and she needs to feel safe."

Clementine placed a gentle hand on Rose's forehead, brushing back a damp curl.

"She can stay here as long as she needs. We'll take good care of her."

"John and Lizzie agree," Shane added. "I already spoke with them before coming here. They told me they won't force her to come home tonight. John said he has a suspicion about what's upsetting her and has likely shared it with Lizzie by now."

Grant let out a breath he hadn't realized he'd been holding.

"Thank you, Shane."

The doctor gathered his bag but paused at the door, his expression grave.

"Grant... be aware that Rose is not herself right now." His eyes softened with sympathy. "She's hurting. Whatever happened, it cut deep."

When he left, the small room felt very still. Rose slept fitfully, her breathing uneven, her lips dry and cracked.

Clementine sat beside her, gently taking the girl's limp hand in hers.

Grant lingered in the doorway, his heart heavy at the sight of her pale face.

"Poor thing. I think I have a pretty good idea of what she's going through right now, and I'll talk to her about it in the morning. This won't be easy for her to overcome, though. Healing a broken heart takes time," Clementine whispered without looking up.

When Rose awoke, a glass of water sat on the nightstand along with a full pitcher. The dryness in her mouth was unbearable. Her tongue felt thick, the back of her throat raw and burning. She drank greedily until the glass was empty, then let herself fall back against the pillows, exhausted by the simple act of swallowing. Sleep claimed her again, before she could wonder where she was.

The next time she opened her eyes, pale morning light filtered through the curtains. For several disoriented heartbeats she didn't know where she was, but then memory rushed in, and her stomach tightened. *The Adams ranch. Grant carrying her. Ahanu's arms steadying her. Christopher's voice with that woman. His father's words. The kiss. The betrayal.*

Her gaze drifted to the nightstand. Someone had refilled the glass with fresh water. Beside it lay a neatly folded letter. Her hands trembled as she reached for it. She recognized his handwriting instantly. A wave of dizzying dread washed through her, and she forced herself to breathe as she unfolded the page.

Dearest Rose,

*My heart is about to break, but I think deep inside, we
knew this day would come...*

The words blurred, then sharpened again as she blinked
through tears.

*I was never unfaithful...
I never meant to deceive you...
My proposal to Grace was long before I met you...*

Every line pulled tighter at the threads wrapped around her
heart. He explained Grace, her late husband, her fear, her
withdrawal. His own request for reassignment, just to escape the
pain of seeing her. He explained the silence between them, the
distance, the uncertainty.

Then came the words that struck the deepest:

*Then I met you, and everything happened so fast. Your
feisty spirit, your passion, your beautiful heart,
everything took me by storm, and my heart was yours.*

A sob tore from her throat. He loved her. He *had* loved her.
And yet...

*My father is right...
I should never have let you know...
We are both paying for my carelessness...*

Rose pressed a trembling hand against her mouth. The next
paragraph blurred through her tears.

Being a marshal has been my dream since boyhood...
I want to help people...
I know you would never ask me to give it up...
But I would always be torn...
I cannot keep you safe and do my job without risking
everything.

Her vision swam. He was choosing duty, his calling, over her. Choosing a life that could never include her.

I don't want to leave you, Rose, but it is the only way for
us to move on and heal...

My love will be with you always...

I am doing this to protect you...

You deserve more than I could ever give.

Her breath hitched, sharp and painful. Finally, the words she feared most:

Farewell, my love,
Christopher Moore, U.S. Marshal

The page slipped from her fingers as if her strength had been cut away. A broken sob ripped through her chest. She folded over the letter, burying her face in the pillow, her body shaking with grief so raw she could hardly draw breath.

It hurt, everything hurt. Her heart felt carved out and scraped hollow, then shattered into pieces she wasn't sure she would ever be able to gather again.

Christopher was gone. Gone without giving her a chance to speak. Gone after taking her heart in his hands, after kissing her like she was the only woman in the world, after promising her passion and protection and tenderness, after making her believe she could finally, finally be loved. He was gone. And he had taken the best part of her heart with him.

Rose clutched the pillow as her cries filled the quiet room, her sobs rough and devastating. How was she supposed to heal from this... when the man she loved had walked away to keep her safe? How was she supposed to breathe... when the one man who *saw* her, truly saw her, had left her behind?

Rose didn't know how long she had been crying when a gentle hand touched her shoulder. She lifted her head and found herself looking into the compassionate eyes of Clementine Adams. The older woman sat beside her with a soft rustle of skirts, then gently brushed the wet strands of hair from Rose's cheeks.

She helped the girl sit upright and coaxed more water into her trembling hands. Rose drank obediently. Though the sobs had quieted, the tears continued their steady stream.

"It's all right to cry, Rose," Clementine murmured, her voice a tender hush that soothed like warm tea. "Don't force yourself to be strong this moment. Let it out. The heart must empty itself before it can heal again. And I believe I understand exactly what you're going through."

Rose blinked up at her in surprise. The older woman sighed, her eyes soft with memory and something deeper, old pain, old grief.

"You don't have to speak yet, not until you're ready," Clementine promised. "But if it's all right with you, I'd like to tell you what I think is happening."

Rose nodded faintly.

"If you allow me," the woman continued, "I want to share why I recognize your pain so well. But only if it won't burden you further."

Rose took the handkerchief offered, wiping her swollen eyes. Clementine touched her hand warmly.

"You've only been among us a short while, but one thing is already clear, this town treasures you. They admire your courage and kindness. But among all those who care for you, there is one man who earned your trust and your love above all others. Am I right?"

Rose pressed her lips together and gave the smallest nod. Her heart felt like it was splitting open all over again.

"The younger marshal..." Clementine shook her head with a rueful little smile. "He is a handsome man, any woman with blood in her veins would understand how you came to love him. And I suspect he is the first man you've ever cared for that way. Not as a friend... but as someone who made your heart flutter when he entered a room."

Rose nodded again, another tear slipping down her cheek. Clementine reached out and cupped her face tenderly.

"Oh, my sweet girl," she whispered. "I know this heartache more intimately than you think. I was once exactly where you are."

Rose's eyes widened. Clementine drew in a slow breath, her gaze moving not to the room but to the distant years of her youth.

"My mother died when I was ten," she began softly. "She passed during the birth of my youngest brother... and we lost the baby as well. My father's grief swallowed him whole. He became harsh... unkind. He loved us, but he no longer knew how to show it. And I, being the eldest and the one who resembled my mother most, bore the brunt of his anger."

Rose listened intently, her own pain softened by empathy.

"He traveled often for work," Clementine continued. "Those were our peaceful days. But when I was fifteen, he was attacked on the road and killed. My grandparents took us in afterward. Bless their souls, they gave us warmth, safety, and love." Her voice thickened.

"It was then a drunken stranger accosted me one evening. I still shake at the memory. But a soldier, young, strong, brave, saw what was happening and saved me. I thought my heart would burst. He was the most handsome man I'd ever seen. Before long, we met whenever we could. And yes... he gave me my first kiss too." A bittersweet smile touched her lips.

"He was fifteen years older than I was. But I was in love, and he promised to wait until I was eighteen before asking for my hand." Her smile faded. "But my grandfather discovered us. And though he was normally the gentlest of men, that night he was furious."

Rose's breath caught. "He was angry with *you*?"

"Oh no, child. Never with me." Clementine shook her head softly. "He was furious with the soldier, for pursuing someone so young, even with honorable intentions. My grandfather reported him to his superiors. The young man was transferred immediately. And my heart... shattered." She pressed a trembling hand to her chest.

"I was stubborn and proud. I refused to forgive my grandfather. I ignored every attempt he made to mend things. Only years later did I understand—he was protecting me the best way he knew how. But I let pain blind me. I let pride harden my heart. And when he died..." Her voice broke. "When he died, I had not yet forgiven him. It is a regret I will carry for the rest of my days."

Rose reached out and squeezed her hand gently, her heart aching for the old woman. Clementine breathed deeply, steadying herself.

"I know you are hurting, Rose. I know you feel betrayed and raw. But please... don't let anger separate you from those who love you. Your uncle, your aunt, those marshals, they meant to protect you, even if they made mistakes." She brushed a final tear from Rose's cheek with her thumb.

"Give yourself time to grieve, my dear. But once the storm settles, speak with them. Hear them out. Don't let pride prevent healing. Hearts break easily... but they mend beautifully when softened with forgiveness."

Rose swallowed. "Thank you, Mrs. Adams," she whispered. The older woman smiled warmly.

"Oh, sweet child, call me *Nana*. Jennifer is to marry your cousin soon, which makes us family, doesn't it?"

"I've never had grandparents," Rose confessed softly.

"And I have plenty of love to give," Nana replied, drawing her into a soft, grandmotherly embrace. "That is the blessing of grandparents, we never run out."

A soft knock sounded, and Jennifer peeked into the room. "Is it all right if I come in, Nana?"

"Of course, my girl," Nana said, rising slowly. "I'm sure you two have much to speak about." She squeezed Rose's hand one last time, then slipped out, leaving the two young women alone.

16

The Break Before the Mending

"**Y**our grandmother is a wonderful woman," Rose said once they were alone. "You're so blessed to have her."

Jennifer's face brightened with a warmth that made Rose feel, for the first time since waking, a little less hollow.

"She's your grandmother now too," Jennifer replied cheerfully. "Nana doesn't let anyone stay a stranger for long. I think she already adores you."

A small, grateful smile tugged at Rose's lips. Jennifer perched on the edge of the bed, tucking a loose curl behind her ear.

"I'm so glad I get to have you all to myself for a bit," she admitted with a soft laugh. "I've wanted to really know you for ages. Living miles away from town makes it hard to make or keep close friends, and..." She shrugged lightly. "Most girls my age moved on, married, left for bigger towns, or got too busy with children or helping on their ranches and farms. I only had two close friends growing up. One got married and moved farther west, and the other is always working." Her voice held no self-pity, only a quiet longing Rose understood all too well.

Rose listened, something gentle stirring inside her as Jennifer chattered, bright, earnest, and full of easy affection. She couldn't remember the last time another young woman had spoken to her like this, as if she mattered simply because she existed.

She had never truly had a close female friend, only her beloved servants and, for a time, Andrew, who now seemed like a stranger wearing the face of someone she'd once trusted. Before leaving Boston, she had begun forming a fragile friendship with a kind young woman, but that had ended the moment her journey west began.

She swallowed softly, feeling something close to hope. Maybe... maybe Jennifer could become the friend she had been longing for, someone to laugh with, talk to, confide in. Someone who wasn't drawn to her money or her name or the idea of rescuing a helpless girl. Someone who might simply love *her*.

Jennifer scooted a little closer, her expression bright with sincerity.

"So," she said, "once you're feeling better, you and I are going to make up for lost time. I have so much to tell you, and I want to hear everything about you, Boston, your travels, your dresses, everything."

Despite the heaviness still pressing on her heart, Rose let out the faintest laugh.

"I would like that." And she meant it.

Jennifer squeezed her hand, and for the first time since she'd opened Christopher's letter, Rose felt a flicker of comfort, fragile, but real.

The two women talked for a long while, slipping easily into conversation as though they had known each other for years instead of hours. Jennifer's bright, lively chatter filled the room, stories about the ranch, her childhood, her brothers, and the small-town world she loved so dearly. Rose listened with growing fondness, smiling despite the raw ache in her chest.

When Rose finally asked where she could wash up, Jennifer immediately stood and guided her down the hall.

"This way," she said softly, keeping her voice gentle, as though Rose were a wounded bird she feared might startle. She opened the door to the washroom, lit the lamp, and stepped aside.

"Take all the time you need. I'll wait for you right here."

Rose washed her face and hands, lingering as the cool water soothed her swollen eyes and the tightness in her throat. For several minutes she simply breathed, steadying herself, before finally opening the washroom door.

Without hesitation, Jennifer scanned the hallway, making sure no one else was around. Only when she was certain did she give Rose a reassuring nod and walk her back to the guest room.

As soon as they stepped inside, Rose slipped behind the folding screen and changed out of the borrowed nightgown and back into her clothes. Her movements were slow, drained, almost fragile. By the time she emerged, her limbs trembled with exhaustion.

Jennifer guided her toward the big armchair near the window.

"Sit," she said firmly, but kindly.

Rose obeyed. The chair was deep and soft, and she sank into it as if her bones had melted. Jennifer lifted a thick woolen blanket from the bed and draped it around Rose's shoulders with all the tenderness of an older sister, or perhaps the sister Rose had never had.

"There," Jennifer murmured. "You're safe here. Rest."

Rose clutched the blanket a little tighter. Something inside her loosened, something that had been coiled painfully since the moment her world had fallen apart.

"Thank you," she whispered.

Jennifer sat on the edge of the bed, her expression warm and earnest.

"I'm glad you're here with us, Rose. Truly. And I'm not going anywhere. If you need to talk, cry, yell, anything, I'm right here."

Rose swallowed hard. In all her travels, hardships, and heartbreaks, she had longed, truly longed, for a friend like this. Someone kind. Someone close. Someone *safe*. Jennifer's gentle presence kept Rose's mind so occupied, so comforted, that her heartbreak, though still sharp, no longer threatened to swallow her whole. Rose felt she might breathe again.

Not long after the two women had settled comfortably into conversation again, a firm knock sounded at the door. Jennifer looked up with a small frown.

"Who is it?"

"It's Grant. May I come in?"

Rose instinctively began to rise, but Jennifer pressed a gentle hand to her shoulder.

"Stay put and rest. I'll take care of everything." She lifted her voice. "Just a moment, Grant!" Jennifer hurried about the room, straightening the bed and pulling the blanket neatly around Rose's waist. Then she handed Rose the folded letter from Christopher. "Best keep this close," she whispered.

Rose slipped it into her pocket just as Jennifer called, "You can come in now!"

Grant opened the door, balancing a tray loaded with warm biscuits, scrambled eggs, sliced fruit, and a steaming cup of tea. The moment he stepped inside, the comforting scents of breakfast drifted through the room. He set the tray in his sister's hands with a smirk.

"Aw, Grant, how sweet of you to bring *us* breakfast," Jennifer teased, flashing her brother a mischievous grin.

"You're lucky Rose is here," he shot back. "Mom and Dad figured she shouldn't eat alone."

Rose quickly sat forward as far as the blanket allowed.

"I don't want to be any trouble. Truly, I've imposed enough. I—perhaps—I should go home." She began to push herself up again, but Jennifer immediately eased her back into the armchair.

"You're not going anywhere," she said firmly. "Doctor's orders."

Mrs. Adams entered just then, her warm voice filling the room.

"She's right, dear. Dr. Hunter told us you need complete rest. That means breakfast is brought to you, whether you approve or not."

Mr. Adams stepped in behind his wife, tipping his head to Rose with a kind but amused expression.

"Good morning, Miss Williams. I see the color's returning to your cheeks. How are you feeling today, Rose?"

"A little better," she admitted, touched by their kindness. "Thank you for taking such good care of me."

"That's what neighbors do," Mrs. Adams said with a fond pat to her shoulder.

A few more gentle greetings and assurances followed before the family stepped out, leaving Jennifer and Rose alone with the breakfast tray. Jennifer placed it across Rose's lap.

"Now eat," she said warmly. "You need your strength."

Rose let out a breath she hadn't realized she was holding. Surrounded by such tenderness, her heart, though still aching, felt just a little steadier.

The rest of the day passed as pleasantly as circumstances allowed. Though Rose's heart remained heavy, the Adams women did everything in their power to lighten it. Nana drifted in and out of the room with soothing teas, and gentle smiles. Mrs. Adams brought warm blankets and soft conversation. And Jennifer stayed near her almost constantly, filling the quiet with cheerful chatter that gave Rose's thoughts no space to spiral.

Grant and his father stopped by several times as well, each visit brief but comforting in its own way. Even their simple inquiries: '*Do you need anything? Can we get you more water? How are you feeling?*' helped anchor her, reminding her she wasn't alone.

Just past midday, Ahanu and Calian arrived. Their presence eased something deep within her chest, and she managed her first real smile when they teased her gently about her 'escape' from home.

"We will visit often," Calian promised quietly as he squeezed her hand, his dark eyes full of brotherly affection. "Once you are back in town, your Indian brothers will check on you as much as your white ones."

Rose felt comforted, held inside a circle of people who genuinely cared for her. It kept the grief from consuming her entirely.

When Shane arrived not long after the two Cheyenne men departed, Rose braced herself for a stern lecture, but none came. Instead, he studied her carefully, his fingers resting lightly against her wrist as he counted her pulse.

"You're doing better," he said gently. "Still tired, but your color is returning. Are you ready to go home, Rose?"

She nodded. "I miss Aunt Lizzie. And Uncle John. I think..." Her voice wavered, but she steadied it. "I think I'm ready to talk to them."

Shane offered a soft smile. "Then I'll take you. I need to return to town anyway."

Rose rose slowly, still weak, and allowed Jennifer to drape a shawl around her shoulders. She hugged Nana first, longer than she intended, resting for a moment in the woman's warm, maternal embrace. Then she embraced Mrs. Adams and Jennifer in turn, whispering her heartfelt thanks. Last, she stepped up to Mr. Adams, who tipped his hat with a kind grin.

"Take care, Miss Rose. You're welcome here any time."

"Thank you," she said, her voice thick with sincerity. She swept the room with her gaze. "Where is Grant?"

Jennifer frowned slightly. "He left earlier. Something needed tending on the ranch. He hoped to be back in time to see you off, but it looks like he was held up."

"Oh." The disappointment was sharper than she expected. She had wanted to thank him, for carrying her, rescuing her, and never once pushing her toward a confrontation she wasn't ready for. But she forced a small smile. "Please tell him goodbye for me."

"I will," Jennifer promised.

Shane helped her into the buggy, ensuring she was settled before taking the reins. As the horse started forward, Rose leaned back and watched the ranch fade behind them. The Adams family had sheltered her only briefly, yet it felt as if she were leaving a sanctuary.

She drew in a steady breath. Home awaited her. So did answers. So did conversations she had been dreading. And forgiveness she wasn't sure she was ready to give—but knew she needed to find. And somewhere along the road ahead... perhaps a way to mend her fractured heart.

Jennifer and Nana remained on the porch, watching the buggy rattle down the road toward Idaho Springs. Rose sat beside Shane, her bonnet tilted low, her posture exhausted yet composed. From a distance she almost looked peaceful. Jennifer folded her arms.

"Nana... you worked a miracle on her. What did you do to ease her heartbreak so quickly? She was smiling again before she left."

Nana's lips curved with gentle sadness.

"Rose is not over anything, child."

Jennifer blinked, startled.

"She managed to release a small part of the pain weighing on her heart," Nana said, eyes following the buggy until it disappeared over the rise. "But she has not truly faced it yet. She was able to breathe for a short while because this house was new, new faces, new distractions. But once she returns home... where every corner, every room, every path reminds her of that young marshal? Everything will strike her twice as hard."

Jennifer's brows knit with worry.

"Then why are we letting her go back so soon? If she stayed longer, maybe—"

Nana shook her head gently but firmly.

"It wouldn't help her. Sooner or later, she must face what hurts. Running would only delay it, and delaying pain often makes the fall worse. No, sweetheart... she must walk into it so she can walk through it."

A breeze swept around the house. Jennifer hugged her arms around herself.

"You said she has to fall deeper before she'll heal. That sounds terrifying."

"It is," Nana admitted softly. "But healing often begins only after the deepest break. And you must understand something about Rose." Her wise eyes met Jennifer's. "That child has endured more in a few months than most women endure in a lifetime. She has been brave, fiercely brave. She survived abuse, betrayal, humiliation, danger, and more heartbreak than any young heart should bear. She kept standing because she never had time to fall."

Jennifer swallowed. "...And now she does."

"Yes." Nana's gaze turned distant, sorrowful. "Now that Marshal Moore is gone, her strongest protector, the man she trusted most, Rose has lost the anchor she clung to. That young man wasn't just someone she cared for. He was the first person to ever make her feel cherished. Safe. Wanted. And losing that..." Nana exhaled slowly. "It will tear open every wound she thought had healed."

Jennifer's voice trembled. "You think she'll push us away?"

"Oh, she will," Nana said without hesitation. "A broken heart can twist a person's thoughts. It can make you angry at the very people trying to help you. And if homesickness hits her too, missing Boston, her old life, the father she loved... the pain may drag her lower than any of us expect."

"Then what do we do?"

Nana laid a steady hand on her granddaughter's shoulder.

"We do what good families do, even if she isn't ready to call us that yet."

"We stand with her," Jennifer whispered.

"We stand with her," Nana echoed, her voice firm and full of quiet strength. "Through anger, through tears, through silence. We reach out even when she pulls back. We remind her she is not alone. And when the time is right, we help her rise again."

They both gazed down the empty road where the buggy had vanished.

"And pray, Jennifer," Nana added softly. "Pray that her tender, generous heart does not lose hope before help arrives."

Jennifer nodded, feeling the weight of Rose's fragile future settle on both their shoulders.

"We won't let her go through this alone," she said quietly.

"No, sweetheart," Nana agreed, squeezing her hand. "We won't."

Shane dropped her off in front of the parsonage and continued on. Their pleasant conversation during the ride had kept her mind steady for a time, but now, standing alone, everything crashed over her like a collapsing wave. Her knees weakened. Her chest tightened. Christopher was gone. Gone without letting her speak. Gone without giving her a choice. The pain was too much.

Not wanting anyone to see her break, she rushed over to the church and slipped inside, closing the heavy door behind her as softly as she could. Sunlight filtered through the tall stained-glass windows, spreading soft colors across the empty benches. It should have comforted her. Instead, it made her ache.

She walked to a back pew, sat, and then folded forward as the first sob tore through her. Moments later she slid off the bench entirely, sinking to her knees on the wooden floor, clutching the seat for support. Her forehead pressed against the smooth wood, her shoulders trembling violently.

She wanted to scream, to let every shard of agony out, but she was in a holy place. Even shattered as she was, she forced the grief into quiet sobs. God understood. He saw her heart. He knew every reason for every tear.

Still, the tears wouldn't stop. "Christopher..." she whispered into the silence. But the name broke her further. She longed for him, his warmth, his arms, the tenderness in his brown eyes. And knowing he had walked away from her... willingly... nearly crushed her.

A soft footstep behind her. A hand, warm, steady, rested on her trembling shoulder. Rose gasped and lifted her head. Grant stood over her, his expression full of compassion. No judgment. No irritation. Only concern, and something that looked heartbreakingly like sympathy. He didn't speak. He simply knelt and gathered her into his arms.

Rose collapsed against him, with a broken sob. His embrace was firm, protective, asking nothing of her, simply offering a place to fall apart.

Her sobs intensified, muffled against his shirt. Grant held her tighter, one hand braced between her shoulder blades, the other cradling the back of her head the way someone might comfort a frightened child... or a grieving friend.

"You're not alone," he murmured, his voice low and steady. "Not now. Not ever."

His kindness, quiet, gentle, perfectly timed, struck so deeply she could scarcely draw breath. Gratitude swelled inside her, raw and overwhelming. In that fragile moment, Grant became exactly what she had needed: a safe place to land when her world had fallen apart.

17

When Hope Finally Died

G rant had just finished the errands that brought him to town and was about to mount his horse when he spotted a familiar figure. Rose hurried across the street, shoulders shaking, steps uneven, and slipped inside the church as if fleeing a storm.

Something tightened in Grant's chest. Even from a distance he sensed she was unraveling. And without needing to ask, he knew, instinctively that Christopher Moore's sudden departure was the cause. He had seen the way Rose looked at the marshal, the way her eyes lit when he walked into a room... and the way that light had dimmed over the last two days. So, he followed her.

Inside, the church was nearly dark, lit only by a few leftover lanterns from the night before. Grant walked quietly down the aisle, guided by the faint, fragile sound, soft at first, then devastating, of Rose's sobbing. She was kneeling between the benches, folded in on herself, as though trying to disappear into the floor. Her hands covered her face, her shoulders shaking violently.

Grant's heart ached at the sight. No young woman should ever cry like that. Gently, he reached out and laid a hand on her shoulder. She gasped and looked up at him with tear-drenched eyes, eyes so wounded they nearly stole his breath. For a moment she seemed afraid, startled, vulnerable beyond anything he had ever seen. Then she recognized him. Her face crumpled, and before she could draw another trembling breath, Grant did the only thing his heart allowed. He pulled her into his arms. No questions. No explanations. Just quiet, steady strength.

Rose clung to him, her sobs rising as her grief finally found a place to land. He held her firmly, one hand braced at her back, the other gently cradling her head, murmuring nothing, saying everything simply by being there. She trembled against him, releasing the pain she had tried so desperately to bury.

Grant had known she cared for Christopher, but he had not understood, until this very moment, just how deeply she had fallen. When her sobs at last softened, he lifted her chin with two fingers, coaxing her to meet his gaze. Her cheeks were blotched, her eyes swollen and red, but beneath the sadness was something else, gratitude. He felt it as clearly as if she'd spoken it aloud.

"Are you feeling a little better?" he asked, voice low with tenderness. She swallowed and nodded.

"Thank you, Grant." Quiet words, but sincere.

He leaned forward and pressed a gentle kiss to her forehead, only a touch of comfort, nothing she could misinterpret. Then he stepped back, offering her space without abandoning her.

"Do you want me to walk you over to your aunt and uncle's?" Rose shook her head, brushing a tear from her cheek.

"No... I need a little more time to collect myself."

He nodded in understanding. "All right. But if you need anything, you know where to find me." He squeezed her hand, warm, steady, reassuring, then gave her a soft smile before turning and walking out of the church, leaving her with the quiet she needed... but making certain she knew she wasn't alone.

Rose sat down, the wooden pew cool beneath her trembling hands. She knew—deeply, painfully—that this wasn't over. Her heart felt splintered beyond repair, and every thought of Christopher struck like a fresh blade. Still, she forced herself to breathe, pushing against the tightness in her chest, trying, just for a moment, to quiet her thoughts.

When she finally felt steady enough to move, she rose and made her way toward the doors. She had barely taken two steps when they swung inward. Her uncle stood there. He froze. One look at her tear-streaked face, her red-rimmed eyes, her trembling resolve, and something inside him broke.

Before she could speak, Uncle John crossed the distance and gathered her into his arms. Rose pressed her face into his coat, her hands clutching the fabric as sobs shook her once more. He held her with the same gentle strength he had always shown her, as though she were his own daughter, as though her pain were his.

When her crying quieted again, he let her step back but kept his hands lightly on her shoulders, steadying her.

"Can we talk?" she whispered.

He nodded and guided her to a pew. They sat side by side. Rose drew in a shaky breath, remembering Nana's wise counsel. If she wanted peace, this conversation needed to happen.

"Last Sunday," she began softly, "when you preached about marriage... were you trying to encourage Marshal Moore to leave?"

Uncle John's gaze softened with sorrow and understanding. There was no defensiveness in his expression, only weariness, affection, and the weight of difficult choices.

"I wasn't trying to chase him off," he said gently. "But I was trying to make him think. His decisions were affecting both of you. We all liked him, Rose... but this," he exhaled slowly, "...this wasn't supposed to happen."

Rose's throat tightened. "Why didn't you let me make my own decision? Why did Marshal Jones tell his father? Why did his father get involved? Do you all think I'm a child who can't make choices for herself?"

Uncle John shook his head firmly.

"No. We don't think that at all. But we wanted to protect you, your heart, your future. Marshal Jones and I could see how attached you were becoming. And we could see how attached he was becoming too. The longer it continued, the harder it would have been for both of you." He paused, then continued in a low, sincere voice.

"Christopher Moore is a devoted man. He serves his country with his whole heart. And though he might have been willing to give up his dream for you... that sacrifice would eventually have taken a toll on him. On both of you."

Rose blinked through new tears.

"You said you liked him. If he had asked your permission to court me, would you have said yes?"

Uncle John sighed, the sound heavy with conflict.

"I honestly don't know," he admitted. "All I've ever wanted is what's best for you. But Marshal Moore shouldn't have begun a romantic attachment without speaking to me first. He knew the rules. He knew his responsibilities. It wasn't completely fair to you."

She absorbed this in silence.

"Maybe," he added quietly, "maybe your aunt and I were selfish too. We only just got you back. And the thought of losing you again... frightened us. But nothing we did was meant to hurt you. Our choices came from love, only that. And a desire to spare you a deeper heartbreak later."

Her hurt softened. She reached out and took his hand.

"Thank you, Uncle John," she whispered.

Emotion flickered across his face. He pulled her close and pressed a kiss to the top of her head, as if she were still a little girl who needed comforting.

"Aunt Lizzie and I love you more than we can say," he murmured. "When your heart feels too heavy, come to us. Don't carry it alone."

"I will," she promised.

He squeezed her once more, then stood.

"Lizzie is on a walk with the dogs. Do you want me to walk you home?"

"Is Jordan home?" she asked softly.

"No. He's at the Adams ranch today."

Rose nodded. "Then I'll go alone. A few minutes to myself... I think it will do me good."

Uncle John gave her a gentle, understanding nod. As she stepped out into the fading light, the ache in her chest throbbed... but she no longer carried it entirely alone.

Rose inhaled shakily the moment she stepped inside her uncle's house. The familiar quiet wrapped around her like a shroud, and instantly the silence pressed against her chest until she could hardly breathe.

Every room, every shadow, every memory inside these walls whispered of Christopher, his steady presence, his warm voice, his laughter. The ache was too much. Her feet moved before she realized where they were going. Not toward her own room. Not toward the kitchen or parlor. Toward his room.

Her hand trembled as she pushed the door open. The breath punched from her lungs the moment she stepped inside. His scent lingered, warm, woodsy, clean. The room felt like him, as though he had only stepped out for a moment. The thought shattered her. She slipped inside and closed the door quietly, pressing her forehead against the wood as fresh tears blurred her vision. Then she turned.

The bed looked like he had only left that morning. The blanket slightly rumpled on the side where he'd slept. She moved toward it in slow, dragging steps, her heart pounding painfully. A strangled sob escaped as she sat on the edge of the bed. Her fingers curled into the blanket. She lifted it toward her face.

His scent washed over her. Warmth, leather, soap, and something uniquely him. Whatever fragile hold she had on her composure crumbled. With a broken cry, she lay down and pulled the blanket over herself as though she could gather him in her arms. As though, if she wished hard enough, she could pretend he was still there. She buried her face in his pillow, clinging to it like a lifeline, and the sobs tore free, raw, desperate, unrestrained. It felt as though someone had reached into her chest and torn her heart clean out.

"He's gone," she whispered into the pillow, her voice breaking. "He's really gone..." The pillow muffled her sobs, but it couldn't quiet the storm inside her. Memories came in brutal waves, his fierce kisses, his tender whispers, the warmth of his arms, the fire in his eyes when he looked at her like she was the only woman in the world. And now he was gone. Gone because he loved her. Gone because he believed she deserved better. Gone without letting her fight for him.

Her tears soaked the pillow. She curled into the blanket as if she could wrap herself in the last pieces of him. Her body shook with every breath. Her heart shattered all over again.

She cried until her throat was raw. Until her chest ached. Until the line between heartbreak and exhaustion blurred entirely.

But she kept crying—because she didn't know how to stop. Because loving Christopher Moore had awakened something deep within her... and losing him felt like losing the air in her lungs. And alone in the dim quiet of his room, wrapped in the remnants of his warmth, Rose finally let herself break.

<hr />

"Lizzie, is Rose in her room?" John called the moment he stepped through the front door, not finding her anywhere downstairs. Lizzie turned from setting the table, surprise flickering across her features.

"Isn't she still at Jonas' ranch?"

"No. I found her at the church earlier. She said she was coming home, so I sent her here two hours ago. You haven't seen her?"

"No," Lizzie breathed, confusion sharpening into concern. "I came home, aired out the rooms upstairs, and then started supper." Her eyes widened slowly. "You don't think she—"

They called her name in unison, their voices filling the quiet house. No answer. They checked her room again, nothing.

Marshal Jones stepped out of his room when he heard them. "What's happening?"

"Rose is missing," John said shakily. "I spoke to her at the church, and she promised she'd go straight home. Lizzie hasn't seen her, and it's been two hours."

Lizzie's throat bobbed. Her eyes glistened.

"She wouldn't run off... not in the state she's in."

Marshal Jones set a reassuring hand on her shoulder.

"We'll find her."

Within seconds, he and John burst out the front door, mounted their horses, and took off in opposite directions, riding hard into the fading light.

Lizzie stepped outside to watch them disappear, her fingers trembling. As she turned to go back inside, Jordan and Grant Adams approached on their horses.

"How is Rose? Is she feeling any better now that she's home again?" Grant asked, hopeful, as he dismounted, until he saw Lizzie's expression. His face hardened with worry.

"We—we don't know where she is," she whispered. "John said she left the church two hours ago, but she isn't anywhere in the house."

Both young men looked around sharply, as if expecting Rose to appear from behind a tree.

"Did you search the whole house?" Grant asked.

Lizzie nodded weakly. "Well... not every room, but we called for her and checked her room. There was no answer."

Grant tipped his head slightly, thinking.

"Did Marshal Moore share a room with his partner?"

"No," Lizzie replied softly. "He had a room to himself."

Grant's gaze sharpened with sudden certainty.

"Then I think I know where she is." Without waiting for permission, he strode past Lizzie and into the house.

After a moment's startled hesitation, she hurried after him, guiding him toward the room Christopher had occupied, her heart beating faster with every step.

The two dogs sat faithfully in front of the closed door, their tails thumping anxiously when Grant approached. He quietly turned the knob, and Lizzie let out a shaky breath of relief as soon as the door opened.

Rose lay curled on Christopher's bed, wrapped tightly in the blanket as if clinging to whatever pieces of him remained in the room. Her small form trembled even in sleep. Her cheek pressed against the pillow that still held his scent.

"Oh, thank goodness," Lizzie whispered. Grant stepped into the room, his expression softening.

"Do you want me to carry her to her room?"

Lizzie nodded, unable to trust her voice. With gentle care, Grant leaned over the bed and slid his arms beneath Rose. The moment he lifted her, her body stirred. Her eyes fluttered open, unfocused at first, until she saw him.

"Grant?" she whispered, confusion clouding her gaze for half a second before everything came rushing back. Her face crumpled, and she dissolved into tears.

Grant's heart clenched. He drew her closer against his chest.

"It's okay, Rose," he murmured, lowering his head so she wouldn't feel ashamed of her tears. "We're here. You're safe. You're not alone."

Her fingers fisted in his shirt as she buried her face against him, her sobs soft but agonizing.

"I miss him so much," she choked, each word slicing through what composure she had left. "I can't... I can't stop hurting."

Grant held her tighter, his arms strong and steady around her trembling body.

"I know," he whispered. "I know." His voice thickened with emotion he didn't bother to hide. "I wish I could take that pain from you."

Lizzie pressed a hand to her mouth, tears filling her own eyes at the sight of the girl she loved so dearly breaking apart in Grant's arms. But she also saw how carefully, how reverently, he held Rose, how his entire presence became a shield.

Grant adjusted his hold so he could carry her more securely. Rose didn't resist. She just clung to him as if she might drown if she let go.

"Let's get you to your own bed," he said softly. "You don't have to be strong right now. Just let us take care of you."

Rose didn't speak, couldn't speak. But her head rested against his shoulder, and she let herself be carried, fragile and grief-stricken, while the two dogs padded faithfully at their heels. And Grant held her as though she were something precious that needed to be protected from a world that had already taken too much.

Grant gently laid Rose on her bed, and she immediately curled into a tight ball, drawing her knees up as if trying to protect the shattered pieces of her heart. She hid her face in the pillow, shoulders trembling with quiet, exhausted sobs.

Lizzie sat on the edge of the mattress and tenderly stroked her niece's hair, murmuring soothing words, soft, motherly, steady. Her voice was a gentle anchor in the storm, but Rose barely responded, the pain too deep to reach with simple comfort.

Grant and Jordan stood nearby, unsure and helpless. They were strong men, capable in every crisis, from rounding cattle to facing down danger, but heartbreak was a battlefield they couldn't fight for her. Both looked stricken, wishing they could protect her from this too.

"Shh, sweetheart," Lizzie whispered. "We're here."

Still, Rose shook, grief rolling through her in silent waves. Then, with soft whines, Lucy and Sally hopped onto the bed. They nudged their warm bodies against her, weaving between her folded arms until her hands brushed their fur. Sally pressed her nose under Rose's palm, and Lucy curled against her stomach. Their instinctive, unwavering loyalty finally broke through the storm.

Rose's sobs slowed. Her fingers tightened around their silky ears, clinging to them as though they were the only solid things left in her world. A moment later, John and Marshal Jones stepped into the room. Relief washed over both men the instant they saw Rose safe in her bed. John's shoulders eased, and some of the tension along the marshal's jaw softened.

"Thank heaven," John breathed quietly.

No one spoke loudly. It felt as though even a raised voice might fracture her all over again. They simply remained near, Grant with his arms folded tightly, Jordan pacing quietly at the foot of the bed, John standing with one hand braced against the doorframe, Marshal Jones watching with solemn compassion. For a few minutes, they just stayed. A silent circle of protection around her.

Gradually, Rose's breathing eased. Her eyelids fluttered. Finally, exhaustion began to pull her under, her hands still tangled in the dogs' fur. Only when she drifted into sleep did the group slip out, one by one, moving as quietly as if the slightest sound might stir her pain. Lizzie, however, stayed. She adjusted the blanket around Rose's shoulders, brushed a stray curl from her damp cheek, and settled into the chair beside the bed.

"I'm right here, sweetheart," she whispered. And she remained by her niece's side, determined that Rose would not face one more moment of heartache alone.

In the days that followed, Rose grew apathetic. Her body remained in the house, but her spirit seemed far away, lost somewhere between pain, longing, and numbness. She wrapped herself in the blanket that had belonged to Christopher as though it might shield her from the hollow ache inside. Her gaze often drifted unfocused across the room, her expression empty. She barely ate. She barely spoke. Nothing stirred a response, except the dogs.

Sally and Lucy refused to leave her. They lay beside her, pressed against her legs or curled against her stomach, nudging her hands whenever she sank too deeply into silence. Only they could coax the slightest movement from her: a twitch of her fingers, a small sigh, a faint stroke through their fur. They seemed to know she was fighting invisible wounds, and they remained vigilant.

Then Ahanu and Calian began visiting. Every day they came, sometimes in the morning, sometimes in the afternoon. Their presence, calm, steady, unhurried, slowly began to draw Rose back toward life. They took her on quiet walks through the woods, speaking gently, telling stories about their people's history, customs, and teachings. With them, she felt no pressure to pretend she was healing. With them, she could simply exist, hurt and fragile, without judgment. And slowly, the darkness around her heart began to thin.

Jennifer visited whenever she could as well. She was cheerful, talkative, and endlessly patient. Rose found that spending time with another young woman soothed something deep inside her. Jennifer's warm personality, her lively chatter, her sincerity, everything helped Rose feel connected again. They talked for hours, strolled through town, explored the woods, and visited families in need.

Jennifer even introduced her to the two oldest granddaughters of Mable Colton. To Rose's surprise, she found herself laughing again, small, hesitant laughs, but real. Each new friendship was another thread gently pulling her back into the world.

She avoided her uncle's house whenever possible. Every hallway, every shadow, every room there whispered of Christopher—his voice, his smile, the warmth in his eyes. The memories were too sharp, too fresh, too unbearable. The woods and the company of her friends felt safer.

As October neared its end, Rose realized she had reached a turning point. Four weeks had passed since Christopher's departure, four long weeks of grief, reflection, and slow mending. Her heart still ached, but she could carry that ache now without collapsing beneath it. It was time to face the remaining pieces of her hurt.

One evening, after returning from a walk with Ahanu and Calian, she stepped into the house, removed her shawl, and headed toward the kitchen in search of Aunt Lizzie. She walked softly, still feeling the calm of the crisp autumn air, until she passed her uncle's office. The door was slightly ajar. She would have gone on, but a familiar name stopped her cold.

"—Christopher—" Marshal Jones's voice carried into the hallway.

Rose froze. The sound of his name felt like a blade sliding between her ribs. Her breath caught. Tears stung her eyes. She swallowed hard, willing herself to move—forward, away, anywhere—but her feet refused to obey. Something in her, instinct, fear, desperate longing, compelled her to listen. She stood perfectly still, hardly daring to breathe, as the two men continued speaking behind the partially open door...

"So, you received a telegram from Marshal Moore?" Uncle John asked.

"Yes," the marshal replied. "He and Grace are officially engaged, and they're planning to marry in the spring."

A sharp, invisible blade twisted inside Rose's chest. Her fingers trembled.

"I thought Grace wasn't sure about marrying him because of his occupation," John said, confusion threading his voice. Marshal Jones sighed.

"She wasn't, at first. But her feelings for Moore were stronger than her fear. And she has supportive parents who promised to take care of her whenever he's away on assignment."

Rose pressed a hand over her mouth, swallowing back the small sound that clawed at her throat. *Engaged.* The word echoed through her like a cannon blast.

"Did he write to invite you to his wedding?" her uncle asked quietly.

"He asked me to be his best man," Marshal Jones said.

Uncle John sounded genuinely surprised.

"That is quite an honor, considering he wasn't too pleased with our interference."

"He said," the marshal continued, "that informing his father was the wake-up call he needed. In his letter, he admitted that as much as he cared for Rose, it had been infatuation on his side. He wrote that he was taken in by her beauty, her fire, her generosity, and that he'd let himself cross boundaries he never should have crossed."

Rose's vision blurred. Her lungs burned with each shallow breath. *Infatuation. Taken in.* Was that all she had been to him? Just a moment of weakness? A spark he had snuffed out the instant duty called?

"Imagine if he had reached that conclusion months or years into courting her," Uncle John said gravely. "It would have broken Rose's heart even more."

Broken? She was already shattered. What more was there left to break?

Marshal Jones hesitated. "Should we tell her about the engagement?"

"No," John said firmly. "She's finally beginning to move in the right direction. Telling her now, before her wounds have truly begun to heal, would only drag her back into the depths. She doesn't deserve that. Better to let her move on and let time help her forget."

18

When Laughter
Returned

Rose felt as if an invisible blade had driven straight into her heart. She staggered back from the half-open office door, her breath catching painfully. Though she would never have admitted it, not to her uncle, not to Nana, not even to herself, some small, desperate part of her had still hoped Christopher might return for her one day. That hope, fragile as spun glass, shattered at the words *officially engaged*.

Her pulse roared in her ears. She couldn't breathe. If she stayed one moment longer, she would scream. She rushed toward the front door, but before she could reach the knob, it swung open. Jordan and Grant stepped inside, their conversation dying instantly at the sight of her face.

"Rose?" Jordan's voice was low with worry. "What happened?"

She couldn't speak. She couldn't even shake her head. Tears surged violently, blinding her, and she tried to push past them, but Grant caught her gently and gathered her against his chest. His arms wrapped around her, strong, steady, and she collapsed into him, sobbing openly.

"Easy... I've got you," he murmured, holding her while Jordan hovered anxiously at her side.

Uncle John and Marshal Jones hurried out of the office moments later, alarm etched across their faces.

"Rose?" her uncle said, stepping toward her. "Sweetheart, what is it? What happened?"

But she couldn't form a single word. All she could hear was the echo of Marshal Jones's voice: *He and Grace are officially engaged... He realized it had been infatuation...*

He shouldn't have gotten Rose's hopes up... Her stomach twisted. It made her physically ill.

Grant held her until she found enough strength to stand on her own. When she finally did, she pressed her hand to his chest, a silent plea to release her. He loosened his arms immediately, concern still warm in his eyes.

"Rose," Uncle John tried again softly, "please talk to us."

She shook her head fiercely. If she opened her mouth, she feared she would break apart entirely. She clutched her arms around herself and backed away.

"Rose, wait—" Jordan began, but she couldn't.

Before anyone could stop her, she turned and fled down the hall, up the stairs, and into her room, slamming the door behind her as the tears came all over again.

Rose remained in her room the rest of that day and the next, refusing to come out. Lizzie and John tried everything, soft pleading, gentle knocking, quiet conversations through the door, but Rose wouldn't open it. Her silence frightened them more than her sobbing ever had.

Sunday morning arrived with a heavy quiet, the kind that made every clock tick feel louder. John and Jordan went to church alone while Lizzie stayed behind, unwilling to leave in case Rose finally emerged. After the service, the Adams family joined them for lunch and supper, hoping their presence might give Lizzie and John strength, or at least a small distraction from their worry.

When they sat down for lunch, Jonas studied Lizzie's strained face.

"How is Rose today?" he asked softly.

Lizzie shook her head, tears filling her eyes.

"No change," she whispered. "It's breaking my heart. I want to help her... but I don't know how. She won't come out of her room, and she won't talk to us. We don't even know what happened."

Grant exchanged a meaningful glance with his father, then looked toward John.

"She was beside herself when Jordan and I came into the house that night," he said quietly.

Jordan nodded. "I've never seen her so shaken."

Jennifer's face fell. "Rose was doing so much better... or at least I thought she was. She was smiling, even joking sometimes. And Ahanu and Calian worked so hard to cheer her up. The three of them have become such good friends."

Lunch ended heavy-hearted. As Lizzie gathered plates, Clementine gently laid a hand on her arm.

"Would you mind," the older woman asked softly, "if I tried talking to Rose?"

Lizzie blinked through fresh tears. "Of course not." She led Clementine to Rose's room and knocked.

"Rose, Mrs. Adams is here and would like to speak with you. Will you please let us in?"

For a long moment, silence. Then the faintest shifting inside. The door cracked open, and the two dogs peeked out first, tails wagging but unwilling to leave her side. Clementine stepped inside and immediately drew Rose into her arms.

"We're so worried about you, honey," she murmured. "Tell us what's hurting you."

Rose nodded against her shoulder. Lizzie attempted a reassuring smile.

"I'll give you two some privacy."

"No. Please stay, Aunt Lizzie." Rose's voice trembled. "I can't keep hiding from you. You and Uncle John have been so kind to me."

Relieved, Lizzie and Clementine settled into the two armchairs while Rose sat on her bed, the dogs snuggled close against her hips as if guarding her heart.

"What happened, child?" Clementine asked gently. "Everyone said you were feeling better."

Rose's chest heaved before she forced the words out.

"I heard Marshal Jones and Uncle John talking. Marshal Moore... got engaged." She lowered her gaze, shoulders curling inward. The two older women shared a quiet, knowing look.

"Oh, Rose," Lizzie breathed, her voice breaking.

"When I heard... I realized he's not coming back." Rose's voice wavered. "Deep inside, I kept hoping he might return someday. That maybe... maybe he might even marry me. You know... if things didn't work out here."

Lizzie frowned softly. "What do you mean, sweetheart?"

Rose twisted her fingers in the blanket.

"I know you love me, but... what if something happens, and you don't want me here anymore? What if you died, Aunt Lizzie, and Uncle John couldn't bear it? And I reminded him too much of you? It's happened before. It could happen again."

Lizzie gasped. "Oh, Rose... your uncle is not like your father. Not even a little." Her voice softened, thick with emotion. "Your uncle has always been a loving, devoted husband and father. He doesn't run from pain. He meets it head-on. And I'm the same. Your father... he was very different." She paused, gathering herself.

"Edward was always reserved, serious, used to having others handle things for him. Your grandparents catered to him his whole life. He was an excellent doctor, but he leaned heavily on his family and servants for everything else." She touched Rose's hand tenderly.

"Your mother was perfect for him. She made him laugh. She softened him. She gave him joy. When she died... the world he depended on shattered. He couldn't cope with the grief. Your uncle and I begged him to move to Colorado so he wouldn't drown in loneliness. But he refused."

Clementine nodded gently. "Your father left you in kind, capable hands, dear."

Rose swallowed. "After my mother died, he was so lost he nearly sent me to a boarding school for girls. He already had it arranged. But the butler and servants begged him not to. I was so young." She looked at Lizzie. "He listened, finally, and hired my governess instead."

"And that's why you're afraid we might send you away?" Lizzie asked softly.

Rose nodded again, small, fearful.

"If even my father thought about it... then it's not impossible you and Uncle John might think about it too. I'm only your niece."

Lizzie's eyes shone with fierce, maternal love.

"*Only* our niece? Oh, Rose..." She gathered her into her arms, voice breaking. "...you are so much more to us than that."

The three talked for a long while before Lizzie and Clementine finally left Rose to freshen up and gather herself. When they returned to the sitting room two hours later, everyone downstairs was visibly on edge. Clementine caught her granddaughter's eye and smiled.

"Jen, off you go."

Jennifer hurried upstairs to check on Rose. John leaned forward the moment the two women sat at the table.

"How is she?" he asked anxiously.

"She should be able to join us for supper tonight," Clementine replied.

A wave of relieved sighs swept through the room. Lizzie gently shared what Rose had confided, grateful that Rose had given her permission.

"*Just* a niece?" John echoed softly, shock flickering across his features. "She was never just a niece to us."

"That's exactly what I told her," Lizzie said, her voice trembling. "She *wants* to trust us, but the fear runs very deep."

"That poor girl," John murmured. "I had no idea she'd been carrying that burden." He looked at Clementine. "How do we help her move past something like that?"

"Right now," the older woman said kindly, "her heart is convinced she's an orphan. You must show her—more than ever—that she truly belongs to this family. She needs to *feel* safe... not just be told she is. And she needs to laugh again." Clementine folded her hands gracefully in her lap.

"She never grew up with real playfulness. All she's known is responsibility, seriousness, and grief. She told us the teasing and warmth she's found here, it makes her feel alive. Her father was always solemn, and even her friend Andrew didn't joke much. Her servants teased her lovingly, yes, but that isn't the same. She needs friends her own age. She needs joy that belongs to *her*."

Jordan grinned broadly. "Well, that part won't be a problem, right, Pa? Rose can be feisty. She used to jump into our games every chance she got."

John chuckled. "She takes after her mother more than she realizes. Lily could make Edward laugh even on his worst days. She was mischievous in the best ways, exactly what my brother needed." He leaned back, a nostalgic smile lighting his face.

"Once, I challenged Edward to race me while carrying Lily. He refused, too stiff and proper, but she teased him mercilessly until he agreed. He tossed her over his shoulder, I hoisted Lizzie over mine, and we ran across the lawn like a pair of lunatics. Rose was watching, maybe three or four years old. Her eyes were huge, and then she burst into the most joyful laughter."

Lizzie laughed softly. "I remember that. The moment Lily was back on her feet, Rose ran straight to Edward shouting, 'Me next, Daddy!' And of course he couldn't deny her. He challenged you to another race, grabbed her, and you grabbed Jordan. Lily laughed so hard she had tears streaming down her face."

Warm smiles filled the room. Jonas elbowed John, eyes twinkling.

"Well," he said, "what do you think, John? Shall we remind Rose of those days by racing with our wives now?"

Cornelia flushed. Lizzie quickly shook her head.

"Oh no. John couldn't do that anymore. He wouldn't be able to lift me."

"You wanna bet?" John shot back, and before Lizzie could protest, he swept her up and slung her over his shoulder. Lizzie shrieked, pounding lightly on his back while everyone roared with laughter.

Cornelia pointed a stern finger at Jonas. "Don't you dare!"

But Jonas dared. He lifted his wife over his shoulder with the same ridiculous determination, and Grant, Jordan, and Clementine burst into laughter.

"We should race with our wives," Jonas announced, "and then grab Jen and Rose after! What do you say?"

"I say absolutely," John replied, grinning like a boy half his age.

As if summoned by fate, Jennifer and Rose appeared at the bottom of the stairs at that exact moment. Both froze, wide-eyed, as the men marched toward the front door with their squirming wives slung over their shoulders.

"Dad, why is Mom over your shoulder?" Jennifer demanded.

"I challenged John to a race," Jonas said proudly. Jennifer blinked, then grinned.

"Come on, Rose. Let's go watch. Not every day the old men decide to act like schoolboys."

"Old men?" Jonas gasped dramatically, earning more laughter.

Everyone hurried outside. With much cheering, dramatic groaning, and two protesting wives, the men took off running toward the lake—legs pumping, laughter echoing across the yard.

Rose watched with wide, startled eyes. The laughter, bright, carefree, unrestrained, rippled through the autumn air like something alive. A faint tug of recognition pulled at her heart, like a forgotten melody drifting back into reach, but she couldn't quite place it.

She felt eyes on her, Grant's warm gaze, Jordan's amused smirk, even Marshal Jones's quiet smile, and heat rushed up her neck. She barely had time to process any of it before movement blurred beside her.

Suddenly strong arms wrapped around her waist. She gasped as her uncle swept her clean off her feet and tossed her over his shoulder as though she weighed nothing.

"Uncle John! Put me down!" she cried, kicking lightly in protest.

"No chance," he said, voice bubbling with mischief. "Jonas beat me last time, and I *will not* end this day a loser. I'm getting my rematch!"

Beside them, Jonas had scooped Jennifer up again, to his daughter's shrieking delight.

"Dad! If you drop me—!"

"You'll bounce. Probably," Jonas teased. Cornelia gasped in outrage. Jordan nearly fell over laughing.

The men lined up again, two grown, respectable adults transformed into competitive boys. With a shared nod, they bolted forward.

John's strides were long and determined, and Rose felt the rhythm of each pounding step. Despite her shock, something warm and fragile flickered in her chest, something she hadn't felt in weeks. Joy. Jennifer's laughter rang like bells. Rose didn't laugh, not yet, but something inside her loosened. Between the pounding footsteps, the cheering, the silliness... her empty heart stirred. A memory bloomed. A sunlit lawn. Her mother's laughter, bright, musical, unrestrained. Her father carrying her mother exactly like this while Uncle John ran beside them. Her tiny self, racing after them shouting, "Me next, Daddy!"

Warmth flooded her chest, melting something brittle and fragile inside her. When Uncle John finally slowed to a victorious halt, he set her gently on her feet. Rose swayed, overwhelmed, not from being carried, but from the wave of emotion washing through her.

Her uncle grinned, breathless.

"Told you I'd win."

Rose stared up at him, her throat tightening, her eyes burning, but not with grief this time. With something softer. Something healing. She understood now. It wasn't playfulness. It wasn't foolishness. It was love, joyful, ridiculous, unreserved family love.

Something she'd had once... and something she had again.

"Father did that with Mom and me, didn't he?" Rose whispered, her voice barely steady. Uncle John's expression softened.

"Yes," he said gently. "I'm glad it helped you remember. Your mother teased your father until he gave in to my challenge, and he could never resist your big smile. He adored finding any excuse to make you laugh."

Aunt Lizzie rubbed her arms as a breeze rolled across the yard.

"All right, you men. You've had your fun. Let's get inside before we all catch our deaths." She cast her husband a look equal parts gratitude and exasperation before heading toward the door.

Rose and Jennifer exchanged breathless smiles and followed, until two tall figures blocked their path.

"What now?" Jennifer demanded, narrowing her eyes at her brother. Grant didn't answer. With a wicked grin, he scooped Jennifer clean off her feet and slung her over his shoulder.

"Grant Adams!" she squealed, pounding his back. "What is wrong with all of you today?"

Grant only laughed, securing his hold as she squirmed. Rose barely processed the chaos before Jordan moved toward her, grin far too confident.

"No," she said, backing up quickly. "Absolutely not. Stay away from me, Jordan." She bolted, skirts flying, but she made it only three steps before Jordan wrapped an arm around her waist and hoisted her over his shoulder.

"Jordan!" she gasped, half outraged, half breathless. "Put me down!"

"Nope," he said cheerfully, already jogging after Grant. "Grant and I have a race to win."

Grant shot ahead with Jennifer shrieking indignantly. Jordan followed, laughing, and Rose bounced helplessly in his hold, caught between embarrassment and a flutter of startling, unexpected joy. Behind them, the older family members cheered so hard that Uncle John had to lean on Jonas just to stay upright.

For the first time in weeks, maybe months, the cold ache inside Rose's chest loosened. Her heart, once bruised and hollow, felt... full. Full of voices, laughter, warmth. Full of love that wrapped around her as securely as the crisp mountain air.

As Jordan carried her back toward the house, a quiet realization settled over her. She had been carried by grief for so long. But now, finally, she was being carried by family. And it felt like hope.

Jennifer slapped her brother's arm when Jordan and Grant finally set the girls down, though the gesture was more playful than scolding.

"I cannot believe you two did that," she huffed, though her eyes sparkled. "Truly, something is not right with any of you today."

Grant only grinned, brushing dust from his shirt as though tossing girls over his shoulder were a normal afternoon chore.

"Perfectly right, if you ask me. It's been a long time since this family had a good laugh."

Jordan crossed his arms smugly. "Besides, you should thank us. Consider it practice, for when you have children of your own. They won't always walk willingly."

Jennifer scoffed and swatted at him again, earning a dramatic yelp.

"Oh please. If my future children inherit your stubbornness, I'll need divine intervention."

Everyone burst into laughter, including Rose. She hadn't meant to laugh. The sound slipped out soft at first, then warm, then full. She covered her mouth, startled to discover joy still lived inside her.

Grant noticed. His smile gentled, full of relief and something like pride. Then he let the moment be, turning back to the teasing uproar around them. Jennifer looped her arm through Rose's and dragged her toward the house, muttering about 'wild mountain men.' Laughter followed them like a blessing, thawing a corner of Rose's heart she thought might never feel warm again.

In the weeks that followed, the two families spent more and more time together. Jennifer and Rose visited one another nearly every day, sometimes for errands, sometimes just to walk or sit beneath the trees by the lake.

Rose fought hard against the shadows still clinging to her heart. She tried to follow Nana's advice, one day at a time, one step at a time, even when those steps felt unbearably heavy.

Nana had urged her to make small goals each day. It felt silly at first, but Rose quickly realized how grounding it was. The goals kept her moving, kept her from sinking too deeply into the quiet ache of her thoughts. Her first goal was also the hardest: speak to Marshal Jones about Christopher.

She had barely spoken more than a few polite words to him since overhearing the conversation, but he was scheduled to leave at the end of the week. If she didn't talk to him now, she would carry the questions and resentment forever.

One crisp morning, she sat on the bench beside the lake, twisting a corner of her shawl as she rehearsed what she would say. Her resolve wavered with every thought.

I can do this, she told herself. *Just one conversation. One truth. One step.* She was about to rise when she saw Anthony Jones walking toward her. He slowed a few feet away, asking permission with his eyes. She gave a small nod.

"Marshal Jones," she said quietly. "I'm glad you're here. I... I was about to come find you."

He sat beside her, leaving space out of respect.

"What's on your mind, Rose?"

She inhaled deeply. "Why did you do what you did? Why did you interfere?"

He let out a long, weary sigh and rubbed his jaw.

"I didn't feel I had a choice. Moore broke several rules, and not small ones. I tried talking to him, but he wouldn't listen. At first, I thought it was harmless affection. But when he let it go further..." He shook his head. "I couldn't stand by and watch him risk his career. And I didn't want either of you hurt."

"Hurt?" Rose echoed softly. "It seems like everyone keeps deciding that for me. Why does everyone think I can't make my own choices? I'm not a child."

"No," he said gently. "You're not. But you're still young, and you'd already endured more loss than most girls your age. Pain like that leaves wounds we can't always see." His voice softened further.

"After all you'd been through, none of us wanted to watch you walk into a situation that could shatter you all over again."

She swallowed hard. "But death can take people no matter what we do. No job or distance can guarantee safety. No one can promise that the person we love will grow old with us."

"No," he agreed quietly. "But the risk is far greater for a marshal than for most. This job demands everything, your time, your loyalty, your safety. Families suffer. Wives suffer. Mothers and children suffer. The fear never leaves them. I didn't want that for you. Not again." The apology in his expression was unmistakable.

"I know you're angry," he said. "But I hope, one day, you'll forgive me."

Rose looked down at her hands, clasped tightly in her lap. The ache was still there, but so was the slow healing she'd been fighting for.

"I *have* forgiven you," she whispered. "I don't like what happened, and part of me wishes everything had gone differently... but if Christopher and I had truly been meant for each other, nothing you, or anyone else did, could have stopped it." She took a shaky breath. "I suppose God has different plans for us. And maybe... maybe that has to be enough."

Anthony bowed his head, relief softening the tension in his shoulders.

"You're a remarkable young woman, Rose. Stronger than you know."

She gave him a small, trembling smile. "I'm trying."

"And that," he said, rising, "is more than enough for now."

After Marshal Jones left Idaho Springs, Rose poured her energy into building her friendships with Ahanu, Calian, Jennifer, and Grant. Jordan often joined them as well. Their companionship became a balm to her aching heart, and though the wound was still tender, the sharpness of her grief slowly began to dull.

She cherished every hour spent riding or walking with Ahanu and Calian, who taught her Cheyenne stories, traditions, and the meaning behind small details she had never noticed before. Jennifer often swept her away for 'girl-time'—cooking, sewing, exploring the woods, or sitting by the river sharing secrets.

Rose had never known female companionship like this. In Boston, her 'friends' had been polite acquaintances, and the servants, though kind, could only fill the void so much. Here, laughter came more easily. Here, she was learning what it meant to belong.

Not every girl in town welcomed her, however. Rose tried to be friendly and approachable, but most of the young women her age grew cool or guarded the moment they realized she spent time with Jennifer and Grant Adams. Jealousy flickered in their eyes, so she kept her distance. She didn't want conflict, especially not now.

Unfortunately, one young woman seemed determined to be near them whenever she could. Tara Philipps, beautiful, outspoken, and notorious for pursuing the most desirable young men in town, had her sights set squarely on Grant. Everyone knew it, including Jennifer, who could barely stand being in the same room as her. Rose always felt tense around Tara, never sure when the girl's temper or envy might flare.

One brisk afternoon, Rose and Jordan were outside walking the dogs when Tara rode up on horseback. She didn't spare Rose a glance, her dazzling smile was fixed entirely on Jordan.

"Jordan, darling," she drawled, batting her lashes with practiced sweetness, "do you know when Jennifer and Grant will be coming into town next?"

Jordan folded his arms. "Rose and I are expecting them. They should be here soon."

Tara's smile snapped like a thread, her pretty features twisting sourly. She turned her glare on Rose, who bit the inside of her cheek to keep from laughing. Jennifer had once mimicked that exact expression in private, and seeing it in real time nearly broke Rose's composure. She quickly looked away, but Tara noticed.

"Are you smiling at my expense, Miss Williams?" Tara demanded, her voice sharp as glass. "If you're judging my riding, perhaps remember you've no business criticizing something you can't do yourself. Unless..." Her gaze swept Rose disdainfully. "You're mocking my riding habit? Not everyone grew up wealthy, you know."

Jordan stiffened beside her, jaw tightening. He drew breath to answer, but Rose lifted a hand, she could handle this.

"I wasn't smiling about your riding or your outfit, Miss Philipps," Rose said gently. "I was amused by something else."

"Oh?" Tara leaned forward, eyes glinting. "Then do share your amusement, since you claim it has nothing to do with me."

"I don't think I should," Rose said softly.

"So, it *was* about me," Tara snapped instantly, indignation flaring so quickly it startled even Rose. She looked ready to dismount and continue the argument on foot, until she caught sight of Grant and Jennifer approaching on horseback.

At once she straightened, lifted her chin, and fussed with the curls under her hat. Then she gave her horse a sharp, unnecessary slap. The startled animal bolted, and its flank slammed directly into Rose. Rose stumbled with a cry, losing her footing and hitting the ground hard. Tara shrieked dramatically as her horse galloped out of control.

Jennifer went pale. She spurred her horse into a full run toward her friend while Grant followed Tara with his eyes. Since the sheriff and Shane were already racing after Tara, Grant veered toward Rose.

"Rose, are you hurt?" Jordan was already kneeling beside her. Jennifer dropped to her knees moments later.

"I... I think so." Rose tried to sit up, but the world tilted. Pain throbbed at the back of her head. She pressed her hand to it, flinching.

"Good grief, Rose, you're bleeding," Jennifer whispered.

"Shane!" Jordan called urgently. "We need you over here!"

The young doctor turned at the sound of his name. Leaving the sheriff to handle Tara and her runaway horse, he rode over and knelt beside Rose.

19

Humorous
Interactions

"This needs stitches," Shane said calmly. "Rose, can you walk?"

"I think so." She tried to stand, but her knees buckled. Jordan and Shane both reached for her, but it was Grant who caught her—firm, steady, careful.

"I'm sorry," she whispered, embarrassed through the pain.

"There's absolutely nothing to apologize for," Grant said softly. His warm, reassuring tone steadied her.

"This wasn't your fault," Shane added. "Your body's reacting to the shock. Grant, take her to the clinic. I'll follow right behind you."

As Grant lifted her fully into his arms, Rose glimpsed Tara returning with the sheriff. Tara's face was flushed, not with worry, but with indignation. She wasn't looking at Rose at all. Her eyes were locked on Grant, with fury, with jealousy, and something inside Rose twisted. Had Tara done this... on purpose?

"Don't forget what Shane told you," Aunt Lizzie reminded once they'd settled Rose on the sofa with pillows and blankets. "No physical activity for several days."

"That could have ended so much worse," Uncle John said gravely. "How did this even happen?"

"I don't think that was an accident," Jennifer said, certainty tightening her voice.

"What do you mean?" Uncle John asked, concern sharpening his tone.

"Tara Philipps is an experienced horsewoman. Very experienced. She *knows* how to control her mount. A sudden lunge like that doesn't just happen, not unless she let it." Jennifer folded her arms, her expression grim.

Aunt Lizzie pressed her hand to her chest.

"Jennifer... are you saying she did that on purpose?"

"I think so."

"Those are hard accusations, Jen," Grant said, though the frown tightening his face showed he wasn't dismissing the idea. "Why would Tara do something so dangerous and foolish?"

"I believe jealousy is the problem," Jennifer said without hesitation.

"Jealousy?" Grant blinked, baffled.

"Yes, brother dear," she said pointedly. "Ever since you invited her to the town dance after Rose arrived, she's been trying to secure you for herself. She's practically been throwing herself at you, showing up everywhere you are, batting eyelashes, making sure no other girl gets too close."

"That's ridiculous," Grant muttered, but the discomfort in his eyes betrayed him.

"Maybe not," Jordan added, leaning against the wall. "It's been obvious Tara is interested in you. Very obvious. And I'm not the only one who's noticed."

Grant looked between them, stunned.

"But would a girl really go that far?"

Silence settled. Rose watched quietly, her head aching, her body exhausted, but her mind sharp enough to catch the undercurrent.

Jennifer sighed. "I don't think Tara *meant* for Rose to be injured," she admitted reluctantly. "But she wanted Grant's attention. And she would have gotten it too, if the sheriff and Shane hadn't seen the whole thing and gone straight to help her." Her voice softened with weary exasperation.

"When that didn't work, she panicked. And Rose got caught in the middle."

Grant's jaw tightened. Jordan's frown deepened. Aunt Lizzie shook her head in disbelief. Uncle John muttered something that sounded suspiciously like a prayer for patience. Rose sat quietly through it all, piecing the truth together with a sinking heart. Tara's glare. The purposeful flick of her hand. The hard slap to her horse's flank. And the way she'd stared, not at Rose, but straight at Grant. It all made terrible, perfect sense.

When Rose's head injury had finally healed, she threw herself into her second goal with new determination. She visited Jennifer at the ranch one crisp autumn morning, and the two girls sat on the front porch, their skirts brushing the wooden planks as they talked.

"Nana suggested I make goals so I can distract myself," Rose said, twisting a loose thread at the edge of her shawl. "I want to buy a horse, but I need to learn how to ride first. Boston never gave me the opportunity, and now I feel as though I've been missing out my whole life. Could you teach me, Jen?"

Jennifer's eyes widened, and she laughed.

"I don't think I'd be a good teacher, not for a beginner. I can ride, but you need someone who can catch you if you slip." Her grin turned sly. "Grant could teach you."

Rose's cheeks flushed instantly, hot, burning, impossible to hide. Before she could argue, a familiar deep voice sounded right behind her, warm enough to melt her bones.

"What can I teach?"

Jennifer bit her lip to keep from laughing as Rose stiffened like a startled kitten. Grant stepped beside them, his presence large, steady, and much too close. His warm brown eyes flicked to Rose's blushing face before shifting to his sister.

"Rose wants to learn how to ride," Jennifer announced. "You can teach her, right?"

Grant's grin was nothing short of devastating.

"It would be my honor." He even winked at Rose, an unmistakably playful wink, before extending his arm toward her in an exaggerated gesture of gallantry. "Shall we begin at once, my lady?"

Jennifer burst into laughter. Rose wished she could sink through the porch boards and vanish.

Before she could recover, a sharp, sugary voice cut through the yard. Tara Philipps nearly tripped over her own skirts in her haste to reach them.

"But Grant, I thought you would assist my father and me to choose a horse today." She pouted up at him, batting her eyelashes dramatically. Rose's stomach tightened. The last thing she wanted was to be the reason Tara shot daggers at her every time she walked into town.

Jennifer's expression darkened. "Dad and your father are perfectly capable of helping you, Tara." She pointed toward the enclosure, where, indeed, their fathers were already choosing a horse together.

"I wasn't talking to you, Jennifer."

Grant rolled his eyes. "Sorry, Tara, but I never planned on helping you pick a horse. Our fathers arranged that, and they're handling it just fine. Now, if you'll excuse me, I have a new student."

Tara huffed, spun sharply, and stomped away. Her retreat made Rose uneasy.

"Perhaps you should help her," Rose whispered. "She... already doesn't like me."

Grant studied her, steady, warm, unbothered.

"That's not your problem. Tara gets away with everything because people let her. Jen's right, she needs to learn the world doesn't revolve around her."

Jennifer nodded firmly. "Tara wants attention. She throws fits to get it. Don't take her nonsense personally."

Grant offered his arm again. "Shall we?"

Jennifer smirked and rose. "I'll leave you two alone. Grant, don't let her fall." She fluttered her eyelashes dramatically and sauntered off.

"Traitor," Rose muttered. Jennifer only laughed harder. Grant looked thoroughly amused.

"Will you be using one of your uncle's horses?"

Rose shook her head. "No. I'd like to buy my own, if possible. Something gentle."

"Gentle ones, hmm?" He raised an eyebrow. "All right. Let's see what we can find."

He led her to a paddock of grazing horses. Autumn sunlight shimmered across their sleek coats. Rose climbed onto the fence rail and scanned the group until her eyes settled on a dark brown mare with soft, intelligent eyes.

She called softly, and to her delight, the mare approached and nudged her hand. Grant handed her an apple.

"Here. See if she likes you."

Rose offered it, smiling as the mare took it delicately between her lips. But before she could blink, another horse darted forward, ears pinned, and bit the mare hard. The startled mare kicked back and jumped sideways—straight into the fence. Rose lost her balance. She felt herself tipping, but strong hands caught her around the waist and steadied her instantly. Grant.

His hands were firm but gentle, fingers curled securely around her hips. Her breath caught, sharp, unsteady, completely involuntary. One heartbeat passed, then another, and Rose suddenly became acutely aware of every place his warm hands touched her.

"Thank you," she whispered, too embarrassed to meet his eyes.

"You're welcome," he murmured, his voice low behind her. "And sorry about that. Those two need to be separated." He guided her chosen mare into the next enclosure. Rose followed, still flustered, still trying not to think about how effortlessly he had caught her.

Grant retrieved a saddle, his movements practiced and confident. Rose watched him, her heart thudding in a way she did not want to analyze. There was a softness in the moment, something shifting, something new. Something she wasn't sure she was ready for... but could no longer pretend she didn't feel.

While Grant prepared the mare, Rose couldn't help watching him. She had always known he was handsome, but only now did she realize how strikingly *manly* he truly was. His broad shoulders shifted under his shirt as he tightened the straps, and the muscles in his arms flexed with each movement. Heat rushed up her neck. She ducked her head quickly.

My word, she thought. *Will my face ever not be red around him?*

Grant finished saddling the mare and opened the gate. But before Rose could step inside, Tara swept toward them again.

"What a beautiful animal," she exclaimed, running a hand along the mare's neck. "Father, I think I'd like this one instead. It's perfect for me."

As Mr. Philipps and Jonas joined them, Grant shook his head.

"Sorry, Tara, but Rose claimed this horse."

"She doesn't even know how to ride," Tara snapped, glaring at Rose. "An animal like this needs an experienced rider."

Mr. Philipps turned to Rose. "You wouldn't mind choosing another horse, would you?"

Rose stared at him, stunned. Her mouth went dry. And when she glanced at Tara, who wore a triumphant, vicious little smile, something inside Rose straightened. Her back lifted. Her heart steadied.

Before she could speak, Mr. Adams stepped forward.

"Oliver, I don't believe it's your or your daughter's place to decide what horse Rose should ride. Tara already chose hers."

Grant nodded. "Rose will do just fine. I'll teach her." He didn't look at Tara, only at Rose. And when she met his gaze, warmth flickered there, subtle but unmistakable. Encouraging. Protective. Rose faced Tara's father again.

"Actually, I do mind," she said, her voice firm. "This horse came to me when I called her. I believe I deserve the chance. Just because Tara has more experience doesn't mean I can't learn." She turned her gaze to Tara, lifting a brow.

"How odd that you only noticed this horse after you saw I wanted her. Is that a habit of yours? Wanting things that already belong to someone else?"

Tara gasped. Grant and Mr. Adams both turned away to hide their grins, and even Mr. Philipps allowed a reluctant smirk.

Mr. Adams cleared his throat loudly.

"Well, that settles it. Tara, if you're unhappy with your original choice, you may look at the other horses again."

Tara shook her head furiously and folded her arms, sulking. Her glower could have cut glass, but no one seemed concerned.

Grant turned back to Rose, all business, yet soft somehow, attentive.

"Come here," he said gently. "I'll show you how to mount."

Standing beside the mare, Rose suddenly felt very small. She lifted her foot into the stirrup and tried pulling herself up. The horse shifted, her skirts tangled, and she slipped back down. She tried again, but before she could fall, two strong hands caught her by the hips. With one smooth, effortless motion, Grant lifted her into the saddle. Her breath left her in a rush.

"I—I'm sorry," she whispered, face blazing.

"No need to be," Grant murmured with a warm smile. "It takes time to learn. I could've had you mount from the fence, but you won't always have one nearby." He stepped closer, resting a steadying hand on the mare's neck. "Ready?"

Rose nodded, though her heart was pounding so hard she felt sure he could hear it.

"All right. I'll walk her in a circle so you can get used to the movement. Don't be surprised, your backside might protest tonight. Your muscles have to adjust."

It felt strange at first, but soon Rose found herself smiling, gently patting the mare's neck as they moved. Grant's voice drifted up to her—low, warm, reassuring—correcting her posture, explaining each step with patient calm. She was just about to signal the mare to walk when the horse jolted violently. Grant lunged forward to calm her, but the mare reared. At that exact moment, Tara let out a theatrical scream and toppled dramatically to the ground. A riding crop flew through the air and landed near the mare's feet. The horse bucked, and Rose was thrown, straight into Grant's waiting arms.

Her breath caught. His arms wrapped around her, steady and certain.

"What—what happened?" she gasped.

"I don't know," he said, voice taut with concern as his eyes met hers. On the ground, Tara moaned like she'd shattered half her bones. Mr. Adams and Mr. Philipps rushed toward her. Jennifer and Jordan hurried after them.

Grant gently set Rose back on her feet but didn't step far, hovering protectively behind her.

"Tara, are you hurt? Can you stand?" her father asked, kneeling beside her.

"Tara is an all-right actress," Jennifer said dryly. "She's not hurt at all. She did it on purpose."

Mr. Philipps stared at her. Jonas stiffened and turned sharply.

"Jennifer Louise Adams, that is completely out of line. How dare you accuse an injured young woman—"

Jennifer scoffed.

"She's right, Mr. Adams," Jordan cut in. "Tara threw that rock, right there, at the horse's back leg and pretended to fall while tossing her crop. We saw everything."

Mr. Philipps' face turned scarlet. He snapped, "Tara. Open your eyes."

She obeyed, teary, trembling, a little too perfectly.

"Why would you do something like that?" he demanded.

Jennifer folded her arms. "Because she's jealous of Rose spending time with Grant. She wants him for herself."

"Buggy. Now," Mr. Philipps ordered. Tara scrambled to her feet and hurried away. He turned back to Rose and Grant and exhaled heavily. "I sincerely apologize. She won't trouble either of you again." With a curt nod to Jonas, he followed his daughter down the drive.

"Jennifer," Mr. Adams said once they were out of earshot, "that was rude. Why put her on the spot like that?"

Jennifer folded her arms. "What was I supposed to do, Dad? Pretend she wasn't playing her manipulative games? This was the second time she's tried to hurt Rose."

He frowned. "And how do you even know she's jealous?"

"It's painfully obvious," Jennifer replied without hesitation. "The moment Tara realized Grant spends more time with Rose than with her, she's been desperate to get his attention."

Jordan turned to Rose with concern. "Are you all right?"

Rose tried to steady her trembling legs. "I think so."

"It looks like she needs to sit," Mr. Adams murmured. "Perhaps we should fetch the doctor."

"No," Rose insisted quickly. "We don't need a doctor. I'm fi—" But the moment she stepped forward, her knees buckled. Strong arms caught her again before she hit the ground. Grant swept her up without hesitation, lifting her against his chest. Her face burned.

"No, Grant, please put me down. I can walk," she protested weakly.

He ignored the protest entirely.

"Your body's reacting to the shock. Give yourself a minute to breathe. I'll carry you to the porch, and Jennifer will bring water." His tone allowed no argument.

Jennifer darted toward the house, and Grant carried Rose across the yard. He set her gently into a chair, and the men stayed with her until Jennifer returned with a large glass of water.

As Rose drank, Jennifer leaned back with a dramatic sigh.

"You know," she said with a smirk, "even though Tara is a terrible, selfish woman, something good did come out of this."

Grant lifted a brow. "Oh? And what good would that be, Jen? If I hadn't been standing there, Rose could have been seriously hurt."

Jennifer grinned wickedly. "Exactly, but she *wasn't*. Because you caught her. In your strong arms. Like some hero from a dime novel. Honestly, Grant, do you have any idea how many girls in town would faint dead away just to be rescued like that?"

Grant stared at her flatly.

"You make no sense whatsoever. What's romantic about almost getting trampled?"

"Oh, for heaven's sake." Jennifer rolled her eyes. "The way you grabbed her, like she weighed nothing! If Tara had landed in your arms, she'd be telling the whole town by sundown."

Rose's cheeks ignited. She stared hard at the porch boards, wishing they would open and swallow her whole. Even worse, the memory of how she'd stared at Grant earlier, his shoulders, his arms, flashed painfully through her mind. She shot to her feet.

"I—I have to go."

"Whoa, hold on." Grant reached out, caught her hand, and gently drew her back. "You're not going anywhere." His voice lowered, steady, warm, and far too calming. "We were in the middle of a riding lesson. You took a fall, and the best thing you can do is get right back in the saddle."

"Grant, I'm too embarrassed—"

"You don't need to be," he said softly.

Rose kept her gaze down, but he lifted her chin with gentle fingers, guiding her eyes back to his. His brown eyes held warmth, reassurance... and something else she couldn't quite name.

"We're friends," he said. "Friends tease each other. Jen was being dramatic with all her romance talk. There are no girls staring at my shoulders or muscles."

"Oh yes, there are," Jennifer cut in smugly. "Plenty of them."

"Jennifer Adams," Grant warned, glaring, "you are one word away from being tossed in the water trough."

She only stuck her tongue out at him. Grant suddenly realized his hand was still beneath Rose's chin. He released her quickly and stepped back with a sheepish, yet undeniably charming, smile.

"All right," he said. "Shall we continue our lesson?"

Rose swallowed, her heart thudding as she nodded.

Grant and Rose continued their riding lessons every day for the next two weeks. Rose improved quickly, and she was practically glowing the morning Grant finally stepped back, folded his arms, and declared her capable enough to take her horse home. She had named the beautiful mare *Willow*, and she was already deeply attached to her.

Accompanying Mr. Adams and Grant to the bank felt strangely empowering. She didn't have access to her dowry, but her father had ensured she had personal funds, enough to live comfortably, enough to give generously when her heart urged her to. For the first time in a long while, she felt in control of her own future.

Inside the bank, arrangements were made to transfer the payment to Mr. Adams. Rose signed the purchase contract with steady hands, and when she turned to shake hands with the ranch owner, her radiant smile was impossible to miss. Grant exchanged a proud glance with his father, both men grinning as though *they* had accomplished something grand.

She owned a horse. *Her* horse. As they stepped onto the street, the late-afternoon sun stretching warm light across the town, Rose felt something unfurl inside her, something fierce and hopeful.

For the first time, she was grateful for the inheritance her father had left her. And with that gratitude came a new resolve: She would not let marriage, any marriage, strip away the freedom she had finally tasted. She would not give her life over simply because the world expected it. If she ever married, it would be to a man who respected her dreams, her independence, and the fire she had fought so hard to reclaim. No one would ever take that from her again.

20

Free to Choose Her Heart

One evening, just before the Williams family sat down to supper, a knock sounded at the door. Aunt Lizzie was still in the kitchen, and Uncle John sat in the sitting room reading the paper, so Rose set down the stack of dishes she had carried into the dining room and went to answer it.

At that exact moment, Jordan barreled down the stairs. Their eyes met, then both sprinted for the door. Rose reached for the knob first, but Jordan swept an arm around her waist, pulled her back, spun her around, and slung her over his shoulder like a sack of potatoes.

Rose shrieked with laughter. "That's not fair! Put me down, Jordan! You cheated. I reached the door first, which means I won!"

He ignored her and, with Rose still hanging helplessly over his shoulder, opened the door.

"Evening, Shane," he greeted casually. Heat shot straight into Rose's cheeks.

"What's all this?" the young doctor asked, amused.

"Jordan, put me down right now," she demanded, pounding lightly on his back.

"Oh, nothing much," Jordan said breezily. "Rose challenged me to a race and thought she could win. Clearly, that was wishful thinking."

"Ha! I *did* win," Rose protested. "You used your manly strength against me, completely unfair!"

"She's just a sore loser," Jordan announced, giving Shane a mischievous wink.

"Uncle John, I need your help!" Rose cried.

Her uncle appeared in the doorway, taking in the scene with a lift of his brows.

"What did you do now, Rose?"

"*Me?* I was just trying to open the door! Are you seriously taking his side?"

Aunt Lizzie joined them, shaking her head but smiling.

"Jordan, if you want supper tonight, you'd better put that girl down."

With exaggerated reluctance, Jordan lowered her to the floor. Rose stuck her tongue out at him.

"Welcome, Shane," John said, stepping forward to shake the doctor's hand. "I'm glad you could join us for supper."

Rose and Jordan exchanged a startled look just before Uncle John slipped an arm around her shoulders.

"Shane has asked if he may court you, Rose," he said gently. "I thought it best to invite him over first, so you two can get to know one another a little more, away from prying eyes."

Rose's entire face erupted with heat.

"Pa," Jordan objected, "don't you think you might've told Rose that ahead of time instead of announcing it at the door?"

Rose shot her cousin a grateful look. It was nice to know he'd defend her, even while tormenting her relentlessly.

"It's just supper, Jordan," John replied, trying to sound stern, though his eyes sparkled with amusement. "They're not getting married tonight."

"My word..." Rose gasped and wished the floor would swallow her whole.

"John," Aunt Lizzie muttered warningly.

"All right, all right," he said, raising his hands. "I'll behave. Let's eat."

They all sat around the table. Rose whispered a silent prayer of gratitude when Shane chose the seat across from her rather than beside her. Jordan took his usual place at her side, still wearing a grin that promised further torment. After saying grace, supper began, and John and Shane quickly fell into a lively discussion about medicine and recent happenings in town.

When everyone finished, they moved toward the sitting room. John and Shane entered first, but Jordan tugged Rose gently back in the hallway.

"So..." he whispered mischievously, "you and our handsome doctor, huh?"

She shoved his shoulder. "Keep your voice down!"

Jordan merely smirked. "Why? There's nobody here but us. Didn't you hear what Pa said? He wants to give you two some time alone."

Rose groaned.

In the sitting room, Shane patted the cushion beside him, and Rose sat down, smoothing her skirt. He talked easily about Boston, its streets, its theaters, his favorite bakeries, and Rose soon found herself relaxing. His gentleness put her at ease, even if the idea of courting still frightened her.

The evening passed quickly. As Shane prepared to leave, he turned to her with a hopeful smile.

"Rose... may I take you out to supper tomorrow evening?"

Rose glanced at her uncle. John gave a small nod. She swallowed, then nodded.

"Yes... I would like that."

Shane's smile warmed the room, and Rose felt a flutter in her chest, soft, tentative, and not painful like before. Maybe... just maybe... life was beginning to shift again.

As soon as the young doctor left, the family gathered in the sitting room. Rose gave her uncle a puzzled, slightly wounded look.

"Why didn't you tell me Shane wanted to court me?" she asked quietly. "And why didn't he ask me himself first?"

Uncle John folded his hands, leaning forward with tenderness and seriousness.

"You're still very young, Rose, and the last thing Shane wanted was to make you uncomfortable. He felt it proper to ask my permission before speaking to you openly."

Rose frowned slightly. "I don't think I like him *that* way. He's kind, and I enjoy talking to him, but I don't feel... anything romantic."

"That's all right," John said gently. "This isn't courting with marriage in mind, not yet. This is simply getting to know one another. What matters is that you learn what *you* want. That you set boundaries. That you learn what sort of man is, or isn't, right for your heart."

He squeezed her hand warmly.

"Shane is safe, respectful, steady. Your aunt and I want you to experience what it's like to be courted properly, without pressure, and with room to say no if you wish." His expression softened even more.

"And whether you realize it, you're beginning to draw attention from quite a few young men in town. We want you to feel capable of handling that, to speak your mind, to decline a suitor kindly, but firmly if needed."

Rose's expression gentled. "And if nothing changes with Shane?"

"Then you tell him," John said. "Gently. Honestly. You're not bound to him."

A warm swell of affection rose in her chest. She stood, leaned down, and pressed a soft kiss to his cheek.

"Thank you," she whispered, giving him a small, grateful smile that eased the last of her confusion.

Rose smiled as Sally and Lucy chased each other along the lake, their barking drifting across the cold November air like deep, echoing bells. The sound warmed her, even as her breath curled in faint white clouds before her. She pulled her shawl tighter around her shoulders.

Behind her came the sharp, familiar neigh of horses. She turned to find Grant and Jennifer riding toward her. Rose stood just as Grant swung off his horse with effortless grace. He reached up to help his sister down, his strong hands steadying Jennifer before she hopped lightly to the ground.

The two dogs bounded over, tails wagging wildly as they circled the newcomers in noisy enthusiasm. Jordan, crouched over a growing campfire, brushed wood shavings from his palms.

"Jordan," Jennifer said as she dismounted fully, "do you know when Paul will be home again?"

"Oh, you *miss* him," he teased, mischief dripping from every syllable. She nudged him sharply in the arm.

"Of course I do, silly. I love the man. So, when can we expect him?"

"Next weekend, I believe." Jordan smirked. "Don't worry, the old pastor retires at the end of the month. Once Paul takes over, you'll be married before you know it. Then you can turn into a good little pastor's wife."

"Ha-ha." She shot him a deadly glare, which only widened his grin.

Rose laughed softly. "I don't know how you do that, Jen. Being separated from him must get to you." Her voice gentled. "I think I finally understand what everyone tried to tell me about Marshal Moore. His occupation would have kept him gone for long stretches... and I would have been somewhere far from family." The words tasted bittersweet. She still missed him, the friendship, the warmth in his eyes, the feeling of being cherished, but the ache no longer consumed her every waking moment. She was beginning to understand that fate had spared her heart from an even deeper wound.

Almost timidly, her gaze drifted toward Grant. He was brushing down his horse, sleeves pushed up, the muscles in his forearms shifting with each practiced stroke. A cold wind swept across the lake, but warmth bloomed in her chest, sudden, fluttery, impossible to ignore. Then the butterflies came. A whole swarm of them, sharp, nervous, startling, burst to life in her stomach. She dropped her eyes at once, nearly stumbling over her own breath.

She had noticed Grant's handsomeness before, of course, but this... this was different. This made her pulse skip. Jennifer smirked knowingly. Rose willed her cheeks not to blush. She failed.

"It isn't easy," Jen finally responded, snapping Rose from her thoughts. "I miss Paul so much. But once he's officially the new pastor and we're married, we'll be together all the time."

"True, but that also means you'll move to Denver and away from here," Rose said, scrunching her nose. "I'll miss you."

"I'll miss you too. But both our parents live here, we'll visit often, I promise." Then, with a mischievous glint, "Besides, you still have Grant and your goofy cousin Jordan."

"Goofy cousin?" Jordan repeated with mock offense. He crossed his eyes and made a ridiculous face, drawing giggles from both girls. "In truth," he added smugly, "Rose has nothing to worry about. Shane is more than capable of keeping her company."

Rose felt heat flare across her cheeks, especially when she sensed Grant's startled gaze snap toward her.

"Jordan," she hissed under her breath, "you better watch what you're saying."

"You and Shane are *courting*?" Jennifer's eyebrows shot up. "He asked Uncle John for permission to court you?"

"He did," Rose admitted, trying to steady her voice, "but it isn't really courting, more like getting to know each other."

"Yes, getting to know one another," Jordan echoed, "which could very well end with a kiss."

Rose glared at him. "Don't you have something else to do? Shouldn't you be at the café admiring Mable Colton's granddaughter, Alice Baker?"

His neck instantly flushed pink. Jennifer and Grant burst into laughter.

"Fine, you got me there," Jordan conceded with a grin. "I mean, what can I say? She *is* beautiful."

"She is," Rose agreed softly.

"Is it just me," Grant asked, stepping toward the fire, "or is it freezing today?"

"It's not just you," Jennifer said, shivering dramatically. "I hate this type of cold."

Jordan leaned back on his hands. "Why don't you ladies go inside and get us something warm to drink?"

Rose and Jennifer turned slowly toward him.

"Excuse me?" Jennifer snapped. "Do we look like maids to you?"

"You *are* women, are you not?" Jordan replied with a perfectly straight face. "The kitchen is your natural territory."

Rose nearly choked trying not to laugh. She knew exactly what he was doing, poking Jennifer just to watch her explode.

"Why don't you get up and get it yourself?" she suggested sweetly.

Grant chuckled. "Careful, Jordan. Jen will claw your eyes out if you say one more word about where a woman's place is."

His sister's glare could have melted stone. Sensing imminent disaster, Rose grabbed Jennifer's hand and tugged her upward.

"Come with me," she whispered urgently.

Jennifer resisted. "Are you seriously going to serve them?"

Rose snuck a glance at the two men, who watched them with identical wolfish grins.

"Aunt Lizzie made tea earlier. Would that be agreeable, gentlemen?"

"Tea sounds good," both men said at once.

"Rose?" Jennifer hissed, baffled. Rose leaned close with a conspiratorial smile.

"Just come with me. I'll explain."

⤙

Jennifer huffed as they entered the house.

"Why didn't you give Jordan a piece of your mind?"

"Because he wasn't being serious. He loves pushing your buttons." Rose smirked. "But that doesn't mean we can't give him exactly what he asked for." She wiggled her eyebrows mischievously. Jennifer's indignation melted into a startled laugh.

In the kitchen, Rose poured the still-warm tea into two cups. Then, with a wicked glint, she reached, not for the sugar, but for the *salt*.

Jennifer slapped a hand over her mouth, stifling laughter, as Rose added two heaping spoonfuls of salt into each cup before topping it with a splash of milk.

"We can sip real tea afterward," Rose whispered, downright impish.

By the time they returned, their expressions were perfectly angelic. Jordan and Grant accepted the cups with mild suspicion, but the moment they took generous sips, identical sputtering eruptions followed. Both spat out their mouthfuls in synchronized sprays, choking and coughing violently.

Jennifer shrieked with laughter and bolted. Jordan shot to his feet and tore after her.

Rose managed, barely, to keep a straight face as Grant continued coughing beside her. She widened her eyes innocently.

"Oh dear... is something wrong? I didn't grow up doing kitchen work. We had servants, you know..." She clasped her hands sweetly. "I only wanted to add an extra bit of love to my aunt's tea."

Grant's glare sharpened, narrowing on her like a hawk spotting prey. She lost the battle against laughter and darted away. Grant recovered in half a heartbeat and chased her. Rose was nearly to the house when a warm, calloused hand caught hers. Grant tugged gently but firmly, spinning her toward him. She stumbled into his chest, her hands bracing against him. His grip softened but didn't release her. She looked up—and instantly regretted it.

His brown eyes locked onto hers, warm, intense, far too close. Her breath caught. Heat shot through her as the world softened to a hush, the only sound her thundering heartbeat.

Grant's fingers loosened, sliding from her hand only to settle lightly at her waist, barely there, yet enough to send a shiver racing down her spine. His face dipped toward hers, slow, unthinking, drawn by a force neither of them seemed able to resist.

For one breathtaking moment, Rose forgot how to breathe. Then—panic. Her gaze dropped to the ground, breaking the spell. Grant blinked, stepping back as though waking from a dream. He instantly gave her space.

Her heart pounded painfully against her ribs. What had that been? Grant was her friend, her steady, warm, teasing friend. She couldn't risk another heartbreak. Not now. Not again.

"I—I have to go," she stammered, retreating. "I'm meeting Shane later." It wasn't much more than an excuse, and they both knew it, but she needed distance, she needed air.

Grant released her, though confusion and something deeper lingered in his eyes. Rose hurried into the house before he could speak.

* * *

Left alone in the yard, Grant ran a hand through his hair and exhaled hard.

"What was that?" he muttered. He prided himself on composure, on restraint. But one glance into her blue eyes and he had nearly... he shook his head. He had almost kissed her.

And heaven help him... a part of him wished he hadn't stopped.

As Rose brushed out her hair and pinned it into a simple but elegant style for her supper with Shane, her thoughts betrayed her, slipping back to Grant's warm hand closing around hers. Had she imagined it... or had they truly almost kissed?

Her stomach fluttered just remembering the way his eyes had locked onto hers, steady, sure, and far too intense for a simple friend. The butterflies swirling inside her answered the question well enough. But how could she feel that for Grant... when she had loved Christopher? Or... had she?

Rose sat on the edge of her bed, hands trembling slightly as she tied the ribbon of her gown. For the first time, she allowed herself to examine that painful, beautiful, confusing chapter with a clearer mind.

She had cared for Christopher. More than cared; she had adored him. He had made her feel safe at a time she'd been terrified and lost. He had protected her, made her feel seen, fought for her when she hadn't had the strength to fight for herself. He had awakened something in her, a warm blooming in her chest and a spark that made her feel alive. But... was that love? Or had it been the desperate grasp of a lonely heart clinging to the first man who had shown her gentleness?

Her breath caught. For the first time, she wondered if it had been infatuation, fierce, emotional, consuming... but perhaps not the deep, steady love she had believed it to be.

Her heart still ached when she thought of him. She missed him. She missed their friendship. She missed what she *thought* their future might have been. But the pain was different now. Less sharp. Less like the world had ended. And then... there was Grant.

Her face warmed as her thoughts wandered, uninvited, back to him. The memory of his arms around her as he'd caught her falling from Willow still made her pulse race. Her fingers tingled remembering the strength in his hands as he steadied her. And when she thought of how close he'd come to kissing her, how his breath had brushed her cheek before he pulled away, her own breath left her in a shaky rush.

For a moment, she wondered, what would it feel like... to kiss him? Immediately, her mind conjured the image of his solid shoulders, the warm rasp of his voice, the deep brown of his eyes when they softened, focused only on her...

Heat curled low in her stomach, surprising and terrifying.

"No," she whispered to herself, shaking her head. "Don't do this. Don't be foolish." She forced herself to stand, smoothing down her skirt with more force than necessary. He had told her plainly that he wanted to be her friend, only her friend, when he invited her to the dance. And Rose knew better than anyone what it felt like to fall for someone who did not love her back. She would not allow her heart to make that mistake again.

Taking one last steadying breath, she tied the final ribbon of her dress and reached for her shawl. Shane would be there soon. Supper with him would help keep her mind from wandering where it shouldn't. Still... as she stepped toward the stairs, her heart whispered what her mind rejected.

But what if he had wanted to kiss you? What then? Rose pressed a hand over her fluttering heart.

"I will not fall in love with a man who doesn't want me," she murmured. But her heart, traitorous, hopeful, confused, wasn't entirely convinced.

Rose enjoyed spending time with Shane. His upbringing, manners, and education made him one of the few people in Idaho Springs who could discuss the world beyond Colorado with ease, and their conversations often stretched for hours. He was handsome in a calm, refined way, and yet, no matter how hard she tried, there was no spark. No flutter. No breathless warmth. Only friendship.

One afternoon, as they rode together through the sparsely wooded hills, Shane guided them along a narrow trail she had never seen before. When they broke through a curtain of aspens into a secluded clearing, Rose gasped. A waterfall spilled over a rocky ledge, its mist catching the sunlight like drifting silver. Willow tossed her head, whickering eagerly as she stepped toward the water.

Shane dismounted first, then came to Rose and lifted her gently from the saddle. For a brief moment, she was held securely in his arms before he set her on her feet. When his hands slipped into hers, her breath caught, not with excitement, but with sudden worry.

Please... don't propose. Not here. Not like this.

He looked into her eyes, searching.

"What do you think about us, Rose? How do you feel our courtship is going?"

Her heart thumped uncomfortably. *Courting.* That word carried an expectation she knew she couldn't give.

"I'm... not sure what you mean," she said carefully. "What are you trying to find out?"

His smile was gentle, reassuring.

"I want to know how you see us. Whether you think of this as friendship... or something more. Can you imagine us as a married couple one day?"

"Shane—" she began, but he lifted a hand slightly.

"It's all right. Say exactly what's in your heart. Don't think about sparing my feelings."

She studied him for a moment. He deserved honesty—kind, respectful honesty.

"Truthfully?" she said quietly. "I like you very much. You're a wonderful friend, and I love our conversations. You understand things about Boston and the East that no one else here does. I enjoy every moment we spend together." She swallowed. "But there's no... romantic pull. No spark. My heart isn't involved."

Shane's shoulders relaxed, as though he had expected her answer, but needed to hear it aloud. A warm smile softened his features.

"Thank you for telling me," he said, giving her hands a light squeeze. "I feel the same way. You're a remarkable young woman, and I value you more than I can say, but we are better friends than anything else."

Relief washed through her. He hesitated only a moment before adding, "May I still call on you? As a friend? I'd hate to lose that."

Rose smiled, genuine and warm. "Of course. I'd like that very much."

Their hands fell apart naturally, and for the first time since the waterfall came into view, Rose felt entirely at ease, free in a way she hadn't expected. Free to be Rose, free to choose her future, free to let her heart heal... and perhaps, one day, free to let it love again.

Paul returned for the weekend, and Jennifer was absolutely over the moon. Their little group gathered by the lake as they always did, Grant, Jordan, Jennifer, Paul, Alice, and Rose, enjoying the crisp November air and the warmth of the campfire. Jordan had invited Alice Baker to join them, and Rose liked her immediately. Alice was soft-spoken and sweet, with a shy smile that surfaced whenever Jordan looked her way. It was obvious, even in the flicker of firelight, that she adored him.

Laughter drifted through the air as Grant tossed another log onto the fire. Rose felt content in what seemed like ages. The cold stung her cheeks, but friendship warmed everything else. Even the dogs curled happily at her feet.

Uncle John's familiar footsteps approached from behind, and Rose turned with an easy smile, one that froze when she saw there was someone with him.

Another man stepped into the circle of firelight. Tall. Broad-shouldered. Blond hair perfectly combed back. And when he lifted his chin, the flames revealed piercing green eyes, the same eyes she remembered from Boston society functions. The same eyes that had once followed her like a hunter tracking prey. Her blood ran cold.

No... no, it couldn't be.

"Rose," Uncle John said, unease threading his voice, "I have someone here to see you."

The man smiled, slow and self-assured.

"Mr. Foster," she whispered, horror creeping up her spine. "What are you doing here... in Colorado?"

He spread his arms as though greeting an adoring audience. "I've come for you, of course."

"For... for me?" Her voice cracked. "Why?"

"Oh, Rose." He stepped closer, and Grant instantly shifted, placing himself subtly between them. Bradley Foster pretended not to notice. "Surely your father told you he agreed to an engagement between us."

Her stomach twisted. The world tilted. She shook her head.

"My father died," she said firmly.

"I know," he replied lightly. "My condolences. Before he passed, he and I exchanged many letters. We were finalizing wedding plans when, tragically, he succumbed to his illness."

Rose's hands curled into fists. "Mr. Foster, I don't know what game you are playing, but—"

"Game?" His voice dripped honey. "My dear girl, I have pursued you since your debut into society."

"You pursued my dowry, not me," she snapped, anger finally breaking through her shock. He chuckled—actually chuckled.

"Ah, yes. The vicious tongues of society. They delight in painting me as some villain who chases wealth. Lies, of course.

Your father gave full consent to our engagement in his final letter."

Her breath caught. Falsehoods—every word stank of deception. Rose's gaze shot to her uncle. He cleared his throat and stepped forward.

"Mr. Foster," Uncle John said stiffly, "I made myself clear earlier. I will not consider anything without that letter from my brother. You claimed you left it at your hotel in Denver. Retrieve it, or there will be no further conversation."

Bradley dipped his head, unfazed. "Very well. I must return to Denver for business regardless. I shall fetch the letter and return within one week."

He reached for Rose's hand. She stepped back so sharply that Jordan and Paul moved behind her protectively.

"There is no need for you to return," she said, her voice finally steady, cold as the November wind. "I am not engaged to you. And I will never agree to marry you."

Something dark flickered in his eyes—irritation, maybe even hatred, but his smile remained eerily intact.

"As you wish... for now," he murmured. "Good evening, Rose."

Uncle John stepped in quickly. "Let me direct you to your hotel, Mr. Foster."

The two men disappeared into the dimming light, leaving Rose standing stiffly beside the fire, her heart pounding so hard it hurt. Paul immediately stepped to her side. Jennifer rushed to her other. Jordan glared toward the path Mr. Foster had taken.

But Rose hardly noticed any of them. All she could feel was the old familiar terror she had thought she'd left behind in

Boston. And the fire in her chest, rage, fear, and something far stronger... defiance.

Rose let out a breath she hadn't realized she'd been holding. She stood frozen where Foster had left her, her fists clenched at her sides and her heart pounding wildly. The night air suddenly felt too thin to breathe.

Grant, who had been standing close to her, turned so abruptly that several heads swiveled toward him. His jaw was tight, his expression unreadable, but his brown eyes were filled with something sharp and accusing.

"So *that's* why you and Shane ended your courtship so quickly." His voice was clipped, cold. "You knew your fiancé would come for you. Why didn't you tell us you were engaged?"

Rose's head snapped up. "I'm not engaged to that man," she said, her voice trembling with indignation. "I never was and I never will be. My father would never have agreed to any such thing. Bradley Foster may have taken an interest in me during my first Season, but my father shut him down immediately. Foster is twelve years older than I am and—"

"So Foster is the reason you needed protection on your way here?" Grant cut her off, his brows pulled tight. "You were trying to escape him because you were angry your father agreed to his proposal?" he demanded loudly.

Her stomach dropped. Uncle John and Mr. Foster had apparently doubled back, they were now standing a few yards away, both wearing taut expressions. Foster wore a triumphant, poisonous smile, drinking in every word of Grant's accusation like proof he'd been right all along.

A sickening heat washed over Rose. She couldn't believe Grant, her friend, the man she had trusted more than almost anyone these past weeks, would say such things. And in front of *him*. She waited until her uncle ushered Foster away and they were well out of earshot. Only then did she turn to Grant, her breath shaking, her blue eyes shining with hurt and disbelief.

"What is your problem?" she demanded, voice low but fierce. "You don't know that man. You know *nothing* about him. How could you take his word over mine?"

Grant stared at her, his jaw flexing.

"Because it all makes sense now," he snapped. "You never wanted to get married in the first place. What you want is your money. That's what this has been about all along."

Her eyes widened in horror.

He continued, bitterness dripping from every word, "You care only about the inheritance your father left you. Once you're of age, you'll be wealthy and free, and you've been playing all of us, so we'd feel sorry for you. The tears, the fear, the talk about being abandoned—" he scoffed, shaking his head, "you used those to soften your uncle. To soften *all* of us, didn't you?"

"Grant!" Jennifer shoved herself between them, her face blazing with fury. "What is wrong with you? Apologize. *Now.*"

He didn't even blink. "No." His gaze flicked back to Rose, cold, distant, full of wrongheaded certainty. "You can all believe whatever lies you want. But I won't."

The world tilted beneath her. She opened her mouth, but no words came, only a wounded breath. The ache in her chest tightened, sharp and unbearable, as if he'd reached inside her and torn something vital loose.

Without another word, Grant turned, mounted his horse, and disappeared into the darkness, leaving Rose standing in the firelight, stunned, humiliated, and more heartbroken than she had been since Christopher left.

Rose breathed through her teeth, fighting the tears burning at the corners of her eyes. Anger pulsed hot beneath her ribs, nearly overwhelming her. Jordan immediately wrapped his arms around her, holding her steady as her emotions threatened to spill over.

"Don't listen to Grant, Rose," Jennifer said, fury stiffening her voice. "I don't know what has gotten into him, but *we* believe you. Did anyone else get a horrible feeling when that man joined us? Because the feeling I got was pure evil."

Alice nodded, as did Paul and Jordan. Their collective agreement steadied Rose enough that her legs didn't give way. When she finally managed to sit, Paul gently slipped an arm around her shoulders, and she leaned into him, grateful for the comfort.

"You said something about a reputation," Alice asked quietly. "What kind of reputation?"

Rose drew a slow, shaking breath. "Bradley Foster is one of the worst dowry hunters in history. He has been married four times already. If I'm forced to marry him, I'll be wife number five."

Jordan's jaw dropped. "What? How is that even possible? What happened to his wives?"

"They all died," Rose said softly. "Every single one. Under suspicious circumstances. But he always manages to escape blame. He's a powerful attorney, wealthy, respected, connected, and he has access to some of the richest families on the East Coast."

She hesitated before adding, "His first wife died in childbirth. The baby died, too. His second wife supposedly fell ill shortly after the wedding and passed away within months. His third wife was kidnapped and later found dead in Virginia. His fourth wife died in a fire at her family's home in Washington. Everyone in the house perished except for the two men who set the fire, and they were conveniently shot while fleeing."

Jennifer's eyes flashed with fury. "So this monster loses wife after wife... and gains their fortunes?"

Rose nodded grimly.

Paul shook his head. "How has he not been arrested? Why would any father agree to marry his daughter to a man like that?"

"Because the press protects him," Rose replied bitterly. "Every article I've ever read paints him as a tragic widower cursed by fate. There's never enough proof to convict him. And three of his wives came from out of state. I think he changes identities and charms families who don't know his history." She paused, swallowing hard.

"I met his fourth wife, Cassandra, at a ball," she murmured. "I found her crying in the lavatory. At first, I thought it was because he was ogling every girl in the room... but when I asked if she was all right, she asked me to follow her." Rose shivered. "She took me to a private parlor and told me everything."

Paul and Jordan exchanged troubled glances.

"Cassandra said that from the moment she married him, he became violent. He forced her to be with him every night. If she refused, he beat her until she feared he'd kill her. She showed me bruises on her arms." Rose hugged herself. "She told me she knew he was pursuing me too, and she begged me to stay away from him."

"Oh, my goodness..." Jennifer whispered.

"She was planning to leave him," Rose continued. "She told her father everything, and he took her home to Washington while Foster was traveling. Her father refused to let Foster see her. Bradley threatened them, said they would all pay if they kept Cassandra from him."

"How do you know the details?" Jordan asked gently.

"Cassandra wrote me a letter," Rose said quietly. "She sent it the same day Foster came to Washington to take her back. She overheard everything from a hidden room beside her father's study and wanted me to know the truth. She asked a servant to mail it before anyone realized she'd written it." Rose swallowed hard. "But that same night, the fire broke out. Her entire family was killed."

Silence fell, a heavy, stunned silence.

"And Foster's house in Boston conveniently caught fire that same night," Rose added. "Enough to confuse investigators. The Boston *Codex* later claimed Cassandra's father had set the fire himself, and that the robbers who broke into Foster's home were unrelated. The press practically turned him into a tragic hero."

Paul rubbed her back gently. "Do you still have Cassandra's letter?"

"No." Rose's voice wavered. "I gave it to my father. He said he'd make sure it reached the right hands... but then he got sick, and he never had the chance. I never saw it again."

Jennifer closed her eyes in disbelief.

"All of that... and now this man claims you're engaged to him?"

Tears gathered in Rose's eyes. "I'm terrified. What if Uncle John doesn't believe me? What if Foster finds a loophole to drag me back East?"

Paul immediately pulled her into a steady embrace.

"Don't worry, Rose. We'll talk to Pa. He would never agree to anything that endangers you."

Jordan nodded fiercely. "And maybe—just maybe—that snake won't return at all once he realizes there's no hope."

Rose nodded, but her hands trembled as she wiped her tears. It was the first time she had spoken the full truth aloud, and now that she had, the weight of it felt heavier than ever. But at least she wasn't carrying it alone anymore.

21

Daughters Are Not
Debts to Be Paid

The following days slipped by quickly, though for Rose each one felt heavier than the last. She had no idea what Paul and Jordan had discussed with her uncle behind closed doors, but she trusted them. She had to. Even so, the unspoken topic hung over the household like a storm cloud, growing darker with every passing day. And with it, her anxiety grew.

She avoided Grant entirely. If she spotted him in town, or saw him riding beside Jennifer and Jordan, she turned the other way. She couldn't bear the memory of his accusations, the disbelief in his eyes, or the sting of his words. Her pride and her heart still throbbed from the blow.

Instead, she kept to herself or rode with Shane whenever he was free. His calm, steady presence made it easier to breathe, even if her heart was somewhere else, somewhere it had no business being.

One afternoon, while riding Willow along a quiet ridge, Rose spotted two riders approaching from the opposite direction. For a fleeting moment she thought of retreating into the trees, but it was too late. They had already seen her.

Mr. Adams reached her first. Grant stayed several lengths behind him, his posture rigid, his gaze unreadable.

"Rose, what a pleasure to see you," Mr. Adams greeted warmly. "We're on our way to meet with your uncle. It's been too long since you last visited the ranch. My mother keeps asking about you, she misses you terribly."

Rose's throat tightened. She missed Nana too, her gentle wisdom, her warm laughter, but the thought of stepping foot on that ranch with Grant there...

She kept her eyes fixed on Mr. Adams's reins.

"Please tell her I send my regards," she murmured.

"Why don't you come by sometime this week?" he encouraged, hope softening his features. Rose shook her head, blinking rapidly as tears gathered.

"I... I can't."

Before she could pull away, Mr. Adams dismounted with surprising agility and stepped beside her. With a tender firmness, he lifted her gently from Willow's back and drew her into a fatherly embrace. Behind them, Grant's voice cut through the air, clipped and distant.

"I'll meet you in town, Dad." He turned his horse and rode away, never once looking back.

Only when Grant's figure disappeared over the rise did Mr. Adams tilt Rose's chin upward. The moment her eyes met his, the dam broke. Tears streamed freely, and he pulled her close again, holding her the way a loving father would.

"My dear girl," he soothed. "What's wrong?"

Rose forced herself to step back, brushing her cheeks with trembling fingers.

"I just... I don't feel like myself at present." Her voice cracked, but she tried to offer him a grateful smile. "Thank you for your kindness. Truly."

He squeezed her shoulders gently before helping her remount, Willow.

"Anytime, Rose. You're family, whether you realize it or not."

She watched him ride away, her heart aching in too many directions at once, fear of Bradley Foster, grief over the past, and longing for something she wasn't ready to name.

Rose wished she could talk to someone, anyone, about her fears and tangled emotions, but what could she possibly say?

I'm terrified of a man who wants to marry me because he's after my dowry and will kill me as soon as we wed. Or: *I can't come over because your son treated me horribly and betrayed our friendship?* No. She could never burden Mr. Adams with that.

She shook her head sharply, blinked back the sting in her eyes, and nudged Willow onward. She needed air, space, and the comfort of familiar faces. It had been too long since she'd visited her friends on the reservation. Maybe Ahanu's quiet humor or Calian's steady patience would soothe the storm raging inside her.

But when she reached the reservation half an hour later, an eerie stillness greeted her. No laughter drifted between the lodges. No children ran past. The air felt wrong, heavy, tense.

Rose's stomach tightened. She guided Willow toward the gate, but a soldier stepped directly into her path.

"Sorry, Miss Williams," he said, raising a hand. "You can't come in. We have a typhus outbreak and must keep it contained."

"No..." Rose's breath hitched. The blood drained from her face so fast she gripped the saddle horn to stay upright. Memories slammed into her. Her father's fevered skin before he was taken to the hospital, his fading breath, the helplessness. Not again. Please, not again.

The captain emerged from a nearby tent, his expression grim. She didn't wait.

"Are Ahanu and Calian all right?" She leaned toward him, voice cracking with desperation. "Please, I must see them. Please let me pass."

He walked toward her horse. "You can't go in there, Miss Williams."

"You don't understand," she whispered as tears spilled down her cheeks. "My father died of typhus. I never got to say goodbye. Please—please let me see them."

"I'm sorry. No one is allowed to enter or leave. Dr. Hunter is here assisting the sick. His nephew is in town securing supplies when needed."

"I don't care," she cried, trying to push Willow forward. "I *need* to see my friends!"

The soldiers caught Willow's bridle and held her firmly.

"Miss Williams," the captain said more sternly, though not unkindly, "your friends are very ill. They wouldn't even recognize you right now."

A roaring filled her ears, drowning out the world. Her vision tunneled. Darkness pressed at the edges, threatening to swallow her whole. She clenched her jaw, focusing on breathing until the ground steadied beneath her again. She was about to wheel Willow around when she spotted the elder Dr. Hunter exiting a tent.

"Dr. Hunter!" Her voice cracked. "Please—please let me inside. I need to see Ahanu and Calian."

He approached slowly, his lined face burdened with sorrow.

"I'm sorry, Rose. It's far too dangerous. We've already lost several people. You must stay away."

Her heart hammered painfully. "Then... then tell me how they're doing. Please. Just tell me."

Dr. Hunter hesitated, then exhaled softly and removed his spectacles.

"Ahanu is fighting, but..." His voice trailed off. "It's not looking good."

Rose's breath stilled.

"And Calian..." Dr. Hunter's throat worked. "Calian passed away earlier this afternoon."

The cry that burst from her was raw and devastating, echoing across the silent grounds. Willow shifted anxiously beneath her, but Rose barely felt it. The captain stepped closer, his voice gentle.

"Let me escort you home, Miss Williams."

Rose shook her head fiercely, wiping at her tears with trembling hands.

"No. I don't need you." She dug her heels into Willow's sides. The mare leapt forward, tearing down the path, carrying Rose away from the heartbreak behind her, though no matter how fast Willow ran, the grief stayed, clinging to her like a shadow.

Rose hardly remembered the ride back, only the cold wind stinging her cheeks and the roar of Willow's hooves against the frozen earth. When she rounded the bend and the parsonage came into view, Uncle John's porch came into focus. Mr. Adams and Grant stood with him, deep in conversation. All three turned at the frantic sound of hoofbeats.

Rose slid off Willow before the mare had even fully stopped. Her legs nearly buckled, but she forced herself forward, stumbling toward the lake. By the time she reached the bench, the sob inside her chest tore free, and she collapsed onto the wooden seat, trembling violently. The men rushed after her.

"Rose!" Uncle John called. "Rose, what happened?"

She shot to her feet and threw herself into his arms with such force he nearly staggered. Her fingers clutched desperately at the back of his coat.

"Calian died," she choked out, the words shattering her. "They have a typhus outbreak at the reservation, Ahanu is dying too, and they won't let me in. I can't see him, Uncle John, I can't—" Her sobbing dissolved into ragged, uncontrollable cries. Uncle John wrapped his arms around her and held her tightly against his chest while she shook.

"Oh, sweetheart..." His voice was thick, aching. "I'm so sorry. I'm so, so sorry."

Mr. Adams placed a trembling hand on her back, and even Grant, who had kept his distance for days, stood just behind her, his face pale and stricken.

When her sobs finally subsided into broken, uneven breaths, the men gently guided her back toward the house. She tried to walk, but her knees were weak, her vision swimming. Grief pressed in on her from all sides, suffocating, merciless.

Halfway across the yard, the familiar ringing sound filled her ears again, an overwhelming, rushing hum as though the world were collapsing inward. Rose blinked, trying to breathe, but darkness crawled in from the edges of her vision, swallowing the porch, the men beside her, the sky overhead.

"I... I can't—" she whispered. And then her legs gave way.

"Rose!" Uncle John caught her just as her body sagged, lifeless, into his arms. He swept her up at once, fear flashing across his features.

"Get the doctor," he ordered, voice hoarse. "Now."

Grant didn't hesitate. He tore off toward Willow, and Uncle John carried Rose, pale, unconscious, and still trembling, into the house.

When Rose next opened her eyes, a cool, damp cloth rested on her forehead, and Aunt Lizzie sat beside the sofa, her expression tight with worry.

"How are you feeling, sweetheart?" she asked softly.

Rose blinked, her vision still swimming a little. Behind her aunt, Uncle John, Mr. Adams, and Grant stepped into view. The moment her gaze met Grant's, she shut her eyes again. She had seen the concern on his face, genuine, startled concern, and it twisted something painful inside her. Why was he even here?

He had made it very clear what he thought of her. Was this sudden worry nothing more than an act for his father's and Uncle John's sake? None of it made sense, his accusations, his temper, the harshness she had never imagined he was capable of. For weeks he had been kind, attentive, and gentle. He had almost kissed her. At least it had certainly felt that way. And then Bradley Foster had arrived and everything in Grant had turned sharp and ugly. Had he only been pretending before? Was there a temper beneath the surface that she simply hadn't seen?

A sickening thought struck her, was he more like Grayson than anyone wanted to admit? A rush of gratitude filled her that a kiss never happened. She still felt drawn to him, even now, but her heart ached with wariness. Attraction meant nothing if a man could turn so cruel without warning.

"I think I'm all right now," she murmured without opening her eyes. "Just dizzy... and numb." She took a slow breath, but her voice trembled anyway. "I can't believe Calian is gone. He and Ahanu were some of my first friends here, and they made me feel welcome after..."

She stopped abruptly, swallowing hard as Grayson's outburst flickered through her mind. There was no reason to bring that up, especially not with Mr. Adams standing there, looking so worried. None of this was his fault.

"I mean," she corrected gently, "they were always there when I needed cheering up. After what happened with the colonel, they held that special ceremony for me." Tears welled again, blurring her vision. "Calian chose the name for me. Takoda was his idea."

Her throat tightened painfully. She turned her face toward the back of the sofa, unable to bear the weight of all those sympathetic eyes. Aunt Lizzie shifted closer and began stroking her back in slow, comforting circles as Rose fought the fresh wave of grief rising inside her. But she knew crying couldn't bring Calian back. Nothing could. And the thought made her feel utterly, devastatingly alone.

After examining Rose, Shane assured Aunt Lizzie that, aside from being severely shaken, she was physically unharmed. He prepared a mild dose of medicine to calm her nerves and help her sleep, then stepped aside to let John and the Adams men rejoin them. Lizzie tucked a blanket around Rose's shoulders and settled beside her, gently rubbing her arm.

"So, what's this business about a typhus outbreak at the Indian reservation?" John asked the moment he stepped back into the room. His voice was tight with worry. "Why wasn't the town informed?"

Shane let out a slow sigh. "According to the army, they believed they had it contained. The mayor didn't want people panicking unnecessarily."

Jonas Adams frowned deeply. "How is typhus even showing up out here? Nobody in these parts has had it, at least not that I've heard."

"They had a small outbreak at a fort near New Orleans," Shane explained. "A soldier was transferred to Idaho Springs before anyone realized he'd been exposed. By the time symptoms appeared, he'd already been in contact with people at the reservation."

A heavy silence fell over the room. John rubbed a hand over his face.

"What is the army doing to keep it contained?"

"They've separated the healthy from the sick," Shane said. "Clothes, blankets, and tents are burned after use. They're also burning the bodies of those who die."

John stared at him as if he hadn't heard correctly.

"Burning the bodies? Shane, the Cheyenne believe, a body must remain above ground so the spirit can pass on in peace. Burning it is... it's a violation of everything sacred to them."

Shane's expression softened. "I know. They don't approve. But the captain and my great-uncle have done their best to explain the danger. It's the only way to keep the disease from spreading any further."

John shook his head slowly, grief tightening his jaw.

"As if they haven't suffered enough. First, we take their land, then force them onto small patches of ground that are no good and tell them to live the way we want them to. And now, even in death, we take their traditions from them." His voice trembled at the edges, anger, sorrow, and shame mingling together.

"This country is enormous," he continued softly. "There was room enough for everyone. They lived in peace on their own terms for generations. I will never understand why it was necessary to push them into corners, treat them like prisoners, and strip them of the life God gave them."

Lizzie reached for his hand, her eyes shining with quiet sympathy. Grant and his father stood silently, both clearly unsettled. The only sound was Rose's soft breathing as she drifted toward the sleep the medicine promised, her tear-stained cheeks still damp.

Outside, the wind rattled against the windows, a lonely, mournful sound, echoing the ache in every heart inside the room.

"I have had enough of the *Boston Codex* and men spreading lies and trying to take advantage of me," Rose snapped, the telegram trembling in her hands.

Uncle John, Aunt Lizzie, and Jordan looked up at her in surprise. They had all been quietly reading in the sitting room, and none of them had expected such an outburst.

"What's happened?" Uncle John asked.

Rose read the telegram aloud, her voice sharp with fury.

"Rose, the following announcement was published in the Boston Codex today. We thought you should know.

Mr. Bradley K. Foster is pleased to announce his engagement to Miss Rose Julianne Williams. Details about the upcoming wedding are forthcoming."

She lowered the slip of paper, shaking her head, in outrage.

"Who does he think he is? I am not engaged to him. I never was. He is a despicable human being and doesn't deserve another wife."

"We don't know that yet," John said cautiously. "Foster claims your father arranged everything with him, and if he returns with the letter, I'm not sure how much we can do."

Rose stared at him, stunned. "So, you will simply marry me off? You're my guardian."

"I am," he replied soberly, "but if he provides written proof that your father agreed to the match, the law will acknowledge his authority over mine. Foster could take us to court, and he would likely win."

"My father would never have agreed to such a thing," Rose hissed. "He despised that man. When I was introduced to society, Foster approached him immediately, begging permission to court me. I was sixteen, Uncle John, sixteen. His third wife had died mere weeks earlier, and he already had his eyes on me. My father was livid and sent him away in terms I do not dare repeat." Her voice shook with ice and fire.

"Besides... why are we, as women, not allowed to make our own decisions about marriage? We aren't livestock to be bargained over or handed off from one man to another. People were outraged at the reports of white slavery spreading across the country, but how is this any different?"

John blinked. "What do you mean?"

"I mean," she continued, pacing as her anger gathered strength, "that a father can treat his wife and daughter, like property. He may not force his daughter to share his bed, but if he alone decides who she must marry, how is that any different from a man selling a woman to a brothel, saloon, or wealthy brute? If a young woman has a dowry and her father chooses her husband, it's like saying, 'Here, take my daughter and some of my money. Do whatever you please with her.' Once a woman marries, her dowry is no longer hers. It becomes his. And in high society, men hunt dowries more eagerly than they hunt wives."

She gestured sharply, her eyes blazing.

"Who created this system? Who decided daughters were debts to be paid off? 'Oh, I only have daughters, so I must pay men a fortune to convince them to marry.' Perhaps it isn't this extreme in poorer communities, but in wealthy circles? It absolutely is. Men don't even need to be attracted to their wives. They will marry a girl who does not appeal to them at all, as long as she comes with money. Wealth and power turn men into scoundrels. They can take a plain wife for her fortune and purchase a pretty mistress for their pleasure."

Her voice dropped to a venomous whisper. "It is despicable."

When she finally stopped to breathe, she discovered the room had fallen silent. Her relatives stared at her as though she had grown wings, or flames.

"I need some air," Rose muttered, turning on her heel. Jordan immediately set down his book and followed her outside.

"Let's just wait and see," Jordan said gently, falling into step beside her as she strode across the yard. "Perhaps Foster won't come back for you."

Rose stopped and turned her face toward him, her expression a mixture of fear and fury.

"If he's already telling all of Boston that he has secured me, of course he'll come back." Her voice shook with restrained outrage. "Men like Bradley Foster don't give up easily. They tighten their grip."

Jordan opened his mouth as if to argue, then closed it again. He knew she was right.

"It doesn't matter," Rose continued, shaking her head firmly. "I won't marry him. I don't care what he wants, what my father supposedly decided, or whether Uncle John feels obligated by some letter Foster claims to have. None of it matters!" Her voice grew steadier and stronger. "I will never become his wife." She lifted her chin, her eyes bright with conviction.

"I would rather lose every penny of my dowry, every scrap of inheritance, every comfort I have, than bind myself to a man like him. I won't be bought, bullied, or bargained away."

Jordan's expression softened, pride flickering through his features.

"That's the Rose I know," he murmured, placing a reassuring hand on her shoulder. "And no matter what happens, I promise, you won't face him alone."

Rose exhaled slowly, letting the cold air cool her burning thoughts. Somewhere deep inside, a spark of courage steadied itself.

"I won't be afraid of him," she whispered, more to herself than to Jordan. "Not anymore."

A week before Jennifer Adam's and Paul's wedding, Uncle John called Rose downstairs. It had been nearly two weeks since Foster had left Idaho Springs, and she had finally begun to breathe again. Relax. Sleep. Believe that he might not return. She should have known better.

In front of his study door, Uncle John held out a folded letter. His face was grave.

"Mr. Foster has returned, Rose. And he has a letter from your father."

Her head swam. Tears stung her eyes.

"That can't be legitimate. Please, Uncle John... you can't do this to me."

He pulled her into his arms, his voice low and pained.

"I'm sorry. He insists on speaking with you alone. Just talk to him, tell him how you feel, and we'll go from there. Nothing is decided yet."

Rose wiped her eyes, steadied her breath, and stepped into the study.

Bradley Foster sat comfortably behind the desk as if it were his own home. He smiled, a slow, pleased, poisonous smile.

"Well," he said, "it looks like we'll be married sooner or later."

"Mr. Foster, I have already told you I will not marry you. Nothing has changed. Just because you have a letter, which you most likely forged, does *not* make us engaged. Your pathetic announcement it in the *Boston Codex,* changes nothing."

He chuckled softly. "That wasn't the first time the Codex printed something in my favor. You'd be amazed at what generous donations can buy. Why do you think you were targeted so viciously in Boston?"

Rose stiffened. "That was your doing?"

He rose from his chair, his smile sharpening.

"But of course. I intended to intimidate you... make you vulnerable enough that marrying me would seem like the natural solution. I admit, your new town proved inconvenient. And when I learned two journalists from Colorado Springs were poking their noses into matters concerning the Codex and you, I had to step back temporarily."

"You should have given up then," Rose snapped. "Because all your schemes have failed. I will *never* be your wife."

Before she could move, he seized her wrist, yanked her forward, and dragged her into his lap as he sat. Rose struggled, panic surging through her, but his grip was iron.

"You don't have a choice, sweet Rose," he murmured. "The law is on my side."

"Let me go!" She shoved, twisted, but he held her pinned. When his lips grazed her neck, she slapped him hard across the face, wrenched herself free, and scrambled several steps away.

"I will *always* have a choice," she said fiercely. "You will never own me. One day you'll pay for your arrogance, your greed, and your *murders*. I know you killed your wives."

He laughed and shoved her against the wall, his face inches from hers.

"You have no proof. Your uncle will marry us, and we'll return to Boston, together."

"No!" she cried. "I would rather die than go anywhere with you. I'll tell my uncle to give away my entire inheritance before any wedding can take place. You won't touch a cent of my dowry. Your greed is the only reason you want me."

He tsked, softly. "You poor, naïve girl. You truly don't understand the law. Women have little say in anything. If a marriage must be forced, then forced, it will be. You're not yet of age, you belong under a man's authority." His eyes gleamed. "And yes, I want your dowry. But I also want *you*. I look forward to · taming that fiery little spirit."

"Monster," she whispered. "One day someone will stop you. Someone will find the proof. Cassandra tried. She told me what you did. She showed me the bruises."

Something flickered across his face, brief, dangerous. Then his hands clamped around her wrists again.

"If you know all that, then I advise you to make a very wise choice... before your dear aunt, uncle, or cousin suffer unfortunate accidents. You wouldn't want to lose them, would you?"

Rose's stomach twisted, but she lifted her chin, refusing to shrink.

"Listen to me, Mr. Foster. A Williams does not bow to threats, they *fight* them. My uncle will never allow you to harm me. And if you so much as breathe wrong in our direction, the sheriff and every judge in this territory will know it was you. Cassandra's letter is safe. If something happens to me or my family, it will be used."

His jaw tightened. "I will not be blackmailed. And let me tell you a secret..." He pointed to a document on the table. "Your uncle already agreed to this marriage. He signed it. So even if you run or refuse, the law favors me. Nothing can protect you now."

Rose's breath vanished. Her uncle... signed it? He had given her away? Not fighting for her at all? Cold despair washed through her, but she refused to let Foster see it. Slowly, she straightened.

"You're wrong," she said, her voice steadying. "I am not unprotected. And I am *not* afraid of you."

"This piece of paper means and changes nothing," she continued, her voice sharpening like steel. "I will not marry you. You might as well kill me now, though we both know you won't. You want my money, and you can't touch a cent of it until we're wed." Fury, not fear, flared in her eyes. "This document is worthless, see?"

Before he could react, Rose shoved past him, snatched the document from the table, and flung it into the fireplace. The flames caught instantly, curling the edges and devouring the signatures with greedy hunger.

Foster lunged forward. "Your uncle will sign another one!" he snarled. But shock flickered across his face, brief but unmistakable. He recovered with a vicious glare, grabbed her face in both hands, and forced her back against the wall.

"You foolish girl," he hissed. "You think you can ruin my plans? I will tame you if it's the last thing I do." He tried to crush his mouth against hers.

Rose didn't think, she reacted. Her hand flew to the table, knocking over the vase. She seized it, ripped the flowers free, and threw the water into his face. Foster roared, momentarily blinded. Before he could regain his grip on reality, or her, she swung the porcelain jug with all her strength. It shattered against his temple with a sharp crack. Foster staggered, clutching his head.

Rose didn't wait. She bolted from the study, her heart pounding like a war drum, raced down the hallway, and fled up the stairs two at a time.

22

Flight Before the Truth

In her room, she slammed the door, locked it, and ran straight to her shelf. Her hands shook violently but worked quickly as she grabbed her saddlebags and stuffed them with clothing, her diary, her money, anything she might need. Panic clawed at her throat, but determination drove her. She would not be caged. She would not be bought. She would *not* be handed over.

When the bags were full, she pushed open her window. Cold air rushed in, carrying the faint sound of Foster's shouting downstairs. Without hesitation, she tossed her bags into the bushes below, swung a leg over the sill, grabbed the tree branch outside, and climbed.

Her skirt snagged once, nearly sending her off balance, but she steadied herself and continued downward until her boots hit the ground. Then she ran. Straight to the stable.

Inside, Willow lifted her head with a soft whinny, sensing Rose's terror.

"I know," Rose whispered, her voice breaking. "We have to go. Now." With frantic fingers, she saddled the mare in record time, not caring about perfect straps or tidy buckles, only what would keep her alive. She mounted, dug her heels in, and Willow surged forward.

Rose didn't look back, never once. She rode hard, her hair whipping behind her, every beat of Willow's hooves pounding the same vow into the earth: *No man owned her. No man ever would.* And if she had to run for a week, a month, or the rest of her life, she would. Because freedom, her freedom, was worth everything.

John Williams pushed himself into his study, only moments after Rose fled. The instant he saw Bradley Foster, disheveled, blood dripping from the gash on his head, rage flared in his eyes.

"Rose is right. You are a monster, Foster," he spat. "The game is over. You won't see the light of day ever again."

Foster blinked, stunned. Before he could reply, the side door of the study swung open. The sheriff entered with two deputies. A heartbeat later, the closet door creaked and Jordan Williams stepped out, fury blazing in his face. Jonas and Grant Adams followed through the side door, grim and silent. Two U.S. marshals came behind them, and then, to Foster's utter disbelief, the President of the United States himself, Chester A. Arthur.

"You're under arrest, Mr. Foster," one marshal said flatly. "Stand up."

"This is absurd!" Foster barked, scrambling to his feet. "What are you accusing me of?"

Jordan scoffed, the sound sharp as broken glass.

"I was in that closet the entire time, Foster. I heard every word you said to Rose. Every threat. Every lie." His hands shook with fury. "You trapped yourself."

Grant stepped forward, eyes burning.

"Playing the victim won't work anymore."

The marshal snapped the handcuffs around Foster's wrists.

"I believe you know exactly how long your list of crimes is," he said. "But since you insist on pretending, allow us to enlighten you."

Another marshal stepped ahead. "We've been monitoring you for a long time, Mr. Foster. Every time you left on your convenient 'business trips,' we searched your home, quietly, legally, and with cause."

Foster's face blanched.

"It wasn't until we received the last letter your wife sent Miss Williams," the marshal continued, "that we knew where to look. Under the carpet in your study, the one you believed no one would ever lift, we found a hidden door. And beneath it..." He paused just long enough for fear to flicker across Foster's eyes.

"...we found the evidence. Your wives' diaries. Letters you never allowed them to send. Personal belongings. Records of money transfers after each death. Everything they tried to hide from you, and everything you tried to hide from the world."

Bradley cursed under his breath. Cassandra had been far more cunning than he ever imagined. He should have burned those incriminating papers, but arrogance had clouded his judgment. He kept them all, believing they might one day serve as leverage to silence Rose or any future wife.

Now those hidden trophies had betrayed him. His gaze flicked to the uniformed men, then to the distinguished man whose presence suddenly made the room feel unbearably small.

"And why is *he* here?" Foster snapped, jerking his chin toward the President. Chester A. Arthur stepped forward, his expression carved in stone.

"Because this is personal," he said, voice low and dangerously steady. "And you will pay for it."

The air crackled. Foster's bravado wavered.

"You preyed on women with no power to protect themselves," Arthur continued. "You used the law to trap them. Money to silence them. Fear to control them. You thought no one would ever connect the dots." His voice hardened. "Unfortunately for you, someone finally did."

Bradley's breath caught.

"You've destroyed families across multiple states," Arthur said. "Including the daughter of one of my dearest friends." His gaze sharpened like a blade. "That alone makes this very personal to me."

Foster opened his mouth to argue, but the marshal shoved him toward the door.

"And rest assured," Arthur added, following him with measured steps, "you will not escape justice this time. Not with the evidence we have. Not with the testimony you so generously provided moments ago." His eyes gleamed with cold finality. "You will spend the remainder of your days behind bars... if you're fortunate."

Bradley Foster paled. For the first time in his carefully curated adult life, the indestructible façade cracked. And he finally understood: The game was no longer his to play.

Rose was near the reservation when she spotted movement between the trees. Her heart lurched with fear, until the figure stepped into the open. Ahanu.

She pulled Willow to a halt, dismounted before the mare had fully stopped, and ran straight into his arms. He staggered slightly, he was clearly not yet fully healed, but he wrapped his arms around her with a faint, warm smile.

"It is good to see you too, Takoda," he said softly.

Realizing what she'd done, Rose stepped back at once, cheeks flushing in embarrassment.

"I'm so sorry, Ahanu. I didn't mean to make you uncomfortable. I'm just—" Her voice broke. "I'm just so happy you're alive."

He lifted her chin gently, his touch steady and kind.

"I'm not uncomfortable, Rose. Truly. You only continue to amaze me. I don't think I will ever grow used to how freely you show your heart, to me, or to people like me."

"Why shouldn't I?" she whispered. "You and I are both human. Both friends. Skin, tradition, culture, none of that decides a person's worth. The heart does." Her eyes grew soft. "And you have one of the best hearts I've ever known."

Ahanu's expression warmed, then dimmed with quiet grief when she added, "I'm so sorry about Calian."

He nodded, pain flickering in his eyes before he mastered it.

"He is where God needs him now. And he would not want us drowning in sorrow." He studied her more closely. "So... where are you going in such a hurry? To the Adams' ranch?"

She shook her head. Tears welled. "No. I'm leaving."

"Leaving?" Alarm sharpened his voice. "Why?"

So, she told him—everything. The rumors. Foster's claim. The forged letter. Grant's cold accusation. Her uncle's supposed consent. Foster's threats. The horrifying certainty that her life was no longer safe or her own.

Ahanu's jaw tightened as she spoke. By the time she finished, his eyes were burning with protective fury.

"I thought I had finally found a real home," Rose whispered. "A real family. I should never have let my guard down. Maybe... maybe I don't deserve what I've been wishing for."

"Don't say that, Rose." Ahanu's voice was firm. "You deserve peace. You deserve love. And you deserve safety, more than most." He placed a steady hand on her shoulder. "This is not the end of your story. Everything will work out."

She glanced toward town, fear and heartbreak warring in her chest.

"I have to go before they start looking for me."

"Will you return?" he asked softly.

Rose swallowed. "I don't know. If they force me to marry Bradley Foster, it will only be a matter of time before he gets rid of me. And I will not... I will not die by his hand."

Her voice shook. "Farewell, Ahanu."

Before she could lose her resolve, she stepped forward and hugged him one last time, brief, tight, desperate. Then she mounted Willow, wiped her tears, and rode into the trees without looking back. Ahanu stood watching her disappear, a silent prayer forming on his lips.

"I think Rose is gone," Lizzie exclaimed breathlessly as she rushed down the stairs. John, Jordan, Jonas, and Grant all turned toward her at once, alarm tightening their faces. President Arthur stood just behind them, arms folded, watching with grave concern. The two marshals, the sheriff, and his deputies had already escorted Bradley Foster to the jailhouse.

"What do you mean gone?" John demanded. Lizzie pressed her hand to her chest, trying to steady her breathing.

"She's not in her room. Her window is wide open, and her closet and drawers look as though she pulled things out in a hurry. She took clothes... and anything else she thought she'd need."

John's stomach dropped. He glanced at the men gathered around him. He should have told Rose the truth—that this had all been a setup, a trap to catch Foster legally and publicly, but they'd agreed that the fewer who knew, the safer it would be. Now he wondered if they had miscalculated.

Before he could speak, Jordan bolted out the front door. Moments later he returned, breathless.

"Willow is gone too."

A heavy silence fell. Grant stepped forward first, jaw tight, eyes dark with determination.

"Then there's no time to waste. We need to split up and search for her."

Jordan nodded quickly. "I'll ride into town and get Shane. Maybe the sheriff or one of his remaining deputies can join us."

He didn't wait for a reply, he sprinted outside and leapt onto his horse.

Jonas turned to the president. "Chester, do you have time to come home with us? Cornelia would be delighted to see you again."

But President Arthur slowly shook his head.

"I'm afraid I must return to Denver at once. I was on my way to California when word reached me that Foster would be here today. I detoured only long enough to see the trap sprung, and to ensure justice could finally begin." His gaze fixed on John, firm but sympathetic. "I pray you find your niece quickly. She's endured far too much."

John swallowed hard and nodded. "We'll bring her home."

With that, everyone rushed into motion, mounting horses, gathering supplies, scattering into the cold November air, each man silently determined to find Rose before fear, danger, or desperation carried her somewhere she could not return from.

Rose knew darkness would fall soon, but she was only an hour from her destination. She silently thanked heaven, and Mrs. Colton, for the detailed directions the older woman had given her in her last letter. The Coltons had moved to the outskirts of Denver only a few months earlier, far enough from Idaho Springs to feel like another world. Rose had clung to that letter like a lifeline as she fled her uncle's house.

Now twilight settled over the land. The forest grew shadowy and dense, the fields stretched out like pools of ink, and the steady rhythm of Willow's hoofbeats kept Rose grounded when her thoughts threatened to splinter.

At last, a warm golden glow appeared ahead, a single lit window. Relief washed over her like sunlight breaking through heavy clouds. She urged Willow up the final hill. The Coltons' home sat proudly atop it, overlooking miles of forest, an expansive lake shimmering faintly beneath the rising moon, and mountains standing guard in the distance.

She pulled Willow to a halt, her throat tightening when she saw Mrs. Colton's familiar outline through the window. A safe place. A refuge. Who would have imagined that her gentle, grandmotherly friend would become the haven she needed most?

Rose swung down, wrapped the reins around a fence post, grabbed her saddlebags, and hurried to the door. Before knocking, she turned for one last look at the breathtaking view, a brief reminder that the world still held beauty, even in the midst of fear.

She took a steadying breath and knocked. The door opened almost immediately.

"Rose!" Mrs. Colton gasped, pressing a hand to her heart before pulling her into a warm embrace. "What a pleasant surprise! Is your uncle with you?"

Rose shook her head. "No. Just me. May I... may I put my horse in your stable?"

"Of course, sweet girl. Walter will take care of her." She glanced over her shoulder. "Walter, dear?"

Mr. Colton appeared behind his wife, offering Rose a kind smile.

"I'll see to her. It's good to see you again, Rose."

"And you," she replied softly.

Mrs. Colton guided her inside. "Come now, let's talk before supper." The warm, tidy sitting room enveloped Rose in the soothing scents of fresh bread, herbs, and woodsmoke. Mrs. Colton motioned for her to sit.

"So," she said gently, "what brings you here, my dear? I'm not complaining, but you look troubled."

Rose hesitated. Would she believe her? Doubt her? Turn her away? But Mrs. Colton's steady, kind expression broke open the dam. Rose told her everything, from Foster's arrival to his threats, from the forged letter to the terror of the study. She didn't hold back. Mrs. Colton listened quietly, never interrupting, never doubting.

Mr. Colton returned just as she finished.

"So, your aunt and uncle have no idea where you are?" Mrs. Colton asked.

"No," Rose whispered. "I had to leave as quickly as I could."

Mr. Colton frowned. "That doesn't sound like John. There must be some explanation."

Rose's shoulders slumped. "Maybe... but it doesn't change how it felt. It doesn't change that he betrayed my trust."

Mrs. Colton rose and rested a comforting hand on Rose's arm.

"Come help me finish supper, dear."

Grateful for the distraction, Rose followed her into the kitchen.

"Are you sure it's all right for me to stay?" she asked softly. "Just until I can figure out where to go next?"

"Of course," Mrs. Colton said firmly. "Walter and I are happy to have you here. Stay as long as you need." Then she flashed a warm smile, one that eased Rose's tight chest more than she expected. "Now, tell me, the latest gossip from Idaho Springs. Alice wrote to me and raved about a certain cousin of yours."

Rose laughed. "Jordan seems just as smitten. Alice is a darling girl. They'd be wonderful together."

"She's your age, isn't she?"

Rose nodded. "Yes. I'd hoped to grow close to her, but... things haven't exactly gone the way I expected."

"Has Jordan begun courting her yet?"

A mischievous smile tugged at Rose's lips.

"Not yet. He's working up the courage to speak to her father. Jordan isn't shy, but your son-in-law is rather... intimidating."

Mrs. Colton chuckled as she stirred the pot on the stove.

"That he is. Martin may be a sweetheart, but those broad shoulders of his have scared off many a suitor. And he's a fiercely protective father." She winked. "Still, he's always had a fondness for your uncle and cousins. I suspect Jordan has little to fear."

Rose's heart eased, warmth blooming in the space where panic had lived for hours. For the first time since fleeing, something other than dread stirred within her: Hope.

Right after supper, Rose excused herself, and Mrs. Colton kindly led her to the guest room. Rose was grateful the older couple understood her so instinctively, they asked no unnecessary questions, offered no advice she wasn't ready to hear. They simply let her be.

Once the door closed behind her, the silence rushed in. She had pushed the memories of the day into the farthest corners of her mind ever since arriving and confiding in Mrs. Colton, but the seesawing of her emotions finally demanded their toll.

With trembling fingers, she undressed, slipped into her nightgown, and crawled beneath the soft quilt. The moment her head touched the pillow, the dam broke. Hot tears spilled freely, soaking the linen as sob after sob shook her. Her heart felt shattered, splintered into a thousand jagged pieces she wasn't sure she'd ever gather again.

What was she to do? Where could she possibly go? Every familiar place suddenly felt dangerous. She could flee to Boston, to her former governess and butler... but that would be the first place anyone searching for her would look. The thought sent another wave of dread rolling through her.

She squeezed her eyes shut and hugged the blanket to her chest, as if the soft fabric could anchor her against the rising tide of fear. A suffocating cloud of despair settled over her, cold, heavy, consuming. It made her feel small, lost... like a frightened child rather than the young woman who had already survived so much.

Her breathing gradually slowed, though tears continued to slip down her cheeks. She cried until exhaustion overtook her trembling limbs. Only then, drained and heartsick, did her body surrender to restless, uneasy sleep, one filled with shadows that clung to her even in dreams.

Walter Colton stepped into the kitchen, rolling up his sleeves as he joined his wife in clearing the supper dishes. Mable glanced over her shoulder, worry etched in every line of her face.

"I sent a telegram to Rose's uncle," Walter said quietly. Mable froze, clutching a damp dish towel.

"Walter... I don't know if that was the right thing to do." Her voice trembled. "I feel like we're stabbing poor Rose in the back."

He set a gentle hand on her shoulder.

"Mable, we had to let them know. Lizzie must be beside herself with worry. And something tells me what Rose told us wasn't the full truth of what happened today."

Mable turned to him fully, her eyes softening.

"John loves that girl like a daughter," Walter continued. "He'd fight like a cornered lion to protect her. Whatever happened, I can't believe he simply cast her aside. Not John."

"I know..." Mable sighed, folding the towel with shaking hands. "I just worry about her. That girl has been carrying heartbreak after heartbreak, and her spirit is more battered than she lets on. She tries so hard to be brave, but..." Her voice broke. "She's so young, Walter."

He nodded, jaw tightening.

"I hope that man, Bradley Foster, gets exactly what he deserves. What kind of monster schemes like that? To trap innocent girls... women barely into adulthood..." He shook his head, fury flickering beneath his calm exterior. "No wonder Rose felt she had to run. Marrying that scoundrel would be signing her own death sentence."

Mable reached for his hand, squeezing gently.

"I hope John gets here quickly. That girl needs truth and comfort... and she needs her family."

Walter nodded, his expression firm.

"And she'll have both," he promised softly. "One way or another."

"We haven't found her, I'm afraid," John said quietly as he stepped back into the house, Grant and Jordan following behind him. Dust clung to their boots and coats, a clear sign they had searched every possible road until darkness made it impossible to continue.

"We ran into Ahanu," John added, closing the door. "He saw her earlier today, but he didn't know where she was headed."

Lizzie's strength finally crumbled. She burst into tears and pressed a shaking hand to her mouth.

"I wish we could have told her what was truly happening. If something happens to her now, it's our fault."

John pulled her firmly into his arms.

"We had no choice, Lizzie. That man had to be caught, and secrecy was the only way. Under the circumstances, we did what we had to do." His voice trembled despite his effort to stay strong. "We *will* find her. I promise you, we will."

Lizzie nodded against his chest, though her eyes remained full of fear. Accepting that nightfall had ended their search, she slipped into the kitchen to prepare a late meal, anything to keep her hands steady.

A short while later, just as John and the two young men sat down at the table, a knock sounded at the door. Jordan hurried to open it, but his father was right behind him. A messenger handed John a telegram, then disappeared into the night. John tore it open and scanned the words. Relief washed over his features so quickly it stole his breath.

"Rose is safe," he whispered. Then louder, "She's safe. She's staying with Mable and Walter Colton tonight."

Lizzie dropped her dishcloth and sagged with relief.

"Oh, thank the Lord..."

Jordan let out a long breath, raking a hand through his hair.

"I knew she had to be somewhere sensible. She wouldn't run blind."

Grant had gone completely still, too still. His hands hung at his sides, but his jaw flexed tightly, the only sign of the turmoil twisting inside him. Guilt darkened his features, raw and unguarded. He looked like a man standing at the edge of a cliff, unsure whether to step forward or fall apart.

John glanced at him, then folded the telegram with deliberate care.

"Maybe you and I should go alone in the morning to bring her home, Grant," he said gently. "She... she may be the angriest with the two of us right now." A pause, then his voice dropped. "And it's only right that we're the ones to explain everything, to tell her the truth together."

Grant swallowed hard, gaze dropping to the floor. His shoulders tightened with remorse.

"I agree," he murmured, though the tension in his frame revealed far more than his words. He wasn't only bracing for Rose's anger, he was bracing for the moment he'd have to face the pain he'd caused her.

John set the telegram on the table, sealing the decision.

"We leave at sunup."

Silence swept through the room. Lizzie wiped her eyes. Jordan let out a breath he seemed to have been holding for hours. And Grant stood there, motionless beneath the weight of regret, his thoughts already miles away, with the girl who had every reason to hate him. But beneath it all pulsed one truth, like a heartbeat: Rose was safe, but her heart was far from healed. And come morning, it would fall to them to try to mend what had been shattered.

23

At the Edge of Fear

When Rose awoke, the room was already bright with morning light. For a moment, she lay still, disoriented, the heaviness in her chest reminding her of everything she had run from. Despite her heartbreak, exhaustion had granted her a few hours of merciful, dreamless sleep.

She rose, dressed quietly, and moved toward the window, intending only to breathe the crisp morning air before facing the Coltons. But when she glanced out over the sloping hill, her blood turned cold. Two riders approached the house at a steady trot. Even before they came fully into view, she recognized the broad frame of her uncle... and the second rider, the last man she wished to see, Grant Adams.

Her heart slammed against her ribs. *No. No, no, no.* They couldn't see her. They couldn't take her back. If they brought her home, everything she feared would become her prison again. Foster would find a way. Men like him always did. And she would not become the fifth name on his list of dead wives.

Panic sharpened her senses. Rose stepped back from the window, barely breathing as she listened. The moment she heard a firm knock at the front door and Mrs. Colton's surprised greeting, she knew it was her only chance.

She shoved the window open. She didn't care that she left everything she had brought with her behind, survival mattered more than belongings. With a small jump, she landed on the soft earth outside, steadied herself, and sprinted for the stable.

Willow lifted her head the moment Rose burst in. The mare must have sensed her fear. She pawed at the ground anxiously. Rose grabbed the halter and reins with trembling hands and looped them into place.

"I'm sorry, girl," she whispered, throat tight. "We must go now. Right now." There was no time for a saddle. Buckles would make too much noise. With a desperate, practiced swing, Rose mounted bareback.

Meanwhile, John and Grant approached the Coltons' front door. John knocked firmly, though his hand trembled with worry. Moments later, Mable opened the door, her eyes filled with relief and concern.

"Come in," she urged gently. Walter stepped beside her. "Rose told us what happened, though..." Her brows pinched. "We can't help feeling there is more to the story than what she witnessed."

John nodded, weariness settling into his posture.

"I'll explain everything," he promised. "But first, please tell me how she is."

Mable let out a soft sigh. "She is heartbroken, John. Truly heartbroken. And she feels deeply betrayed." Emotion flickered in her voice. "I'm glad she came to us. If she hadn't..." She lowered her voice. "In the state she was in last night, I fear she might have done something desperate. She told us about Foster, about the letter, but after supper she went straight to the guest room. I heard her crying for nearly an hour before she finally slept."

John closed his eyes as anguish tightened his jaw. Grant stood stiffly beside him. Guilt etched across every line of his face.

"We never meant for her to suffer," John said quietly. "It was a trap for Foster. Everything that happened after Rose fled the study..." He shook his head. "She didn't know. She wasn't supposed to know."

Walter and Mable exchanged looks of shock and dawning comprehension as John explained the entire sting operation, the sheriff, the marshals, Grant, Jordan, Jonas, and even President Arthur. How Foster had been arrested minutes after Rose fled in terror.

Mable gasped softly. "Oh, John... I knew you wouldn't betray that girl. I told her last night." Relief washed through her features, followed by a determined set of her shoulders. "Let me check on her. If she's awake, I'll bring her out so you can explain everything together. She deserves to hear it from you both."

Grant swallowed hard, tension radiating from him. John placed a hand on his shoulder, not in rebuke, but reassurance.

"Thank you, Mable," John said.

She nodded and headed toward the hallway, leaving the two men waiting in the warm, quiet parlor, hoping there was still time to repair the damage that had been done.

As Rose rode out of the stable, a sharp chill bit through her thin dress. She shivered hard. In her frantic escape, she had forgotten her coat, and now the cold clung to her skin like ice. She urged Willow faster, and they dashed down the hill.

Clouds rolled in from the west, dark and heavy, swallowing what little light the morning offered. A storm was coming, she could feel it in the air, in the eerie stillness that fell over the fields.

Willow slowed, muscles bunching beneath Rose's hands, ears flicking with agitation.

"What is it, girl?" Rose whispered, dread rising. Willow was usually steady. This kind of tension meant only one thing: *danger*.

Before Rose could decide which direction to flee, something flickered at the edge of her sight. She turned sharply. A blur of tan and muscle cut across the far field, lightning-fast. A mountain lion. Large, lean, deadly. Charging straight toward them. Rose's breath died in her throat.

She slapped Willow's flank and kicked hard.

"Go! Go, girl!"

Willow exploded forward, hooves tearing into frozen earth. The sudden burst of speed nearly unseated Rose, who clung to the mare's mane with both hands, her heart hammering. Riding bareback had been reckless, but she hadn't expected to face a predator.

Wind burned her cheeks as Willow raced toward the narrow trail skirting the lake, a dangerous path even on calm days. The lake glimmered like dark glass on her right. The mountain rose sheer on her left. The path narrowed ahead, barely wide enough for a horse.

Behind them, the mountain lion released a chilling, guttural roar.

Ice shot through Rose's veins. "Faster, Willow!"

The mare flew. Rose jolted violently with each stride, her grip slipping once, almost throwing her into the dirt. She forced herself upright. If she fell at this speed, she wouldn't survive. They tore toward the narrow passage. Rose risked a glance over her shoulder. The mountain lion was closing in. If they didn't reach the trail before it cut them off, if the cat caught them in the open... they were done. Rose tightened her grip, heart thundering a frantic prayer.

Mable knocked softly before easing open the guestroom door. The moment she stepped inside, her breath caught. Rose's bed was empty. The window stood wide open, curtains fluttering like frantic warning signals.

Mable hurried to the window and scanned the sweeping landscape below their hilltop home. And there, so far, she almost doubted her sight, was the silhouette of a rider on a galloping horse. Rose. Barely clinging to Willow's back. And then she saw it, the blur streaking after them across the field. Low. Fast. Predatory. A mountain lion.

"Heaven forbid..." Mable stumbled back, then rushed into the hall, her voice sharp with panic.

"Rose is gone! I saw her from the window. Something is chasing her. I think it's a mountain lion!"

John and Grant were on their feet before she finished. Chairs scraped. Boots thundered against the wooden floor. Walter hurried in from the porch, startled by the commotion.

"What happened?" he demanded.

"She's being chased," Mable panted. "Down by the western field, heading toward the lake path. She won't be able to hold on for long."

John and Grant didn't hesitate. Without another word, they sprinted out the front door, vaulted onto their horses, and launched into a breakneck gallop, hooves pounding through the cold morning air. They raced down the hill toward the narrow trail by the lake, where one slip could send horse and rider tumbling into icy waters. And where a mountain lion was already closing in.

"Grant!" John shouted over the pounding of hooves as their horses tore across the field. "I'm going around the lake this way. You go straight after her. If she gets past the lion, she'll try to outrun us. I'm hoping to cut her off before she gets away, or before something worse happens."

Grant nodded once, fierce determination tightening his features. With a sharp jerk of the reins, he urged his horse forward, racing toward the narrow trail that hugged the lake's edge. Cold wind knifed past him. Hoofbeats thundered through the ground and up into his chest, syncing with the frantic tempo of his heart. Branches clawed at his coat as he leaned low over the saddle, eyes locked on the trail ahead.

Please, let me reach her in time. He could already picture her, terrified, unsteady on Willow's bare back, with the mountain lion closing the distance. His stomach twisted. Every muscle in his body braced around a single purpose: He had to reach her. Before the lion. Before the lake. Before she disappeared from him forever.

Grant pushed his horse even harder, breath stinging his lungs.

"Hold on, Rose," he whispered fiercely into the wind. "I'm coming."

Rose tried to steady herself, but her trembling body refused to obey. She was slipping, inch by inch, as Willow's frantic strides jostled her. It was only seconds now. Seconds before she fell.

She was nearly on the narrow path when a blur of tan shot past her. The mountain lion lunged ahead, landing directly in front of them. Rose's heart lurched painfully. Willow skidded, hooves scraping desperately against rock as she tried to turn. But the trail had already claimed them. On one side: the icy, merciless lake. On the other: the steep, unforgiving rise of the mountain. The lion crouched low, muscles coiling.

Willow reared violently, striking out with her hooves. Then the mare lunged forward and connected with the lion's shoulder. Rose flew backward. She hit the ground hard, air exploding from her lungs, then tumbled helplessly into the freezing lake.

The shock was instant, brutal. Her breath vanished. Darkness swarmed her edges. Her arms flailed wildly, searching for anything to grip. Gunshots cracked through the air. The lion snarled, then fell silent. A moment later, strong hands plunged into the water, seized her, and hauled her upward.

Rose surfaced with a violent cough, water streaming down her face. Her vision blurred, then sharpened, revealing Grant. Breathless. Terrified. Before she could fully absorb the sight, her panic surged again. She scrambled upright, disoriented, and staggered toward Willow, who stood trembling in the clearing.

"Rose, wait—stop—"

She reached for the mare, with the intent of fleeing again. But Grant grabbed her arm and pulled her back.

"No, let go of me!" she cried, thrashing wildly. "I'm not coming with you!"

"Just calm down and listen—"

She shoved him harder, trying to break free, but Grant lunged forward and tackled her gently to the ground, pinning her arms so she couldn't hurt herself. Hot, furious tears burst forth. She met his eyes with raw anguish.

"Why are you doing this to me?" she choked. "Why does everyone hate me? Why can't anyone just let me go? Why do people say they love me if it's all a lie?"

"Rose." His voice broke, quiet, urgent, aching. "Nobody hates you. Nobody is trying to get rid of you. And your uncle did not betray you. Everything that happened yesterday was part of a trap, to finally bring Foster down and get justice for Cassandra and the others."

She blinked, shaken. Hope warred with exhaustion.

"Then... why are you here?" she whispered. "Why *you*, Grant? Why not Jordan? You made it clear I wasn't worth trusting. That I deserved all of this."

"It was an act." His voice thickened with guilt. "I never meant a word of it. Foster had to believe we trusted him. My mother's distant cousin needed him to think everything was going his way."

Confusion flickered across her face.

"What does your mother's cousin have to do with Cassandra? Did you... know her?"

"No." Grant shook his head. "But Mom's cousin was her godfather."

"What?" She stared. "Who are you talking about?"

"Chester A. Arthur."

The name hit like a blow, but she immediately rejected it.

"You're telling me the *President of the United States* is your mother's distant cousin?" she snapped. "Do you honestly expect me to believe that?"

"You don't believe me?" he asked softly.

"No, I don't," she said sharply. "Just like I don't believe your cruel words were an 'act.' You sounded sincere. I'm tired of being mocked. Tired of being a joke. I don't know what I ever did to make you hate me." She pushed him off and scrambled up, but he caught her wrists and pulled her gently back against him.

"Rose," he breathed, "I never hated you. I could never hate you."

"Then why?" Her voice broke. "Why try so hard to drag me back?"

His hands softened, sliding from her wrists to her arms, steady, warm, grounding.

"Because I was worried about you," he said softly. "Because you mean more to me than you could ever imagine."

She shook her head, overwhelmed, not thinking clearly. "Nobody cares about me. They care about my dowry. I matter only because of money."

"That isn't true." His voice gentled into a caress. He lifted her chin, guiding her eyes to his. "Your aunt and uncle love you fiercely. Your cousins adore you. And Rose..." He swallowed. "Everything I said about Foster was the truth. Your uncle has been terrified ever since he received a letter from your father months ago, begging him to protect you at all costs and see Foster brought to justice. Cassandra's letter was already in his hands."

Her breath caught. "My uncle... knew?"

Grant nodded. "Your father sent a telegram straight to the President after you gave him Cassandra's letter. Arthur wanted Foster stopped at all costs, and they all knew he'd come after you next. Your father did everything he could to protect you, and your uncle finished the job." He drew a steady breath.

"President Arthur met with me in Boston, told me everything, and asked me to step in if it came to it. That's why I was there when we crossed paths at the station. If Foster planned to come to Colorado for you, I would have to make him believe I'd turned against you, so he'd drop his guard. What we didn't expect was that he would bide his time."

Rose stared into Grant's eyes, warm, earnest, remorseful. No lies. Just truth... and something deeper. He stepped closer, voice dropping to a tender whisper.

"I care about you, Rose. I'm in love with you." His admission trembled with sincerity. "Hurting you was the hardest thing I've ever done."

Her heart stumbled. "Why... why would you love me?" she whispered.

His hands cupped her face, thumbs brushing her damp cheeks.

"Because you are brave and fierce and kind. Because you see people for their hearts, not their circumstances. Because you defend others even when it costs you everything. Because you came to Idaho Springs and changed every life you touched." His voice softened further. "Because you're beautiful, inside and out."

Heat flushed her skin. Her pulse fluttered wildly.

"And that day we teased each other," she whispered, "when you chased me... did we almost—"

"Kiss?" he finished gently. She nodded. "Yes," he breathed. "And I wanted to. From the moment I saw you at the station in Boston, I needed to protect you. And somewhere along the way... you stole my heart." His gaze burned into hers, and she trembled. "I love you," he whispered. Then his lips found hers.

The kiss began soft, tentative, warm, then deepened into something slow and hungry, unraveling every barrier between them. His arms tightened. Her hands slid into his damp hair, pulling him closer as the world melted away. When they finally parted, breathless, he rested his forehead against hers.

"I love you too," she whispered, shy but certain. Grant's answering smile was radiant, pure, unrestrained joy.

Rose had utterly forgotten everything that had happened before the kiss, her fear, her desperation, even the icy cold clinging to her soaked clothes, until the distant thunder of hooves pounded across the earth. Her breath caught. The trance Grant had wrapped her in dissolved as she blinked past him. Her uncle was riding toward them, fast.

The moment she recognized him, something inside her broke loose. All the tension from the chase, the terror of the mountain lion, the heartbreak and confusion of the day before, every emotion she had held back, crashed over her at once. Her knees weakened, and she shivered so violently her teeth clicked together.

Grant reacted instantly. He turned, hurried to his horse, pulled a rolled blanket from behind the saddle, and wrapped it around her soaked shoulders. His hands lingered there for a heartbeat, steady, warm, protective, before he stepped back just enough to let her breathe.

"So..." Rose swallowed, her voice thin and raw. "So, I... I won't be forced to marry Bradley Foster?" She turned to her uncle, who had already dismounted and reached her in only a few strides. "I can come back home?"

"Yes, Rose." Uncle John gathered her into his arms with such gentleness it shattered the last of her composure. He cupped the back of her head as if she were a frightened child again. "You can come home. And you will never be forced into anything, ever."

"That man is in jail," Grant added behind her, his voice firm with conviction. "He'll stand trial for every crime he's committed. I swear to you, none of us would ever have allowed him to hurt you. Everything we did, every painful moment, was to protect you."

24

Belonging at Last

S he couldn't hold back anymore. Her body sagged against her uncle's, and sobs burst free, raw and uncontrollable. She clung to him, her guardian, her last living tie to the family she had lost, as he held her tight, anchoring her with all the love and strength she had doubted she still had.

When the storm inside her finally loosened its grip, Uncle John eased her back and gently lifted her chin with his work-roughened, tender fingers.

"I am so sorry," he murmured. "We hated deceiving you. Hated watching you suffer because of it. But Lizzie and I had to keep the investigation secret. We love you, Rose. More than we can ever say. You have become our daughter in every way that matters. And we will never let anyone harm you again. Please... trust that."

Fresh tears pooled in her eyes, soft this time, full of gratitude rather than fear. And then she glanced at Grant. He stood a few paces away, his expression unguarded in a way she had never seen before. The warmth in his brown eyes sent a flutter deep into her chest. She blushed so fiercely she had to tug the blanket higher, hiding half her face.

Her uncle followed her gaze and smiled, a slow, knowing, fatherly smile. And in that moment, Rose felt something she hadn't felt in months, perhaps years: Safe. Wanted. Loved. Her heart, battered and bruised, felt impossibly full.

"The wind is picking up, and heavy clouds are rolling in," Grant said, glancing toward the darkening sky. "We should get back to the Coltons' before the storm breaks."

Uncle John nodded. "I think we may have to stay overnight." He turned toward Rose with a gentle smile, and a teasing glint in his eyes. "Since you're soaking wet, shivering like a leaf, and without a saddle, I think it's safest if you ride with Grant. I'll lead Willow."

Rose's face ignited with heat. Had he seen the kiss? Did he know? Would he give his blessing for Grant to court her? The warm, knowing curve of her uncle's mouth only deepened the blush burning across her cheeks.

Grant loved her. Truly loved her. The realization still wrapped her heart in a glow so new and overwhelming she scarcely knew what to do with it. Everything with him had collided all at once, danger, fear, anger, longing, and yet her heart had already woven itself around his far more deeply than she'd ever imagined possible. Her uncle's voice broke gently through her spiraling thoughts.

"Yes, Rose," he said, grinning openly now, as though he could read the truth in her eyes. "I already gave Grant permission to court you."

Her lips parted in shock. For a moment she could only stare at the two men who loved her, one like a father, the other like something far more wonderful and terrifying.

Grant lifted her onto his horse with steady, careful hands, making sure she was secure before swinging himself up behind her. His arms came around her to take the reins, and heat seeped through the damp fabric of her dress. Her heart fluttered wildly, unsteady and elated.

With John leading Willow, they rode through the rising wind. When they reached the Coltons' homestead, Grant dismounted first, then turned to lift her down. Instead of setting her immediately on her feet, he held her for a heartbeat, his arms firm around her waist, her hands braced against his chest. The world narrowed to just that, the warmth of him, his breath mingling with hers, the storm forgotten. Then he slowly lowered her to the ground.

"Go on inside, Rose," her uncle urged gently. "We'll take care of the animals."

She hurried to the porch, her dress clinging to her legs. Before she could knock, Mrs. Colton opened the door, her eyes widening.

"Good heavens, child, you're drenched!" Mable exclaimed, ushering her inside. "Did you fall into the lake?"

Rose nodded, still trembling from cold, and from everything else. The storm outside was nothing compared to the one inside her chest.

"Let me draw you a hot bath," Mrs. Colton said at once, her voice full of concern as she shut the door firmly against the rising wind. "Fetch some dry clothes, sweetheart. You must be freezing."

Still shaking, Rose hurried down the hallway. Her wet skirt clung heavily to her legs. She gathered her warmest dress, undergarments, stockings, and shawl before returning to find the Coltons preparing the bath together.

Walter poured cool water from the pump into the copper tub while Mable carefully added steaming kettles from the stove. Warm fog filled the air.

"There," Mable murmured, testing the heat. "Just right." She sprinkled Epsom salts, then uncorked a small vial and let droplets of lavender oil fall into the water. The scent drifted upward, soft, soothing, almost tender.

"Lavender will help settle your nerves," she said gently. She laid out towels and Rose's clean clothes. "Take your time, dear. Let the warmth do its work."

Rose swallowed a knot of emotion. "Thank you," she whispered.

Mable brushed her cheek affectionately, then stepped out, closing the door with quiet care. Alone in the lantern-lit room, steam curling in golden light, Rose let out a long, shaky breath.

Sinking into the steaming bath felt heavenly. The heat wrapped around her like a balm, melting the cold that had settled in her bones since she'd fallen into the lake. Lavender curled through the air, calming her breath and easing the tight knot in her chest.

It soothed her limbs, her muscles slowly unclenching after the fall from the horse. The trembling eased. Her mind, always racing, finally began to slow.

She leaned back, eyes closed. Grant's arms flashed through her thoughts. The desperate chase. The mountain lion's roar. The shock of ice-cold water. Grant dragging her to safety. His voice when he said he loved her. His kiss.

The truth about everything unfurled slowly in her mind, a banner she wasn't quite ready to look at directly. Lavender softened her thoughts, tugging her toward sleep. She nearly drifted off right there.

When the water cooled enough to raise goosebumps along her arms, she reluctantly stood, dried off with the soft towels, and dressed in warm clothes. A new steadiness settled over her, not perfect, but enough. Enough to face what waited beyond the door.

When she entered the sitting room, every conversation stopped. Every pair of eyes lifted to her. The three older adults sat around the fire, leaving only one vacant seat. Beside Grant. He looked at her with warm eagerness, his dark eyes glowing in a way that made her pulse skip.

Rose froze, etiquette whispering warnings. She and Grant hadn't officially started courting. Yes, they'd spent months laughing and talking in fields and forests, but sitting beside him... letting him hold her... Would it be improper? Would it look forward? Her thoughts tangled like knotted yarn. Her time with Christopher had always been private—hidden, sheltered from the eyes and expectations of others. But this? This was different. Not fully public, yet far from private. What would the Coltons think? What would her uncle think?

"Oh, for heaven's sake, sit next to him, Rose," Mrs. Colton said, exasperation spilling into her tone. She waved a dismissive hand. "We're not blind. We all know you two are in love. There's no shame in sitting beside the man who adores you."

Heat rushed up Rose's neck. She glanced at her uncle for confirmation. He nodded gently, even encouragingly. Still, she hesitated.

Mrs. Colton threw up her hands. "Honestly... Grant, go get her."

Grant laughed under his breath, stood, and crossed the room. Startled, Rose instinctively stepped back, but he only reached for her hand, careful and reverent, his touch warm and grounding.

"Come here," he said softly.

She let him lead her. He sat first on the sofa, then lifted his arm to draw her close. His arm slipped around her shoulders with natural familiarity, as though holding her was something he'd longed to do for ages.

Embarrassment burned her cheeks. She kept her gaze lowered, afraid to look up and see tenderness she wasn't ready for.

"There," Mrs. Colton said with smug satisfaction. "Isn't that better?"

Conversation resumed. Gradually, Rose relaxed. Her shoulders softened. She dared lean, just slightly, into the warmth of Grant's arm. After a few minutes, she finally looked up. Grant was watching her already. The smile he gave her, soft, warm, certain, unraveled the last of her resistance.

She was so lost in those stormy brown eyes that when hail suddenly roared against the roof, she jumped violently. Laughter rippled around the room, even from Grant, though he tightened his arm around her instinctively, protective without thought. He lowered his head, pressed a lingering kiss to the top of her hair, and murmured against her temple: "You're safe."

Her breath hitched, but she truly believed it.

Even though it was nearing lunchtime, Mrs. Colton and Rose prepared a hearty breakfast, and once everyone had eaten, they returned to the sitting room. Walter and John settled in for a chess game, while Grant wasted no time drawing Rose down beside him, his hand lingering at the small of her back, as though he still couldn't quite believe she was truly there, safe and warm.

Mrs. Colton sat across from them with a knowing sparkle in her eye.

"I imagine this year will end rather well," she said with a mischievous lift of her brows. "Jennifer and Paul are getting married the day after Thanksgiving, and something tells me you two won't be courting very long either." She winked openly at Grant.

Grant grinned, completely unbothered. Rose felt her cheeks warm at the teasing, especially when Grant's thumb brushed lightly over her knuckles, a gentle, absent-minded caress that made her breath catch.

"And once Jordan finally gathers the courage to ask for my granddaughter's hand," Mrs. Colton continued, "I suspect we'll have another wedding not long after. So much to look forward to."

Uncle John glanced over his shoulder.

"Well, I suggest Grant and Rose begin with some proper courting first."

"Yes," Mrs. Colton agreed. "Grant, make sure the other young fellows in town know that this girl is yours now, and that they should keep their distance. And any young ladies with an eye on you will need discouraging as well."

Grant snorted. "There are no young ladies with eyes for me."

"Oh, I beg to differ." Mrs. Colton smirked. "I've seen plenty staring your way. And one young woman who visits her grandparents regularly has been trying to get her hands on you for quite some time."

Rose stiffened. She turned quickly to Grant.

"Is this about Tara Philipps?"

He squeezed her hand. "No."

"Then there are more?" Rose wrinkled her nose despite the blush rising across her cheeks. She hated the thought of anyone else pursuing him, far more than she was ready to admit.

"Just one," Mrs. Colton said. "But determined as a mule and completely fixated on Grant."

"I have no feelings for her," Grant said at once. "She's stubborn and relentless, yes, but that doesn't change anything about how I feel for you. If anything, it's simply annoying watching her try so hard."

Rose pouted unconsciously. "I don't like the sound of this. Do I have to fight other women for your affection?"

Grant leaned in and kissed her forehead, his thumb brushing her cheekbone with tender certainty.

"No. My heart is yours, Rose. No other woman could claim it, even if she tried."

Her pulse fluttered wildly at the possessive warmth in his tone.

"Who is she?" Rose asked.

"Her father is a doctor," Mrs. Colton replied. "They moved from Boston to Denver earlier this year. Her grandparents live just outside Idaho Springs. Catherine Mildred Evans."

Rose gasped.

"What? You know her?" Grant asked, brows lifting.

"Not well," Rose said, "but well enough to tell you to stay far away from her. She's... trouble."

"What do you mean?" Uncle John asked.

Rose hesitated, she disliked speaking ill of anyone, but Catherine Evans was not a woman to underestimate.

"There were three women in Boston with reputations like hers," she said at last. "They're essentially the female version of Bradley Foster. Their parents spoiled them so thoroughly that they despise their social standing and will do anything to marry into wealth. People often assume only men hunt for wealthy brides, but these women hunt wealthy husbands with equal greed."

Everyone leaned in as she continued.

"Catherine's last... pursuit caused a tremendous scandal. Likely the reason they left Boston. Her father worked with mine, he was a kind man, but they let their daughter get away with everything."

Mrs. Colton clicked her tongue. "That sounds about right."

Rose nodded. "Women like Catherine don't care about love. Only status. She's destroyed relationships left and right. Once, at an engagement party, she wrote a fake note to the man she wanted, pretending to be his fiancée and asking him to meet her in a private sitting room..."

Rose shook her head at the memory.

"When he entered and saw Catherine instead of his fiancée, he told her to leave. But the moment the door opened again, she threw herself in his arms and kissed him. He tried to push her away, but of course nobody believed him. His fiancée was devastated. Her parents were furious. His own family shamed and humiliated. They disowned him."

Grant stared. "Why would they side with her so quickly?"

"Because Catherine still carried the appearance of a well-mannered lady," Rose said. "Nobody knew Cassandra and I were hiding behind a screen and witnessed everything. When the room emptied, I found the fake note near the fireplace." A faint smile tugged at her lips.

"I visited the poor young woman the next morning, showed her the note, and told her everything. Cassandra confirmed it. The couple confronted his family, who were horrified by what they had done. Unfortunately, her parents refused to believe it and ended the engagement anyway. So, the couple eloped, and they're happily married now."

Mrs. Colton beamed. "At least there's a happy ending."

Grant shook his head. "How do women like that get away with it?"

Rose sighed. "Most women have very little power. Those who discover how to manipulate society's expectations can twist them into weapons. Catherine is one of them. She's capable of blackmail, threats, and lies if she doesn't get what she wants."

Uncle John frowned. "Do you truly believe she's pursuing Grant, Mable?"

"I know she is," the older woman responded firmly.

Rose nodded. "And she won't stop unless someone finally stands up to her."

Grant pulled Rose closer, his thumb sweeping slow circles along her arm, a quiet reassurance echoing everything he'd told her by the lake. Rose leaned into him, her heart warming, despite the uncomfortable subject. Whatever storms still lay ahead, she knew now she wouldn't face them alone.

Grant and Rose made their courtship official the moment they returned to Idaho Springs. Word spread through town with almost comical speed, and the excitement was overwhelming in the best possible way. Jennifer squealed like a little girl when she first saw them ride in together, Grant's arm protectively around Rose as if daring anyone to challenge their happiness.

Rose still thought about Christopher now and then, but the once-blinding ache had softened into something gentle, fondness, gratitude, friendship. She knew now it had never been love the way she believed. Not like this. Not like Grant.

Her heart skipped whenever he appeared in a doorway without warning, whenever he walked toward her with that warm, intent gaze that promised strength and tenderness in equal measure. When his arms came around her, steady, secure, reverent, her breath caught and the world felt impossibly right.

The butterflies in her stomach had taken up permanent residence.

Her uncle and Grant's father teased them endlessly, insisting they'd known from the beginning that Grant and Rose were meant for each other. And perhaps they had been right. The more time she spent with Grant, the more she realized her heart had recognized him first, long before her mind admitted it.

Though they had only just begun courting, everyone spoke of an engagement as though it were inevitable, simply waiting for its proper moment. Rose felt it too—that quiet promise in Grant's eyes whenever he looked at her, as if he already held her future in the palm of his hand.

And she loved him. Fiercely. Joyfully. With a certainty that warmed her entire being. Their love had been forged through danger, heartbreak, and fear, but what remained between them now was steady, bright, and breathtakingly real.

Preparations for Paul and Jennifer's wedding were finally coming to an end. Rose, honored to serve as maid of honor, had spent the morning helping Jennifer dress and soothing her nerves. Jennifer had chosen Alice and Paul's two sisters-in-law as her bridesmaids, and the four young women had shared a sweet, giggling moment before the ceremony, one Rose knew she would treasure forever.

Uncle John and Aunt Lizzie's two older sons had arrived the day before with their families, filling the house with laughter and cheerful commotion. Rose was delighted to meet her other cousins and felt a warm thrill each time one of them drew her into conversation as though she had always belonged among them.

Paul's oldest brother, Benjamin, and Grant stood as his best men, while Grayson, Jordan, and her cousin Kyle completed the wedding party. When the ceremony began, the music softened the crowd, and Mr. Adams walked his daughter down the aisle with such tenderness that Rose felt her throat tighten. Uncle John performed the ceremony with heartfelt sincerity, so much so that even the most stoic men discreetly blinked back emotion.

As Rose watched her friend glow with happiness, a small ache tugged at her heart. A part of her longed for her own father, for the chance to feel his arm linked with hers as he guided her down an aisle someday. But that dream would never be. Loneliness brushed against her, fragile and unwelcome.

Then her gaze drifted to Uncle John, standing strong and proud, his eyes warm as they met hers across the gathering. And in that moment, she knew—deep and certain—that when her time came, she wanted him to be the one to walk beside her. Not from obligation, but because she loved him dearly. Because he had filled the empty spaces of her life with compassion, strength, and unwavering devotion.

Her aunt, uncle, and cousins had become her anchor. They had taken the quiet ache of being an orphan and steadily replaced it with belonging. With love. With family.

When the ceremony concluded, laughter and applause drifted through the crisp air as the guests spilled out of the church and crossed the street to the hotel for the reception. Lamps glowed warmly through the windows, and music floated out onto the boardwalk, promising an evening of dancing and celebration.

Rose lingered near the entrance, watching as Paul and Jennifer, radiant and smiling, were ushered inside by friends and family. The atmosphere was lively: white linens, garlands of winter greenery, and the joyful hum of conversation.

Mr. and Mrs. Colton approached with affectionate smiles, and Rose greeted them happily. They spoke about the ceremony, Jennifer's gown, and the lovely decorations. Rose listened contentedly, grateful for the familiar comfort of the older couple.

But out of the corner of her eye, she saw Grant approaching. He wore his new black suit, sharp, handsome, and entirely distracting. When he reached her side, he leaned in close, his breath brushing her ear.

"Meet me outside when you're finished," he murmured, low enough for only her to hear. A flutter rippled through her stomach. She nodded, unable to stop herself from watching him as he stepped away, weaving through the crowd with quiet confidence. Anticipation warmed her cheeks.

Mrs. Colton chuckled. "My, my... someone has a suitor who's rather eager this evening."

Rose ducked her head, smiling shyly.

"Well," Mr. Colton said with a wink, "don't keep the young man waiting too long. He looked like he had something important on his mind."

Her heart skipped. Perhaps he did. Perhaps tonight held more than dancing and celebration.

When the conversation reached a natural pause, Rose excused herself politely and headed toward the door, her pulse quickening with every step. Grant was waiting. And the soft, hopeful look in his eyes earlier had told her everything she needed to know.

Grant leaned against the large oak tree beside the hotel, the music and laughter from the reception drifting softly into the night. He closed his eyes briefly, letting the quiet steady him. His thoughts were fixed entirely on Rose, on her smile, her laugh, the way she fit so perfectly in his arms. Soon, he told himself. Soon he would ask her the question that had lived in his heart for months.

Then suddenly, arms looped around his neck, a pair of lips pressing urgently against his. His entire body went rigid. This wasn't Rose. Grant's eyes snapped open. He immediately grasped the woman's arms and pushed her away, not roughly, but firmly.

Catherine Evans stood before him, wearing what she clearly believed was a seductive expression. The moonlight glinted in her green eyes and across the overly tight, revealing gown she wore. The neckline plunged indecently low, so low she resembled more a saloon girl from Denver than a respectable wedding guest.

"I'm so glad I finally found you alone," she purred, brushing a perfectly arranged curl toward her cheek. "I think it's time you acknowledge your attachment to me... and that I'm the only woman who will ever meet your needs." She stepped closer, angling her body provocatively. Her perfume was overwhelmingly sweet. She tried to press herself against him, leaning in for another kiss.

Grant stepped back immediately, hands raised in clear refusal.

"No," he said, firm and unyielding.

But Catherine wasn't deterred. Her lips curved into a practiced pout, and she blinked rapidly until false tears glossed her eyes, tears Grant recognized instantly as calculated.

"Grant," she whispered dramatically, "I don't understand why you keep pretending. I know you want me. Everyone can see it."

"That's enough," he said sharply. Under normal circumstances, her persistence was merely irritating. But tonight, it felt suddenly dangerous. They were alone. No witnesses. And women like Catherine wielded false innocence like a blade.

She took another deliberate step toward him, voice slipping into a low, breathy murmur.

"If you admit it now, we can leave this silly little party together. I promise you won't regret choosing me."

Grant stiffened. Every instinct screamed that something was about to go terribly wrong.

She had him cornered, and she knew it. Worse still... at any moment, Rose could appear from inside the building. And if she saw this, saw Catherine pressed close, her heart would shatter.

25

Love Is in the Air

R ose stepped out of the building and scanned the lantern-lit
street. Her gaze found Grant almost immediately. He
stood beneath the sprawling oak beside the hotel, his tall frame
relaxed against the rough bark, eyes closed, a faint smile
softening his lips, as though he were thinking of her.

Her breath caught. She would never tire of looking at him,
his strong jaw, broad shoulders, and the quiet confidence that
made her heart flutter. She started toward him, warmth
blooming in her chest, when a flicker of movement to her right
stole her attention.

A young woman approached Grant with purposeful strides,
her hips swaying in a way Rose instantly distrusted. Before she
could make sense of it, the woman reached him, then flung her
arms around his neck and pressed her lips to his. Rose froze.

A sharp, familiar ache speared through her, an echo of the
day she'd seen Grace kiss Christopher. The world tilted, her lungs
forgot how to work... but only for a moment. The pain didn't
linger this time. It hardened, swift, hot, unyielding. Her spine
straightened. Her chin lifted. A quiet fire lit behind her eyes. Oh

no. Not again. Not with Grant. He was hers, and she was done letting anyone trample her heart.

With a fierce, determined stride, Rose marched toward them, every step radiating fury, certainty, and a bold, unmistakable claim. The heat that surged through her veins wasn't jealousy, it was instinct. A raw, protective instinct for the man her heart had already claimed.

She knew Catherine Evans's kind too well, women who wielded tears like weapons, who twisted moments and reputations until innocent men paid the price. If Grant tried to defend himself, Catherine would twist every word, cast herself as the victim, and paint Grant as the villain. But another woman, one who would look her in the eye? Catherine would not win that battle.

Rose picked up her pace, fists tightening, jaw set with unshakable resolve. Her heart pounded, not from fear, but from conviction: she was fighting for the man she loved. And this time, she would not run. He was worth standing for. He was worth fighting for. And Heaven help the woman trying to pry him from her.

"What are you doing, Catherine?" Grant snapped, stepping back as though her touch had scorched him. "I have never shown the slightest interest in you. And surely, you've heard that I'm courting someone."

She lifted her chin with a slow, self-satisfied smile.

"As long as you aren't married, I consider you available." Her gaze swept boldly over him. "You can't truly want someone else when I'm standing right in front of you." She stepped back as if displaying herself, clearly expecting him to falter. But Grant's gaze stayed fixed on her face, not admiring, but cold.

"There is no future for us," he said flatly. "I'm in love with someone else."

Catherine's smile sharpened into something venomous.

"Are you?" she purred. "And do you honestly believe she'll take your word over what she *saw*?" She gestured behind her, as though the kiss she had forced on him was damning proof. "Be smart, Grant. I would rather not cause a scene, but I will if I must." Her voice dropped, low and threatening. "You'll lose this game."

"I wouldn't be so sure about that," Rose said coolly. Her voice, steady, cutting, unmistakably furious, made Catherine jump as if stung. She whirled around, green eyes widening at the sight of Rose who pushed herself between them.

Confusion flickered across Catherine's face, quickly replaced by a polished, sugary smile she had perfected years ago. Rose didn't move. Didn't blink. She stepped forward, and Catherine was forced to retreat a matching step, her heeled shoes crunching against the frosted ground.

"I know you think highly of yourself, Miss Evans," Rose said, her tone sharp as sleet, "but I strongly suggest you leave before you make an even greater fool of yourself. Boston should have taught you something, yet here you are, repeating history."

Catherine inhaled sharply. "You don't know what you're talking about." She flicked a disdainful glance over Rose. "Who are you, anyway?"

Grant opened his mouth to answer, but Rose lifted one hand, quiet, authoritative, stopping him instantly.

"Rose Williams," she said, chin high. "Daughter of the late Dr. Edward Williams."

Recognition flickered in Catherine's eyes, along with irritation. Clearly, she disliked being reminded of a social circle she had once tried to claw her way into.

"And there's no need for further introduction," Rose added, voice like steel. "I know exactly who you are, and I'm very familiar with your reputation."

Catherine bristled. "We have never met."

"Not formally," Rose agreed. "But your father worked with mine, a kind, respectable man. He deserved far better than a daughter who uses his name to further her own schemes."

Grant stared at Rose in awe. He had never seen her like this, fierce, composed, utterly unshakeable. Admiration swelled in him until it was almost overwhelming.

Catherine huffed and looked past Rose toward Grant.

"You're just going to stand there and let her speak to me like this?"

Rose answered before he could breathe.

"He's letting me because every word I've spoken is true. I know your kind."

Catherine's face reddened with fury. "My kind? How dare you?"

"Oh, I dare," Rose said, stepping forward again. "You are one of those women who hunt wealthy men to elevate themselves. Who destroy reputations and engagements. Who manipulate tears and pretend innocence while ruining good people. Boston remembers your scandals well, and so do I."

Catherine blanched, her composure slipping. Rose gestured toward Grant without breaking eye contact.

"Take a good look at him, Miss Evans. Because a look is all you will ever have."

Catherine's breath hitched indignantly.

"That handsome, honorable man behind me," Rose continued, her voice pulsing with fire, "is mine. And I will not allow someone like you to ruin his life or drag his name through the mud."

Grant's heart thudded. If he hadn't loved her already, that moment would have sealed it. Completely.

Catherine stared, stunned and humiliated. Rose didn't waver. She stood her ground, small, fierce, and utterly fearless. And Catherine Evans, notorious manipulator and self-appointed belle of every room she walked into, finally understood: She had met her match.

Grant couldn't help the slow grin curling across his face. Of all the outcomes he had imagined when Catherine ambushed him under that oak tree, this, Rose storming toward them like a warrior queen, was the last he expected. And the best.

Her fire humbled him. Thrilled him. Undid him. Watching her defend him with such ferocity stirred something deep inside, protective, possessive, reverent. Her small frame stood between him and Catherine like a shield, yet she commanded the moment with a confidence that stole his breath.

He folded his arms, arms warm with quiet pride, letting the scene unfold. Rose had Catherine Evans cornered without ever raising her voice. It was almost worth being ambushed and forcibly kissed. Almost. But the true reward... was watching Rose stand her ground that fiercely, for *him*. And he reveled in every second of it.

"Would you like to know what happened after the scandal you caused?" Rose asked, her voice low but edged with iron.

Catherine lifted her chin. "You don't know anything about that situation. He lured me into the parlor because he didn't want to marry his fiancée. He used me to—"

"No, he didn't," Rose cut in sharply. "You went after him because he was wealthy. You created that scene so his fiancée would break off the engagement. What you didn't expect was for it to backfire, or for his family to disown him when they believed you were the injured party." Rose folded her arms. "For your information, he and his fiancée married anyway."

Catherine blinked, her confidence wavering.

"How would you know any of that?"

"Because," Rose said, stepping closer, eyes blazing, "I was there. Cassandra Foster and I were in the room. We saw everything. We picked up the fake note you forged, pretending to be his fiancée, and I delivered it to the poor young woman the next morning."

"You're lying," Catherine whispered, though the tremor in her voice betrayed her.

"I'm not," Rose replied coolly. "His family believed us too. We pleaded with the girl's parents, but they refused to listen. So, the couple eloped and built a happy life together, without you interfering." She tilted her head. "And you? You vanished the moment you realized he wasn't wealthy anymore. How tragic... and predictable."

Catherine's face twisted with anger.

"You know nothing of my life, Miss Williams. You've always been a rich heiress. You've never had to worry about anything."

"If you're trying to gain my sympathy, it isn't working," Rose said bluntly. "Your father wasn't wealthy, no, but he is a good man. A generous one. You weren't deprived, Miss Evans. You were spoiled. And now you've convinced yourself the world owes you whatever you want."

Catherine scoffed. "Oh, look at you, poor rich orphan." Her glare shot toward Grant. "Is that how you won him over? Surely, he doesn't find you attractive enough—"

Grant stepped forward, outrage flaring in his eyes, but Rose lifted a hand and spoke first.

"Just because I don't cheapen myself by flaunting my body does not make me less attractive," she shot back fiercely and before Grand could even say anything. "Yes, you're... well-endowed." Her gaze slid pointedly to Catherine's scandalous gown. "But beauty without goodness becomes ugliness very quickly." Her voice dropped to a cutting whisper.

"Maybe it's time to stop throwing yourself at every wealthy man you see and work on the woman you actually are."

Catherine gasped as if struck. Her eyes darted desperately to Grant.

"And you let her speak to me like this?"

"Yes," Grant said flatly. "Because if the roles were reversed, if a man treated Rose the way you treated me, I would've beaten sense into him. You're fortunate you're a woman, Catherine."

Her mouth fell open.

"Why are you so offended?" Rose asked, voice soft but unwavering. "You hand out cruelty as easily as breath, but the moment someone pushes back, you crumble? Perhaps it's time you consider why."

"I don't have to listen to this," Catherine muttered, turning away.

"No," Rose agreed. "You don't. You can continue living miserably, chasing money, breaking hearts, and destroying reputations. But I want to know something, Catherine." Her tone softened, not kind, but honest. "Why do you have so little self-respect? Why do you think your body is the only way to get a man's attention? Why chase men who don't want you instead of letting a good man chase you?"

For the first time, Catherine faltered. Her voice cracked.

"Men don't look at me as someone worth chasing."

Rose nodded sadly. "Because you trained them not to. Respect is mutual, and you demand admiration without giving any in return. You can change that, but you must want it."

"It wouldn't matter," Catherine whispered brokenly. "The law is always on the side of men. The law degrades us."

"Yes," Rose said softly. "It often does. But if we want that to change, we must be better than the men who mistreat us. Uphold the good ones. Fight the evil ones. And stop copying the methods of those who hurt us. You're not helping women. You're making things harder for us."

Catherine stared at her, speechless, shaken, stripped of her usual armor.

"You created this reputation," Rose finished gently. "You can unmake it. Wealth won't buy you happiness. But respecting yourself might."

Grant let out a quiet breath beside her, admiration warming his expression. Rose's words had struck deeper than any scolding could, and Catherine Evans had nothing to say.

Catherine's eyes glistened, real tears, Rose realized with a faint jolt. Then a soft sniff broke the moment. All three turned.

Standing just a few yards away were Catherine's parents. Her mother held a handkerchief to her face, eyes wet, while her father stood stiff-backed beside her, grief and regret written plainly across his features.

Rose's heart softened. She stepped closer to Catherine, gently taking her hand.

"I don't know if your tears are genuine," she said quietly, "but they look like they are. And even if they aren't, everything I've said still stands." Her voice gentled even further. "Change is frightening. It means facing what we've done. But you deserve more than the bitterness you've been clinging to. You deserve a life you can be proud of."

Catherine swallowed hard, her throat working as though she could not speak. For the first time, she didn't look like a rival, she looked like a young woman who had never been told she could be more.

Slowly, Catherine nodded. Then she turned toward her waiting parents. Her mother immediately wrapped an arm around her shoulders, guiding her gently away. Her father followed, laying a steadying hand on her back.

Rose watched them go, silently praying her words had planted something real. Beside her, Grant exhaled, awe and pride brightening his gaze as he looked at Rose.

Rose drew in a slow, trembling breath, and the tension that had held her rigid finally released. Grant didn't hesitate. He pulled her into his arms, holding her as though he needed her as desperately as she needed him. Her body softened against him. When he tipped her chin up with two fingers, her pulse fluttered.

"If I weren't already in love with you," he murmured, voice warm and low, "I would have fallen for you tonight." A teasing smile tugged at his lips. "Remind me never to end up on your bad side."

Rose's cheeks warmed, though her smile matched his. "You have nothing to fear if you give me no reason to be put on my bad side," she whispered.

He laughed softly, the sound rumbling beneath her palms.

"Do you think you got through to her?" he asked, glancing toward Catherine's retreating figure. Rose followed his gaze.

"I hope so," she said. "She has a long road ahead. But if she truly wants to change... she can."

Grant twined his fingers with hers, holding her hand firmly, possessive, tender, unashamed.

"Come on," he whispered. "Walk with me."

They strolled toward the church, bathed in the soft glow of lamplight spilling from the windows. When they reached the doorway, the world seemed to hush around them. Grant slowed, turning toward her. His thumb brushed across her knuckles, slow and warm. He lifted her chin and Rose leaned closer, longing for another kiss, but the hotel doors burst open.

Jordan hurried toward them. "Jennifer is about to throw her bouquet," he called. "You're needed inside, cousin."

Rose groaned. "Let the other girls have fun. They don't need me."

Jordan raised his brows. "The bride insists. You are the maid of honor."

Rose rolled her eyes. Dramatically. Grant laughed, then nudged her gently forward, his hand warm at the small of her back.

"Come on," he teased. "It's tradition. And who knows..." His voice dropped, intimate, "maybe it'll land exactly where it should."

Heat rushed to her cheeks, her heart stumbling delightfully. She sighed but didn't resist. Grant's hand remained securely around hers as he guided her inside. And she did not pull away. She wasn't sure she ever would again.

When they entered the ballroom, Jennifer rushed toward Rose at once and wrapped her in a tight, breath-stealing hug.

"I heard what you did outside," she gushed, pulling back just far enough to meet Rose's eyes. "You are incredible, defending my brother and your relationship like that. Honestly, Rose, perhaps you and Grant should get married today as well. You two look more than ready to start your lives together."

Rose laughed softly. "I think that's a bit early, Jen, and Grant hasn't even asked me yet." She lowered her voice. "Besides, such a fast courtship is frowned upon in society."

Jennifer groaned dramatically.

"Oh, Rose, you need to let go of those tedious rules. This isn't Boston. Out here, the whole town adores you both. They'd celebrate a wedding tomorrow. You deserve every bit of happiness, and I want you as my sister as soon as possible."

Before Rose could respond, Jennifer's grin widened.

"All right. Are you ready? I want you at the front."

"Jen—"

"No excuses," Jennifer interrupted, already taking Rose by the wrist and leading her through the crowd. "Come."

Rose stumbled after her, laughing under her breath, until Jennifer planted her firmly at the front of the cluster of unmarried young women. Alice stepped beside her, offering an encouraging smile.

Jennifer walked a few paces away, bouquet raised high, and turned her back to the group. The room quieted, tense with anticipation. She held perfectly still.

Then, without warning, she spun around, marched straight to Rose, and pressed the bouquet into her arms. Rose stared at her, stunned.

"Jennifer, you can't cheat the other girls out of their chance to be the next bride."

Jennifer only smiled... then glanced behind Rose. Puzzled, Rose turned, and her breath caught. Every unmarried woman who'd been standing behind her had stepped aside, forming a clear path. And down that path walked Grant. Slowly. Confidently. Warmth in his eyes that made her heart give a startled flutter. He stopped in front of her, and then, with a smile that melted straight through her, he went down on one knee.

The bouquet slipped from Rose's arms and hit the floor. Her hands flew to her mouth as tears rushed to her eyes. The entire room fell silent.

"Rose," Grant said softly, his voice warm, steady, full of feeling. "I know you didn't expect a proposal tonight, but my sister was... very insistent on adding a little excitement to her wedding." He cast Jennifer a playful glance. She nodded enthusiastically, making the room bubble with laughter. Grant's gaze returned to Rose, focused, tender, sincere.

"The moment I saw you, I knew you were special. Your beauty, your kindness, your courage... it didn't take long before you completely captivated my heart. I knew I couldn't let you go. I knew you were the one."

Emotion thickened his voice.

"So, Rose Julianne Williams... will you do me the honor of marrying me?"

The entire ballroom held its breath. Rose's tears spilled over as she nodded, unable to speak. The room erupted, cheers, applause, delighted shouts. Jennifer squealed loud enough, to make people jump.

Grant rose quickly, swept Rose into his arms, and kissed her, gentle, joyful, overflowing with love, before lifting her off the ground and spinning her in a circle. Laughter and celebration filled the ballroom, but Rose felt only him, Grant, steady, strong, hers. And she was his. Forever.

26

When Joy and Grief Collide

After everyone had hugged them and offered heartfelt congratulations, Grant took Rose's hand and guided her away from the noise and laughter of the hotel. They crossed the quiet street toward her uncle's house and followed the familiar path down to the lake.

The night was still and dark, but the moon hung full and bright above them, spilling silver across the water. The cold air nipped Rose's cheeks, yet it felt fresh, clean, as though the world itself had been washed new.

Grant stepped behind her, wrapped his arms around her waist, and drew her back against his chest before leading her to the bench. He sat first, keeping one arm snug around her as she settled beside him. He held her close, as if he might wake from a dream if he let go. His voice was warm against her ear.

"You know... my heart is still trying to understand that you said yes."

Rose smiled, leaning into him. "You planned the proposal with Jennifer's help?"

He chuckled. "Very much so. The only reason I asked you to meet me outside was to give Jen the chance to spread the word and get everyone ready."

Rose laughed softly. "That explains their suspiciously eager expressions."

Grant shifted to see her better, his thumb brushing gently over her knuckles. Happiness shone in his eyes, steady, warm, certain.

"Have you thought about when you want to get married?" she asked quietly.

"Unless you have grand ideas," he murmured, "I was thinking... two weeks. Nana leaves before Christmas to visit my uncle, and I want her there. Once the snow sets in, travel becomes difficult. But what about you? Is there anyone you want at the wedding? Any dreams you need fulfilled?"

Rose shook her head. "I only want a simple wedding. We have everyone I need right here... except my former governess and butler. I'd love for them to be here. But I doubt they can afford the journey, and they'd never accept money from us."

Grant smiled. "Then we simply won't give them the chance to refuse. We'll buy the tickets, send them with a letter, and tell them their presence is required."

Rose brightened. "That might work."

Grant followed her glow with a slow, affectionate grin.

"Nana asked me to meet her for lunch tomorrow."

He nodded, his grin widened. "I'm excited for you two to spend time together."

Rose narrowed her eyes. "What?"

"Nana does this with all her granddaughters before they get married. Perhaps I should join you. Watching your reaction would be entertaining."

Rose blinked. "I... why my reaction?"

Grant gave her a falsely innocent look.

"Because Nana is the one who gives the talk."

Rose's whole face flamed. "The... the talk?"

He nodded solemnly, though his lips twitched.

"She covers how marriage requires daily effort, how to solve disagreements, the importance of compromise—"

Rose sagged with relief. "Oh. Well... that's not so bad."

Grant leaned in, his breath warm against her cheek.

"What did you think I meant?"

Her blush deepened to scarlet. He saw it. He loved it. Rose stood abruptly, flustered.

"I should get home before Uncle John sends a search party."

Grant stood too, stepping close until their bodies nearly touched.

"Rose... I was teasing." His voice dipped low. "You're so lovely when you're embarrassed."

He tilted her chin up with gentle fingers and kissed her, slow at first, tender, then warmer, deeper, until the breath fled her lungs and her hands clutched the lapels of his coat. When they parted, he rested his forehead against hers.

"We're staying at the hotel tonight. Tomorrow, after lunch with Nana, may I take you for a walk?"

Rose nodded shyly. "Yes. I'd like that. Will Paul and Jennifer leave tomorrow?" she asked.

"No," he said with a soft smile. "They'll stay until Monday. I think all our relatives will stay through Sunday, too. The town will be very lively... and I plan to steal you away every chance I can."

The warmth in his voice sent her heart fluttering again. The night was cold, but wrapped in his love, Rose had never felt warmer.

Rose was excited about her lunch with Nana the next day. It warmed her heart that the older woman already considered her a granddaughter, Rose felt exactly the same.

They met at the café just before the lunch rush. The lamps glowed softly. The room was warm and quiet, with only a few locals lingering over coffee. Alice took their orders with a smile before hurrying back to help her mother in the kitchen.

Nana reached across the table and gave Rose's hand an affectionate pat.

"Now, my dear, you know why I asked you here today. A happy marriage doesn't just happen because two young people are smitten. It takes patience, forgiveness... and a good bit of humor."

Rose listened, drawn in. Her governess had taught her many things, but never with this level of tender clarity.

"Intimacy between husband and wife is nothing to fear," Nana continued. "It is something God sanctified. It may feel strange at first, but closeness grows into comfort, and comfort blossoms into something beautiful." She smiled warmly.

"And true love, child, isn't the flutter in your stomach. Those feelings are sweet, but they're only the beginning. Real love is built one day at a time."

Rose's throat tightened. "I hope I can make Grant happy."

"Oh, sweetheart," Nana chuckled, "Grant is already happy. And he's very much like his grandfather, steady, loyal, fierce in love and protection. He will never raise a hand against you or hurt you on purpose. He is a God-fearing man who'd die for his family. And you," Nana squeezed her hand gently, "are exactly the woman he needs at his side. You are kind and brave and gentle where he is strong."

Rose blinked rapidly, overwhelmed by sincerity. "I love you, Nana."

"And I love you, child. I cannot wait to officially welcome you into—"

The café door slammed open so violently the hinges rattled. Both women jumped. A filthy, wild-eyed man staggered inside, brandishing a gun. Gasps rippled through the room as he pointed the weapon toward Rose and Nana.

"Nobody move!" he barked. "Put your money and jewelry on the tables, everything you got! Then get to the back where I can see you!"

The café froze. Silent. Breathless. Rose's hands trembled in her lap. But Nana... Nana stood. Rose tried to grab her hand, but the older woman slipped free and stepped forward with astonishing calm.

"Young man," Nana said, her voice firm yet gentle, "don't do this. You look hungry and desperate. Whatever drove you here, robbery won't fix it."

"I ain't hungry!" he snarled. "And I don't want your advice! Sit down or I'll shoot."

"Please, Nana," Rose whispered, tears welling. "Sit down. Please."

But Nana didn't move. Her chin lifted, unafraid.

"You won't get away with this," she said steadily. "The sheriff will be here shortly, and you'll lose everything you think you're gaining."

"Shut up, old woman!" he shouted, the gun shaking in his hand. "Sit down!"

"Alice Baker," Nana called toward the kitchen, "go fetch the sheriff and his dep—"

Two gunshots cracked through the café like thunder. Nana crumpled.

"No!" Rose fell to her knees, catching her before she hit the floor. Hot blood soaked Rose's hands at once, pooling across the wooden planks in deep red streams. "Nana, please... Nana—" Her voice broke as she pressed her palms over the wounds, frantic, desperate. "Hold on. Please hold on. Dr. Hunter will be here any moment."

Nana's eyes fluttered once... then stilled. The breath left Rose's lungs as if she had been struck. She drew Nana into her arms, sobbing into her shoulder, rocking her gently as though movement alone might keep life from slipping away. But the café was silent. Too silent. Nana was gone.

Rose barely heard the shouting and gunfire around her. The world had collapsed to the frail, still body in her arms. She clung to Nana, rocking slightly, her fingers trembling, her sobs broken and raw, the sound of a heart shattering in real time.

It wasn't until strong arms wrapped around her and gently pulled her back that she realized someone was speaking. Shane's voice reached her first, low, steady, trying to anchor her to a world that no longer made sense.

"Rose... let go. Come on, sweetheart. Let me help you."

She blinked up at him as though seeing him through water. Only then did she notice the sheriff and two deputies restraining the filthy man who had fired the shots. The criminal was shouting, cursing, but his voice was muffled beneath the roaring in her ears. The sheriff barked orders, securing the scene and returning inside to question the witnesses.

The elder Dr. Hunter knelt beside Nana, grief etched deep across his face. He gently closed her eyes with two fingers, murmuring something Rose couldn't hear. Moments later, two men stepped forward, lifted Nana's lifeless body with reverence, and carried her toward the door. The emptiness that rushed in behind her felt colder than any winter storm.

"Miss Williams," the sheriff said gently, approaching her. "I need you to tell me what happened."

Rose forced herself to stand. Her legs trembled, but Shane kept an arm around her to steady her. She stared at the floorboards as she spoke, quiet, hoarse, shaking, detailing every moment from the man's arrival to the terrible instant Nana fell.

When the sheriff nodded and moved on, Shane looked down at her with quiet concern.

"Rose... do you want me to take you home?"

She couldn't answer. Her throat burned too much to speak. Instead, she shook her head, stepped out of his grasp, numb and drifting. Without looking back, she pushed open the café door and walked out into the sunlight, though the world felt steeped in shadow.

Rose didn't remember leaving the café. The voices, the shouts, the scrape of chairs, all of it blurred into a hollow roar in her ears. Her legs carried her on their own, numb and unsteady, as if she moved inside a nightmare she couldn't escape.

By the time she came to herself, she was standing in her uncle's stable, her hand pressed against Willow's warm neck. The familiar scent of hay and horses surrounded her, and the last sliver of strength inside her broke.

A ragged sob tore free. She buried her face in Willow's mane, gripping fistfuls of hair as if the mare were the only solid thing left in a world that had just split open beneath her feet. Her entire body shook, grief, shock, fury, terror, crashing over her until she could hardly breathe.

"Nana..." The whisper cracked with anguish. "Oh... Nana..." Her knees buckled, and she clung to Willow to stay upright. The horse whinnied softly, nudging her shoulder as if sensing her torment, and the gentle sound only made her cry harder. Hot tears spilled onto Willow's coat.

She had to get out. She couldn't stay here. She couldn't face Grant. She couldn't endure the pitying looks or the condolences she knew were coming. Not now. Not with her heart ripped open and her mind reeling from what she'd witnessed.

Her hands moved without thought, habit, instinct, desperation. She grabbed the saddle, threw it over Willow's back with trembling arms, and fumbled with the girth. Her vision blurred, and she had to stop more than once to scrub her sleeve across her eyes.

"Just... go," she whispered, voice shaking. "Take me anywhere but here." With a frantic motion, she mounted. Willow sensed her distress, pawing the ground anxiously, but Rose tightened her grip on the reins. Then she kicked the mare forward. Willow surged out of the stable and into the cold air.

Rose didn't care where they went, only that the trees swallowed her, only that the world behind her faded, only that she could outrun the crushing pain in her chest. She rode straight into the forest, the wind tearing at her hair as tears streamed freely, her heart splintering with every hoofbeat.

"I am so sorry, Jonas," Henry Hunter said softly, placing a steadying hand on the grieving man's shoulder. Jonas nodded once, jaw clenched, his face carved with sorrow. Cornelia and Jennifer stood together, openly weeping, while Paul wrapped an arm around his new bride as if shielding her from the pain in the room. As word spread, more relatives filled the clinic, each face mirroring the same stunned disbelief.

Grayson lingered near the table where Nana's body rested beneath a white sheet. He stared at the outline of her small frame as if refusing to accept it. The clinic, usually scented with herbs and antiseptics, felt suffocating under the weight of loss.

"I've already sent for a coffin," Shane said quietly from the doorway, his expression grim. Grant stood beside him, barely hearing the murmured conversations. Then a thought struck him like lightning.

"Where's Rose? She was with my grandmother."

Shane exhaled, grief and worry flickering in his eyes.

"Rose saw everything happen, Grant. She must have tried to stop the bleeding. Her hands and arms were covered in blood."

Jennifer broke down again, burying her face in Paul's chest. The sound tore through Grant like a blade. Panic surged in him, sharp, immediate, unyielding.

"Do you know where she is?" he demanded, voice rough with fear.

"I asked if she wanted me to take her home," Shane replied. "She said no. I saw her walking toward her uncle's place before I left to tell you."

Grant's blood ran cold. Rose, covered in Nana's blood. Rose, who loved so deeply it hurt. Rose, who carried others' pain as her own. She wouldn't be thinking clearly. And she wouldn't be safe. Without another word, he tore out of the clinic. He had to find her, before she broke completely.

Grant sprinted across the property, heart pounding like a hammer. He barely felt the bitter wind cutting past him or heard the shouts behind him. There was only Rose. Only the terror tightening around his chest. He leapt up the porch steps and hammered against the door. Lizzie opened it within seconds, her eyes red, grief-stricken.

"I'm so sorry, Grant," she whispered. "I just heard."

He swallowed hard. "Where is Rose? She was with Nana."

"I—" Understanding widened her eyes. "I thought she was with you. I assumed you'd bring her home after... after everything."

27

Grayson's Story

Grant felt the ground tilt beneath him. Without another word, he bolted toward the stable. The doors were open. The stalls were silent. Willow's stall was empty. His pulse thundered painfully. He snatched the nearest saddle, threw it onto a horse with shaking hands, and fastened the bridle with frantic speed.

She had run. And he knew exactly where she would go. There were dozens of trails... but only one place she sought when she needed to breathe. When she needed quiet. When she needed safety. The waterfall. Her sanctuary. If she was hurting—truly hurting—that was where she'd be.

Grant swung into the saddle and spurred the horse forward.

"Hold on, Rose," he whispered into the wind, pushing the horse faster, desperation clawing at his throat. "I'm coming. Just... hold on." He tore into the trees, toward the distant thunder of falling water, toward the girl he loved, praying he wasn't already too late.

Just as he'd hoped, he soon found Willow grazing quietly near the rocky edge of the clearing, and moments later, he heard the broken sobs of the woman who held his whole heart. Grant swung off his horse before it even slowed. He sprinted toward the sound, rounding the bend to find Rose collapsed at the base of the familiar pine, her shoulders shaking violently with grief.

He dropped to his knees and gathered her into his arms without hesitation.

"I'm so sorry, Grant," she choked out, her voice raw and shredded. "If I hadn't met Nana at the café... she might still be alive."

Grant cupped her face in both hands, gently but firmly guiding her gaze to his.

"Rose, my love," he whispered, steady and tender, "this was not your fault. Not even a little. You are not to blame." His thumbs brushed away the tears streaming down her cheeks. "Terrible things happen, and only God knows the moment He calls us home. Nana loved you with all her heart. And as hard, so painfully hard, as it is to have her taken from us, she would want us to keep living... not carry guilt that was never ours."

Her breathing hitched, and he drew her closer until her forehead rested against his chest.

"When my grandfather passed," he continued softly, "Nana made sure his funeral was a celebration of his life, not a day drowned in sorrow. She always said death is a separation, not the end. We will see her again." He tipped her chin upward. "She's with my grandfather now. And she's happy."

Rose's tears spilled faster. Grant kissed each one away with reverence, his touch so gentle it nearly undid her.

"She won't be at our wedding in person," he murmured, brushing a damp strand of hair behind her ear, "but I know we'll feel her there. Standing right beside us. She adored you, Rose. You were already a granddaughter to her."

Rose closed her eyes as his forehead came to rest lightly against hers. His breath mingled with hers, steady, warm, anchoring.

"My family loves you," he went on, his voice thick with emotion. "You've taken hold of their hearts just as you've taken mine. They're hurting for you right now... hurting because you had to witness something so horrific." His fingers slid into her hair, holding her as if afraid she might slip away. "You're already a daughter-in-law, a sister, a niece, and soon you'll be my wife. In every sense of the word."

He kissed her then, slow, tender, then deepening into something fierce, as if he could draw her pain into himself. Rose melted into him, clutching the front of his shirt as the world softened around her. When he finally pulled back, his lips lingered against hers for a trembling heartbeat.

"God wanted you to meet Nana before she left this earth," he whispered. "He knew you needed her, her strength, her love, her wisdom. She helped you through trials you should never have had to face alone."

Rose nodded, her voice a fragile whisper.

"She was one of the brightest lights in my life... a lighthouse in a terrible storm. I'll carry her with me forever."

Grant pulled her against his chest again, holding her as the wind stirred the trees, two hearts mourning, healing, and binding themselves ever tighter beneath God's sky.

Rose drew a steadying breath before stepping into the clinic. The moment the door opened, the heavy stillness inside pressed against her chest. Grant walked behind her, his arm wrapped protectively around her shoulders, solid, steady, grounding her when she felt she might collapse.

Jennifer rushed toward her and wrapped her in a tight embrace. Rose clung to her, the two of them crying softly. Mr. and Mrs. Adams joined them, enveloping both girls in their arms.

Rose closed her eyes and leaned into their comfort. It stirred another wave of tears from deep within her. Then a sharp, cutting voice sliced through the room.

"What is she doing here?" Grayson snapped, glaring at Rose as though her presence alone offended him. "She isn't part of our family."

"Grayson!" Mrs. Adams gasped, horrified.

Mr. Adams squared his shoulders. "Rose is family. She is your brother's fiancée."

"She shouldn't be here," Grayson bit out, anger flashing beneath his grief. "Being engaged to Grant doesn't make her family. And why is she even crying? She knew Nana for, what, five minutes? She knows nothing about us."

The words struck Rose like a physical blow. Her breath caught. Her throat burned. She stared at him for a long, stunned second, her heart fracturing in a new and unexpected place. Then she turned and slipped out of the room before anyone could stop her.

Grant followed her instinctively, catching her hand in the hallway and pulling her gently back toward him.

"Don't go," he whispered, his voice raw with pleading.

Tears blurred her vision. "He's right," she whispered. "I don't belong here. Go back and be with your family. They need you now. You all need each other."

Grant stepped closer, cupping her face in his hands with heartbreaking tenderness.

"You are my family, Rose. I love you, and you belong to us. With me."

She shook her head, her voice barely audible.

"Why does your brother hate me so much? What did I do to him?"

Grant exhaled slowly, pain flickering in his eyes.

"I think..." He hesitated, then nodded. "I think it's time I told you about his past."

Rose swallowed hard. "Not now. Please. Go be with them. Nana would want you all together, comforting one another, not chasing after me."

Grant pressed his forehead gently to hers, eyes closing for a brief, aching moment.

"I'll come to you as soon as I can," he murmured. Then he turned back toward the room, leaving Rose standing alone in the hallway, heartbroken, aching, and wishing she could somehow fill the space Nana had left behind... for all of them.

Grant found Rose inside the church when he went searching for her several hours later. She sat quietly in one of the back pews, her hands clasped in her lap, her eyes distant and red from crying. When she looked up and saw him, she didn't speak, but she didn't turn away either.

Without a word, Grant extended his hand. She slid hers into his, and together they walked to the lake behind the church. The air was cool, the water still, reflecting the lavender blush of the evening sky. The bench where they had shared so many tender conversations waited for them.

Grant sat first and gently pulled Rose down beside him, tucking her beneath his arm. She leaned into him instantly, seeking the warmth of his body and the steady beat of his heart. He rested his chin on the crown of her head, letting the quiet settle around them. Then, with a soft breath, he began.

"Grayson wasn't the oldest in our family," Grant murmured. "We had an older brother—Jackson."

Rose lifted her head slightly, attentive and gentle.

"Jackson and Grayson were inseparable," Grant said, emotion tightening his voice. "Two years apart, but you'd think they were twins. Wherever Jackson went, Grayson followed." He paused, his chest rising and falling slowly.

"Jackson moved to Denver first to attend college, business and agriculture. He paid all his tuition himself. He worked as a deputy sheriff in his spare time. Grayson followed him a year later, studied law, and became a deputy as well." Grant's voice wavered. Rose reached for his hand.

"One day, while Jackson and Grayson were on duty, Jackson tried to stop a bank robbery," Grant continued softly. "He... he was shot. He died before Jackson could get to him."

Rose's breath caught. "Oh, Grant... I'm so sorry."

"His death broke all of us," Grant whispered. "But Grayson... it destroyed him. He blamed God, fate, the world. He started drinking, gambling, getting into fights, falling into debt deeper than he could pay."

Rose's eyes filled with sorrow.

"A professor eventually contacted my dad," Grant said. "A young woman was expecting a child... and Grayson was the father. Dad and Grandfather went to Denver, demanded he marry her and take responsibility. He refused." Grant's jaw tightened. "Grandfather told him if he wouldn't do right by that girl and their baby, he couldn't live under their roof."

Rose swallowed. "What happened to her?"

"She lost the baby," Grant said quietly. "And Grayson still didn't change. He cut ties with all of us. Mom and I tried visiting, but he wouldn't hear it." He took a shaky breath. "Nana was the only one who ever reached him. She kept trying, lovingly, patiently... but after a terrible argument, he cut her off too."

Grant exhaled, weariness shadowing his face. "When Grandfather died suddenly, Grayson realized what he had lost. He apologized to Nana and Dad. They forgave him, but... the bitterness never really left. He's been fighting himself ever since."

Rose's eyes glistened. "Poor man... Grant, I truly had no idea."

"So, when he lashed out at you today," Grant said gently, "it wasn't personal. He lashes out at everyone. He's drowning in guilt and grief. And now, with Nana gone..." He shook his head. "He's falling apart."

Rose rested her forehead against his temple. "Is there any way we can help him?"

"We've tried for years," Grant murmured. "He only opens the door a sliver at a time. But maybe... one day."

Rose nodded softly. "Thank you for telling me. I understand him better now."

Grant cupped her face and kissed her, gentle, slow, full of devotion.

"Will you be all right?" he asked.

"Yes," she whispered. "Go be with them. Your family needs you. Your brother needs you."

He hesitated. "Rose—"

"Go," she said, brushing her thumb along his cheek. "Nana would want it."

He kissed her again, one lingering kiss, then stood and walked back toward town. Rose watched him go, grief heavy in her chest, but a quiet resolve rising slowly in its place. Something had to be done about Grayson. If only she knew how to reach a man who no longer believed he deserved love.

Darkness settled over Idaho Springs when Rose wrapped herself in a warm shawl and took the dogs for a walk. The cold breeze stung her cheeks, but the quiet gave her space to breathe. She wondered how Grant and his family were coping, but she didn't want to cause more tension with Grayson.

As she rounded the bend toward the lake, she slowed. A tall figure sat hunched on the bench, elbows on his knees, and his head lowered. Even from a distance, she sensed the storm simmering inside him. His posture radiated a loneliness so sharp it felt tangible. She stepped closer.

"Grayson."

"Go away and leave me alone." His voice was harsh, cutting, but beneath it, she heard the tremble of grief. She didn't retreat.

"I know you're hurting," she said gently. "But I'd like to talk. You don't have to speak. I only hope you'll listen."

He didn't move, didn't glare or scoff, but he didn't walk away either. That was enough.

"You were right earlier," she continued softly. "I'm not part of your family by blood. And yes, compared to you, I barely knew Nana." Her voice thickened. "But I loved her. And I'm not trying to take love from anyone. I just want to be loved too."

His jaw tightened, but he said nothing.

"My mother died when I was five," Rose whispered. "My father... fell apart after losing her. He left me with servants. They loved me, but they weren't him. I missed him every day. We could have helped each other, but instead, we grieved separately." Her heart tugged painfully, but she pressed on.

"I wish I'd known my grandparents," she whispered. "Your Nana was the closest thing I ever had to a grandmother. She helped me when I was hurting. I'll miss her deeply."

Still no response, but the air around him shifted.

"I know we may never be friends," she said gently. "But I'm worried about you. Your family is worried about you. They love you, and they're terrified of losing you the way you lost Jackson."

She moved a step closer, but still kept a respectful distance.

"Death took my mother from me," Rose continued. "But it took my father too, in a different way. I don't want that for you. You still have your parents, your sister, your brother. You have people who love you fiercely."

A wind rippled across the lake. Rose pulled her shawl tighter.

"You lost faith in God when Jackson died," she said softly. "Anyone would struggle after that. But I don't believe God abandoned you. Even in your anger and grief, He's still trying to reach you." She gathered a breath.

"When I came here, my aunt and uncle gave me a home... and more love than I thought possible. I hope someday you let your family do the same. Let them carry part of your burden. You weren't meant to walk this alone."

Still nothing, but he wasn't stone anymore. She saw the trembling in his shoulders. Rose managed a small, aching smile. She whistled, and the dogs bounded toward her.

"Goodnight, Grayson," she whispered. "Thank you for listening." She walked back toward the house, the dogs at her heels. Grayson remained on the bench, still grieving, still hurting, but no longer completely shut away. A crack had formed. A small one. But a crack, nonetheless.

Aunt Lizzie stood in the kitchen when Rose returned, her hands stilled over a towel as soon as she saw the girl.

"Are you all right, Rose?"

Rose exhaled slowly, the weight of the day settling heavily across her shoulders.

"I am... or I will be," she whispered. "It was a terrible day. I'll miss Nana more than I can say, but I'm grateful I got to know her. Even for a short time." Her eyes shimmered. "She was the closest I've ever had to a grandmother." Her voice trembled.

"I want to hold on to her faith. I want to believe, like she did, that we'll see our loved ones again. That I'll hug my mother someday. That maybe... one day... I'll reconcile with my father. Losing them both has been the hardest trial of my life, but it also brought me to you and Uncle John. I can't thank you enough for loving me."

Aunt Lizzie's eyes filled instantly. She crossed the kitchen in two steps and pulled Rose into a fierce, motherly hug.

"Oh, sweetheart..."

They stayed like that until Jordan peeked in, eyebrows raised dramatically.

"What about me, Rose? Aren't you grateful for me? I've worked incredibly hard to be charming and lovable. I think I deserve an honorable mention."

A watery laugh escaped her. "Of course I'm grateful for you. You're more of a brother to me than a cousin."

Jordan grinned triumphantly and pulled her into a hug. Uncle John appeared in the doorway then, looking perplexed.

"What's all this?"

"We're just grateful for each other," Rose said softly.

John tugged her gently from Jordan's arms and folded her into his own, a protective, fatherly embrace.

"You're our angel," he murmured, voice thick. "Not just for this family, for the whole community. Your strength, your courage, your compassion... they inspire people. You inspire people. We love you, Rose, not only as our niece." His voice dropped even softer.

"Lizzie and I will forever be grateful that Lily and Edward brought you into this world... and that you became part of ours."

Rose's throat tightened. "You're going to make me cry, Uncle John," she sniffed, though tears were already forming. He chuckled and hugged her tighter.

And there, wrapped in the arms of the people who had become her home, Rose felt something deep and quiet begin to mend. The emptiness inside her no longer echoed. It overflowed, warm, full, brimming with the truth she had longed for her entire life: She was not alone. She was not an orphan. She belonged. She was loved, deeply, unconditionally, completely.

Mr. Adams wished for Nana's funeral to be held two days later. It was soon, far sooner than Rose had imagined, but with so many relatives still in town from the wedding, there was no reason to delay what everyone dreaded yet needed to face together.

When Rose stepped into the church the next morning, Aunt Lizzie and Jordan just behind her, the soft murmur of grieving voices faded. She hesitated for a heartbeat, until Grant crossed the aisle in long, purposeful strides and drew her into his arms. His embrace was strong and steady, anchoring her. When he pulled back just enough to meet her gaze, his warm brown eyes searched hers with quiet devotion. Her heart fluttered painfully.

Uncle John's sermon was tender, reverent, full of hope. Rose knew he had prayed long and hard the night before. His words struck deep: "Death is not the end of our story. It is merely the turning of a page. Love does not die, it waits."

Rose blinked rapidly, fighting tears. She could almost hear Nana humming beside her.

As she scanned the congregation, her gaze caught on the empty space where Grayson should have been. A small ache formed in her chest. She had hoped—truly hoped—that the words she'd spoken to him the night before had softened at least one corner of his hardened heart. Not just for his sake, but for the family that longed to pull him close.

After the service, the Adams family, everyone except Grayson, walked with the Williamses back to the house. Rose found herself between Jennifer and Grant along the familiar road. The cold wind nipped at their cheeks, but the warmth of shared memories wrapped around them like a comforting quilt.

Lunch and supper blended into one long gathering. Laughter broke through the tears as they shared stories of Nana, her soft kisses after scolding a child, the hymns she hummed while working, the sparkle in her eyes whenever someone she loved walked through her door.

"She was our glue," Mr. Adams murmured as they sat around the parlor fire. "The one who kept us close, even when life tried to scatter us."

Rose nodded, her voice tender.

"She brought people together," she said softly. "Even me."

Grant reached for her hand beneath the armrest of the settee, giving it a gentle squeeze. His thumb brushed her knuckles, soft, steady, full of silent devotion. Warmth unfurled inside her chest.

Sitting among them with Aunt Lizzie humming in the kitchen, Uncle John deep in conversation with Mr. Adams, Jennifer curled against Paul's shoulder, and Grant's presence comforting beside her, Rose realized something profound: Nana was gone, but her love had not gone anywhere. It lingered in this home, in these hearts, in the young woman Rose had become because of her.

And as she leaned her head lightly against Grant's shoulder, breathing for the first time in two days, she knew Nana would walk with them all for the rest of their lives.

Mrs. Adams folded her hands, a warm yet determined smile brightening her face.

"So," she said, eyes landing squarely on Rose, "we need to get you a wedding dress. How about a day trip to Denver?"

Rose shook her head quickly. "I don't need a special dress. I can just use one of my old ball gowns."

"Oh no, darling." Mrs. Adams reached out and squeezed her hand. "You deserve a dress chosen just for your wedding day."

"I actually have an idea," Aunt Lizzie said suddenly, her eyes sparkling. "Come with me."

Cornelia rose at once. Rose followed, though uncertainty fluttered in her stomach. Jennifer practically bounced to her feet, only to whirl around when she saw the men beginning to follow the women.

"No, gentlemen," she said firmly, one hand raised like a traffic officer. "You stay right here. Anything concerning the bride is absolutely none of your business until the wedding day."

Grant smirked, as if tempted to protest, but Jennifer narrowed her eyes in warning. He surrendered immediately.

"That's what I thought," Jennifer said smugly, before scampering after the group.

Rose felt her cheeks grow warm as excitement buzzed around her. The realization that she was soon to be married settled over her in a flutter of nerves, thrilling and overwhelming all at once. She clasped her hands together as she followed her aunt upstairs.

"Come along, dear," Aunt Lizzie said warmly. "It's time we see whether a certain something in my cedar chest will fit you."

Jennifer gasped dramatically. "You mean that dress? Oh, Rose, you're going to LOVE this!"

Rose's heartbeat quickened. She still wasn't sure what her aunt had in mind, but suddenly she couldn't wait to find out.

Aunt Lizzie led them to Paul's old bedroom. Once inside, she crossed to the closet, opened it, and carefully lifted out a gown wrapped in linen. When she unfolded it, soft satin shimmered beneath lace so delicately stitched it seemed almost ethereal. Rose froze where she stood.

"It's beautiful," she whispered. "Where did you get it?"

Aunt Lizzie's expression softened with tender nostalgia.

"This was my wedding dress," she said quietly. "I always hoped a daughter of mine would wear it someday... but the Lord blessed me with sons. When you came into our lives, I dared to dream again. If you would like it, Rose, it is yours."

Rose's eyes widened, shimmering.

"Are you truly sure?"

"Absolutely," Aunt Lizzie replied, smiling warmly. "I'm taller than you, but that's easy to fix. Why don't we step outside and let you try it on?"

Cornelia and Jennifer eagerly ushered Aunt Lizzie out, leaving Rose trembling with excitement. She undressed quickly and lifted the gown, her fingers brushing the lace that had once been part of one of the happiest days of her aunt's life.

When she fastened the last hook and turned toward the mirror, her breath caught. The dress fit beautifully, almost perfectly. The hem was long, but the bodice hugged her gently, the sleeves framed her shoulders, and the lace lay soft against her collarbone. She barely recognized the young woman staring back.

And for the first time, she saw herself clearly: A bride. A daughter. A woman loved and cherished, and about to begin a new life.

Not long after supper, Mr. and Mrs. Adams excused themselves. Grant's father had a eulogy to finish, Paul and Jennifer left for the hotel, and the house slowly quieted, until Grant brushed his fingers over Rose's hand and murmured, "Walk with me?" She didn't even try to hide her smile.

Down by the lake, the air was crisp and the stars glittered above them. The dogs tore along the shoreline as though the whole world belonged to them. Rose pulled her shawl tighter. Her cheeks flushed from the cold... and from him.

"What exactly were you ladies whispering about earlier?" Grant asked, hands tucked in his pockets, his tone deceptively casual. Rose lifted her chin with exaggerated innocence.

"I have no idea what you're talking about."

"Oh, you do," he countered, his voice dipping into a teasing drawl. "And if you don't tell me, I'll just have to... persuade you."

Her heart tripped. "Persuade me? And how would you do that, Mr. Adams?"

He stepped closer, close enough for his warmth to spill into the cold around her.

"I can think of several ways. All highly effective."

"Well," she said primly, "there is absolutely nothing to persuade. And even if there were, it is none of your concern."

"That so?" His grin was borderline sinful.

"Yes." She nodded with great dignity. "Now, if you'll excuse me, I should help my aunt inside—" She yelped softly when he caught her hand and spun her gently but swiftly into his chest.

"You," he murmured, sliding an arm fully around her waist, "are not excused."

"Grant..." Her voice barely formed as his warmth enveloped her. "You—let me go."

"No," he said simply, wickedly. "Not until you tell me."

"There is nothing—"

He brushed a single knuckle down her jaw. "Rose Williams, you are a terrible liar."

"I am not lying," she insisted, breathless.

"Mm." He leaned in. "Then prove it." Before she could blink, he lowered his head and kissed her, deep, warm, and consuming. When he finally drew back, she swayed against him, breathless and dazed.

"Now," he asked softly, "are you going to tell me?"

Rose shook her head, stubborn even as her lips tingled. "No."

Grant kissed her again, longer, more determined. When he stopped, she gasped for air and pushed weakly at his chest.

"This isn't fair," she managed. "You... you are entirely too good-looking to kiss me like that. I can't think when you do that."

His chuckle vibrated through her. "Is that so?"

"It is," she pouted, leaning back just enough to glare up at him. "You're playing with fire, sir. A very dangerous fire. And I still won't tell you."

He brushed his thumb tenderly across her cheek.

"If fire burns this sweetly, I'll risk it."

"Grant..." Her knees went weak, and his arms tightened around her, steadying her effortlessly. His nearness, his warmth, his scent of cedar and leather, made her dizzy. He pressed a soft kiss to her forehead.

"I have to say... I quite like the effect I have on you."

"Well, I don't." She scrunched her nose, irresistibly endearing. "Please accept that I will not tell you anything. You'll find out at our wedding."

He let out an exaggerated sigh. "You wound me, Rose. Truly."

She giggled, and he offered her his arm.

"Come on," he said warmly. "Let's get you inside before you freeze. And before I try kissing the truth out of you again."

Rose lifted her chin proudly, slid her hand through his arm, and whistled for the dogs, even as her lips still tingled from his kisses and her heart felt far too light to be entirely proper.

28

A Mare's Last Gallop

Uncle John, Aunt Lizzie, and Jordan were in the sitting room reading when Grant and Rose returned. The warmth of the fireplace drew Rose immediately, and she stepped toward it, letting the heat seep back into her chilled fingers.

Grant crossed the room, took her hand, and gently tugged her down beside him on the settee. She had barely settled when an unexpected knock echoed through the quiet house.

John lifted his head, surprised.

"Who could that be at this hour?" He rose, crossed to the front door, and opened it wide. "Jonas, Cornelia, please, come in." Concern knit his brows as he stepped aside. "Did you forget something?"

Within seconds, they returned to the sitting room, except Cornelia didn't walk. She hurried. Straight toward Rose. Before Rose understood what was happening, Mrs. Adams took her by the shoulders and pulled her into a fierce, trembling embrace. Rose stiffened in shock. Cornelia had always been a pillar of strength, seeing her undone carved fear straight into Rose's chest.

"Mom?" Grant stood instantly, worry tightening his features. "What's wrong?"

When Cornelia finally loosened her arms, Mr. Adams stepped forward and wrapped Rose in another warm, fatherly hug. His eyes glistened.

"Mr. Adams?" Rose whispered, unable to breathe. "Please, what happened?"

He tipped her chin gently, his expression softening into pure tenderness.

"You darling girl," he murmured thickly. "You spoke to Grayson yesterday, didn't you?"

Rose blinked. "Not really a conversation," she said quietly. "I just... talked. I wasn't sure he heard anything."

Mr. Adams shook his head, emotion choking him.

"He heard every word. We just spent the last two hours with him. He opened up, fully. Apologized for everything since Jackson's death... the drinking, the anger, the distance. He asked us to let him be part of our lives again."

Cornelia dabbed her eyes. "We thought we had lost him forever. But you, somehow, you reached him. You gave him hope." Her voice trembled. "We have our son back because of you."

Rose's breath caught. Warmth flooded through her, disbelief, humility, and awe all tangled together until her eyes stung. Grant stepped behind her, resting both hands on her shoulders, pride radiating through his touch.

"I knew you would make a difference," he whispered.

Rose swallowed hard. Her life, once fractured and uncertain, seemed to be stitching itself together, piece by piece. For the first time in so long, she felt as though everything wasn't merely settling... but beginning to bloom.

Mr. Adams delivered a touching, at times even gently humorous, eulogy the following day, and Uncle John's sermon wrapped the congregation in a deep, quiet peace. But the hardest moment came when everyone followed the Adams family to the ranch, to the small cemetery beneath the pines where generations rested.

Six of Nana's oldest grandsons served as pallbearers, Grant and Grayson among them. Rose stood beside her aunt, tears slipping silently down her cheeks as the young men carried Nana toward her final resting place. Uncle John offered a quiet blessing, and then, with reverent hands, they lowered the casket into the earth.

Jennifer trembled in Paul's arms, shaken with sobs. Even Mr. Adams wiped his eyes as he held his grieving wife. One by one, Nana's children stepped forward, their goodbyes full of aching love.

When it was Grant's family's turn, Rose hesitated several steps behind. This grief belonged to them. She didn't want to intrude. But Mr. and Mrs. Adams turned, seeking her. Before she could retreat, Grant reached back, took her hand, and drew her firmly into the circle of his family. His arms wrapped around her from behind, holding her close to his chest.

"Grant," she whispered, "this moment is for your family. I can say goodbye later."

He only tightened his hold, his breath trembling against her hair. Mr. Adams reached out and took her other hand.

"You *are* family, Rose. We love you. And my mother loved you."

Grayson stepped forward, his expression softened, earnest in a way she had never seen.

"I'm truly sorry for what I said to you," he murmured. "Dad is right. You're family. You'll be my sister soon. Thank you... for helping me realize what I still have before I lose even more."

Rose's throat tightened painfully as emotion rose in her chest. One by one, they each released a shovel of earth onto the casket, the muted thuds echoing through the still afternoon. Red roses followed, creating a gentle blanket of color. They lingered in silent unity before stepping aside for the next group to say farewell.

Grant pulled Rose into his arms the moment they moved away. She melted against him, her quiet sobs muffled against his chest as he held her tight.

After the burial, everyone returned to the ranch for a funeral luncheon. Voices were hushed but warm, memories shared through tears and soft laughter. Rose, however, could barely touch her food. Her heart felt tender and raw. Slipping out the back door, she stepped onto the porch. The cold wind cooled the tears tracing down her cheeks.

"I miss you already, Nana," she whispered. "If you see my mother and father... please tell them I'm all right. Tell them Uncle John and Aunt Lizzie are the best family I could wish for. Thank you... for making me feel like I belong. I promise I'll hold onto hope—that we'll see each other again." She drew in a long breath, pulled her coat tighter, and looked through the window. Grant stood inside speaking with his cousins, warm in the glow of lamplight. And then—

A hand clamped over her mouth. An arm yanked her backward. Rose only had a fraction of a second to gasp before she was dragged off the porch into the dark brush lining the forest's edge. The world spun. Panic clawed up her throat. She tried to scream, to fight, but the man's grip was merciless, and the trees swallowed them whole. When they were finally out of earshot, the man spun her around violently. She stumbled, breath choking in her throat.

"Andrew?" she gasped. "What are you doing here? How did you even find me?"

He smiled, a cold, warped mockery of the boy she once knew.

"Hello, Rose. I traveled to Denver, rented a horse, and arrived this morning. I hid in the trees around your uncle's place until you all left for the funeral."

Her stomach twisted. "You need to leave. Now. Because this time, I won't stop anyone from throwing you in jail."

Andrew laughed, harsh, hollow.

"You didn't stop anything. You were only trying to protect your precious reputation. You knew if you dragged me into court, I'd take you down with me."

Rose winced. "Why are you doing this? Where has my best friend gone?"

"The best friend grew up," he spat. "And realized what you really are, a selfish, manipulative woman who uses her looks and wealth to get attention. I was just a distraction to you. A shoulder to cry on because you can't stand being alone."

Rose stared, stunned. "Andrew... what are you talking about?"

"Oh, don't pretend." His glare sharpened. "You used me. And now it's payback time."

"I never used you," she said, her voice trembling. "We were friends. I didn't know you only became my friend so you could throw it back at me."

"You were never there for me," he hissed. "I listened to your pathetic whining about being an orphan, about wanting peace with your father. I had needs too, Rose."

Anger flared through her, cutting through her fear.

"That's not true," she snapped. "I was there for you. I defended you at school. When your mother died, I sat with you every day. I mourned her too, she was—"

"Don't you dare talk about my mother," he growled. "She loved you more than she loved me. But you never deserved it."

"Your mother loved you with her whole heart," Rose insisted. "Before she died, she begged me to look after you."

"And did you?" he snarled. "No. You left. Even after I told you how I felt, you still left."

"Andrew... I couldn't force feelings I didn't have," she whispered. "I cared for you deeply, but not the way you wanted."

"You didn't even try." Suddenly he yanked her against him from behind, arms clamping around her waist. His breath brushed her ear. "You never gave me the chance to show you what real passion feels like."

She shuddered—and instantly regretted it.

"There," he said darkly. "I knew you'd respond."

Rose tore away, lungs burning. "Leave me alone. Nothing you say will change anything. You're the selfish one, not me. And you need to disappear before the people in this town find out you're here."

He grabbed her wrists.

"Nobody will know," he hissed. "And I know you're alone. The marshals are gone. Everyone is inside mourning that old hag."

"Don't you dare speak of Nana that way," Rose snapped.

"Nana?" He barked a laugh. "Are you collecting old people as substitutes for a real family now?"

"You know nothing about family," she shot back. "And ever since you discovered my dowry, all you've cared about is money. Let. Me. Go."

But before he could respond, two men stepped from the shadows. One wore a reverend's collar. The other, leading her horse. Rose's blood ran cold.

"Mr. Foster?" she whispered. "But... he was awaiting execution."

Andrew smirked. "Brad bribed a guard. I helped him escape. We planned this together. You're going to be *his*, Rose."

"No," she breathed. "I will never be his. Why would you stoop so low? If you're after my dowry, why work with someone like him?"

"Because we're splitting the money."

"You actually trust him?" Rose scoffed.

"I don't need to trust him," Andrew muttered. "If he crosses me, I'll turn him in."

"You're a fool," Rose said coldly. "He'll kill you before you ever get the chance."

Foster stepped forward, lip curling. "Hello again, Rose, ready to get married?"

"I'm engaged," she said firmly. "And not to you."

"You're engaged," he said with a shrug. "Not married." He nodded at the clergyman. "Reverend Jacobson."

"I will never agree to this."

Foster's grin grew sharp and terrible.

"Oh, you will, if you want your horse to live." He tied Willow's reins to a low branch. Rose's heart stopped.

"No," she whispered. "Leave her out of this."

"Marry me," Foster said, "and she lives."

Rose looked into Willow's gentle, trusting eyes. Her heart cracked open. She turned to Andrew.

"Please," she pleaded. "Don't let him do this."

For a heartbeat, Andrew hesitated. Then Foster seized Rose's arm.

"He won't help you. Choose. Marry me... or watch her die."

Tears blurred Rose's vision. She knew she could never agree to this, but sacrificing her beloved horse? Her heart was already beginning to shatter.

When Foster struck the horse, Willow reared, screaming. Rose lunged to protect her, but Foster shoved her into Andrew's arms and pulled out a knife.

"No!" Rose screamed, thrashing against both men. She seized Foster's wrist, fighting with every bit of strength she had left. He stumbled over a rock and went down hard. Rose lunged, fingers brushing Willow's reins for a fleeting moment, but Foster was on her again almost instantly. He slammed her to the ground, knocking the breath from her lungs.

And the reverend? He just stood there several feet away, watching as if none of it concerned him. He didn't shout, didn't intervene, didn't so much as lift a hand. His silence was damning, proof enough that Foster had promised him a glorious treasure.

Andrew pulled her upright, but Rose jerked free just as Foster drove the knife into Willow's shoulder.

Rose screamed. Her legs buckled, and she nearly collapsed as Willow tried desperately to flee. Andrew wrapped his arms around her trembling body.

"I'm sorry," he whispered, brokenly. "I'm so sorry..."

Rose clung to him, sobbing, searching desperately for the boy he once had been, for the friend she had lost.

"Are you ready to give in now?" Foster demanded. "Or should I finish the job?"

Rose forced Andrew to release her and staggered closer.

"You kill my horse," she choked, "and you'll never escape what's coming for you. You are a vile, sick demon. A piece of prairie coal. And God will judge you for every wicked thing you've done."

Foster laughed, a cold, merciless sound, and plunged the knife straight into Willow's heart. The mare collapsed. Rose screamed again, collapsing with her. She reached out, but Foster grabbed her before she could touch Willow's still body, yanking her back into the nightmare waiting for her.

Andrew shoved himself between Foster and Rose, his movement fueled by desperation rather than strength. His fist connected hard with Foster's jaw, snapping the man's head to the side. For one suspended heartbeat, Rose dared to hope it might be enough. It wasn't.

Foster staggered only a step before regaining his balance. His face twisted with pure malice as he lunged, driving his knife into Andrew's side. The young man gasped, folding to his knees as his hand clutched the wound. Rose cried out, her voice hoarse and broken.

Foster advanced, breath heaving, eyes blazing with victory. He reached into his coat and pulled out a pistol. The metallic click as he cocked it echoed in the forest, cold and merciless. Then he leveled it at Andrew's head.

"NO!" Rose screamed.

The world fractured into chaos. Several gunshots cracked through the air, sharp, deafening, final. Birds scattered from the trees in a panicked burst. Rose flinched, her hands flying to her mouth as she stared at Andrew, who was still alive, then Foster.

He stood frozen for a moment, shock widening his eyes. Then he fell backward, hitting the ground with a heavy thud. He didn't move again.

Rose trembled violently. From all sides, behind trees, from brush, from shadows, marshals emerged, rifles still raised. The sheriff of Idaho Springs and his deputy sprinted into view, arresting the reverend, faces carved with grim resolve.

"It's done," one marshal called out as he holstered his gun. Another rushed to Andrew's side.

Rose's breath shuddered out of her. Alive. Andrew was still alive. She dropped to her knees beside him. He was bent over, one hand pressed hard against his bleeding side, his breaths ragged and wet.

"You'll be all right," a marshal said, kneeling beside them. "Knife missed anything vital. He'll hurt, but he'll live."

Relief slammed into Rose, stealing her strength. The deputy ran toward the ranch to bring help, his boots pounding against the ground. The marshals lifted Andrew carefully, supporting him between them. He groaned but stayed conscious as they carried him toward the house.

Rose turned back. Willow lay still, her beautiful dark eyes already glazed. The sight of her beloved mare broke something inside her. Rose crawled to the horse's side and lowered herself against the warm neck, sobs erupting from deep in her chest, raw, aching, unstoppable. She pressed her cheek to Willow's mane, whispering apologies and love through the tremors of her grief.

She didn't know how long she clung to her horse before strong arms swept her up from the ground. Grant. She recognized his scent before she registered the strength of his hold or the tremble in his breath. His arms wrapped around her with a fierce protectiveness that made her collapse against him.

She didn't speak, couldn't speak. But when she buried her face in his chest, letting the tears fall freely, Grant held her tighter, as if he could shield her from every horror in the world.

It didn't erase the pain. But at that moment, with his warmth anchoring her and his heartbeat steadily beneath her cheek, Rose felt that she wasn't alone.

"Andrew will be fine, but he has a long road of recovery before him," Shane said gently.

"Why?" Rose asked, her brows drawing together. "Was the stab wound that bad?"

Shane shook his head. "No. The wound will heal well. That's not what concerns me. Andrew has a morphine addiction."

Rose stared at him, stunned. "Morphine? Is... is that why he changed so much?"

"I believe so," Shane replied. "The addiction took control of his mind and made him do things he never would have done in his right senses. He wanted your dowry because he needed money to buy more of the substance he craved. Truthfully, he's fortunate it didn't kill him."

Rose's voice trembled. "But how did he even become addicted? Morphine is for pain... isn't it?"

"Yes and no," Shane said with a slow exhale. "Morphine numbs pain, but it numbs everything else, too. It dulls the heart, the mind, and eventually the conscience. I just finished speaking with him at length. After his mother died, his grief was unbearable. He was very near to taking his own life. His father's abuse only made it worse. He eventually sought help from a physician who prescribed morphine to help him cope with both the physical and emotional pain."

Grant and Rose exchanged shocked looks.

Shane went on, "There has been a morphine addiction epidemic since the Civil War. Thousands of soldiers were left dependent on it after battlefield injuries. Over the past decade, there have been countless studies and warnings, but many physicians still think it harmless." He shook his head.

"Uncle Henry and I have watched the problem spread, and we've begun developing treatments. We're going to try the Keeley Cure, also known as the Gold Cure. Jordan and John volunteered to stay with him to help him through the worst of the withdrawals."

Rose swallowed hard. "Can... can I see him?"

"Not yet," Shane said softly. "Andrew wants to get through the most severe stage before he faces you. He's ashamed, Rose. Deeply."

"So, his behavior toward Rose wasn't because he was wicked," Grant said carefully, "but because the addiction took over?"

"Yes," Shane confirmed. "An addiction can twist a man's mind. When the drug leaves their system, they can become violent, desperate, hateful, even toward the people they care for. It can turn a kindhearted person into someone unrecognizable."

Grant frowned. "How did he snap out of it enough to defend her?"

"Pain," Shane replied. "Real, emotional pain has a way of breaking through the haze. When Foster threatened Rose's horse... when he saw her heart breaking... something pierced through the fog of the addiction. For a moment he was himself again, enough to step between them."

Rose let out a trembling breath. She hadn't lost Andrew completely. Beneath all the anger and the twisted words, her friend was still there, buried but not gone.

"And there's something else," Shane said suddenly. "Andrew helped the U.S. Marshals finish this. He assisted Foster during the escape, but Foster never paid him a dime. Halfway across the country, when he had a moment of clarity, he secretly contacted a sheriff, who sent word to the marshals. They met with him in Denver, without Foster knowing, and Andrew told them where Foster was headed." Shane exhaled.

"One of the marshals was a former soldier and recognized the signs of Andrew's addiction. He gave him just enough money to get some morphine. But he told him that once Foster was no longer a threat, he'd take Andrew to a doctor."

Grant nodded. "So, if Andrew hadn't gotten injured, that marshal would have taken him to a hospital?"

Shane nodded.

"Will he be well enough to come to our wedding?" Rose asked quietly.

Shane's expression softened. "The battle won't be finished by then, but he should be past the worst of the withdrawals. If his recovery continues well, yes, he should be able to attend."

Relief washed over her. "Thank you," she whispered. "Please tell Andrew I'm thinking of him... and that I'm praying for him."

Shane nodded. "I'll be sure to pass that along."

When Grant and Rose stepped out of the clinic, the cold air hit her cheeks, sharp and stinging, but it was nothing compared to the ache inside her chest. She exhaled a long, trembling sigh, as if releasing part of the weight she had carried since the attack.

Grant immediately turned her to face him. His hands settled warmly on her arms, steady and grounding, and his deep brown eyes searched hers with a tenderness that made her throat tighten. The simple way he looked at her, so present, so fiercely protective, made her heart flutter despite her grief.

"How are you feeling?" he asked softly. Rose tried to smile, but it wavered.

"Knowing that my best friend was there this whole time... trapped inside himself... it makes me grateful he's still in there somewhere." Her voice cracked, and she brushed at a tear. "But losing Willow is just..." The words crumbled in her throat. She swallowed hard, unable to finish.

Grant didn't make her. His expression softened, full of understanding, and he drew her closer.

"I know," he murmured. "I'm so sorry, sweetheart."

She leaned into him, letting herself feel the warmth of his chest, the steady rhythm of his heartbeat under her cheek. For a moment, the world quieted. Then Grant gently lifted her chin with two fingers. The gesture was so tender that her breath caught.

Before she could say anything else, he bent his head and pressed a kiss to her lips, soft, sweet, and full of aching compassion. Right there on the steps of the clinic, in full view of half the town, he kissed her as if she were the only person in existence.

Heat rushed into her cheeks, but she didn't care. She kissed him back, clinging to him as if he were the only thing keeping her upright. His hand slid up her back, holding her close, steadying her as her world shifted beneath her feet. When he finally pulled back, their foreheads rested together, breaths mingling in the cold air.

"You don't have to pretend you're all right," he whispered. "Not with me. I'll carry as much of this with you as you need."

A shaky breath escaped her. "Thank you, Grant."

He gave her a faint, bittersweet smile. "Always."

And for the first time since the nightmare began, Rose felt a small spark of warmth easing through the fractures in her heart. She had lost so much, but she hadn't lost everything. Not while Grant was here, holding her together, piece by piece.

29

A Hearth for Her Heart

"This is where we will live." Grant slowed his horse to a stop in front of a charming blockhouse nestled beside a quiet, snow-dusted lake. Tall pines framed the clearing like loyal sentinels, and the air smelled of fresh winter and woodsmoke. Rose felt her breath catch as Grant dismounted, then reached up for her with those steady, capable hands she loved so much.

As her boots touched the ground, she took in the peaceful little homestead, the glimmer of the lake, the thick shelter of the forest, the serenity she could almost feel settling into her bones.

"It's beautiful," she whispered.

"It was my parents' first home," Grant said softly. "They lived here before my dad built the ranch house. He had it renovated this year. Since Jennifer and Paul will be living in Denver... this place is ours now."

There was quiet pride in his voice. Not boastful, tender. It made Rose's heart swell.

He guided her up the steps and opened the door. Rose gasped. Inside was warm, spacious, and inviting, more than she had ever expected. To the right, a handsome stone fireplace anchored the room. To the left stretched an airy open space perfect for a dining area. Behind that, framed by broad archways, was a kitchen large enough to make any homemaker sigh in contentment. To the other side of the fireplace was a washroom, complete with a bathtub. A bathtub. In their own home.

A broad staircase led to an upper floor with a beautiful railing overlooking the sitting room. Large windows flooded the space with light, showcasing a breathtaking view of the lake and winter forest. Her breath trembled. It wasn't just a house. It was a future.

Grant took her hand and led her upstairs into the largest bedroom. Soft light spilled across the floorboards, and Rose drifted toward the wide window overlooking the frozen lake. Snowflakes danced past the glass in slow, quiet spirals.

Grant's arms came around her as they stood before the window, the hush of falling snow wrapping the world outside in soft white. Rose felt the warmth of him at her back, steady and solid, an anchor in a storm that had nearly broken her. His breath brushed the side of her neck, and her pulse fluttered wildly.

"So," he murmured, his voice low and warm, "do you like it?"

Rose swallowed hard, unable to keep the shimmer of emotion from her voice.

"Like it? I love it." She turned just enough to meet his gaze, and the look he gave her sent a fluttering heat through her entire body.

Grant lowered his head, brushing his lips over hers, soft at first, almost reverent, as though he feared she might vanish like a dream. But when she rose on her toes, fingers clinging to the front of his coat, his restraint broke. He kissed her fully, deeply, stealing her breath, making her knees weaken. His hands slid to her waist, pulling her anchored against him, and Rose felt her heart race so wildly she thought it might lift her right off the floor.

"This," he whispered against her lips, "will be our room."

Her blush flared instantly, he felt it, she knew he did, because his quiet laugh came warm and wicked and far too knowing.

"What about the other two rooms?" she managed, though her voice was still unsteady from the kiss. His eyes darkened with tenderness and something that made her pulse skip.

"Guests... for a little while."

"And after?" she whispered.

Grant's gaze swept her face, lingering on her lips, and the slow smile that curved his mouth nearly unraveled her.

"After," he murmured, brushing his thumb over her lower lip, "we'll need space for a growing family."

Rose's breath caught. Heat rose in her cheeks, heat that spread through her whole body in a way she couldn't control. She looked away, flustered, but he tipped her chin back up with one gentle finger.

"Rose," he whispered, voice lower now, almost hoarse, "you're my future. My home. Everything."

Then he kissed her again, longer, lingering, coaxing, a kiss that promised a lifetime of devotion and shared dreams. She melted into him, her fingers curling against his chest, her heart overflowing with a love so strong it nearly overwhelmed her.

When they finally drew apart, breathless and flushed, he rested his forehead against hers once more.

"I love you, Rose."

Her smile trembled with emotion but shone radiant.

"I love you too."

Outside, the snow continued to fall softly, but inside that warm, quiet room, Rose felt as though spring had bloomed in her heart.

Grant and Rose stood beside the horse enclosure, watching the animals mill about in the soft winter light. Snowflakes drifted lazily through the air, settling on the rails and catching in Rose's hair. Grant slipped an arm around her waist, sensing the tension in her body even before she spoke.

"Are you ready to pick a new horse?" he asked gently, searching her eyes rather than the corral.

Rose swallowed hard. The simple question squeezed her heart. She missed Willow terribly, her gentle snorts, her familiar gait, the bond they'd formed since the day Rose first chose her. But she also knew Grant was right. She couldn't walk everywhere for the rest of her life, and Willow would have wanted her to move forward. She nodded, though her throat tightened.

"I think I'm ready."

They walked the fence line slowly, Grant letting her set the pace. Rose studied each horse carefully, her gaze lingering on the mares. She didn't want a replacement, no creature could ever be Willow, but she needed a companion she could trust. One with spirit... and loyalty.

After several minutes, one mare stepped forward with a toss of her head, as if demanding attention. Her coat was a striking near-black, glossy as ink, with a sharp white star on her forehead. Her eyes were bright, bold, observant, perhaps a touch stubborn. Rose felt her breath catch.

"I think this one," she said softly. "She looks a lot like Willow... but her personality seems different. She looks a little sassy."

Grant chuckled, his grin spreading wide.

"Oh, she's perfect for you then."

Rose lifted a brow and nudged him with her elbow.

"Ha-ha. Very funny."

"It's true," he said with an innocent shrug, though his eyes sparkled. "You'll keep each other out of trouble."

Rose rolled her eyes, but a small, genuine smile found her lips, her first since the funeral. It warmed Grant's heart to see it.

"Do you want to try riding her?" he asked after a moment.

Rose hesitated, nerves fluttering in her stomach. Riding had always felt natural, freeing, joyful, but since losing Willow... she wasn't sure she trusted her courage. Grant saw it instantly.

"I'll be right here," he murmured, brushing his knuckles along her cheek. "I won't let anything happen."

Something inside her steadied at his touch. She nodded. Before she could brace herself, Grant placed his hands at her waist and lifted her onto the saddle in one smooth, effortless motion. Rose gasped, grabbing the horn, her heart flipping at both the sudden height and the warmth of his hands lingering for just a moment too long.

"Warn me next time," she breathed.

He gave her a wicked grin. "Where's the fun in that?"

A soft snort from the mare drew Rose's attention, and she reached down to stroke the velvety neck.

"You are beautiful," she whispered. "And brave. I can tell."

The mare flicked an ear back, as though acknowledging the compliment. Rose clicked her tongue gently. To her surprise, the horse responded at once, stepping forward with energy, testing the reins but respectful of Rose's hold.

Grant's smile deepened. "Looks like she chose you."

Rose's throat tightened again, but this time not from grief alone. Hope flickered there too, quiet, fragile, but real.

She glanced down at Grant, who watched her with adoration and pride shining in his eyes.

"She'll never be Willow," Rose murmured.

"No," Grant agreed softly. "But she'll be yours. And she'll carry you into our future."

Rose nodded, blinking back tears, not heartbreak this time, but healing.

"Then... I think I'd like to take her for a ride."

Mr. Adams joined Grant at the fence, folding his hands over the top rail as he watched Rose circle the enclosure with the new mare.

"That's the perfect horse for Rose," he said with quiet certainty. Grant nodded, his gaze fixed on his fiancée as though the rest of the world had fallen away. Rose guided the horse toward them, her posture straight, her expression calm yet glowing with a spark he hadn't seen since before the attack. When she reached the fence, Grant stepped forward and lifted her easily out of the saddle. She let out a soft laugh as her boots touched the ground.

"Do you have a name picked out?" he asked, his hands lingering at her waist a heartbeat longer than necessary. Rose stroked the mare's velvet nose.

"Meadow," she said softly. "She's so delightful, calm, and beautiful... but I can sense her wild spirit." Her voice wavered slightly, but hope shimmered there, more than there had been in days.

Mr. Adams smiled, the kind of smile that softened every line in his face.

"You two are perfect for each other. Both beautiful, and you share a feisty spirit."

"Mr. Adams," Rose began gently, cheeks pink. He shook his head with mock sternness that only made him look more fatherly.

"What did we talk about, Rose? I want you to call me Jonas." His gaze warmed even further. "And once you two are married, I'm Dad."

Emotion tightened her throat. So much loss in her life... yet so much unexpected gain. She nodded.

"All right... Jonas," she said softly, testing the name with affection. "I'll try to remember. And... Dad, when the time comes."

He reached out and squeezed her hand with a tenderness that nearly brought tears to her eyes.

"You're already part of this family, sweetheart. Titles will catch up in time."

Grant wrapped an arm around her shoulders, pulling her gently against his side. Meadow nickered behind them, as if approving of the moment, and a faint breeze stirred Rose's hair.

"Rose," Andrew said the moment she and Grant stepped into his small room at the clinic. Uncle John and Jordan sat nearby, both keeping watchful, supportive eyes on him. Rose stepped forward, her expression softening.

"How are you feeling?"

Andrew gave a tired but sincere smile.

"It's been rough," he admitted, voice hoarse. "Rougher than I expected... but I'm blessed to have your uncle and Jordan here to keep me steady when I feel like I might lose my footing." He reached for her hand, hesitant at first, as though afraid she might pull away. When she didn't, he gently drew her closer.

"I'm truly sorry for how I treated you. I never wanted to hurt you. I never imagined morphine would turn me into such a horrible version of myself. Looking back... I can't believe the things I said. The things I did. I don't know how you can even stand in this room with me, let alone speak to me with kindness."

Rose squeezed his fingers. "Yes, you hurt me," she said honestly, her voice steady but warm. "But it wasn't the real you. The addiction clouded everything, your feelings, your thoughts, your conscience. I'm grateful you're still alive... and that I have my friend back. One day, we'll look at these last months as a terrible nightmare we both woke from."

Tears gathered in Andrew's eyes as he managed a small smile.

"How did I ever get so lucky to earn your friendship?"

Rose glanced toward Uncle John and Jordan, feeling both bashful and relieved.

"Have you made any plans for once you're released from the hospital?"

Andrew nodded. "It'll be a while before I feel like myself again... but I want to stay here, if that's all right. I want to build a new life. I need people who won't give up on me, and I don't have that in Boston."

"We'll help you in any way we can," Uncle John assured warmly. Jordan nodded.

"We're glad the real you is back," Jordan added.

Rose brightened. "And once you're stronger, you need to meet Alice's older sister, Cathleen."

Andrew blinked. "Cathleen?"

"Yes," Rose said, grinning. "She isn't shy like Alice. She'll give you a piece of her mind if you deserve it."

Andrew let out a true laugh, one that finally sounded like him.

"You think I need that?"

"Definitely!" Rose and Jordan said in unison, then exchanged surprised laughs. Andrew threw up his hands.

"Hey, what's that supposed to mean?"

"I think you already know," Jordan teased.

Rose added, "You need a wife someday who won't hesitate to put her foot down."

Andrew rolled his eyes dramatically.

"Fine, fine. I'll keep that in mind." He paused. "So, when do Thomas and Charlotte arrive?"

"Tomorrow," Rose said with genuine excitement. "I can't wait to see them again." Her joy made Andrew smile fondly.

"That reminds me," Grant said, stepping closer and placing a hand on Andrew's shoulder. "Before Rose and I head to the church to meet Uncle John about the ceremony... there's something we'd like to ask." He exchanged a look with Rose, who nodded. Grant took a breath.

"Andrew... we would be honored if you would stand with me as one of my groomsmen. Would you do that for us?"

Andrew stared at him, stunned. His lips parted but no sound came at first. Then, eyes brightening with emotion, he whispered, "I... I would love that. Truly."

Rose beamed. "Wonderful. And if it's all right with Dr. Hunter, we'd love for you to attend the rehearsal today. Only for as long as you're able."

For the first time since she'd entered the room, hope lit Andrew's face, not borrowed, not forced, but real.

Rose and Grant joined Uncle John and Aunt Lizzie as they made their way toward the saloon, where the stagecoach had just come to a stop. The moment the door swung open and Thomas stepped out to help Charlotte down, Rose let out a delighted squeal that turned every head.

Thomas barely had time to brace himself before Rose flew into his arms. He caught her mid-rush, laughing as he twirled her once. When he set her back on her feet, he pulled her into another tight squeeze.

"That was very selfish of you, Thomas," Charlotte scolded lightly, though the wide smile spreading across her face betrayed her amusement. "I should have been the first to greet Rose."

She immediately enveloped Rose in a fierce, lingering hug, rocking her gently before leaning back to study her face. Her expression softened with affection.

"Just look at you, Rose. I always knew you were beautiful, but my word, you're glowing. Moving here has done you more good than a thousand doctors ever could."

Rose's cheeks warmed, and she lowered her gaze shyly. Needing the familiar steadiness of Grant beside her, she reached back, clasped his hand, and guided him gently forward.

"May I introduce my fiancé?" she said proudly, her voice trembling with excitement. "Grant Adams, this is Charlotte and Thomas Graham."

Charlotte's smirk was immediate, mischievous, approving, and more than a little teasing.

"Well done, Rose," she declared boldly. "You caught yourself a very handsome man."

Thomas nodded solemnly, though his eyes sparkled.

"You're getting a jewel, Grant. This girl was given the perfect name. She truly is a rose, beautiful and loving, but watch out for the thorns when her feistiness comes out."

Laughter rippled through the group, and Grant slid his arm around Rose's waist, pulling her close enough that she could feel the warm rumble of his amused exhale.

"Oh, I know," Grant said, giving Rose a look so filled with adoration it made her knees weaken. "She's already taken over every corner of my heart. I can't picture my life without her, and I can't wait to marry her so we can spend the rest of our lives together." He lifted Rose's hand and kissed her knuckles in front of everyone, his gaze never leaving hers.

"I promise," he said softly, "I will love, cherish, and protect her with every fiber of my being."

Charlotte sighed dramatically and dabbed at the corner of her eye.

"Oh dear. Rose, I like him already."

Rose laughed, leaning into Grant as warmth flooded through her. For the first time in a long time, everything felt beautifully, perfectly right.

Everyone who needed to be at the rehearsal was already in place. Grant's parents and Aunt Lizzie sat on the front bench, hands folded, watching with soft smiles as Jennifer glided down the aisle when the pianist began the wedding march. Her steps were slow, graceful, full of joy, though her misty eyes betrayed the lingering emotions of the past few days.

Rose stood in the church doorway, holding her small bouquet, her heart fluttering wildly. Something tugged at her, where was Uncle John? She drew in a steadying breath, trying to calm her nerves as she waited for her cue. Then she sensed a presence beside her.

Startled, she turned, and there he was. Uncle John, eyes warm and full of affection, smiling at her as though she were the brightest star in the heavens. He extended his arm.

"Rose," he began softly, "I know I am not your biological father..." His voice broke. He paused, gathering himself before continuing, gentler still. "But Aunt Lizzie and I cannot express how deeply we love you... how much we truly see you as our daughter."

Her breath caught. She stared up at him, wide-eyed, already trembling.

"These past few months," he said tenderly, "you slipped right into our hearts and settled there before we even realized it. And although you never said anything aloud, your aunt and I saw it, the sadness in your eyes during Paul and Jennifer's wedding... when you realized you would have no father to walk you down the aisle." His voice thickened.

"Nothing would make me happier than stepping into my brother's place and bringing you to the man you love. Rose... would you allow me the honor of walking you down the aisle?"

The world blurred. Shock, love, longing, the ache of years without a father, every emotion rushed through her at once until her knees nearly gave way. Tears spilled before she could stop them. She turned as if to flee, to gather herself, but Uncle John caught her immediately. He drew her into his chest, wrapping both arms around her in the way only a father could, holding her as though she were the most precious soul in the world. Her quiet sobs echoed through the stillness of the church.

Something holy settled over the room. Everyone watched, eyes glistening. Grant swallowed hard and wiped his cheek. Jennifer's bouquet trembled in her hands. Even Grayson lowered his gaze, blinking rapidly, jaw tight.

When Rose's sobs finally eased, Uncle John gently lifted her chin with one fingertip. He kissed her forehead, slow, reverent, tender.

"I love you, Uncle John," she whispered, voice trembling. He smiled through his own tears.

"I love you too, sweetheart. More than you will ever know." Then he straightened, clearing his throat with exaggerated seriousness. "Now... shall we finish this rehearsal? We can't keep Grant waiting. He looks like he might faint if you don't take a step soon."

Rose let out a shaky laugh and nodded. She slipped her arm through his, and together they moved toward the aisle. Her eyes immediately found Grant, and the look on his face stole the air from her lungs. Pure admiration. Awe. A love so steady and blazing she felt her knees weaken. His slow, breath-stealing smile sent her heart fluttering wildly.

Paul waited at the front, officiating the rehearsal with quiet pride, the groomsmen lined beside him, Grayson, Jordan, Andrew, and Ahanu. The bridesmaids stood across from them, hands folded, smiles soft.

When Uncle John placed her hand into Grant's, she instinctively wrapped her arms around her fiancé in a brief, heartfelt embrace. Grant kissed her cheek before she stepped into place beside him.

Jennifer, desperately trying not to cry again, handed Rose the flowers with a dramatic sniff.

"All right," she said, blinking furiously, "you need to stop making us all puddles. I just watered those flowers enough to keep them alive through winter."

Laughter rippled through the church, easing the emotional tension. Rose lifted her gaze to Grant. He was already looking at her. And his smile, full of wonder, devotion, and quiet awe, made her feel as though she had hung the moon.

❦

Rose stood in the small back room of the church, surrounded by the women who had shaped her heart, and the women who were quickly becoming family. Aunt Lizzie dabbed her eyes with her handkerchief, Charlotte tried and failed to keep her composure, and Mrs. Adams sniffed softly, her expression glowing with motherly pride.

Rose stood in the center of them all, hands folded over her gown, her cheeks warm and her smile radiant.

Alice, Cathleen Baker, and Ahanu's bride, her three bridesmaids, waited near the door, bouquets in hand, ready to walk down the aisle first. The older women circled Rose once more, checking every detail of her dress and smoothing the veil with tender, trembling fingertips. It wasn't fussing, it was love poured out in small gestures. Aunt Lizzie kissed her cheek, Charlotte followed, and Mrs. Adams cupped Rose's face gently before kissing her forehead.

"You're perfect, sweetheart," Mrs. Adams whispered.

Aunt Lizzie lowered the veil carefully, her fingers lingering on Rose's cheek before she followed the others out to join the congregation. Jennifer slipped in and stood beside Rose, eyes gleaming with excitement.

"Are you nervous?" she asked softly, just as the first familiar chords of the wedding march drifted through the church walls. The bridesmaids lifted their bouquets and glided from the room.

Rose exhaled shakily.

"So nervous," she whispered, though joy glowed right through her skin.

Jennifer grinned. "You look beautiful. Grant will faint when he sees you."

Rose laughed softly, nerves fluttering like moth wings in her stomach. Jennifer winked before slipping out to take her place.

Left alone, Rose placed a hand over her heart and breathed in deeply. This is real, she thought. I'm about to marry the man I love. The music changed, her cue. She stepped toward the main doors, where Uncle John waited. He stood tall and proud, but the emotion shimmering behind his eyes nearly undid her.

"You ready, sweetheart?" he asked gently. She nodded, and he opened his arms. Rose fell into his fatherly embrace, letting herself savor one last moment of simply being held. His arms steadied her heart, soothed her fears, and filled her with a warmth that felt like home.

He pulled back and offered his arm with a loving smile. Rose placed her gloved hand atop it, breath catching. Beyond those doors waited Grant—her future, her happiness, her forever. Together, they stepped toward the aisle.

Charlotte reflected on that distant morning at the train station, the day she and Thomas had sent Rose off with trembling hearts and whispered prayers. Rose had been so frightened then, her gloved hands clutching her ticket as though it were both lifeline and doom. She'd feared meeting relatives she barely remembered, feared being an imposition, feared never finding a place where she truly belonged.

And now... now she stood here safely in the arms of the man she had once dreaded meeting, held with such tenderness that Charlotte's vision blurred. A moment later Grant embraced her with the devotion of a husband long before the vows were spoken. Watching Uncle John give her that same fatherly hold, one Rose had been denied for so many years, made Charlotte's heart swell until it ached with joy.

"...joining two families together—but mostly joining this man and woman to become husband and wife. Grant, you may kiss your bride."

Rose lifted her gaze, shy but radiant beneath her veil. Grant raised the veil gently, then lowered his head, his eyes soft with reverence as his lips met hers. Their first kiss as husband and wife was gentle yet full of promise, sweet enough to melt every heart present, strong enough to silence the pasts that had haunted them both.

The church erupted in cheers. Aunt Lizzie dabbed her eyes, Mrs. Adams clutched Jonas's arm, and Charlotte pressed a hand over her racing heart. Even Grayson managed to smile.

Grant rested his forehead against Rose's, then wrapped an arm around her waist and guided her toward the back doors. Rose clung to his hand, glowing from the inside out. Together, Mr. and Mrs. Grant Adams walked down the aisle, not as the lost, heartbroken girl Rose once was, but as a cherished bride... a beloved daughter... and now, the center of a love she had waited her whole life to find.

Rose was in heaven. Grant never left her side, not for a single moment, and each time he leaned down to kiss her, her heart fluttered as though she was experiencing love for the very first time. The young man who held her heart so completely seemed to know precisely how to make it race. And when he whispered into her ear that he was looking forward to kissing her later without restraint, her entire face flamed into the deep, breathtaking shade of a sunset sky. Her breath caught, and her nervousness soared.

Grant only grinned, looking terribly pleased with himself, while Rose desperately attempted to steady her thoughts so her complexion would return to something less conspicuous than the fiery glow she currently wore. To distract herself, her gaze wandered through the bustling reception—and soon fell on Andrew and Cathleen Baker.

They sat close together near the corner of the room, deep in conversation. Just as Rose and Jordan had hoped, Alice's bold and perceptive older sister and Andrew had bonded quickly. Cathleen understood more than most the pain Andrew had endured, and she seemed determined to support him through his recovery.

A gentle warmth flickered between them, an unmistakable spark, but to her admiration, they had agreed not to rush anything until Andrew felt steady and sure. Rose's heart swelled with hope for her friend's future.

Her gaze drifted then to Uncle John and Aunt Lizzie. They stood watching her, eyes misty, smiles soft. Pride radiated from them, pride, love, and something so tender Rose had to blink back tears. For the first time in her life, she felt completely, unquestionably cherished. She curled closer to Grant's side, his arm tightening around her, and for the first time ever, Rose Williams, now Rose Adams, felt entirely, beautifully complete.

When Grant woke, the room was still and hushed, washed in the soft silver glow of moonlight spilling through the window.

Shadows shifted gently across the walls, and the faint crackle of the dying fire whispered from the hearth. He looked down, and his heart clenched with a warmth he knew would never fade.

Rose was curled against him, her cheek resting over his heartbeat, one arm draped across his waist as though she instinctively sought his nearness even in sleep. Her golden hair spilled over his chest like a silken cascade, faintly illuminated by the moonlight. She looked so peaceful, so trusting, so heartbreakingly lovely that Grant felt a tightness in his throat.

He would never tire of waking like this, he knew that to his very bones. One week. They had only been married for one week, seven days, and yet it felt as though his world had never fully existed before she stepped into it. A slow smile warmed his face as he brushed a strand of hair away from her cheek. His smile deepened when he remembered the night before. His sweet, gentle wife had turned into a mischievous sprite.

They had been lounging together on the sofa in front of the roaring fire, snow drifting outside like feathers falling from heaven. He had teased her relentlessly, about her blushing, how adorably flustered she became when he whispered something suggestive, how he could make her heart race with just a look.

Rose had pressed her lips together, fighting every reaction. He had seen the spark in her eyes, the challenge, but she pretended otherwise. Until she struck. He had gone to the washroom for only a moment. When he returned, bending to place another log on the fire, she slid a handful of snow straight down the back of his shirt. His yelp had startled even him. Her laughter, bright, pure, and unrestrained, filled the cabin as she dashed up the stairs. She almost managed to lock him out, but he was too quick.

He caught her, tossed her over his shoulder, carried her outside, and dropped her into a bank of fresh snow. She squealed, kicking and laughing, until he pulled her into his arms, cold snow melting against their clothes, warm breath mingling, and kissed her until she melted all over again.

Now, in the moonlit stillness, Grant watched her chest rise and fall, felt the soft puff of her breath against his skin. A fierce protectiveness surged through him. Knowing she felt safe in his arms, safe enough to sleep deeply, was a gift he would never take for granted. He pressed a tender kiss to her forehead.

"I love you," he whispered, even though she couldn't hear him. As much as he wanted to stay wrapped around her, he needed to check the fires. The winter cold was ruthless, and their warmth depended on his vigilance. Slowly, carefully, he eased his arm from beneath her and shifted her onto her pillow. She murmured softly but didn't wake, her fingers curling loosely in the blanket as if still reaching for him.

Grant tucked the covers snugly around her, then rose quietly from the bed. After one lingering glance at his sleeping wife, he stepped into the hall to tend the fires that kept their home warm through the night.

Rose opened her eyes just as he disappeared beyond the doorway. She watched the last glimmer of him vanish down the hall, and her heart skipped with its familiar wonder. Grant Adams, broad-shouldered, steady-handed, tender-hearted, was her husband. Her home. Her safe place.

She lay still, listening to the rhythm of his distant footsteps, and felt warmth fill her chest. What a year it had been, heartbreak, danger, unexpected kindness, and moments that had changed everything. Through it all, Grant had been the unwavering presence she didn't know she needed. With him, she no longer had to fear the world. She no longer had to prove her worth. She was protected. Cherished. Loved.

Tears pricked her eyes as her thoughts drifted back to her rehearsal. The moment Uncle John had stepped beside her, offered his arm, and asked if he could walk her down the aisle... that moment had mended something deep inside her. It had filled a hollow place she had carried since childhood. From then on, she knew she would never again be alone. Uncle John, Aunt Lizzie, Jordan, each had claimed her as family with a love she once believed she would never deserve.

Yet her heart tugged gently when she thought of Christopher Moore. Not with regret, she had never doubted that Grant was the man meant for her, but because she missed his friendship. His kindness. He had helped her rediscover her worth at a time she desperately needed it. She prayed he had found joy, and that the woman he married would treasure him completely.

Her thoughts shifted to Andrew, and a soft shiver ran through her. Remembering what he became under the grip of addiction still pained her. Yet she could not hate him. Morphine had twisted his mind, drowning the boy she once knew beneath a darkness he could not control.

But he wasn't lost. Not truly. She was grateful he fought his way back, grateful she had not lost her childhood friend forever. Rose closed her eyes again, letting the warmth of the blankets and the faint crackle of the fire soothe her. Grant would return soon, his arms warm, his voice gentle, his heartbeat steady. And as she waited, a soft smile curved her lips. Her life had not unfolded as she once imagined. It had unfolded better.

Grant returned to their bedroom, the glow from the fire outlining the breadth of his shoulders as he added a log to the grate. Rose lay still, admiring him with quiet wonder. Even simple movements, the flex of his hands, the ease of his stride, the care he put into every small task, made her heart swell.

When he turned and saw her awake, his expression softened instantly. In a few long strides, he slid beneath the blankets and drew her against him. His arm slipped beneath her shoulders and pulled her close, enveloping her in warmth. He looked down at her, eyes dark and tender in the firelight. The intensity of his gaze made her breath catch. She felt her pulse flutter wildly beneath her skin.

"I love you," she whispered, barely more than a breath. The words were still hanging in the air when he kissed her, slowly, reverently, savoring each second of closeness. Rose melted into him, her fingers curling in the fabric of his shirt, pulling him nearer. His kiss deepened, warm and consuming, sending a tremor through her.

Grant gathered her closer, holding her as though the world beyond their room did not exist. The heat of his embrace chased away all lingering fears, all old shadows. She answered his kiss with tenderness and longing, her heart beating wildly against his.

And then another realization washed through her, warm, steady, profound: Her heart was whole again. Her heart was home.

She pressed her forehead to his, their breaths mingling as he pulled her even closer. Grant brushed his thumb across her cheek and kissed her once more, gentler, lingering, full of devotion. Wrapped in his arms, Rose knew with certainty: Nothing in this world had ever felt more right.

The End

Epilogue

"Try to breathe through it," Aunt Lizzie encouraged softly, brushing damp tendrils of hair from Rose's forehead. Rose forced a shaky breath past her lips, trying to stay with the rhythm of her body as another wave of pain crashed through her. It felt as though her lower body were splintering apart, and despite her efforts to be brave, moans slipped out, raw, strained, uncontrollable.

"You're doing wonderfully, Rose," her mother-in-law murmured, squeezing her hand with warm, steady strength. "You're stronger than you think."

"We're almost there," Dr. Hunter added, his calm voice anchoring her frayed nerves. "Work with me when I tell you to push." Beside him, the nurse moved efficiently, preparing everything for the moment the child arrived.

Another contraction tore through her, hot, sharp, demanding. Rose gasped, clutching the sheets. The baby was determined. It was Thanksgiving, and the faint scent of the holiday feast still lingered in the air downstairs, where laughter and chatter filled the house. No one had expected Rose to go into labor that day.

Through the pain, she heard Jennifer and Paul's little boy crying on the floor below, a familiar, strangely comforting sound.

She pictured Grant pacing anxiously in the hallway with Grayson, Jordan, Uncle John, and her father-in-law hovering beside him, no doubt trying, and failing, to keep him calm.

"All right, Rose," Dr. Hunter said, leaning closer. "When the next contraction comes, push as hard as you can. I can see the head. We're moments away."

Aunt Lizzie took Rose's left hand. Her mother-in-law held her right.

"Don't hold back, sweetheart," Aunt Lizzie whispered, her voice thick with emotion. "Scream if you need to."

The contraction hit.

"Push!" Dr. Hunter urged. Rose obeyed, giving every last scrap of strength she possessed. Her body trembled, one push, then another, her vision blurring with exhaustion. But then the pain shifted, fading into something distant, overtaken by fierce determination.

And then... a cry. Loud. Healthy. Demanding. Rose let out a broken sob of relief as Dr. Hunter lifted a slick, squirming newborn into the air. He cut the umbilical cord, and the nurse quickly washed and wrapped the tiny, furious miracle before placing her gently into Rose's waiting arms.

Rose laughed and cried at once, her heart splitting wide open. Aunt Lizzie covered her mouth with trembling hands. Her mother-in-law pressed a palm to her chest as tears spilled freely. The room filled with nothing but joy, awe, and the soft, insistent wails of new life. Once the afterbirth was taken care of and Rose was cleaned and settled back into bed, they invited Grant and the two grandfathers inside.

"Grant," Dr. Hunter said with a warm smile, "you have a beautiful little girl."

Grant froze in his tracks. His breath caught audibly. Rose watched his face transform, shock, reverence, wonder, and a tenderness so profound, it nearly undid her. He lowered himself onto the chair beside her, and when she guided the tiny bundle into his arms, he held his daughter as though she were made of spun glass.

He kissed the baby's forehead, soft, lingering, and Rose thought her heart might burst at the sight of this strong, rugged man undone so completely by love.

"Have you settled on a name yet?" Uncle John asked, his voice reverent. Rose brushed her thumb gently over the baby's cheek.

"We had chosen a name... but when Dr. Hunter placed her in my arms and I saw her face, another name came to me." She looked at Grant. "What do you think about the name Lily Clementine?"

Grant's eyes shimmered. He swallowed hard, emotion tightening his jaw before he leaned in and kissed his wife, tender, grateful, full of wonder.

"I can't think of a more perfect name, Rose," he said, voice thick. Uncle John placed a gentle hand over the small, blanket-wrapped form.

"Lily Clementine Adams," he said softly. "A perfect name for a perfect little angel."

Did you love *Healing the Orphaned Heart*? Then you should read *Flames of the Fire*[1] by Rebecca Lange!

She was a fierce spitfire and would protect her family with her life.

Her heart raced and she kept staring at the burning building before her. Pure Panic caused her heart to beat faster and Joy ran closer, yelling her sister's name. She heard a toddler crying somewhere and after what seemed like forever, her sister's voice. Joy's heart sank. Alice was still in the house. Where was her sister's husband? Why had the house caught fire? One look was

---

1. https://books2read.com/u/b6Jgzy

2. https://books2read.com/u/b6Jgzy

enough. It wouldn't take long before the entire building collapsed.

About the Author

Rebecca Lange is a devoted romantic at heart. Though she has explored a variety of genres throughout her writing journey, her deepest passion lies in historical fiction—particularly stories set in the 1800s American West and the Regency era.

A passionate advocate, Rebecca uses her stories to raise awareness of abuse, human trafficking, and the devastating impact of drug and alcohol addiction. These themes are not woven in for suspense alone, but as a reminder that such struggles are tragically real—and that victims are never to blame.

She is also a firm believer in women's rights, inspired by the courageous women of the 1800s who fought to prove they were not the property of their husbands but their partners and equals. Rebecca upholds the conviction that violence has no place in relationships or marriage.

Originally from Germany, she was born and raised there before moving abroad in 2002 to serve a mission for her church in Scotland. A member of The Church of Jesus Christ of Latter-day Saints, she now lives in Utah with her husband, their two sons (ages 18 and 20), and two lively Yorkie puppies.

Her writing motto is: *Never Smut, Always Sizzling Kisses, Consistently Closed Door.* Rebecca delights in weaving passion and tenderness into her stories, offering what she calls "sweet and diet spice" romance. Diet spice—what is that, you ask? It's the thrill of longing gazes, passionate kisses, and close embraces that build anticipation without ever crossing into explicit territory. For her, the most powerful love stories are those that remain tasteful and teasing, proving that romance can be both heart-stirring and wholesome.

Read more at https://authorrebeccalange.wixsite.com/bookstolove.